PUNISHMENT
OF A HUNTER

YULIA YAKOVLEVA is a writer, theatre and ballet critic and playwright. She was inspired to write *Punishment of a Hunter* by her love of St Petersburg, where she grew up. The novel subsequently became a bestseller in Russia.

RUTH AHMEDZAI KEMP translates literature from Arabic, German and Russian into English. Her work has been shortlisted for the Helen & Kurt Wolff translator's prize, The Saif Ghobash Banipal Prize and GLI Translated YA Prize.

YULIA YAKOVLEVA

PUNISHMENT OF A HUNTER

TRANSLATED FROM THE RUSSIAN BY RUTH AHMEDZAI KEMP

PUSHKIN VERTIGO

Pushkin Vertigo
An imprint of Pushkin Press
71–75 Shelton Street
London WC2H 9JQ

Punishment of a Hunter was first published as
Вдруг охотник выбегает by Eksmo in 2017

The publication of the book was negotiated through Banke,
Goumen & Smirnova Literary Agency (www.bgs-agency.com).

First published by Pushkin Press in 2021
This edition first published in 2022

This book has been selected to receive financial assistance from English PEN's
PEN Translates programme, supported by Arts Council England. English
PEN exists to promote literature and our understanding of it, to uphold
writers' freedoms around the world, to campaign against the persecution and
imprisonment of writers for stating their views, and to promote the friendly
co-operation of writers and the free exchange of ideas. www.englishpen.org

  Supported using public funding by
**ARTS COUNCIL
ENGLAND**

1 3 5 7 9 8 6 4 2

ISBN 13: 978-1-782276-791

Internal Illustrations © Credit: Myakonkina Vlada

Designed and typeset by Tetragon, London
Printed and bound by CPI Group (UK) Ltd, Croydon, CRO 4YY
www.pushkinpress.com

PUNISHMENT OF A HUNTER

Chapter 1

I

Zaitsev glanced back at the top of the report. Again that feeling that his eyeballs were being rubbed with sandpaper. His gaze ran back down the page, but again he took nothing in.

Victim: Faina Borisovna Baranova, thirty-four, no party affiliation. Bookkeeper at an industrial co-operative. Unmarried.

Hmm, that's a shame, thought Zaitsev. The spouse is usually the first on the list.

So—no suspects. Nothing to go on. Not even the hint of a lead.

Zaitsev switched on the green-shaded desk lamp. Not that it made any difference. A soft blue sky peered in at the window. The usual deception of Leningrad's white nights. Without even pretending to get dark, the June evening had long since closed the shop doors and swept the traffic off the roads. The city's residents had their thick curtains drawn tight, as they tried to make room for some troubled sleep amid the ceaseless expanse of light that day and night had been for the past month. The somnolent streets were as bright as day.

Zaitsev laid out the photographs under the lamp.

Faina Baranova was killed in her room. In the black-and-white photographs, the pinkish wallpaper became a light grey. The murdered woman was slumped in an armchair by the window. The heavy curtains were pushed to the side. He could see the Public Library through the window.

Zaitsev turned the sheet of paper over and checked the address: 25th October Prospekt. On the corner of Nevsky and Sadovaya, then.

Again the letters jumbled into meaningless symbols. Zaitsev suppressed a yawn. He could barely hear himself think: there was too much noise coming in, interference. The Leningrad Criminal Investigation Department was bustling on all floors with the usual nocturnal activity. Someone was being led away; someone was being interrogated. From one direction there were sobs, from another furious swearing. And in all the corridors and offices, yellow light bulbs glowed needlessly. The air reeked of tobacco smoke.

So, Faina—Faina Baranova. Zaitsev picked up the photo again. He forced his mind to visualize the black-and-white image in colour, to recall what he had seen earlier that evening. His mind's eye turned the edges of the picture into a door frame—the doorway through which Zaitsev had first glimpsed this woman. Or rather, her corpse.

"So, Vasya, do we force it open?" Agent Martynov had asked him as they arrived at the victim's door that evening. He pushed his cap back from his forehead to wipe off the sweat. His eyes were red, with bags underneath. Martynov had been up all night on a stake-out in one of the large tenement blocks on Ligovsky Prospekt. Then he'd had to do the write-up. He hadn't managed to get home before a new day started and now the squad had been summoned to 25th October Prospekt.

"Wait a little longer, and you shall have a rest," sang Demov in a strained falsetto, as he dragged along the case containing their crime-scene-investigation kit. In his other hand he clutched a folded camera tripod.

"Sod off, Demov," snarled Martynov. He blinked; the air was thick with steam from about a dozen different dinners being cooked at once. You could barely walk down the narrow, shared corridor for junk left there by the residents who couldn't fit it in their rooms. This had once been a spacious, bourgeois apartment. Now there was a family squeezed into each room. A typical Leningrad communal flat. The corridor was suddenly crowded with personnel arriving on the scene. The neighbours' doors opened as they gingerly peeked out. Zaitsev felt someone brush against his back. He turned around to see a little woodland gnome of a man.

"Is there a problem, comrade?" Zaitsev snapped.

"Comrades, there's nothing to see," Demov told the neighbours who were emerging into the corridor, including those who had initially planned to sit tight until the police came and knocked at their doors. Curiosity had got the better of them.

Zaitsev examined the flimsy lock. The two witnesses loitered behind him: the janitor for the block and the house manager.

"She hasn't opened her door since yesterday," mumbled the woodland gnome. He was the one who had called the police. Their colleague Samoilov emerged from the steam emanating from the communal kitchen.

"I called the co-operative. Baranova didn't show up at work."

Zaitsev nodded. Martynov leant against the wall and paused with his eyes closed. I should have sent him home, thought Zaitsev. He had barely got a word of sense out of Martynov today.

"Might she have gone somewhere?" suggested Agent Serafimov, standing behind him. Zaitsev turned around. His colleague had a rosy blush and golden curls, like an angel from a pre-revolutionary Easter card. And the surname to match.

"Get away!" spluttered a peasant in a traditional smock, a *tolstovka*. "Don't you think we'd know if she had?"

"She reports to you, does she?" Zaitsev looked him in the eye briefly.

11

"Oof, look at him gawping like that," muttered an old woman. Zaitsev pretended not to have heard.

"What would she need to report to us for?" said the man in the long *tolstovka*, offended. "As if we neighbours can't see with our own eyes. We're all on good terms here, I'll thank you very much. This lot'll tell you so. Our relations towards Faina Borisovna are of the most respectful kind, notwithstanding her being of Jewish origin and all. She's an earnest woman, neat and tidy."

"A dog! Ooh, a dog!" Along the corridor, there was a rustle of whispers and gasps as the police dog slipped through the crowd of onlooking neighbours. This large German shepherd with a black patch on its back was a descendant of the legendary Ace of Clubs, a star player in the Leningrad CID around a decade ago. It had inherited the same ancestral name.

The handler quietly gave the dog a command.

Ace froze for a second—as though the scent had become a sound and demanded absolute silence—then started scraping its claws against the door.

"Open it up, Martynov," commanded Zaitsev.

The handler took the dog by the collar as Martynov inserted a short crowbar between the door and the frame and pressed. At first the crowbar slipped, tearing off a strip of veneer from the door. Martynov seemed to wake up with a jolt and gave Zaitsev a sheepish glance. This time, he put the crowbar into position more carefully.

The door to Faina Baranova's room welcomed them with a crunch as it burst open. Behind them was a muddle of excited voices.

"Neighbours, please back off!" barked Zaitsev. "Witnesses, is this Citizen Baranova?"

"It is," confirmed the janitor, diligently stretching his neck to peer over Zaitsev's shoulder.

"Thank you, comrade. Citizens, nothing to goggle at here!" Zaitsev boomed at the neighbours in the corridor as he stepped over the threshold into the room. "Everyone will be interviewed in turn."

"Stand back, comrades." Serafimov firmly manoeuvred the curious neighbours back into the gloomy corridor.

"Off you go, Serafimov. You start working through the neighbours," Zaitsev whispered to him. Serafimov nodded and left the room, closing the door behind him.

Zaitsev focused on Faina Baranova as though she and he were alone in the room. Before Demov started sprinkling his black powder everywhere in search of fingerprints, and before Martynov started yanking open drawers and banging cupboard doors, Zaitsev wanted to take in the entire scene with one glance. The first impression counts for a lot.

The room was cluttered but large, with two tall windows.

Faina Baranova was sitting in an armchair by the window. One arm lay on the armrest. The other lay draped across her stomach. In her right hand was a white rose. In her left, a feather duster. The kind used more by cleaners than by housewives.

"A black rose is a symbol of grief," Martynov observed. But the rose Baranova was holding was white. Still, Martynov had a point: the woman had an aura of disquiet and drama. Behind her, the silk curtains formed a scarlet backdrop. Against the deep red, her velvet dress seemed even blacker and the white rose even more dazzling. There was something almost theatrical about the contrast of scarlet, black and white, a contrast that was softened by the iridescence of the silk, the softness of the velvet and the tenderness of the petals.

Baranova's posture was so natural that at first Zaitsev could almost believe she was alive. The corpse's eyes were open.

"Looks like heart trouble," said Demov with a nod. He was the oldest in the squad. "One minute you're fine, the next you're a goner."

"Demov, don't assume everyone's past it just because you are. She's not that old."

Demov shrugged his bony shoulders. "OK, she's not exactly a pensioner, but she's not particularly young either. It's a plausible hypothesis."

"Call for the transport, Martynov."

Martynov went into the corridor to ring for someone to fetch the body.

Zaitsev noticed a thin, scarlet line on the dead woman's neck. "Hmm. Bit early to think about calling it a day, then."

With one finger he pulled back her white collar to show Demov: a neat red line ran across the neck, like a cut.

"Her husband's doing—as clear as day," said Samoilov, without a moment's reflection.

"Hmm. Could be a man or a woman—either would be strong enough," suggested Demov, as he set up the tripod. "Even a teenager or an old man—we can't rule anyone out. But most likely a husband or cohabitant, according to the stats. Statistics are a force to be reckoned with." He paused to look Zaitsev in the eye. "Vasya, it's time you told the boss I can't keep on lugging all this heavy equipment around. I have to think of my health. It's time we had a photographer in the squad."

Demov nagged his boss constantly about the need for a dedicated photographer, and it was true: they didn't have enough personnel. But while he was the oldest in the squad, Demov wasn't as frail as he made out. He still had plenty of strength left in him. When Zaitsev had joined the squad, Demov had introduced himself as "Demov—old man, hypochondriac, misanthrope". But when he shook Zaitsev's hand, he gave it such a squeeze his fingers crunched.

Demov held up the camera flash.

"Samoilov, have a look for a string or wire or something, will you?" said Zaitsev. And seeing that Martynov was back, he glanced quickly at his wristwatch with its scratched face and began to dictate: "Body discovered at 6.48…"

Samoilov banged about, rifling through the drawers of the dresser and the dressing table, flinging open the wardrobe doors.

"Cause of death: asphyxiation," Zaitsev dictated mechanically.

The flash went off, instantly filling the room with light.

They didn't find any string.

Not exactly old… but not particularly young either, thought Zaitsev, as he sat in his office that night, poring over the case. Faina Borisovna Baranova was thirty-four years old. There was also a small photograph of her. Very stiff, lips pressed tightly shut—a typical ID-card pose. She lived alone. A female cousin in Kiev; the neighbours didn't know of any other relatives. Those neighbours again!

Zaitsev held the photo at arm's reach, as if trying to see Faina Baranova with his own eyes, rather than the neighbours'.

Perhaps Demov was right: Faina Baranova did look older than her years. If not old, then at least marked by pain. Her face was puffy and she had dark bags under her eyes. Mind you, who looked healthy these days? Everyone was malnourished, overworked. Everyone's day was a constant cycle of work, queues, domestic chores and getting up at the crack of dawn to squeeze on the tram to work again. "And yet she looked after her eyebrows," Zaitsev muttered to himself.

And the feather duster. The kind cleaners used. At home, most people used a plain old rag.

Zaitsev went to the door and shouted into the corridor, "Serafimov, come here a minute!" Zaitsev listened out. He could hear him coming. He went back to contemplating the photographs.

Serafimov appeared in the doorway.

"Ah, Serafimov. Find out if Baranova had a cleaner, will you? Seems unlikely... A cleaner who also happens to be an informant?"

"The neighbours have confirmed that nothing's been stolen."

"They know everything about each other in that flat," grumbled Zaitsev. "We'll also need to find out if they're really as chummy as they make out."

Serafimov didn't answer.

Zaitsev pressed his fingers against his closed eyelids: the yellow light from the electric lamp bore into his temples. A red rose is a symbol of love, he thought. When he opened his eyes again, a sheet of paper lay neatly on top of the file on his desk. Serafimov lurked at his side. At the top of the sheet was written in perfect handwriting: "NOTICE OF RESIGNATION".

"OK, Serafimov, that's all for today," said Zaitsev, not looking at it. He got up from his chair. "I'll have the rest of the statements by tomorrow. For now let's call it a day." The chair grunted as he stood up. "I'm dead beat. Can't think straight today."

"This is my resignation."

"What?" Zaitsev strained his eyes to read. "...MADE VOLUNTARILY". He looked back at Serafimov. "Is this a joke?"

Serafimov certainly had something angelic about his appearance, like his namesake, the biblical seraphim. It was easy to be taken in by his blue eyes and soft rosy cheeks. Serafimov had been transferred to the squad about five years ago, when there were still shots being fired in the dark streets of Leningrad, and the city was swarming with gangsters. He was straight in at the deep end, spending whole nights waiting in ambush or running through a hail of bullets.

Zaitsev read the statement, then dropped the sheet onto the table.

"Serafimov, you're exhausted. It happens. But there's no need to do anything reckless. Here, take it. Off you go and sleep it off. I haven't seen this."

But Serafimov grabbed his sleeve. "I'm serious, Vasya."

Zaitsev wasn't yet thirty, like most in the Criminal Investigation Department. But they worked on more cases in a year or two than most teams were faced with in ten years. Zaitsev was none other than Detective Vasily Zaitsev. Comrade Zaitsev. Known only to his close colleagues in Squad 2 as Vasya.

"Serafimov, we don't have enough men. Martynov is going from all-nighters straight on to call-outs, Demov is taking photos instead of interviewing neighbours, and you—you want to quit?"

Zaitsev was surprised by the look on Serafimov's face.

"I'm serious," he repeated softly.

Zaitsev looked at him. Hmm, so it seemed.

"OK, sit down." Zaitsev closed the office door, slicing off the tentacle of tobacco smoke which was swirling in from the corridor.

Serafimov sat down on the sofa, sinking into the velour cushions. Zaitsev sat on the windowsill. The window was wide open. On the tidal river below, there was a quiet, steady splash of waves against the granite parapet. The River Fontanka gave off wafts of both fresh and rotten smells at the same time.

"Vasya, don't waste your time. I've already decided," said Serafimov. His voice was melancholy. The pistol on his hip showed through his skinny jacket. On Serafimov, with his curls, his blue eyes and his rosy cheeks, the weapon looked like a toy.

"You've decided. OK, you've decided. I won't argue with you, you're a big boy. I'm just curious. What are you going to do? Tram driver? Clerk? What is it? Your girl's had second thoughts? Wants to marry an accountant? Less of the night shifts and the criminal underground?"

Serafimov stood up. He walked over to the window. He gestured with his eyes to the closed door. Zaitsev slid off the windowsill and closed the window.

"What do you think? It's hardly my choice. They'll purge me if I don't go first," Serafimov explained quietly.

"Ha!" Zaitsev was surprised. "Purge you? And what dirt has the commission got on you, eh? That you were wounded on duty? That you risked your own life carrying your comrade Govorushkin to safety after he was shot by bandits? That you barely sleep at night? Everyone knows your biography, Serafimov. Men like you are worth their weight in gold here in CID."

"It's fine for you to talk!" exclaimed Serafimov.

"What about me? How am I different?"

"It's all straightforward where you're concerned."

"And what isn't straightforward about you?"

They were interrupted by the phone. Zaitsev picked up the receiver and held his hand up to Serafimov, as if to say, "Wait a second."

"Zaitsev speaking. Yes, I'm writing it down. Uh-huh. OK, thanks."

Irritated, Serafimov stared out of the window.

Zaitsev hung up. He was animated.

"Interesting! Baranova's neighbour called—from the flat. She's remembered something. Says she wants to talk tomorrow."

He checked the file. "Olga Zabotkina. Hmm, a music teacher. Good. Smart old biddies are better at keeping an eye on the neighbours and their admirers than people realize."

But Serafimov didn't share his enthusiasm. "What isn't straightforward?" he repeated sarcastically. "Well, I suppose it is—especially my background."

"What's he on about?" muttered Zaitsev, having apparently already forgotten what they were talking about. His thoughts were now completely taken up by Olga Zabotkina.

He knocked a handful of photos against the table, straightening up the pile. He placed them in the folder and tied it up.

"My father was a priest, Vasya."

"Serafimov, you didn't hide your background from the authorities. You declared it openly on the form," continued Zaitsev as he put the folder away in the safe, "when you applied to join the police. The only people who should be afraid are those with something to hide."

"That was then! It didn't matter back then. Now it does. The purges are real, Vasya. They're going to send me packing. You get blacklisted, you get a wolf ticket on your passport. Then there won't be any jobs on the trams. They send you away, Vasya—beyond the 101-kilometre boundary. For being an anti-Soviet element. Categorized as hostile to the Soviet social order. Whereas if I leave now of my own accord, there won't be any questions. I might be able to set myself up as a shop assistant, or a mechanic."

Serafimov was afraid that his eyes would well up. The injustice of it hurt.

Zaitsev still looked straight ahead with his cheerful, cold eyes. Only now they were more cold than cheerful.

"Don't take it personally, Serafimov."

The tears did well up. Serafimov turned away.

"It *is* personal, Vasya," he forced out. "Why should my dad have anything to do with it?"

"What are you—a baby?" Zaitsev snapped. "Let the real troublemakers get hot and bothered, not you. You know what?" he added, changing his tone. "The only category you come under is police officer, and the most Soviet kind at that. End of story."

Zaitsev saw that what he'd said hadn't made any impact.

"Listen, Serafimov. I've had an idea. There's no point trying to convince our comrades in the commission. They don't understand how much we need you. And there won't be time to explain."

Serafimov looked at him with hope.

Zaitsev once again pressed his fingers to his eyes. This time the pain behind his eyes didn't go away.

"Look. Here's an order. I'm sending you on a posting, Comrade Serafimov." Zaitsev paused a moment to think. "For a skills exchange with your comrades in the provinces. Is your mission clear?"

A rosy colour gradually returned to Serafimov's cheeks.

"Yes, I think so."

"And when you get back, no one will be any the wiser. Whoever they end up purging—good luck to them. But it'll all have blown over by the time you're back. Is that clear, Comrade Serafimov?"

"It is. But where to?"

"Where what?"

"Where am I being sent to?"

Zaitsev thought about it. "Kiev? Magical city—so I hear."

Serafimov nodded. "Kiev would work."

The Remington crunched as Zaitsev fed a sheet of paper in. He began to pelt the keys with one finger, the letters clinking as they jumped about. His message to their Kiev comrades was a brief one, it seemed. Zaitsev turned the wheel, pulled out the sheet and scrawled a loopy signature at the bottom.

"Tomorrow go and collect your ration cards for the trip and they'll issue you with the tickets. So this purge—when's the meeting?…"

Zaitsev turned over the page of the diary on his desk.

"OK, it's at eleven. So, come in tomorrow at eight sharp to get ready. Then off you go."

"Tomorrow morning?…"

"And I'll go to the meeting instead of you. If they want to purge someone, let them pick me. My background's about as prole as you get. They won't find anything on me—nothing but my trousers."

Serafimov opened his mouth, but before he could say "Thank you", Zaitsev frowned at him.

"Girls say thank you—when you give them flowers," said Zaitsev.

Serafimov stopped, unsure what to say.

"I'll gladly go and sit in this meeting instead of you. Give my legs a rest. OK, go. And sleep!"

II

Zaitsev was somewhat surprised to see metal trolleys being wheeled in from the morgue. A gurgling dissonance echoed off the high ceilings and the painted walls, hung with portraits of party leaders. This was the purge itself, Zaitsev realized. The members of the commission were sitting at a table at the front. Zaitsev spotted some comrades from other police squads. He couldn't help noticing his boss Kopteltsev, head of CID, among the corpses. His eyes scanned the room for his team. He saw Samoilov, and Martynov, and old Demov, and even the dog handler—what was his name again? And Serafimov.

"Why didn't you leave?" he asked.

Neither Samoilov, nor Martynov, nor Serafimov seemed surprised by the metal trolleys or the unbearable, dazzlingly bright ceiling lamp that shone its ghastly light straight in your eyes. Nothing ever surprised Demov. Zaitsev suddenly threw off his jacket and slipped off his braces. He realized in horror that he was getting undressed, and quickly. With monstrous, incomprehensible speed and ease. His satin boxers had already dropped to the floor. He stepped out of them, shook them off his foot. And woke up.

The room was chilly in the morning half-light.

"Damn it, I've only slept an hour or two," Zaitsev estimated. How annoying. A metallic glint caught his eye as it glimmered on a huge, delicate spider's web on the ceiling. Quietly, gently, it started to descend towards him. Zaitsev knew then, even before they touched him, that the gossamer threads weren't delicate and sticky, but razor sharp and taut.

At this point he woke up completely, his heart thumping and his pillow crumpled in his hands.

The sun shone low through the window. That must have been the garish lamp in his dream. Light poured onto the white ceiling and the stucco plasterwork, showing up the dust that filled the nooks and crannies: eternal shadows lending a touch of character to the vestiges of former luxury. There was no other luxury in Zaitsev's room.

Zaitsev reached for the crushed cigarette packet on the stool. He tried to pull one out, tapped the box and gave it a blow. He eventually got one out and put it in his mouth. He took it out again right away. He gave up yesterday, he remembered. It always used to be so easy to get up in the summer. Zaitsev threw back the sheet.

Outside, the sparrows screeched. The summery Leningrad morning had already revved up its motor and was rumbling through the streets, chattering with a cacophony of voices. The black hands of the alarm clock stood like an upside-down letter v, or that obsolete letter *izhitsa*. A radio prattled away in the corridor.

Zaitsev pulled out a drawer. He got dressed. As he did so, he nudged the pack of cigarettes under the chest of drawers.

A shame to throw it away completely, but out of sight, out of mind. He pulled out another drawer. Pasha had tidily left his change in a meticulous metal pyramid on top of the unspent ration cards. Yesterday's purchases were in brown paper bags. They rustled as he checked the contents: tea, coffee, sugar. Wrapped in an off-white linen napkin was a loaf of black bread.

At the helm of the sprawling communal apartment, and the front entrance, the entire courtyard and arched passageway through to the second courtyard, indeed the entire house—which legend has it was home before the Revolution to the famous mezzo-soprano Anastasia Vyaltseva, and which now housed ordinary workers—at the helm of the entire building was, of course, Aunt Pasha. Or, to some, Pashka. A large, middle-aged woman, with a large metal badge on her apron, Pasha was to be found on summer and autumn mornings wielding her prickly broom in the courtyard, and on winter and spring mornings sprinkling sand and scraping the snow with her shovel. In her spare time, when not serving the state, Pasha sat at her sewing machine, her stout foot pressing rhythmically on the square cast-iron pedal inscribed with the name "Singer".

And it was she, dear Pasha, who managed Zaitsev's lean bachelor household.

The criminal investigator was so busy with his work that he didn't have time to manage even his very meagre domestic affairs. Zaitsev left Pasha in charge of his money and ration cards and she left his groceries for him in the top drawer. The second drawer housed all of Zaitsev's summer clothes and the bottom one was for his winter clothes. For convenience, he had given Pasha a key to his room. Zaitsev had nothing to steal except a cast-iron kettlebell in one corner and a worn-out armchair in the other. The wiry horsehair was escaping from the fabric. The people in their house lived poor, meagre lives.

But even they were unlikely to be tempted by the kettlebell or the armchair.

For Zaitsev it was all perfectly sufficient.

Zaitsev made himself coffee in the shared kitchen, with its ten Primus stoves and ten tables of all different shapes and sizes. He cut a rough slice of bread and sprinkled it with sugar.

"So, Comrade Zaitsev, still not found yourself a wife? I never see you eat a proper meal," tutted his neighbour Katya as she plonked her frying pan on the stove and tossed in a lump of butter. She wore a chiffon headscarf over her curlers. Katya didn't like to be "untidy" in front of her neighbours: she was an intelligent lady, an accountant at the Krupskaya factory.

"Good morning, Katerina Yegorovna."

The eggs hissed in the butter. Waiting for them in their room were Katya's husband and their daughter, a student. The daughter planned to get as far away as possible from her roots and become quite the aristocrat: a dental technician.

"And what do girls need from a husband? Someone with nothing wrong with him, arms and legs in the right place. Accommodation, a salary, you've even got an officer card—what more can you ask?!"

"Have a nice day, Katerina Yegorovna."

This was their regular morning ritual, where each had their allotted role. Katya played hers with indifference—her daughter was already spoken for.

Looking at Katya, Zaitsev was particularly perplexed: how did these people find themselves a spouse? Who would look at a hulking body like hers and see the girl of his dreams? And yet, supposedly her husband had actually chosen her, this Katerina Egorovna. It just didn't make sense, he mused, munching on his bread. People decide to get married. They sign the register. They fill their rooms with Primuses and mattresses, then cots and washtubs. They build their little nests together. To Zaitsev, this aspect of ordinary human life seemed unfathomable. And all the rituals that went with it. Asking a girl to dance. And then the indispensable draping your jacket over her shoulders, with the endless River Neva as a backdrop. Not to mention the poems, the flowers... Zaitsev shuddered. He brushed the crumbs from his front and downed the rest of his coffee in one gulp.

"What, Comrade Zaitsev? Has the tea gone cold?" His neighbour Palych had just come into the kitchen. "I just had some. Nothing but grass in there. I had a look—all kinds of filth mixed up in there. No more than twenty pro cent actual tea."

Palych said "pro cent". It seemed to make no difference to him if anyone was actually listening. Sometimes it seemed like residents of the apartment purposely steered him towards the kitchen, when they could no longer take any more of his incessant chatter.

"Pure burdock, that is, it's not tea."

"I'm having coffee," Zaitsev answered.

In a world where Faina Baranova was murdered—where such a calm, unnecessary and savage murder was possible—there was no space for bouquets of flowers or asking girls to dance. The brain simply didn't have the capacity to process it all. This strange case of Faina Baranova now occupied Zaitsev's mind to the exclusion of all else.

The neighbours were already swarming in the corridor, queuing for the bathroom laden with towels and soap. As he walked out onto the embankment of the River Moika, Zaitsev slammed the door behind him. Pasha had already swept outside: the ground was still marked by the circular tracks of her stiff broom. It was a long time since there had been any kind of lawn in front of the house.

Spotting the tram turning on St Isaac's Square, Zaitsev sped up, jumped on as it passed and clung on, standing on the footboard. The tram led him through this beautiful city where for the most part people lived a poor, dreary, unkempt life. Squabbling in their communal kitchens, struggling amid the chaos and stench of life to rest from the tedium and exhaustion of work, with hours on end idled away queuing for horrible foodstuffs grandly described as "nutrition products", painfully squirrelling away enough for a pair of shoes or a suit for special occasions, paying off government loans from their meagre salaries, struggling to stay awake through endless party meetings. But you wouldn't know all that from the Leningrad morning with the sun sparkling on the spires and in the windows.

Even at this early hour when all the shops were still closed, the longest queue was a rabble winding its way along the street towards the vodka store. A meandering line of indistinct, crumpled faces that made Zaitsev think of the old euphemism "the green serpent". When he got to 25th October Prospekt, he jumped down from the tram.

III

The copper nameplate for "F. Baranova" had not yet been unscrewed from the front door. Pinned up next to it was a handwritten note saying "Two short rings". The door was dotted with signs giving the names of all the tenants and instructions on how to summon them specifically. Every sign in its own way expressed the character of its owner. Together they made for a motley sight.

The name "Zabotkina" was inscribed with oil paint on a rectangular piece of plywood. Zaitsev pressed the bell as instructed: two long and one short. And then he thought of joking with the music teacher. Why this little ditty and not a more complex composition?

26

Zabotkina came to the door.

"Comrade, are you from the police?" she asked reverently, timidly.

And Zaitsev decided against his joke.

In shape, Zabotkina resembled a large, pale, unripe pear. Her slightly dishevelled hair was tied back in a bun. Round glasses like fish eyes. Zaitsev noted a vague resemblance to Lenin's wife, Nadezhda Krupskaya.

"Zaitsev, investigator."

"Come in, comrade." Zabotkina's voice turned out to be as quiet and pallid as her appearance suggested.

As soon as he stepped into the flat he could tell which was Zabotkina's room from the faltering tones of *Für Elise*. Zabotkina let Zaitsev into the dark corridor, where Elise stumbled along, dragging her feet. And in a mysterious whisper, Zabotkina added, "I knew right away that it was you."

The string with the brown seal was still stretched across the door to Baranova's room from the previous day. Zaitsev turned away.

Most of Zabotkina's room was filled by the piano. An instrument of torture. Its current victim looked to be about ten years old. The girl had her fingers outstretched on the keyboard. A huge bow was fixed to her cropped hair, though it was unclear what physical force held it in place.

"Valya, elbows down," her teacher commanded with a fearful glance at Zaitsev. He gestured as though to say, "Not at all, don't worry."

Zaitsev looked around for somewhere to sit. Zabotkina quickly pulled an oblong cushion away from the couch to make space. Zaitsev sat down and realized it wasn't a couch but a chest covered with a rug. Another rug was nailed to the wall above.

The girl played a wrong note, shook her head, again picked up the slippery, looping melody. From the dripping sound of the notes, Zaitsev could almost imagine it was a rainy autumn evening outside, not a summer morning. His temples filled with heaviness. Keeping her voice low, the teacher gave her student some corrections.

Finally, her victim noisily scraped back the chair and began to gather up her music in a red folder embossed with a golden treble clef.

"Right, now I can speak," said Zabotkina in that pallid, expressionless voice, once her pupil had gone. She sat on a swivel chair with her back to the piano, her large white hands folded on her lap.

Zaitsev imagined her palms to be cold and moist. Like squashing some kind of slimy sea creature.

"The neighbours don't complain about the music?" he asked with a smile.

"No. We're all on good terms in this apartment," said Zabotkina, peering through her round glasses.

A much-repeated phrase, mused Zaitsev.

"She's a funny one, that Valya. And among your students, do you have more boys or more girls?" he asked, just to make conversation.

Zabotkina looked at him in astonishment. "I'll have to check my notes," she answered seriously. She jumped up.

"Oh no, it doesn't matter. I was just curious."

He smiled again. The teacher didn't answer his smile. Her face showed something akin to panic.

"You called and said you had remembered something important," Zaitsev reminded her softly.

Her face immediately came to life. She seemed to light up, to glow with purpose and direction.

"Yes. Or rather, no, I didn't remember it. I knew it from the very beginning. It was just the way the question was worded."

"And what was the question?"

"Your colleague asked if anything was missing. The one with the red eyes."

Martynov. I shouldn't have made him come with us on the call-out, Zaitsev thought.

"And was there?"

"No," Zabotkina replied quickly. "I don't think so. Not as far as I know."

"Are you familiar with the contents of Baranova's room?"

"Yes, I think so. Faina is a kind lady. She was. She liked having me over to tea in her room. Or just to sit and talk. Over some needlework."

"She enjoyed needlework?"

"Me more than her. Perhaps not a lot. But now and then. For relaxation." The music teacher looked frightened again. As if she had found herself back in the middle of a swamp.

"And what was it about the way the question was worded?" Zaitsev asked, carefully guiding her back to solid ground.

"There wasn't anything missing. Something had appeared!" A little colour even came to her cheeks.

"What do you mean?"

"Faina was a very calm, ordinary person," she began, seemingly out of the blue.

Zaitsev let her talk.

"The curtain. It wasn't there before. And the dress. Faina didn't have a dress like that. And the feather duster!"

"Could she have bought them?" suggested Zaitsev. "And you hadn't seen them?"

"No!" she almost shouted. "Sorry, no. She would never have bought such things! Faina wasn't one for anything flashy."

"Might she have been given them as a present? People aren't always familiar with others' tastes when they give presents. Might her colleagues have given them to her, for example? Does that seem likely?"

Zabotkina boldly looked into his eyes and stated almost defiantly, "She would never have even brought them into her home."

"I see," Zaitsev readily agreed. It's fully possible that she's right, he thought. But then this is complete madness.

Suddenly Zabotkina perked up again. "Do you know what, you should ask Uncle Grisha."

"And who's that?"

"Our neighbour, Grigory Mikhailovich Okunev. A very good person."

Oh yes, everyone's on good terms in this apartment, Zaitsev remembered.

"He helps all the neighbours!" insisted Zabotkina as though she had heard him.

Zaitsev was already taking a particular dislike to this unusually friendly apartment.

"He would have had to help Faina hang the curtain."

"What, she wouldn't do it herself?" asked Zaitsev in mock surprise, playing along with her.

"What do you think?! If she even stood on a stool, she'd be dizzy! I'm not exaggerating. And look how tall our windows are! You can't clean the windows standing on a stool, you need to get a stepladder down from the attic. And certainly to reach the cornice!"

"Thank you for that observation. I'll clearly need to visit again to speak with your Grigory Mikhailovich when he comes back from work."

"Oh no, he's a pensioner!" Zabotkina was delighted to explain. "People bring all kinds of things round for him to fix. He can turn his hand to anything. Come on, I'll introduce you now." Zabotkina jumped up with a surprising lack of effort. "Come on! Only do speak up. He's rather hard of hearing."

He certainly won't mind her music, then, thought Zaitsev. That must be why they get on so well.

Okunev lived at the very end of the corridor. His was a narrow room with one window. It had been cut off from another, much larger room: the ceiling rose was divided by the neighbouring wall. Okunev's room seemed even smaller because of all the ironmongery lying around. Zaitsev didn't even spot the man straight away. When he did, he recognized the same little woodland gnome he had seen yesterday.

"Uh?" asked Okunev, looking attentively not at Zaitsev's eyes, but at his lips.

That's right, he's hard of hearing, Zaitsev remembered. He wasn't deliberately getting in the way yesterday, he just hadn't heard anything to be scared off by.

Both of them shouting, he and Zabotkina managed to establish from the old man that no, he hadn't hung any curtains, but he had soldered a Primus. Yes, he had definitely done that. And he had fitted a new handle on the iron. But a curtain? No, he hadn't hung up any curtains.

"And what kind of curtains did Faina Baranova have?" Zaitsev asked. "Before, I mean."

"Plush," Zabotkina answered.

"Brown," said Okunev.

"Yes, brown," agreed Zabotkina.

And then Okunev confirmed. "Yes, plush."

"I see," Zaitsev concluded.

Although he didn't. He was still none the wiser.

IV

Zaitsev only had time for a quick check of the inventory in the Baranova file before he had to dash to his purge meeting. There were no brown curtains mentioned among the things in her room. Neither plush nor brown.

So where were they? Had they been taken away by whoever

hung the scarlet curtains? Was it the same person who killed Baranova?

Zaitsev left the inventory and the photographs on the table and, hastily pulling on his jacket, rushed off to his purge review. He wasn't worried about it. He had no reason to be. Throughout Leningrad, throughout the country, the Soviet government was screening its citizens, purging the ranks. Everyone had to answer to the collective, to everyone else, and especially to the GPU review committees. Who are you? What did you do before the Revolution? Who are your parents? What did they before the Revolution? Were they for or against the Soviet system? Did you own property? Weren't you bourgeois? Aristocracy? What if your relatives had fought against the Soviet regime? There was no room for black sheep in the new Soviet society.

But Zaitsev wasn't afraid for his job. He whistled as he ran up the stairs.

The table in the assembly hall was covered with a red table-cloth. As Zaitsev sat waiting, he idly examined the threadbare patches. The tablecloth was made from an old curtain, probably from a theatre, but it was meant to represent something revolutionary. The militant atmosphere didn't quite come across, though. The long table, draped with this cloth that reached the floor, instead resembled a coffin.

The members of the commission were recruited by virtue of their class: in other words, they were ordinary Leningrad down-and-outs. They had poor nutrition and an even worse quality of life, which you could tell from their unkempt look and the greyish-green tinge to their complexion. In the meagre light of the electric bulb hanging from the ceiling—who knows why it was even on in the middle of the day—the commission-ers at their coffin–table almost had the air of a gathering of vampires. If it weren't for the fact that all six looked scared.

Zaitsev even felt sorry for them.

Poor Soviet lackeys—they were appointed to purge the police ranks of undesirables, but that responsibility didn't make them any less afraid themselves. At the end of the table sat some rank or other from the GPU, or OGPU as the state political directorate was now known, the department that had established the new category of crimes—crimes against Soviet ideology. The GPU officer's shaved scalp glistened. His nose almost rested on his mouth. A blue-topped cap lay on the table in front of him, its scarlet star facing the hall, watching the audience like the all-seeing eye of Gogol's demonic Viy.

Zaitsev's chair was set forward, in front of the table. Everyone in the building had been made to come along to the review meeting. From investigators to the typing pool. The telephone monitors were the only ones left in peace. Someone had to answer the calls.

A combination of perfume and curiosity wafted from the girls. Everyone else was quietly simmering. There was work waiting to be done. The big city didn't slam on the brakes for such an occasion. It lived a life of its own. People didn't stop thieving, robbing, abandoning babies (if not at the Obvodny Canal, then at the front door), running off with public money, knocking down pedestrians, damaging public property, getting drunk, stabbing and bottling, beating women or jumping off bridges. Neither did they lay off the homicide.

While they had to sit here for the purge, there was evidence to gather, witnesses to question, reports to write, crime scenes to photograph, prints to take. Everyone was eager to get away.

"Make a start, comrades!" ordered the GPU officer.

Look at the epaulettes on him, Zaitsev thought. His collar tabs suggested he wasn't some junior ranker.

Zaitsev's face was expressionless.

One of the commissioners gingerly reached out for the carafe of water, slowly poured some into a cloudy glass and took a sip, peering over the glass at each in turn, bewildered.

The pause dragged on.

"You're in charge," the GPU man urged on the commissioners. "Go ahead and ask."

One of the men at the table began to cough and clear his throat. Everyone looked at him, willing him on. But he didn't make another sound. He pulled out a used handkerchief and wiped his mouth. Then he went back to staring at the large, wilting ficus that had been brought for the occasion from the accounting department and installed at the end of the table.

The ficus itself looked up at the dusty, smoky window that hadn't had a wash in a while.

Our northern summer is a caricature of a southern winter, thought Zaitsev. The ficus must think it's an outrage.

Zaitsev tried to shift slightly, but the chair under him howled and creaked, resulting in an even deeper silence.

"And you, Zaitsev, stand up. Get up! Show some respect for the procedure."

The man with the collar tabs and the blue cap gestured with his fat, white hand, as if to say, "Up you get." Zaitsev's chair gave a parting cry. Zaitsev got up in relief, shaking off the stabbing pins and needles.

From here he could see pretty much everyone in the hall. The irritation on people's faces was gradually replaced by a sleepy stupor. These meetings usually dragged on forever, like the Leningrad rain.

"Comrade, state your name!" someone finally hissed behind him.

Zaitsev turned around.

"Speak into the hall," came a sly, haughty voice from behind the ficus. The GPU man was used to those undergoing a purge

34

review being flustered—fidgeting, sweating and stammering. He took a dislike to this fellow, his back straight, with eyes bright as a Yakut dog. He stared straight ahead, eyes wide open, as if to say, "I've nothing to hide, what you see is what you get." And yet instinctively, the GPU man seemed to sense that before him was someone who had plunged the depths, who had swum the dark waters like a fish.

I'll beat that arrogance out of you, he told himself.

"Zaitsev, Vasily."

"Louder," demanded the *gepeushnik*, the GPU officer. He began to get impatient with the cowardly commissioners, the lackeys. "I'm not shy to say my name out loud before the people: Sharov, Nikolai Davydovich," he demonstrated.

"Right. Zaitsev! Vasily!" His baritone roar echoed from the ceiling.

"That's better, Citizen Zaitsev."

They had made a start now. The purging committee visibly perked up.

"Date of birth."

Zaitsev answered.

"Speak up," Comrade Sharov demanded again. He had given up waiting for his deputies in the commission. Yet again, he had to take matters into his own hands.

"Comrades," Zaitsev roared, "is there anyone who can't hear me? I can come and repeat it in their ear."

There was nothing particularly funny about his remark, but the hall broke out into smiles and muffled laughter. Zaitsev could see why they would laugh. How many years they had spent together on stake-outs, confronting armed bandits, burying their comrades who had fallen in action. They weren't the kind to surrender their colleagues. To anybody. And the GPU maggot knew that. Zaitsev couldn't stand all these proceedings, this whole pretence. They heard your case and decided your fate: you were either clean enough to stay or you got the boot. The whole charade was just a waste of time.

The faces before him were all young. No one was over thirty.

But they weren't laughing at a joke. They were baring their teeth to the unwelcome visitor. And he got the message.

"You, Zaitsev, you'll answer properly. Or you'll be working as a circus clown down on the Fontanka, not in the Soviet police."

"And what was the question?"

By this point, the audience were following the duel with interest and a touch of schadenfreude. Sharov rummaged through some papers and pulled out a piece of paper.

Zaitsev recognized it as the form he had filled in at some point, rounded off with his bold signature.

"And why is Comrade Serafimov not here?"

"He's on a work trip."

"He wasn't yesterday, but today he is? Is that what you're saying?" pestered GPU agent Sharov.

Is he really called Sharov? Zaitsev wondered. It sounded more like a party alias.

"It happens in our line of work," Zaitsev uttered clearly.

Now you needed to retell everything from your statement in your own words: that was how the purge review worked. It was no surprise his colleagues were sitting there stewing—as if they cared about Zaitsev's biography.

"Origin."

"Proletarian," Zaitsev answered clearly.

"Father."

"Father: unknown. Mother: laundress. Zaitseva, Anna. I can tell you about my mother."

"Unknown, you say?" Sharov's shaved head glistened as he buried his face in the folder.

Perhaps time for some new glasses, Zaitsev thought spitefully. And then he noticed that the folder he had taken the sheet of paper from wasn't the yellow card one with Zaitsev's personal file, but a good-quality leather one. Such good quality was something Zaitsev didn't like the look of.

"And here we have some other data," Comrade Sharov began enticingly. "An unambiguous entry in the parish registry. Anna Zaitseva was married to Danilov, Pyotr Sergeevich, merchant. St Petersburg, 1908."

Zaitsev didn't flinch. Not a flicker.

"My dad had his way with my mum and scarpered. In all honesty, that's how I came about. I'm sorry, but whoever my dad was, it's shrouded in mystery."

"And yet here it says: Anna Zaitseva..."

"With all due respect, Anna Zaitsevas are as common as muck in Leningrad. What are you hinting at?"

Sharov gave the perfect impression of a distressed sigh. But his voice conveyed nothing: it was metallic, didactic.

Zaitsev remembered the spider's web from his dream that morning. Then out of nowhere he thought of a childhood rhyme: *Fou, fou, fum—nightmare be gone!*

"I'm not hinting at anything, Comrade Zaitsev. I'm saying it as it is, plain and direct. You misled the Soviet police and the Soviet people."

The end of his sentence was drowned out by a loud shriek of laughter. Everyone turned towards the window. The guffaw had come from a rotund, middle-aged woman sitting on the windowsill, her stout booted legs poking out from under her skirt.

"Oh, I can't," she squealed.

Zaitsev hoped his face didn't give anything away.

"You, citizen... Citizen!..." The *gepeushnik* began to fuss. "Is she an employee? If you're an employee then behave like one, or you leave the room this instant!"

He'd have as much success trying to budge a rhino.

Pasha knew how to handle men. The drunkards of Fonarny Lane knew to fear her wrath. She wiped her red face with the hem of her cardigan.

"I'm a witness, actually. What of it? Well, I knew your Nyourka."

"She's not mine. You're referring to the aforementioned Citizen Anna Zaitseva? You knew her?"

He had come out in a rash of raspberry red. His short neck quickly filled with blood.

A short, sharp blow is usually enough, mused Zaitsev. That should finish him off.

"Answer properly, citizen! We're not at the market. State your name and vocation."

The GPU man hovered his cartridge pen over his sheet of paper, poised to make notes.

"Yes, yes, I've nothing to hide. Praskovya Lukina's my name. Vocation: janitor."

Comrade Sharov didn't manage to get a word in before she was off again.

"So you see, this Miss Nyourka Zaitseva. Forgive me, comrade policeman. You're a Soviet man, p'raps you won't catch my drift. How it was in the old times, you know… You don't rake it in working at the laundry, do you? Well, suffice to say, goodness only knows who the father is. That Nyourka were a lively lass, that she were."

Sharov was distracted for a moment from the fact that Pasha ought not to have been in the room.

"Zaitseva was engaged in prostitution?" he asked, hopefully.

"Oh no"—Pasha waved her rough red claw of a hand. "What, are you deaf? A laundry lass, she were, like I said. Washed and scrubbed. Your linen and your smalls, whatever came. That's how she earned her living. No, no, the lads were for the soul. She had a weakness for the lads, let's say, God rest her soul."

Sharov hurled his cartridge pen onto the table, spattering ink. A few drops landed on the blue top of his cap. This sent him into even more of a rage.

"Enough!" he yelped.

What's it to be? thought Zaitsev. Stroke? Heart attack?

"Citizen… You, citizen… You'll express yourself in a civilized fashion here!"

The audience was already chuckling openly. The fear had even lifted from the commission—on their faces appeared the first blush of a smutty, knowing smile.

"Civilized? Well, well, what's that now?" asked Pasha at full volume. A new explosion of laughter.

Zaitsev stared at Pasha. She didn't even look his way.

"Stop fooling around this instant!" spluttered Sharov, the *gepeushnik*.

"I'll say it civilized like," she mumbled in a more submissive tone, throwing a quick glance at Zaitsev. "Forgive me, comrade policeman."

She inhaled deeply, taking air into her expansive chest; at the fullest point, a button burst open. Savouring her words, she continued, "How to describe Nyourka Zaitseva? Well, she was a…"

The familiar, terse profanity clicked deliciously in the air. The entire room collapsed into laughter. Comrade Sharov burst out of his chair, nearly knocking over the flimsy ficus. Someone from the commission grabbed the bell on the table and began to shake it furiously, calling for order. Its ringing also sounded like a shriek of laughter.

"Stop it!" the GPU man yelled in vain. "Leave the room this instant!"

Samoilov made his way through the aisle like Moses across the Red Sea when it parted in the storm. His full body was constrained by his jacket, otherwise he might have spread even more about the middle. Unexpectedly, given his build, Samoilov was as agile as a cat. His short sideburns accentuated the feline look.

"I'm warning you: you're next on my list!" choked Sharov.

Looking around at the raging sea, Samoilov went one better than Moses. He put two fingers in his mouth and let off a loud whistle that cut through the air like a whip. The sea subsided. Everyone fell silent.

Samoilov didn't even glance at the commission.

"All right, Zaitsev. Enough sitting around. Squad 2's about to leave. Mokhovaya Street. A body."

Zaitsev lingered for a moment. He spotted Kopteltsev and asked him with a glance. Kopteltsev merely nodded.

"Off you go," he ordered drily.

The chairs shuffled. Zaitsev jumped from the rostrum. Everyone broke into motion, not just Squad 2. With visible relief, everyone was glad to hurry back to their interrupted affairs.

"We have more important things to attend to here!" boomed the *gepeushnik*, Sharov, leaning towards the audience.

Samoilov once again looked at the CID chief, Kopteltsev. But he had suddenly found something much more interesting under his fingernails.

"What do you mean, comrade?" Samoilov was indignant. "A Soviet citizen has been found dead. What's more important than that?"

"This is Comrade Sharov, Nikolai Davydovich"—Zaitsev quickly filled Samoilov in.

Kopteltsev said nothing. His little cherry eyes didn't even blink. But Zaitsev knew: it wouldn't be long until they knew everything there was to know about this Agent Sharov.

"For interrupting the implementation of the task—" Sharov launched into a running start.

But Samoilov was already racing ahead. "What do you mean, interrupting? When we have a common task? Protecting the peace and the labour of Soviet citizens. A task assigned to us by the state," he enunciated loudly, his palm helping to separate one word from the next. An echo bounced off the empty walls. "A Soviet citizen is dead. And the perpetrator must be found and punished according to Soviet law."

Sharov too turned to Kopteltsev for support—but he too couldn't catch his eye. Kopteltsev merely raised his chubby palm, as if silently saying, "OK, enough."

Interesting, thought Zaitsev, observing their little pantomime.

Kopteltsev's wordless gesture, or perhaps the word "Soviet", silenced the *gepeushnik* like a stake putting paid to a vampire. Samoilov added insult to injury with a final glare. Only then did he turn his back on Sharov. The GPU agent was now left sitting alone at an empty table. He stood up with a jolt, pulling the tablecloth with him. His cap dropped to the floor, rolled away, further than he could reach, and flopped there like a pancake. Nobody rushed to pick it up.

"This is not the last you'll hear from me, I assure you of that," Sharov creaked, struggling to free his legs from the long tablecloth.

V

The police bus was already rumbling and shaking. With his short, stubby legs, Samoilov ran across the cobbled street and pulled himself up on board. He swore when he almost stepped on the tail of the dog stretched out on the floor. Ace of Clubs nuzzled his face against his handler's lap.

Samoilov flopped down next to Demov.

"Loafers," he said. "Making out that it's work, the bastards."

Everyone resented the OGPU presence in the department.

"All they do is get in the way and stop us from working," grumbled Samoilov. "What is it with them and their bleeding class enemies? It's 1930, for fuck's sake! Lyokha, are you asleep or something?" he shouted to the driver without changing his tone in the slightest. "Let's go already!"

The vehicle shuddered into action and turned out of Gorokhovaya Street.

"Hey Vasya," came Martynov's voice from the back. "What was that weasel pestering you about? What's all this about a merchant dad?"

Zaitsev barely turned around. "Don't you get it? We're up to our ears in work, but I guess these parasites don't have a lot on right now—they've got to think up something to keep themselves busy."

Samoilov interrupted. "The little nit will slip his superiors a note, like, look at me, look how hard I've worked. Surely I deserve a room? Or bump up my rations."

"Who knows," said Demov.

"It's obvious, Demov! What kind of class enemies do they think we've got in the fourteenth year of the Revolution?"

Demov turned away and looked out of the window somehow too intently. It was clear that he didn't like the topic.

"And where's Serafimov, anyway?" Samoilov suddenly remembered.

"Listen, do me a favour, swap seats with me," Zaitsev asked. After an awkward little quadrille with Samoilov in the back of the shuddering vehicle, Zaitsev ended up sitting next to Demov.

Demov was a renowned detective long before the Revolution. Infamous, perhaps. He had happened to arrest a minister, an officer of the guards and the owner of the third-largest fortune in the empire. The case resulted in charges being lifted from some ordinary people, destitute even, but Demov was lambasted in the conservative press; his name was hissed in drawing rooms across the city, and he was twice dismissed. And, indeed, stripped of the right to return to public service. Infamy as a kind of Robin Hood, a protector of the poor, was not without its repercussions. But after the Revolution, which ripped apart the lives of millions, Demov's reputation served him well. Unlike most people, he retained the same role in the new life as in the old, as a detective. In 1922, he received a pistol engraved with a dedication. Whenever a party cell needed an example of an old specialist who had served the new regime and could impart his experience to the Soviet cadres, they would call Demov.

Zaitsev wanted to talk to him about the murder of Faina Baranova. He ran through all the strange finds in the victim's room: the goings-on with the curtain and the dress.

"And?" asked Demov, looking away from the window.

"It's just odd, that's my point. If there's a killer, he went to a lot of effort to make the whole scene look pretty. The bastard wasn't in a hurry. Anyone else would get away as fast as he could."

"Perhaps not his first time," Demov suggested.

"That's not the point. Why go to such lengths? That's what I don't understand."

"Firstly, Baranova could have hung up the curtain herself."

"The neighbours say that—"

"Middle-aged women often do things on a whim," Demov interrupted. "And, secondly, of course she would have put the dress on herself and, thirdly, done her own intricate hairstyle—if the killer was her lover."

Zaitsev thought for a moment. Yes, it was plausible.

And yet not quite.

"But the rose in her hand!" he exclaimed. "And that ridiculous feather duster. Yes, and the way she was posed in the chair. Not a pose she would have adopted herself. So the killer sat her like that? What for? It's madness."

"Not necessarily," Demov objected calmly. "First, it could be an extreme emotional response. Remorse. I remember how a certain cavalryman covered his lover with a shawl after killing her, and tidied up her dress."

"You still going on about that Baranova, Vasya?" asked Samoilov from the other seat.

The sniffer-dog handler was dozing with his cap over his eyes.

"Or the mother who smothered her illegitimate baby, and then carefully dressed it. Even a little bonnet. And swaddled it," continued Demov. "What's the difference? Grief and horror at the act committed can take strange forms."

Zaitsev shook his head.

"But that was under tsarism," suggested Martynov.

"Everything possible has already happened. Every crime resembles another," said Demov. "People are always the same. Same under tsarism as under Soviet rule."

"But don't you know, crime is a relic of antiquity?" said Samoilov. "You're too old for the Komsomol, Demov, but when the young people have their political meetings it's all explained."

It wasn't clear if he was joking.

Demov opened his hand and began to bend and flex his fingers. "People love and they hate, they crave money or a profitable position. Fear of being exposed, blackmail, or someone's standing in their way. That's it. The motives are always the same."

"Oh, I don't know," said Zaitsev, not without irony.

"Crime is the product of society," the driver interjected, taking a turn and just managing to catch the folded tripod in the aisle.

"Quite right, Lyokha," agreed Zaitsev. And he continued more seriously. "Demov, your psychological-realism theory doesn't work for everyone. Think about it logically. If our Soviet society—this new, classless society—is without precedent in the world, then it follows that its criminals are new and unprecedented, right? With unprecedented motives. Or are the only criminals these days those who are against the new society?"

"And you got to all that from asking why he put the feather duster in her hand?" asked Samoilov. "He was taking the piss, that's why he stuck it in her hand. What do you think, Martynov? You're sitting there all silent. Enlighten us with your thoughts."

Martynov stopped himself before he spoke. He didn't have a good answer.

"Who knows, who the hell knows," he tried to answer.

"Good God," muttered Demov, looking out of the window. They were just passing the railings of the Summer Garden. The heads of the gorgons didn't turn to watch them go. Behind the fence was a sea of green grass. The waves laughed, catching the glinting sun. Crisp white seagulls hung obliquely in the blue sky.

"What a wonderful, magical city," said Demov sadly. "I don't understand how anyone can commit murder, theft, fraud, when they're faced with this every day."

Samoilov snorted so loudly the dog looked up.

"The facades could do with a lick of paint here and there."

"We're here," shouted the driver, Lyokha, cutting short the discussion.

The police bus turned into Mokhovaya Street.

Zaitsev was very late home again. The clear water reflected the eerily light sky of the white Leningrad night. The houses, it seemed, were only pretending to sleep, visible to the slightest detail in the warm night air.

Through the *fortochka*, the little ventilation window, came Pasha's trumpeting voice, wailing something about love. Through the archway you could see the huge poplar—an unusual sight in the courtyard of a tenement block in the centre of Leningrad. It was much wider and brighter than your classic "well yard". The singer Vyaltseva had lived well. Zaitsev walked past the front door and turned into the yard. In Vyaltseva's time, this was where the poorer apartments were, with lower ceilings and narrower staircases. Here, in the janitor's quarters, was where Pasha had her digs. By the time Zaitsev had crossed the yard, she had reached the chorus.

"*The chrysanthemums…*" she crooned. The singing partially masked the chatter of the sewing machine.

There was a separate entrance to her digs. As usual, her door was wide open. The gauze-mesh curtain fluttered a little in the draught.

"Ah, hello," said Pasha, breaking off her singing as she noticed Zaitsev on the threshold. "The Leningrad police never sleep."

Zaitsev closed the door after him.

"Pasha, you lied today," he said quietly and coldly. "Why?"

"*…have long since faded…*" The machine started up again with its chatter. The garish fabric crept out from under the needle.

Zaitsev leant on the table with both hands.

"Pasha, I don't recommend deceiving the Soviet government."

The chatter broke off. Pasha piped down. She blinked.

"You know that I've had a room here since I came here from the orphanage. That I only know my mother from documents. You can't just claim to remember her."

Pasha shrugged her mighty shoulders.

"Don't shake your shoulders like that—you're not Vyaltseva. Answer me. Come on, what's all this about?"

"Why! Are you offended, or what? I didn't mean to cause offence. I just want to see justice."

"By lying."

"What, do you think I didn't know what that pimple was getting at?"

"How did you hear about that pimple anyway? Tell me."

"Never you mind how. Well, if you must know, Klavka told me—she's the one who sweeps on Voznesensky. And she heard it from Pakhomych on the Fontanka, and he heard it from Lyuska at your place on Gorokhovaya. And Lyuska read it on the noticeboard."

He knew the Leningrad janitors were a close-knit network, but Zaitsev was once again amazed by how they stuck together.

"I see, Pasha. Thanks, of course. Very comradely of you. But that's enough. I've got nothing to hide. And you can stay out of it with your nonsense and lies. Got it?"

Pasha grinned.

"Comradely, ha! I need your comradeship like a dog needs a fifth leg. Yes, I heard about your purges, so I rushed off. It's really not going to work for us if you get whisked off. We need a copper in the house, all right? I know all the hooligans and the drunks around here. And then there's Fonarny Lane around the corner. All kinds of riff-raff that way. Then there's the alkies and wasters down at Sennaya. But right now they wouldn't dare come this way. They give us a wide berth. Yes, until you joined the police, we had smashed windows once a week, it seemed. Goodness knows how much they've stolen from ordinary people… Comradely, that's right." She grinned again. "It's not just me—everyone knows we need our own copper in the house."

Zaitsev was somewhat taken aback at the simplistic zoological pragmatism of the neighbours. Charles Darwin, that great expert on the struggle and coexistence of species in the wild, might have used this example had he lived to see the victory of Bolshevism.

"Pasha, I'm not your copper. If any of you breaks the law, you'll be questioned in all severity. Understand?"

Pasha nodded her head vigorously, like a horse trying to shake off a sack.

"Don't forget to leave me your ration cards for the month," she reminded him gently.

The sewing machine started chattering away again.

"…*have long since faded…*" was again heard drifting into the white Leningrad night.

In his room, Zaitsev slid the latch on the door. He didn't turn the light on. The room was light enough from the nocturnal daylight, from the water. He gripped the edge of the dresser and lifted it. He pulled it away from the wall, trying not to make a sound.

He unstuck the thick envelope from the back of the dresser and pulled out the documents that were inside.

He immediately set aside his employment-record book. There could be no doubt about that: he had received it himself. He had also earned everything recorded in it.

Zaitsev stared for a long time at the small, thick photograph. Time to part with it, it seemed. His heart was seized by grief. Would his memory be reliable enough to hold on to this face? What if one day he could no longer remember? He felt sick at the thought. Surely he couldn't burn it? But what if this picture cost him his life? Zaitsev stared at it as though he hoped to burn the image onto the back of his eyes. He hesitated, but then lowered the picture into the copper bowl.

He tossed his Osoaviakhim membership card onto the table, and with it the small square photograph and his employment book. His library card landed on the same pile.

He brought the birth certificate right up to his eyes. Then he held it up to the light. He turned it over. Everything was as it should be. The document shouldn't raise suspicions. It looked fine. Why would it not be? Mother: Anna Zaitseva. Father: unknown.

His heart was thumping slightly.

The place behind the chest of drawers was reliable enough if Pasha decided to rummage around or some idiot came looking for something to steal. But during a search, a professional search? Zaitsev himself could not recall seeing anyone ever moving the furniture at a crime scene. But who knows what they were taught at OGPU.

He pulled the bowl closer. Holding the birth certificate over it, he fumbled with the matchbox. No document—no questions. He struck a match.

Or perhaps best not to? It was at least some kind of document confirming the existence of the son of an unmarried St Petersburg laundry worker, Anna Zaitseva. In defence against another document, it was at least a document, not just words.

Zaitsev almost burned his fingers, but managed to blow out the match.

He put the photo back in the envelope.

Chapter 2

I

When he arrived, Zaitsev discovered his office wasn't empty.
A visitor was sitting on a chair facing away from the door. A
close-cropped head poked out from a skinny shirt. His slightly
protruding ears glowed red in a shaft of light; it was early but
the sun was already out with a vengeance. The stranger was
holding his jacket on his lap, giving him the look of a passenger waiting for a train.

"Citizen, how did you slip past the duty officer?" said
Zaitsev by way of greeting.

The stranger jumped up. He could hardly have been a day
past twenty. Round little face like an owl.

Zaitsev didn't give him the chance even to open his mouth.
"Follow me."

The kid didn't argue.

In the large, spacious but shabby stairwell, they went
downstairs to the duty officer. The wooden counter was
already crowded with the first visitors of the day.

The duty officer was patiently addressing a woman with a
shawl draped over her shoulders. "Citizen, kindly sit down."

Zaitsev's appearance gave her new hope and she rushed
over. All Zaitsev could make out were the words "attic" and "I
beg you". Her freshly washed sheets had been stolen from the
attic: the same old Leningrad story.

"Citizen, what do you think we're going to do?" said Zaitsev,
trying to get past her. "This is Criminal Investigation. It's the
district police you need."

Zaitsev leant over the counter and whispered to the duty

officer, throwing a glance at his visitor. "What's with this lad here?" Zaitsev understood right away that this was no ordinary citizen who had been let straight into the investigator's office to make a statement—the duty officer would never let a stranger past the counter and upstairs. The only reason Zaitsev had dragged him downstairs was to unsettle him and put him in his place.

"They sent reinforcements," the attendant whispered back. "With Serafimov being away."

"Who did?"

"Comrade policeman, who'll find my sheets?" said the woman, keen that he shouldn't forget that she was there waiting.

"I'm afraid, ma'am, if your sheets were stolen, they'll be in a neighbour's chest of drawers. And unless they're dim enough to hang them up to dry in the same attic, then no one's going to find them, are they?"

She was taken aback.

Zaitsev looked at the newcomer; he was standing quietly at a distance, his blue eyes peeking out from under half-closed eyelids at the queue that was amassing. A Finn, Zaitsev presumed. Or Estonian.

He made his way through the crowd. The reception was steadily filling with the smell of tobacco and unwashed bodies. The Soviet Union was a state of equals. But the ones jostling in the public queues weren't the ones who smelt of mint toothpaste, soap and perfume. And the CID reception was no exception.

Zaitsev beamed at the "Finn" with an excessively broad smile.

"Why are you so quiet, then? So you're the reinforcements?"

"That's right," he answered.

"I'm Zaitsev."

"Nefyodov," said the Finn, holding out his hand.

"Had enough of standing around as a sentry, then, Nefyodov?" he said with a grin.

"Not at all."

"What are you clicking your heels for, then? Just been demobbed?"

"Three years ago."

Not as young as he looks, Zaitsev realized.

"It was time we had some reinforcements," said Zaitsev with a nod, giving him a slap on the shoulder. "Everyone's up to their ears. Come on then, let's go. No time to stand around chatting. We'll throw you right in. You'll meet everyone on the job."

When they reached the right room, Zaitsev knocked on the open door. Demov, sitting at his desk, peered up over his glasses.

"May I introduce you, Comrade Demov? New staff."

"Nefyodov."

"Nefyodov?" asked Demov, as though he were asking a museum guide for more information. "Got a bit of a Chukhna look about you."

Being met with such a comment was no surprise to the newcomer, but it didn't seem to offend him either. Or perhaps it was a surprise and he was offended, only his face didn't give anything away.

"Well then, welcome, Comrade Nefyodov."

Demov realized that Zaitsev was deliberately dumping the new boy on him, but he didn't even raise an eyebrow.

"Bring him up to speed would you, Demov?" said Zaitsev amiably. "Then I'll come and join you."

Demov nodded. Nefyodov leant forward.

"The case is straightforward enough. Two comrades were having a drink together..." Zaitsev heard Demov start up as he walked away.

He slowed down at the typing pool. He could hear the muffled clatter from behind the door. Zaitsev knocked on the closed hatch and turned the handle to open the door. The wooden shutter opened. A ruddy nose and a greying head of curls appeared.

"Natalya Petrovna, would you do me a favour? I need to check something. A new employee has been issued his ID, but it seems the surname's wrong. Would you mind having a look?"

All Natalya Petrovna took in was that there had been a typo. She was aghast. The nose disappeared. There was a buzz and the door clicked open to reveal the cork-lined interior. Zaitsev pushed the door to enter and for a moment was deafened from the clatter of typewriters. The typists were all wearing headphones. No one looked up; no one seemed to notice the visitor. But some tilted their faces even further forward, their fingers flitting over the keyboards. It wasn't hard to distinguish which of the typists were unmarried. In Samoilov's mind, "secretary" was cynically filed under "girls looking for husbands"; besides them, CID was staffed almost entirely by men.

One of the women was first to stop and take off her headphones. The rest followed. The clatter quietened down. Zaitsev quickly established who had been given the appointment letter to type up again. The typewriters started up again. Zaitsev, his nerves frayed by the noise, quickly ran his eyes over the document. His suspicions were confirmed. Klim Prokhorovich Nefyodov hadn't been promoted from the guards, the traffic police or a district precinct. He wasn't from any police department at all. He had been transferred to the Leningrad CID directly from OGPU.

II

"Officially, and from a practical point of view, they're right." Demov blew out a blue stream of smoke, scaring off a dozy fly that had been sunning itself on the railing. Demov crushed the cigarette butt in his small pocket ashtray. "We definitely need more staff."

Zaitsev nodded. He no longer smoked, but the balcony on the facade was the only place left in the building where, under the pretext of a cigarette, you could talk in private.

"Do you think it's because of the purge?"

Demov shrugged. He looked down towards the street. There was a clatter from below. A cart laden with firewood crept along; a truck scurried past. The tops of people's heads bobbed along like peas. The paved surface of the street seemed to exude humidity.

"I doubt it. Things have calmed down since Pyotr-Jacques."

Kopteltsev's predecessor, Comrade Pyotr-Jacques, had come to a sticky end not that long ago. Or rather, he had got off lightly: they packed him off to somewhere in the provinces. But they could have locked him up. Or handed him over to the tribunal. Things had been disappearing from the evidence store, and it had started to mount up: fur coats, trinkets, money. It turned out that the CID chief was a petty thief. When the story came to light, party leaders and the party newspapers called for a tough response. Across the city, there was outrage at the police for covering their own backs (which was partly true). So, to appease the public, there had been demonstrative reprisals against the less senior ranks of CID.

Kopteltsev had been appointed the new chief, transferred from OGPU. He'd be like a new broom, they said. He would sweep out the old, bring in the new, free from the corrupting influence of old feuds and loyalties, old habits and collusion.

Demov lit another cigarette.

"Haven't you had enough?" muttered Zaitsev, squinting at the flame. "Surely you're smoked through by now."

"Well, I outlived tsarism," Demov retorted. "Which is more

than I can say for many of my comrades, for all their workouts and cold rub-downs. I can get away with it. You're the one who's got all the running around to do—better look after your heart."

"Listen, Demov. There's one thing I don't get. Let's say you're right and there're more heads to roll. But who? The entire investigation team was sent packing, remember? The lead detective on the Pyotr-Jacques case ended up somewhere in Novohopersk. Everyone was punished. They got their comeuppance. All done and dusted."

Demov shook his head.

"They seem to have noticed you, Vasya, don't they?"

"Me? Well, I interviewed a few of the pawnshop owners who received the goods, that's all. I helped him out. I was never part of his team."

"Wasn't your signature on the reports, the pawnshop ones?"

Zaitsev didn't answer.

"That'll be it," said Demov. "We all came to their attention to an extent. As accomplices. We're all under suspicion now. That's why they've sent us Comrade Nefyodov. As a mole."

"But you can't keep an eye on everyone."

"What do you mean?" Demov looked at him suspiciously.

"Well, it seems to me Nefyodov's got a very specific task. Just one thing to do."

"You think?"

Zaitsev heard his voice tremble—it was ever so slight, but the old detective's voice definitely trembled. The word "specific" made Demov think of himself.

Zaitsev looked at him.

"What? You were staring at me like a cat," laughed Demov. The smoke went the wrong way; he coughed. "Trying to hypnotize me or something? Vasya, you just need to glance at someone, then turn away. Don't stare like that. It slices right through you. Ouch. The ladies aren't going to like it."

"They don't like me much anyway," muttered Zaitsev, looking away. It was probably too late to remove all the reports from the Pyotr-Jacques case with his signature on.

"Vasya, for all your broad shoulders and sportsman's build, the ladies can tell you'll be too delicate with them. There's something a bit—"

"You what? A load of bull. Better if you just tell me, what am I supposed to do with him? In the team? The guys aren't blind."

"Don't do anything special," said Demov, tossing his cigarette butt down to the street. "So they've sent reinforcements? Well, great. Let him work. Work him to the bone. Get him behind the camera. Running around after witnesses. So what have you got on now? The murder in the *kommunalka* on Nevsky?"

Demov still called 25th October Prospekt by its old name, Nevsky Prospekt. Zaitsev winced at the thought of Faina Baranova: her eyes wide open, the rose in her dead hand.

"There's an entire apartment full of witnesses." Demov turned to escape the heat back into the cool of the offices, corridors and stairs. "Send Nefyodov to go and talk to them."

"Martynov and Samoilov have already interviewed everyone. I have, too."

"So? Let him get on with it. As long as he's out of the way. Maybe he'll dig something up. If he does—great. If not— never mind. What difference does it make? The main thing is keep him at arm's length."

III

"Vasya, what's all this about?" Martynov leant over the table. The dining room was filled with that characteristic noise that wove together the din of voices, the rumble of chairs and the clatter of aluminium spoons.

"Martynov, your hair wasn't on the menu, thank you. Get out of my dinner!" Samoilov shooed him off with a wave, covering his bowl of soup with his other hand.

"Well, what do you know? A free lunch. They didn't take the vouchers for soup today," said Demov, sitting down with his steaming bowl.

"Well, you can hardly call it soup," said Samoilov, his mouth full.

"What are you in a flap for, anyway?" asked Zaitsev, scooping up the fibrous gloop with his spoon. Martynov was clearly anxious about something.

"There's no way this is cabbage," said Demov. He had taken off his glasses and held them over the steaming bowl like a magnifying glass. In an instant the lenses misted over.

"Definitely not cabbage. It's what just fell out of Martynov's hair."

Martynov's voice rose as he all but screeched, "But seriously, Vasya! What did you send Nefyodov out to the neighbours again for?!"

Zaitsev glanced at Demov, as though for backup. But Demov just slurped his soup, as if the conversation had nothing to do with him.

"Sit down, Martynov. No need to yell at the entire canteen."

But Martynov just slapped his hand on the table.

"Martynov, breathe. Sit down," said Demov calmly.

Martynov wore a disgruntled expression, but he sat down. Then he got up again and went off to queue for his soup.

"Anyway," was all Zaitsev said.

"What was all that about?" mumbled Samoilov.

"He's afraid of the competition," Demov answered. "From long-legged young upstarts."

Nefyodov really had been running around for days. Errands just kept on coming from Zaitsev, from Demov, from Samoilov. But the newcomer didn't grumble or show any sign of discontent.

"At the time of Nicholas I, they say, by order of the tsar, soldiers had to be all looks and no brains, so they weren't a threat to their commanders," announced Demov, moving on to his second course: a sloppy mush with a greyish sausage in a puddle of brown gravy. "Our new colleague has come up trumps in that regard. All credit to him."

"No need to take the piss," Samoilov objected. "If it weren't for Nefyodov, we'd be running ourselves ragged, rushed off our feet. Speaking of which, I've a suggestion."

Martynov returned with a steaming tray.

"Martynov, did you hear that?"

His face was as sullen as before.

"What now?"

A cheerful Samoilov answered, "Unless something comes up, I suggest we all go for a civilized beer this evening. There's a new place, I've heard. Who's in, comrades?" Resting his elbow on the table, he opened up his square palm. In his other hand he held a glass of lukewarm sweet tea.

Demov nodded.

"Why not?" Martynov muttered.

"And you, Vasya?"

"Can't."

"Ah, come on."

"I'm going to the theatre."

"Ha! That's a good one!"

"You're going *where*?"

"What? We all need a bit of culture," Zaitsev said, defending himself. "Comrades, you're Soviet Komsomoltsi, don't forget. Not good-for-nothing layabouts."

"Aren't I a bit old for the Komsomol?" added Demov.

"We need to set an example," Zaitsev continued. "What about you, Samoilov? When was the last time you went to the ballet?"

"Ballet?" said Samoilov, his eyebrows raised in surprise. Demov laughed.

"Enough taking the mick. Quit pissing around," said Zaitsev, terse but friendly.

"Vasya," said Demov, pointing his cigarette in the air instructively. "Remember: a quick glance, then look away."

"All right, get lost!"

"What's all this? What's he on about?" fussed Samoilov.

"Demov... if I were you, I'd pay more attention to contemporary Soviet art and culture. Don't get left behind."

"Comrades," Demov announced. "Don't you see what's behind all this Komsomol youth-club nonsense? Comrade Zaitsev has a little *rond-ay-vou*. With a lady."

"Ooh!"

"You're having us on!"

"He's broken his oath!"

"Congratulations!"

Even Martynov forgot that he was annoyed. Zaitsev stood up and threw on his jacket, the sleeves falling into place. He flipped up the lapels.

"You uncultured lot. I'm off."

"Is she from the typing pool?"

"Canteen?"

"Traffic police?"

Zaitsev sped up to get away.

"So this bar I was talking about. There's something you've got to see," Samoilov resumed. "They've got those tall American bar stools like—"

"Yeah," interrupted Martynov, "for you to fall off after your third."

"Who says you're going to have a third?" said Samoilov. "We'll have a little drink and a few bar snacks. All civilized like."

IV

It is amazing how even one small person is entwined with all kinds of friendships, connections and acquaintances. Even the homicide victim Faina Baranova, described in the paperwork as "single", was someone's colleague, acquaintance, neighbour, friend, customer. Nefyodov really was run ragged, rushed off his feet.

Zaitsev listened to his report and understood that the more Nefyodov spoke, the less it made sense.

What would all these people be able to say about the victim? What could shed some light on her death? That she was a diligent worker? That she went to the hairdresser once a month?

They weren't exactly hot on the heels of the perpetrator. They hadn't found a murder weapon. Or any fingerprints. Demov had covered the entire room with black dust. "Hmm. This one's experienced. The fucker."

But even if he knew what he was doing, why would he change the clothes on the corpse? Experienced crooks were quick, efficient.

And what did experience have to do with it if nothing was stolen from the room?

That's what the neighbours say, anyway, Zaitsev told himself. But what did the neighbours know?

He chased away this thought. Doubts didn't help, they were just a distraction. Faina Baranova's murder had already passed into the category of those that would never be solved. But did Nefyodov realize that?

Nefyodov stood to attention by Zaitsev's desk.

All looks and no brains, Zaitsev recalled. Although Nefyodov actually reminded him more of an assiduous student.

He's never once asked where Serafimov is, Zaitsev realized. He's patient, the bastard. Meticulous. Goes about everything with such attention to detail. And yet his face was bright with interest.

"Well, well, Nefyodov," Zaitsev responded, feigning interest but not listening at all.

Nefyodov perked up a little and pulled out a small notebook from his pocket. Smart and elegant, it looked absurd in his large, bony hands. Nefyodov began to report back, reading from his notes, his pale eyebrows knotted in a frown, his nose seeming even longer from his concentration. All that penetrated Zaitsev's consciousness was the word "shepherd", uttered several times. It stumbled and toppled over the edge of his consciousness. Around fifteen years ago, little notebooks like that were used by debutantes to note down the names of gentlemen who had asked them to dance at balls. Unintentionally, Zaitsev found himself wondering where Nefyodov, a former GPU employee, had got his hands on a little object like that of class-enemy origin, but he preferred to chase away this idea. Not tonight.

"Excellent, Nefyodov!" he said sincerely. "Write your report, on my desk by the morning. Keep it up! Now, I think it's time to call it a day. Well done!"

Zaitsev patted Nefyodov on the shoulder, giving his colleague a little nudge out of the door as he left the room. Zaitsev locked the office door behind him.

V

Demov had been right. Zaitsev did have a date. But not with a girlfriend. More a girlfriend to be. He hoped. And if a Leningrad girl invited a Leningrad man to the ballet, then that man needed to pull out all the stops—this was no mere date. In terms of its significance, the ballet was just two rungs below the final judgement: meeting her friends.

A crowd was already rumbling in the lobby, in anticipation of the performance. Waiting for Lelia, Zaitsev smoothed down his hair in front of a large mirror set in an intricate gilded frame, the alloy-coated glass gleaming scornfully from the days when it reflected dress coats, uniforms, bustles and diamonds, not the dreary clobber of Soviet officials. The current reflection was a sea of porridge grey. Zaitsev moved away swiftly. They still hadn't opened the entrance to the auditorium.

Lelia stood by a velvet-upholstered bench, turning the small mother-of-pearl binoculars in her hands. Zaitsev bought a programme from the usher. And from the look on Lelia's face he knew that he had already committed his first error. A well-educated Leningrad suitor was supposed to know, without a programme to help, what they were here to see, who the composer was and the choreographer, and who the principal dancers were. Zaitsev rolled the programme into a tube, tucked it into his jacket pocket and issued a flustered cough.

Lelia pretended not to notice the false start, linked her arm through his outstretched elbow, and together they climbed the broad, white-marble staircase to the upper foyer. The white marble made it seem particularly spacious and bright. Here were the tall doors that led to what was once the Royal Box—the largest private box, in the centre of the house. Instead of the imperial monograms, everywhere was emblazoned with the crossed hammer and sickle. Lelia nodded again and again to her acquaintances. Zaitsev felt stiff and awkward.

"Perhaps they've opened the doors by now?"

"Sh," Lelia whispered with a smile. "They're all twisting their necks to see you. Desperate to find out who you are."

"Will they be disappointed I'm not from Utesov's jazz band?"

Lelia began to tell him about her studies at the institute. She was studying alongside her job as a laboratory assistant. Perfect. Let her chat, thought Zaitsev, relieved. Couples were circling around the lobby as though doing laps of an ice rink. A fat man in a three-piece suit glided by with his companion. Isn't he hot in that? Zaitsev wondered. Out of the corner of his ear he heard the word "nutcracker". Ah, so that's what they were about to see, thought Zaitsev, relieved. He pictured something bright and colourful, with white blizzards of dancers in fluffy skirts, a fir tree, Christmas. A memory of something from long ago, a recollection of something very comforting and familiar.

Lelia was quite chatty now. Zaitsev muttered some kind of well-meaning nonsense. She laughed and seemed even more lovely.

After the second call, the audience jostled into the auditorium. Their seats were in the *baignoire*, at the end by the aisle. It was with a certain enjoyment that Zaitsev gazed around the hall and took in the sounds. The violins tuning up in the orchestra, the discordant hum of the audience, the lustre of the chandelier—it all filled him with a curious anticipation. He smiled at Lelia. But she was busy, having a quick peek at the boxes through her binoculars. The third call. The ushers closed the doors to the auditorium. The lights went out. Finally, Lelia leant back in her seat. The first notes of Tchaikovsky poured into the darkness and the curtain rose.

Tall cardboard shields entered the empty stage. The dancers appeared, dressed in overalls. Zaitsev glanced cautiously at Lelia. She took his hand in hers, but didn't turn her head. He also started to watch the stage.

Apparently, it was a special, avant-garde *Nutcracker*. Or maybe it was constructivist. Whichever it was, Zaitsev soon began to feel like his head was being squeezed from all sides. He stifled a yawn.

Shields shuffled around the stage. The corps de ballet scurried about dressed in sports attire. Huge swathes of fabric stretched across the stage, the dancers' heads bobbing about behind. A flute piped up. And although the orchestra sang, rumbled, chirped and whistled, it seemed to Zaitsev that his arms and legs were getting heavier, hotter, and that the quiet in the hall was getting darker, deeper, more velvety soft. "'The Dance of the Shepherds,'" came a sarcastic whisper to the side. Nefyodov's voice buzzed in his mind, like a fly beating against glass. "The shepherd..." it said over the trilling flute. The shepherd. And a second later Zaitsev heard his own snoring.

He woke with a jolt. "For God's sake!" gasped Lelia. There was a flutter of quiet laughter from behind. "How could you?" hissed Lelia with tears in her voice, before she got up and fled along the dark aisle out of the theatre.

"Lelia, wait!" whispered Zaitsev as he rushed after her.

"Comrades! Please!" hissed everyone they passed. The door opened a second, letting a fleeting rectangle of light into the stalls.

Zaitsev was blinded by the bright light in the foyer.

He rushed out behind Lelia into the lobby. Her footsteps left a hollow echo in the empty hall.

"Lelia, wait!" He finally grabbed her hand. "Please. I feel terrible."

Behind the glass doors loomed the curious faces of the ushers.

"The ballet is clearly boring for you!" She blushed, even stamped her foot.

"I wasn't bored at all! It's just my work. I never get enough sleep. I don't know how it happened!"

"Don't you dare!" She pulled away her hand. "You... You... you're a philistine! Just leave me alone!"

Zaitsev turned to face the ushers. They immediately with-drew into the foyer, pretending that what was happening didn't interest them in the slightest.

Zaitsev exhaled with a noisy sigh. So, that was it for the date, then.

He walked over to the poster. *The Nutcracker* was embla-zoned across it.

You've got to be kidding? thought Zaitsev angrily.

The name of the choreographer was written in small but chunky letters. Zaitsev tossed the programme into the metal bin and left the building. The evening air was warm and clear.

The lanterns near the theatre gave off a dull sheen, like huge white pearls. Across the road, in the Conservatory, some windows glowed with orange electric light: either students were still practising or they had evening lectures.

Lelia had vanished into thin air.

At the tram stop, people huddled together as one, their heads turned towards the bridge, from where their tram was expected to appear.

Zaitsev had nothing to go home for.

He stretched out the walk as best he could. He stood admiring the gloomy, red-brick New Holland Arch. The clear sky was reflected in the stagnant waters. Branches drooped from motionless trees. For the one thousand, one hundred and fifty-third time, Zaitsev regretted giving up smoking. Slowly he trudged home along the Moika embankment. On the way, he entertained himself by composing a letter that he, Zaitsev, "employee of the Leningrad police", would send to the "respected *littérateur*" Zoshchenko with a request that he write about this heartbreaking case from a lifetime of bitter romantic experience. He suddenly felt unbelievably tired. His jaws were pulled apart by a yawn.

The embankment was deserted and you could see ahead

as far as St Isaac's Square. There was just one Ford parked a little way off, snug against the curb. The driver was sleeping, his cap slid down over his eyes.

Zaitsev turned towards his front door, dreaming of lying down and falling asleep. It had been stupid to drag himself out to the ballet when for once he had a free evening and he could have gone to bed early to catch up on sleep. Or had a beer with the guys. Beer and sleep. A grey cat sprang from the stairwell. As usual, it smelt of dishwater.

The door to the apartment wasn't locked.

One of the neighbours must have forgotten to lock it. Zaitsev pulled the key from the keyhole and stepped inside. A candle burned in the corridor, giving a stingy, dim yellow light. The neighbours never forgot to turn off the electric light and had stern words for anyone who left the bulb on. Zaitsev stepped gently, barely noticing how he softened his tread.

He couldn't hear anything unusual. There was no noise at all in the apartment, and this seemed to Zaitsev what was most suspicious. In the evenings, the neighbours fidgeted; there was the creak of floorboards or some unfortunate piece of furniture; there was always someone talking, someone listening to the radio, someone shuffling along the corridor, someone washing in the kitchen, someone yelling at a child. His hand lay across his chest, his palm feeling for the hilt of his pistol under his jacket.

Zaitsev pushed open the door to his room.

On the chair in the middle of the room sat the janitor, Pasha. Her face was grey, wan. And her lips were quivering.

"Pasha, what are you doing here?" asked Zaitsev, still at the door. At that moment, two shadows stepped out from behind the door. The hunched figure of the house manager moved away from the wall.

"The janitor is a witness. And so is the house manager."

In one glance, Zaitsev took everything in: the tunic, Sam Browne belt, blue Gallifet trousers, blue cap.

"Don't do anything stupid. Don't make a scene," the second one added sullenly. He was dressed in civvies and a foul smell wafted from his mouth.

"Citizen Zaitsev?" the first asked, enunciating clearly. Pasha swallowed with a loud gulp.

"Hands behind your back. You're under arrest. Don't try anything clever."

There was no need to ask who he was being arrested by. The blue-topped cap gave the answer before the question had even occurred to him: this was an OGPU officer.

He quickly relieved Zaitsev of his pistol and ID. Pasha sat there neither alive nor dead. They handed her a piece of paper, which she signed without looking; her trembling hand struggled to obey. They gave the house manager the same form to sign; he was also whiter than chalk.

"Let's go, Zaitsev. The car's downstairs."

Chapter 3

I

The hatch in the iron cell door slid up with a clank. There was a knock and a crunch as a key turned in the lock. The inmates rolled over, jumped to their feet, then sat down on their bunks. The cellmates squinted at the door, blinking in the light. Their eyes, whether dark or light, large or narrow, surrounded by smooth skin or wrinkles, expressed no knowledge or understanding, only fear: who was next? Judging by the dark strip visible through the muzzled window, it was still night. Or perhaps it was already morning? Zaitsev had lost track of time here in prison. The days were all alike, and the nights just got worse. It was dark well into the morning now that it was autumn. He rubbed his eyes, reluctant to emerge from sleep. Night was the time for interrogations: that particular form of human interaction in which a uniformed individual could treat the person sitting in front of him—in shoes without shoelaces and clothes without buttons—to a fist in the face, a blow to the teeth, a booted kick; in which the officer could take a chair to your head, could maim you, cripple you. Could do basically anything. The local law that the inmates knew like the back of their hand.

"Zaitsev!" the warden bellowed in a hoarse bark. "You're out."

Zaitsev stood up. Everyone tried not to look at him. It was as though they were afraid to catch the eye of the condemned, as though the curse were contagious.

"Get your stuff," the warden sneered.

"Am I being transferred?" Zaitsev asked.

"Do I look like your information service?"

Zaitsev glanced at his bunk. Get your stuff. He picked up his jacket, which was folded in place of a pillow. He shook it out, pulled it on. That was it, all the stuff he had.

"Out!"

And the door slammed shut with another clang, leaving relief in the cell: not me today.

The bulbs in the corridor gave a dim light. But they weren't interested in saving electricity in the investigators' offices. His head bent forwards, the investigator was scribbling away. The same poster still hung over his head: POLITICAL VERMIN, WE WILL CRUSH YOU. A serpent in a top hat squirmed in the mighty fist of a rosy-cheeked hero. The investigator himself could hardly have looked any more different from his poster counterpart. Zaitsev suddenly realized that although the room was the same as usual, this was a different officer. He tried to commit this new face to memory by following the usual protocol: male, between thirty and forty, sturdy physique—then he stalled. The investigators' faces were all like linen buttons: unhealthy, sunken, doughy white from a lack of daylight. In the Shpalernaya Street prison (although it had a different name these days, like everything), the air was thick and reeked of bad breath.

Gloomily, the investigator handed Zaitsev a folded piece of paper.

"Sign here," he said, jabbing it with a finger. Something in his voice sounded to Zaitsev like regret.

"I should read it first," said Zaitsev with the obstinacy that had already cost him several broken ribs and fingers.

"Well… read it then," the investigator spat out, struggling to overcome his contempt. He pushed the paper to Zaitsev across the table. Zaitsev couldn't help noticing the polite form of the verb the officer used. That was odd. Did it mean something? What? Nobody here ever addressed you in a polite register, until now. The response to any hint of defiance or disrespect was cursing and a beating—or plain old psychological terror: the investigator would storm out, slamming the door and leaving the prisoner for several hours in the oppressive empty room, where the corners began to swirl, a haze of horror that spreads gradually over the room, and then your consciousness. But Zaitsev was unmoved by their tricks. He had even found he could block out the pain. His mind had remained clear, both then and now. And to his mind, this shift in tone suggested a sudden loss of power.

This conclusion was almost immediately confirmed. Because the very next moment Zaitsev read: "Released on bail…"

The next thing to fly across the table to Zaitsev was a non-disclosure agreement.

"I need to read this first," said Zaitsev again, already enjoying the situation.

"What is there to read?" grunted the investigator. "It's the standard format."

Giving the impression that he was reading slowly and carefully, Zaitsev racked his brains, trying to work out what all this could mean.

He signed.

He threaded his boots with the laces he was given, from someone else's boots: they were too short. To Zaitsev they were as disgusting as having worms in his hands. He yanked the bootlaces back out and threw them on the floor beside him.

"Don't lose your clogs, you moron," his guard said quietly. But he didn't hit him.

They led him out through a side door. The courtyard was closed in on all four sides and, above, the sky was still thinking of changing from black to ultramarine. On the inner walls, orange light glowed in the windows: in there, their abhorrent work continued. Zaitsev's shoulders tensed from the cold, but he was immediately shoved into a car. He flopped onto the seat. He felt it in his ribs, which were still tender. An escort in a felt greatcoat squeezed in next to him. The leather of the seats squeaked against the material under his backside. The car had that smell you only get in brand-new cars.

The car shuddered. They drove around the side of the building and the inner gate opened to let them through. The Shpalernaya prison grounds spat the car out onto the street.

The driver was silently focusing on his task, picking out objects with the beams of his headlamps, be it a cast-iron bollard, a stretch of fence, the corner of a house or a bridge in the distance. "Liteyny Prospekt," Zaitsev thought, recognizing it. His escort stared straight ahead with leaden eyes, only moving to clutch the leather loop above the window when he swayed as the car turned a corner. It was as if he were afraid of accidentally touching Zaitsev.

Do I smell of prison now? he wondered. He did have lice.

The hazy street lamps on the bridge flew past. The city was darker on this side. Every now and again there was a rare lit-up window. The city was still asleep. Silhouettes of hulking masses of factories loomed darkly, though they had already begun the morning shift. You could just make out the vastness of the river beneath the bulky indigo sky. The car darted along the deserted riverside embankment.

Best not to ask any questions, Zaitsev decided. He surmised that for all his haughty poise, this OGPU guy was likely just a small cog and presumably knew very little about who he took from one place to another or why. He was probably unnerved by being charged with this unexpected errand.

On the other side of the river, Zaitsev could see the soft texture of trees, light in colour. Aptekarsky Island. A pang of nostalgia crept across his chest as he realized the leaves were already turning. He had been arrested when their sticky foliage was just coming into bud. And now the colour was already fading. Summer seemed to have fallen into a dark pocket of time. For Zaitsev, it was as though summer hadn't happened.

The GPU officer unstuck his narrow lips.

"The gay and carefree dragonfly / Chirped and sang the summer by; / Didn't stop to look around, / As winter crept across the ground," he declaimed.

Zaitsev looked askance, surprised to recognize the lines of Krylov's fable for children. Was the GPU man taking the piss? Apparently not. His voice and eyes were tinged with that melancholy that a more educated person would associate with Pushkin or Baratynsky. Was this the only poetry this guy knew? Perhaps he only finished elementary school, then a bit here and there at adult evening classes. This was the only poetic string he had to pluck. His hand slipped inside his greatcoat and fumbled in his trouser pocket.

"Want one?" he asked, out of the blue offering Zaitsev a crumpled pack of Nord.

Zaitsev didn't turn his head.

"I've given up."

"Good riddance. All you get is wheezy lungs," commented the *gepeushnik*, striking up a conversation.

"And the savings to be made," the chauffeur eagerly chimed in, with a good-natured glance in the rear-view mirror at the passengers in the back. "I've a friend who got the notion of growing his own tobacco!"

What he said was more like "grewing".

This was uncanny. There, in prison, as far as these people were concerned Zaitsev was just a physical substance, utterly lacking in any human attribute: feelings, habits, desires, thoughts, rights. He possessed only a capacity for fear and to experience pain. But now, it seemed, the further he went from the prison, the more he underwent a reverse transformation. He was reincarnated as a man. A Soviet citizen. He could be addressed, with eye contact, offered a cigarette, practical life tips.

Zaitsev didn't answer.

The car turned and slammed on the brakes just before hitting a wall. The driver toggled the gearstick. Zaitsev's GPU escort sprang out of the car with a sprightly bounce. Through the window was an inky darkness. It took Zaitsev a moment to realize that he himself—not a warden or an escort—was expected to open the door. A chilly dampness trickled into him. His shoulders twitched. He was in the summer jacket he had been wearing when he was arrested. The October wind wasn't going to hold back on his account.

Zaitsev felt like Alice after falling into the rabbit's hole— emerging on the other side everything seemed to have changed. A pity there was no one to share that with. Who else in the squad would have read *Alice's Adventures*? Picturing the scene, he grinned. He didn't resent the time he had served, the time he'd had stolen from him. Zaitsev didn't tend to regret what cannot be returned. He wasn't one to look back. Even from a distance, Zaitsev recognized the department's unmarked car. He could just make out a pale female face through the glass. There was the clucking sound of a baby crying. Zaitsev was a little surprised at the presence of an infant—unless he was mistaken. From the other embankment he could hear the swoosh and rustle of leaves of a huge park. This was Yelagin Island. It seemed brighter here, from the vast sky, from the water. A policeman stood waiting on the broad humpback bridge.

The GPU officer leant in to whisper an order to the driver through the open window. The driver frowned at Zaitsev through the windscreen.

"Don't worry, Arkadyev," the officer grinned, revealing a metal crown on one of his teeth. "You'll get a new one at the warehouse."

The driver leant round with his whole body and fumbled with one hand behind his seat. Stepping out of the car, without pleasure he handed Zaitsev a coat folded over twice. Zaitsev accepted, startled by how cold the lining was to touch. The coat smelt slightly of mothballs. The driver had clearly only just got it from the warehouse. It was in good condition, relatively new, but second-hand: it was the kind that successful New Economic Policy men were getting made for themselves two or three years ago in their heyday, full of belief in their freedom to pursue private enterprise, as announced by the Soviet government. The driver looked with regret at the coat as he handed it over. Perhaps he had been a butcher under the NEP, thought Zaitsev. A jovial, ruddy-faced joker— with blood on his hands. Or maybe a cabbie.

"So. All the best. Perhaps we'll meet again. I might have given up by then," said the *gepeushnik*, cordially extending his hand.

Zaitsev shook it.

The officer gave a wave, then dived into the car. The engine purred as the car gave off a puff of smoke and made a sharp turn. Its lights were visible again on the embankment as it hurried along on its return journey.

II

Zaitsev didn't know what to do next. What was he doing here? He walked over to the policeman. The wind on the bridge caught the hem of his coat; the cloth was dense, heavy as it slapped against his legs. Zaitsev pulled the coat tighter around him, raised the collar. His feet were already starting to freeze in his canvas shoes.

"Comrade Zaitsev," said the policeman, raising a hand to the peak of his cap. "Sergeant Kopytov."

"Hi."

Zaitsev still felt at sea. I wonder what day it is? he thought. But what difference does it make? Today's today. I'm alive, and who knows what tomorrow will bring.

"They're all there. Go straight ahead." The policeman waved his hand in the direction of the path, as if he were about to take a run-up from the bridge and dive into the stream. "And then a little to the right."

Zaitsev nodded.

"You don't have a light on you, do you, Kopytov?"

"Not at all," answered the sergeant cheerfully. "I'm in training on the GTO programme. Got to be ready for labour and defence!"

"Ah, a sportsman. Good for you. I don't smoke either," added Zaitsev. He shoved his hands in his pockets and set off along the path, which he could barely see in the half-light.

A soft glint played on the surface of the ponds on both sides of the path. The dreamy view was only slightly spoilt by the piercing, damp cold that wafted in from the water.

Through the soft air he could just make out voices, then an abrupt bark. Zaitsev turned off the path towards the voices. The grass was still standing tall, strewn with damp leaves. Without their laces, his shoes flopped and squelched, almost slipping off at every step. His feet were immediately sodden and numb.

Samoilov was rummaging through the leaves with a torch. The others were waiting for the morning to get going before beginning their search in daylight. At the soggy sound of footsteps they all turned around in concert, each in his own manner.

Zaitsev didn't notice any signs of surprise on their faces. Perhaps his own face didn't show anything either. They all seemed to be acting as though nothing unusual had happened.

"How are you doing, Zaitsev?" Demov asked, as though it was only yesterday that they last saw each other.

Samoilov held up a square palm. Martynov grunted something. Zaitsev saw that Serafimov was back in the squad, too. So the three months hadn't disappeared after all, rubbed out by an eraser.

No one asked him anything. They were tense with him, like he was a stranger—someone they'd heard of and knew by sight, but had never worked with.

"Go ahead, boss," said Martynov, stepping aside to let Zaitsev come forward.

And then he understood why they hadn't been shocked to see him. Every man's mental capacity has its limits, and after a glimpse at what was here by these two large, yellowing trees, anyone would for a time completely lose the capacity for shock.

The first corpse—kneeling—was a black man, in an orangey-yellow shirt so bright you couldn't miss it even in the twilight.

"Who found them?" Zaitsev asked. He coughed. His voice seemed not to want to obey him straight away.

"The nightwatchman," said Demov, nodding to the side. That must have been where they had taken him, deranged with fear. "Says it was around midnight."

"Says it was the crying he heard first. Went to see what it was. Realized it was a baby."

Zaitsev remembered the car at the bridge and the clucking noise.

"Did the watchman touch anything?"

"He nearly keeled over from fear."

"We waited for you."

"The baby's with the medical orderly," Samoilov added.

"We sent the ambulance back," Demov explained. "There's no one left alive."

Demov's tone was eloquent. Here, in Yelagin Park, something had happened that they had decided to hide carefully from prying eyes and unnecessary witnesses. Something that had caused Zaitsev to be hastily cleared of any charges and in a matter of hours brought directly from the OGPU prison at Shpalernaya.

"You can examine the baby in a bit," Samoilov said, interrupting. "We just got him into the warmth, so he didn't freeze to death. He was already almost blue, the poor thing. He was taken away from here, as he was, in just a shirt." Samoilov shone a torch on the ground, as if to direct Zaitsev's gaze.

The centre of the eerie group was a buxom blonde in a long white dress that reached to the ground. Thick braids were piled on her head. A bush behind her propped her up. It looked like she was standing, in a strange, somewhat limp pose. Another woman was leaning against her, dressed in blue, also with intricately braided hair. In front of them knelt the corpse of an old woman in dark clothes. The white collar stood out in the gloom, making the head seem to float separately from the body. Samoilov moved his torch.

As Zaitsev got closer, he saw how the kneeling corpse was held upright. His legs were folded under him and he was prevented from falling forwards by both hands, which were resting on a large trough standing on the grass. It was as though the black man were presenting it to the dead women.

The sniffer-dog handler said they had lost the trail at the water. Zaitsev ruffled Ace of Clubs on the scruff of the neck. The dog wagged his tail, looked into his eyes, nuzzled into his palm. The dog was the only one in the whole team who had acknowledged their acquaintance.

"He got away by boat, the bastard," said Martynov, expressing what they were all thinking.

"Bastard?" asked Samoilov. "Bastards, more like. Shifting four adult corpses—that's hardly the work of one man."

"There's no prints with all the leaves on the ground. Hmm—if only the dog could tell us how many he could smell."

Realizing they were talking about him, Ace of Clubs raised his snout and let out a short howl. Enough to break your heart. It was only out of respect for the service the beast performed as an equal in the team that they didn't give him a kick to shut him up.

"So much for keeping quiet," was all Serafimov said. "Just had to join in."

"The dog's got feelings, too," the handler rejoined with some resentment. And he led his ward towards the path, to the bridge.

"We don't know that he brought them here," Martynov said thoughtfully. "Perhaps they came for a picnic. A nice civilized drink and a bite to eat. And he murdered them all and ran off with the women's coats—sealskin, let's say? Good, solid coats anyway. The guy probably had a fancy jacket from overseas. They're probably being altered as we speak, to be flogged off tomorrow on Ligovsky Prospekt."

Demov walked away from them.

"Could be," agreed Samoilov. "But why would he have laid them out like this? They're not just any old how—the scumbag went to a lot of trouble. He's posed them. Set them up. Like he had some deliberate arrangement in mind."

"To shake us off the trail? Put the fear in us?" suggested Serafimov quietly.

"What, you shitting yourself, Serafimov?" laughed Samoilov.

Serafimov looked at him, seriously.

"What's to be scared of? They're dead." He conceded. "But yeah—it puts the wind up you. Kind of creepy."

"He spared the baby," Martynov commented, stubbornly clinging to the theory that the killer was alone.

"Yeah. Left out on an autumn night with nothing on. Might as well have just put it out of its misery. Bastards." Samoilov frowned.

Zaitsev shot him a quick glance. "And where was the baby? In the washtub?"

"No, in the old woman's lap."

Zaitsev stepped away and looked at the group again in the half-light. Ordinary criminals would bump the baby off like a kitten or puppy, or if they were sentimental they'd leave it at a hospital or orphanage. No, there was something odd here…

"Maybe they didn't notice the little thing?"

"How could they not? With those lungs."

Demov stood at a distance. To Zaitsev, he had the air of someone in a museum, reticently looking at a sculpture: he stood with one leg forward, his hands behind his back. He was about to take off his glasses and lean in closer to read the name of the artist.

Demov changed his posture, and the likeness vanished.

The two of them stood apart from the rest.

"Demov… What the hell?" Zaitsev wanted to ask. But Demov apparently understood before he could say anything, and he didn't give him the chance.

"The fuss is all because of him," Demov nodded at the corpse of a black man. "He's black, so the watchman assumed he must be a foreigner. Not just a foreigner, it turns out. He's an American Communist. Oliver Newton. His documents were lying around right there. Because of him, they get Kopteltsev out of bed, OGPU comes swooping in…" Demov stopped short.

Footsteps rustled in the leaves. It was Martynov. Six people were searching the perimeter of the island, he said. The only route back to the city was via the bridge Kopytov had been standing on.

Demov didn't even need to finish saying what he had been thinking—everyone had understood: OGPU comes swooping in, Zaitsev gets dragged out.

Zaitsev didn't give himself time to feel bitter.

"Martynov," he said firmly, "notify the river police. Get them combing through the nearest embankments. The killer will have abandoned his boat as soon as he reached the other side. Get them to show you on the map where the rivers have a bottleneck. Let them start looking there. If the bodies were found last night, they can't have got here before dark. In which case he can't have had much time. He will have slipped up somewhere."

Zaitsev stepped aside, letting Demov pass with the tripod. The flash doused the group in pale light, showing up all the details, like lightning in a thunderstorm. Demov moved the tripod and began taking pictures of each of the bodies separately, without disturbing their strange postures.

"And if he isn't alone?" asked Martynov, persisting with his theory.

"Even if he's not alone, they don't have many options. River crossings are risky in this weather. They will probably have chosen the least risky option. Judging by the looks of them"—he nodded towards the dead—"they didn't act on the spur of the moment."

Zaitsev picked up a stick from the ground. He used it to hook a swaddling cloth from the hands of the murdered old woman. Serafimov flinched away from her, as if a ghost had swept through his face. He's right, Zaitsev thought, there's something sickening about this.

"Take this. And go and check the baby. Take everything off him and pack it as evidence. Then get the kid straight to the hospital. It'll be a miracle if it doesn't have pneumonia. We don't want any more deaths. Martynov, call the ambulance. And keep an eye out—don't want us missing anything."

Martynov walked slowly towards the bridge.

Zaitsev squatted down.

"Shine the light here, Samoilov."

He examined the bodies. No sign of any wounds or abrasions.

"The medics will say more precisely."

In the east, the sky had turned pink. In the pale light, the corpses no longer looked creepy. They were more pitiful. Samoilov turned the torch off now it wasn't needed.

Zaitsev scanned everything, taking it all in. Again he considered the whole group, resolutely clinging to every detail. He began a terse dictation.

"Serafimov, take notes. Scene inspected by daylight."

The white dress and the old woman's collar seemed to fill with whiteness from the very first morning rays.

Zaitsev suddenly halted.

Serafimov's pencil stopped.

Zaitsev realized he wasn't wearing a scarf. It was someone else's coat; the pockets were empty.

"Serafimov, have you got a scarf or anything? A handkerchief?"

Serafimov held out a crumpled but clean handkerchief.

Zaitsev shook it out and squatted down. Using the cloth, he carefully picked up from the grass a porcelain figurine of a shepherd.

Chapter 4

The locks in their apartment hadn't been changed. Zaitsev used his old key to let himself in. Straight away he inhaled the astonishingly familiar smells of the shared corridor. One neighbour poked a head around their door, then another. Zaitsev felt their silent amazement as a tickle down his spine.

Zaitsev turned around to see a door snap shut like a mollusc shell. He only just had time to jam it open with his foot.

"Katerina Yegorovna, good evening," he said calmly, propping the door open with his hand.

"Ah... it's... You're back," stuttered the neighbour, choking on her own words. "And we thought... They said... They must have been lying... We thought you'd gone."

There seemed to be a question mark hovering at the end of her sentence.

"I was arrested. But they got to the bottom of it and then I was released," Zaitsev said loudly and clearly. "They don't put innocent people behind bars, after all. This is the Soviet Union, not America."

His neighbour blinked. Her eyes darted about like grey mice.

"That's what I said!" she said, finally thinking what to say. "Right away I told everyone: they'll get to the bottom of it, they'll find out if he's guilty or not."

"And indeed it happened," said Zaitsev with a broad smile, hoping that the fetid smell of the prison had been knocked out of him by the wind while they were searching Yelagin Island, and that his stubble, swollen eyes and sunken cheeks were not too evident.

"Indeed! Quite right!" agreed the neighbour, nodding joyfully. A bit too joyful somehow, thought Zaitsev. Never mind—they'll get used to it.

"Well, I've just got back from work," Zaitsev reassured her. "They got to the bottom of it, resolved the misunderstanding. They've even issued me some ration cards straight away."

"There was a tenant living in your room," said Katerina Yegorovna, all too ready to snitch now she knew where the power lay.

"Well, not any more, since he was given it by mistake. I am registered for my own room again. Well, goodbye then, Katerina Yegorovna."

"Goodnight! Goodnight!" the neighbour blurted out, bowing as she backed away.

Zaitsev knew the whole apartment had heard them. And tomorrow the whole house would know. So much the better. He didn't feel at all like the image he had conveyed, though. The objects in the room seemed unfamiliar.

Near the tall, white stove was a bundle of firewood, a box of matches helpfully resting on top. Zaitsev opened the stove door. He built a little wigwam of kindling. He quickly got a flame going. Zaitsev stood by his bed, not daring to sit on it. The striped mattress seemed to him naked and intimidating. Although in comparison with the prison bunk, of course, it exhaled comfort.

Zaitsev went over to the window. Despite the autumnal dusk, he could make out the open expanse over the Moika.

Yesterday, he had fallen asleep in a cell on Shpalernaya; there was no way he could have guessed that he would spend the following night at home. At home? His room was almost the same as he had left it when he set off for work on that June morning. Back then he couldn't have imagined that he would spend that night at Shpalernaya.

Or maybe he would be suddenly taken back there tomorrow?

In the old days, before his arrest, he would have gone mad from all this "tomorrow", from the suspense and not knowing. But prison had taught him to live in the moment and not to second-guess the future.

The furniture was all as he had left it. All that was different were the traces of sealing wax on the door jamb.

"Time to get to bed," thought Zaitsev without much conviction. He pulled out a drawer. Then another. And another. All empty.

He tensed his muscles and tugged the chest of drawers away from the wall.

There was a gentle knock on the door.

"Pasha, it's not locked."

Pasha slipped in sideways. In her hands was a pile of bedding.

"What are you doing sitting in the dark?" she asked, surprised. She flicked on the switch. The economical carbon-filament lamp gave off a dirty, dim light. Pasha dropped the heap onto the mattress.

"What do I need that for?"

"So, then, will you head to the shops tomorrow? Stand in the queues? No, I know you, you'll be off to work tomorrow at the crack of dawn, won't you, what was I thinking?... Yes, well, I suppose we never know what fate has in store for us..."

Pasha was holding the corners of the sheet.

"So you're out, then. That's the main thing."

"They don't put innocent people behind bars," parroted Zaitsev wearily. He felt his eyes drooping shut. But too much had happened in the day: images and thoughts danced about in his mind, and he knew he wouldn't get to sleep right away. Here, in the warmth of the room, he felt like he was giving off a particularly heavy odour of prison.

"Absolutely," Pasha readily agreed. "And then that weasel in the blue cap went and moved into your living space," she added quickly, shaking out the sheet, which caught the air like a sail. Zaitsev noticed the smell of the iron.

Must have been this former tenant who had stored up the firewood, thought Zaitsev. He hoped Pasha would be on her way as soon as possible.

"We realized right away when he got it early this morning. Up the backside."

"Arrested?" asked Zaitsev, amazed.

"God knows. Come on, you get out of the way. Go and sit yourself down instead of getting under my feet."

Zaitsev walked over to the armchair. It let out its usual sigh beneath his weight. Pasha was tucking the edges of the sheet under the mattress.

"Give me the cash on pay day. No funny ideas—just because you're out, don't go thinking this is a hotel," Pasha added sternly. She looked around. "Whose is the bundle? Yours?"

"Don't know. The weasel's, perhaps. Don't touch it, Pasha. He might come back for it."

"He didn't seem to care when he laid his grubby mitts on your things."

Pasha leant forward, her giant skirted rump jutting out, and quickly untied the knot. Pillows and a blanket. Pasha let out a cry of victory.

"See," she said, punching the pillow, "that's not your average hair-and-straw mix. Probably not even any feathers. Pure down!"

She began to shove the prized booty into a much washed and ironed, off-white pillowcase.

Zaitsev felt as though the armchair were sinking deeper and deeper. And Pasha's voice was fading out somewhere above, and he was tumbling down to the bottom of a dark well, along with where the day had gone.

Snatches of his day flickered past. The ambulance with the red cross on the door. The corpses propped up in strange poses by their killer. Cold drips from the bushes as he pushed back branches in search of evidence. The staircase at the CID HQ like a piano keyboard… A swanky Packard, its polished flanks sparkling. Boots.

Someone was shaking him by the shoulder. Zaitsev opened his eyes. And instead of the wall of his cell, he saw Pasha. The day slotted into place again, like a brick in a wall.

"Ooh, would you look at those boots!" Pasha remarked. "Very fancy! The latest prison fashion, is it?"

Zaitsev stared at his boots. A matt sheen on the toes. They looked new. Good quality, pink leather. On a thick ribbed sole. They had to be foreign.

"Would you look at those boots," he echoed.

II

From the island they had all gone back to Gorokhovaya Street for a meeting in the office. The fact that one of the victims turned out to be an American Communist, and a black one at that, had greatly complicated the matter.

"The global bourgeoisie are desperate for a scandal to shout about. Black people are targets in the Soviet Union, they'll say, just like in America," said Demov, looking at Nefyodov. He sat at an aloof distance: with the others, but also slightly apart.

A blue autumn evening leant in against the window. Damp, yellow leaves occasionally streamed past the glass. Under the table, Zaitsev tried to wriggle his feet: they were frozen numb in his sodden summer canvas shoes. They were filthy and soaked right through from tramping around on the grass at Yelagin Park.

Zaitsev scrutinized their faces. None of the men sitting

in the office—not Demov, or Martynov, or Samoilov, or Serafimov—had expressed the slightest surprise when he appeared on the island. They didn't ask anything later, either. Perhaps that was why their faces seemed a little unfamiliar. He had attributed it to those three months when the only people he saw were his cellmates, wardens and interrogators.

"I think the time of the crime is clear," he said.

Puffs of smoke from four cigarettes crawled through the air. Zaitsev was still getting used to the simultaneous presence of Serafimov and Nefyodov. It still seemed like they ought to cancel each other out: plus one and minus one adding up to zero. But here they both were: Serafimov, as ruddy as ever, and Nefyodov, as anaemic as ever.

After a long day of work, the team sketched out the first, approximate picture of the crime.

"Rigor mortis hadn't set in, the medics say. So the murders were less than twenty-four hours ago."

"Did the nightwatchman have anything to show you? When was his last round of the park?"

"What could he have shown?" dismissed Martynov with a wave of his hand. "One watchman for the entire huge park. As good as none at all. The bodies could have lain there until dawn and no one would have seen them."

Although the killer or killers hadn't had much time, Zaitsev had been mistaken in assuming they would have left some tracks. They had left nothing.

The documents of the murdered women had disappeared along with their coats, shoes and handbags.

"But they left the American's ID," said Serafimov.

"Yeah, not much good to them, is it? Black face and a foreign name. Bit too obvious. So they chucked it."

The other three victims were still unidentified.

"So far, the baby is our only clue," said Zaitsev.

"Yeah, he'll fill you in," agreed Samoilov sarcastically, "in about three to four years."

"He's not a witness. He's evidence," continued Zaitsev, not put off.

"They're all evidence," agreed the experienced Demov.

"They look like whores. If they are, I doubt their relatives are going to rush out looking for them," Zaitsev objected. "But I bet the baby's mother's already been round the whole city."

"Unless one of the whores *is* the mother"—Samoilov spoke again from his armrest.

"Serafimov, go and ask the medical examiner."

Serafimov nodded.

A duty officer appeared in the doorway.

"What?" snapped Zaitsev, riled at being interrupted. This set alarm bells ringing: duty officers usually called—they didn't have time to stagger up the stairs.

"The car's downstairs. Waiting." The policeman was flustered. He clearly knew where Detective Zaitsev had been for the last three months. All expressions disappeared from the others' faces.

"I don't understand," Zaitsev managed to utter calmly.

"For Comrades Zaitsev and Demov," said the officer. Everyone stared at Zaitsev. Demov visibly turned pale. But he stood up smoothly.

"Well, if they're waiting, let's go then," he said evenly, enunciating every word with impeccable Petersburg pronunciation. "Shall we?"

They left the office. But the corridor was empty. Apparently, the blue-caps hadn't bothered coming upstairs, confident their victims wouldn't escape from the CID building.

Demov slowed down ever so slightly. His lips had taken on a tinge of blue. Zaitsev's heart was pounding. Behind them rustled the unsuspecting duty officer, unaware of the situation.

Or was he fully aware?

They stepped out of the building.

In the car's black-lacquered flanks, Zaitsev saw two distorted reflections: his and Demov's. The officer's reflection floated behind them like a pale, flattened griddle cake.

"Packard. Seventh series," said the policeman in a reverent tone, fondly adding, "American production. A shiny toy. When we've finished building Communism, comrades," he carried on dreamily, "any worker will be able to head to the store and buy themselves a Packard like this. And our Soviet cars will be every bit their match!"

A portly driver in gaiters hopped out and opened the door. Out came the aroma of expensive, creaky leather. The driver's expression was one of well-trained indifference.

"Are you going to be long?" came Kopteltsev's disgruntled voice from within.

Zaitsev and Demov glanced questioningly at each other. They stared at the "toy", which no ordinary Leningrad worker even dared dream of. They didn't even have cars like this in OGPU.

These Packards were only found in the garages of the upper echelons of the Party.

III

The streets were dark. Some of the street lamps were lit, but only some, here and there. Trams rattled past, black figures hanging on the running boards; more people wanted to travel than could fit inside. Crowds were pouring into the cinemas' well-lit jaws.

Zaitsev mused, ironically, that today was a day of getting to know the automotive capabilities of the Leningrad authorities, starting this morning with one of the OGPU's Fords and ending now with one of the Packards of the Leningrad Soviet.

Kopteltsev didn't say a word. His flabby cheeks trembled as the car shook on the bumpy road. Demov sat facing the window, grim-faced. People stared at their handsome car. As they turned onto Suvorovsky Prospekt, the driver several times pressed the horn to show off. The Packard roared like a stag. Demov shifted across the seat, away from the window. Without any thought, Zaitsev did the same.

The Packard slowed down in front of the gates of the Smolny. The driver flashed his pass at the window.

This was once the site of a private boarding school—what they used to call an "institute for noble maidens". But that was nothing compared to how private and closely guarded the building was now. The officer at the checkpoint had a pistol of gleaming cold steel. The sentry had a rifle. This imperial-era palace was now home to the city administration.

The Packard swung round its elegant snout, rolled through the gates and steered a bold arc up to the main entrance. The black statue of Lenin seemed to have stepped out to receive his guests. His damp shoulders and head glistened. The building and the statue were illuminated by floodlights.

Another guard with a rifle. Zaitsev tried to guess from Demov's face what he was thinking. He knew about the old days, after all; he could compare then and now. Zaitsev could see it, too; Leningrad's rulers guarded themselves even more closely from the grateful masses than the nobility had guarded their daughters' honour from romantic distractions back in the old imperial capital.

Demov stumbled out of the car to the right. Kopteltsev deftly rolled his rotund body out to the left.

Zaitsev jumped out next, slamming the door behind him. He wanted to catch Demov, who was already standing on the damp steps, looking at Lenin, who cast his giant shadow against the building. But as soon as Zaitsev approached him, he moved on.

Yet another unpleasant shock. Zaitsev didn't quite know why he was surprised. But he no longer felt like talking.

The three of them now seemed to be playing a game of who could keep silent the longest.

In the warmth of the building, Zaitsev's frozen feet quickly warmed up and started to throb with pain. His sodden shoes slurped at every step. The stout officer led them along raspberry-red carpets, past many doors, portraits of leaders, slogans and sentries, up the stairs to the desired floor.

All this was so surreal—especially when he considered that he had woken up that morning on his prison bunk, and spent the day on the idyllic Yelagin Island examining corpses—it was all so surreal that Zaitsev was no longer surprised at anything.

The officer nodded to the guard, who opened the door to the reception. He led Kopteltsev, Zaitsev and Demov past the secretary, who sat motionless, and into the office. Kopteltsev walked ahead—the leader of their small delegation.

Zaitsev looked intently at Kirov, the head of the party organization in Leningrad. His face was familiar from the portraits that hung from the tops of columns at rallies on holidays, and that peered out from the newspapers. Comrade Kirov rose from his desk to receive them.

"Good day, Comrade Kopteltsev."

A smile spread across Kirov's broad peasant face. In his convincingly well-planned scruffiness, he looked like the archetypal proletarian from the Putilov factory, who lived in a communal apartment or a workers' dorm. If it weren't for his wife's ostentatious attire, famous throughout the city, people might fall for his masquerade.

"Comrade Demov, our experienced investigator," said Kopteltsev, introducing the guests. "And this is Comrade Zaitsev, to whom this investigation has been assigned. He's the one who's answerable."

Kirov shook their hands in turn.

"Don't let me down, Comrade Zaitsev."

"I won't let you down," Zaitsev promised, not really knowing what they were talking about.

"That's the spirit. And you're a Komsomolets?"

"Yes," Kopteltsev answered for him.

Zaitsev quickly glanced around. There was nobody in the office besides them. Kirov had a reputation in Leningrad for being a great democrat. In his grey suit, coat and cap, he personally did the rounds of the factories and kept an eye on the shops, canteens and hospitals. A kind of Soviet Harun al-Rashid. This meeting was perhaps intended in the same vein.

Kirov jumped up from behind the table.

"Come with me," he waved. And he sped around the office, narrowly missing a lady in a straight skirt bringing in a tray with a pot of steaming tea on it. Zaitsev's nostrils caught the vanilla scent of the biscuits. His stomach convulsed. Kopteltsev behaved as always. Demov's face was filled with the naïve joy of an old man. Zaitsev knew him too well to be taken in: Demov wore an outward expression of tenderness, while behind the facade he lay in wait like a hunter, his keen senses at the ready.

Out of the corner of his eye, Zaitsev, out of habit, quickly scanned the mayor's desk. He noticed a to-do list. A dense typewritten page covered in handwritten comments in ink: call, request, listen, answer. The handwriting was large. It was clear that Kirov needed glasses but was too embarrassed to wear them—a Soviet leader ought to have an eagle eye.

Kirov threw himself into city affairs with the same zealous attention to detail as Tsar Paul I did over a hundred years ago. In this same city where the tsar had come to a sticky end.

But Kirov was popular in Leningrad.

"You're probably wondering why I asked Comrade Kopteltsev to invite you here?"

You don't say, Zaitsev thought.

With a magician's sweeping gesture, he pulled a velvet cloth from a low table.

"Ta-da!" he announced triumphantly. "Comrades! Take a look."

On the table was a tiny model village: a "town in a snuff-box".

"It is my great honour to present to you the Workers' Park of Culture and Recreation!" declared Kirov.

Zaitsev and Demov were both surprised to see a miniature model of Yelagin Island.

IV

The minute trees and bushes looked like broccoli. The green lawns looked so soft you wanted to stroke them. Standing proud like a birthday cake was the old summer palace—once the not particularly beloved dacha of the imperial family and now a museum of the old way of life. The ponds gleamed like mirrors. Minuscule boats floated here and there, rowed by tiny workers, each skilfully crafted. On the tennis court, Lilliputian players held their racquets aloft. You could make out the bowl shape of the tiers of the summer theatre. Couples strolled along the paths. Mothers in colourful dresses stood tall as they pushed their perambulators. Zaitsev spotted a toddler's toy doll. And looming over everything stood a Ferris wheel.

It seemed to Zaitsev that in a moment he would see the corpses from today, artfully sculpted from wax and inserted into the scene.

Kirov flicked a switch and the Ferris wheel began to spin slowly, the cabins swinging.

Demov took off his glasses and held them up to a detail that interested him—a familiar gesture.

"Well, actually..." he muttered, unable to restrain himself. But he thought better of it and exhaled, "Astonishing!"

Kirov again cracked out his Cheshire-cat smile.

"Here, where once parasites of the working classes walked, with all their ladies-in-waiting and bourgeoisie and whatnot, here the workers shall find their leisure! Ordinary townspeople! Soviet Komsomol members, pioneers and schoolchildren!"

And then he dropped his smile in an instant.

"Do you realize, Zaitsev, how much public attention is riveted on the park?" he asked, looking at Demov.

"What do you say, Demov?" he continued, turning to Zaitsev.

Neither took the liberty of speaking on behalf of the other. Both chose to give the impression of shocked silence.

"So, comrades, this anti-Soviet prank by the vile enemy must not be allowed to ruin the people's celebrations," declared Kirov, enthusiastically jutting out his chin and focusing slightly above their heads. "As I said to Comrade Kopteltsev earlier: our foe, the vermin, has constructed a provocation. And must be punished with the full severity of the law. But first, our police will hunt the enemy down."

It apparently made no difference to him whether he were addressing three thousand party members or just two coppers.

"In the shortest! Time! Conceivable!" He chopped at his palm as if to make it clear that, otherwise, it wasn't words that would roll, but heads. "I told Comrade Kopteltsev straight out."

"And I said," broke in Kopteltsev, "we'll put our best man on the investigation. Comrade Zaitsev."

It's all quite clear, love is dear, thought Zaitsev, remembering the song. So this was what got him pulled out of Shpalernaya. Being arrested by OGPU was practically a death sentence. And when you're on death row—you're expendable. If you solve the murder on Yelagin Island—great. If not—they'll send you packing. But no one else in CID is in harm's way. Nicely done, Kopteltsev. Cunning. Taking the long view.

"Why so quiet?" said Kopteltsev, giving him a subtle nudge.

"I'm flattered by the honour and I only hope I can justify the confidence of the party."

"Quite right. The party will help with every resource necessary. As I said to Kopteltsev: work is work, but here we've got to go above and beyond. I says to him: I myself want to demonstrate to our comrade investigator what the former Yelagin Park means to us. So he's imbued with a sense of the task." Kirov placed his palms on his chest. And then he tapped his chest with his fist. "So he responds with a warm heart. And as for you, Demov," he said, suddenly changing the subject.

Demov winced ever so slightly.

"I see your boots."

Demov stared, confused, at the toes of his boots. And Zaitsev realized that Comrade Kirov was again addressing him.

"It's autumn out there. And you're dressed for the summer. How are you going to go chasing after criminals in summer plimsolls?"

Kirov shook his head. He went over to his desk and pressed some kind of button. The secretary's voice crackled over the line.

In an instant, a chit for some new boots landed on Comrade Kirov's desk. And then from there it found its way into Zaitsev's pocket.

"We, for our part, will not scrimp on resources," said Kirov in a tone that reminded both Zaitsev and Demov of the glory that had followed Kirov from the Caucasus, like a trail, steaming and reeking of blood. Back then, when he was first transferred to Leningrad, he just seemed like a bit of a clown. A sort of bumbling janitor for the whole city.

"There'll be you, Zaitsev, and additional personnel. You'll have all the equipment you need. So work can continue day and night," muttered Kopteltsev, looking at Kirov as he spoke.

Kirov concluded, "All so that those responsible will be found! As soon as possible."

There was no need to expand on what would happen otherwise. That was a scenario that did not bear imagining.

Kopteltsev and Demov stayed with Kirov while Zaitsev was led a long way along corridors and staircases. A door was unlocked. Zaitsev recognized it as a storeroom from the smell of cardboard, cloth, fur and mothballs. The aisles stretched back into the distance, as far as the eye could see. There were shelves tightly packed with boxes and piles of various items, and rails tightly packed with hanging clothing.

A soldier of some kind, without any collar patches, crouched down at his feet, deftly manipulating a shoehorn. Zaitsev was amazed to see both his feet were now shod in brand-new boots, obviously foreign.

Dumbfounded, Zaitsev looked at the reflection of his own feet in the floor mirror. He stamped, took a few steps. His feet felt submersed in the fluffy pile of the carpet. It was sumptuous, soft, clearly expropriated from some bourgeois mansion about fifteen years ago.

"The shoe doesn't pinch so much as caress the foot," muttered Zaitsev, ironically quoting from *Anna Karenina*. The soldier didn't respond.

He neatly wrapped the filthy canvas shoes up in brown paper, nimbly tying it up with twine. Then he handed it to Zaitsev.

Zaitsev was then led to the car, where Kopteltsev and Demov were already waiting. It seemed to Zaitsev that they had agreed on something while he was gone. What difference does it make? he reassured himself. He jumped in and sat down beside Demov.

Again, there was silence the whole way.

The Packard, its wipers pushing back and forth across the wet windscreen, dropped them off on Gorokhovaya, where it had picked them up, at the entrance to CID. The Packard took Kopteltsev on elsewhere.

Puddles flickered with reflections of the occasional headlamps. The asphalt had an oily gleam. The black sky was visible in the grey wet patches. Zaitsev shuddered as a chill wind blew right through him.

Demov dashed up the stairs without glancing back, as if running away from Zaitsev's possible questions.

Zaitsev walked through the dark streets towards home, on the River Moika. He played with the key in his pocket and felt his coat growing heavier as it absorbed more and more rain. It was striking that there were almost no shop names any more. A year ago, they yelled and hollered from every corner, every facade crowded with signs and advertisements. And now all of a sudden they had been ripped from the shopfronts. Without them, the city seemed like it had been silenced. It seemed poorer, more austere. Darker. Rain trickled down his collar and dripped from the peak of his cap.

From that directly to the cold stream of the shower.

The shared bathroom was dark. There was no hot water. You could just see the top of the street lamp outside through the small window up by the ceiling. Zaitsev didn't turn the light on.

His reeking clothes that he hadn't changed for three months lay in a heap on the floor. Zaitsev stood up straight in the bathroom. Before the Revolution, it had been opulent and luxurious. Now it was eerie, with enamel peeling here and there, like impetigo scabs. Zaitsev stood under the shower, his body all but screaming from the stinging icy water, and yet he felt blissful. The water washed away the prison, the interrogations, his cell, and with them it washed away Smolny by night and Comrade Kirov with his electric Ferris wheel, and in the darkness of the bathroom it all seemed like a dream.

Zaitsev returned to his room along the sleeping corridor, dead quiet but for the neighbours' snores, sniffles and murmurs. His bed, made up by Pasha, gleamed white. His coat lay in a heavy heap on the chair, emitting an unbearable odour of dog and mothballs.

Zaitsev yanked the window latches and gave the frame a shove. After his icy shower, his body was burning. The rain drummed on the cornice. Water gushed down the drainpipes. Even the black Moika seemed to be seething. There was a break in the clouds, and for a moment the moon peered through like an eye. One glance and it disappeared.

Zaitsev swung his arms and heaved his coat out of the window. It flew down, waving its sleeves, like a bird that hadn't learnt how to fly. It flopped heavily onto the pavement.

Chapter 5

I

The photographs were ready.

Zaitsev could see the retoucher had made an effort. The open eyes looked alive. You'd be convinced they were conscious, if you didn't know the pictures were taken when these people were already dead. Demov insisted on photographing the corpses as they were found, propped up as though they were alive. But still, there was something in the features that was irregular, inanimate somehow. The lips were sunken; the cheeks seemed floppy, the noses sharp. They had the air of those English memento mori photographs from the Victorian era, when families had portraits taken with deceased relatives.

If you didn't know, you probably wouldn't notice anything odd about them, thought Zaitsev.

Three women: two young, in their mid-twenties, and one old. Identities still unknown. What was their connection with the American Communist Oliver Newton? Zaitsev was afraid the answer would be simple: two hookers and their madam. He picked up the telephone.

"Martynov? Take the pictures down to the archives. Have a look and see if we've got anything on the girls. Yep. For their, er, leisurely lifestyle. And the old woman. Demov's right: the younger ones both look like whores. And if they look like whores, most likely they are whores. The older one must have been the madam."

From the settee, Demov reached for the pictures from the table and looked down at them with his head bowed, as if evaluating someone else's interference in his work. "Not bad. Only they could have done brown eyes for the blonde. It's clearly peroxide."

He sat back, crossing his legs. Samoilov was perched on the armrest. Serafimov, as usual, had chosen the windowsill.

Nefyodov had gone to question the staff at Yelagin Island. There was a lot to do, no time to waste—they weren't just giving him tasks for the sake of keeping him busy.

"That was a call from the garage," said the duty officer, who had appeared at the door. "Your carriage awaits."

Comrade Kirov hadn't exaggerated. Zaitsev's team had been assigned two Fords.

"Well, isn't this the high life?" said Samoilov with delight. "No more tramping about on foot."

To his displeasure, Serafimov and Nefyodov were the first to be sent out with the cars.

"Why didn't you transfer Nefyodov to photography?" asked Zaitsev. He remembered Demov always grumbling about this extra workload, which kept him up late at night.

Demov parted his lips in a smile. "Am I complaining? I'm not complaining. I'll always be able to top up my pension—I'll get a job at a photography studio. Demob portraits. Brides and babies."

"Ah," was all Zaitsev said. He handed him the pictures.

"Shall I print them?" asked Demov, getting up.

"Yes, we need to get them out to all precincts, to the district officers. And to the locals. Maybe one of the neighbours will show up."

Still no ID on the three victims.

Virolainen, the pathologist, looked in at the door and waved a yellow file.

"Autopsy."

Zaitsev quickly ran his eyes over the pathologist's report. Two details caught his attention.

"Large dose of morphine in the blood of all four," he read aloud. "Cause of death. Samoilov, check if any pharmacies or factory first-aid posts have reported any disappearances."

Samoilov silently made a few notes in his pad.

Zaitsev looked up at him. Samoilov sat down in silence. Usually, he always had something to say. Morphine, for example. According to the statistics, the biggest group abusing morphine were those who had access to it: doctors. Then came prostitutes—the main dealers.

Zaitsev felt like a circus performer whose partner on the trapeze was suddenly missing.

He didn't let on and carried on reading the report.

There were no tattoos on the corpses. The morphine seemed to support the brothel theory: they were dabbling and had a bit more than they could handle. The absence of tattoos didn't fit with the theory, though: perhaps the girls were new and hadn't been branded yet, but a madam would definitely have at least one tattoo.

"Samoilov, what have you got? Any leads on the mother?"

"They're at reception."

"They? How many?" Zaitsev got up from his desk.

"How to put it," Samoilov answered enigmatically.

Not even the statistics knew how many babies went missing in Leningrad each year. A doctor at the Ott maternity clinic confirmed the baby was three months old. Samoilov had collected all the reports of missing infants for the last three months.

"Call them."

A woman who looked like a worker shyly slipped in and stood at the door, staring down at the floor. A man in a cap quickly sneaked in behind her. They looked like they could be husband and wife.

But appearances were deceptive.

"I was here first!" insisted the man energetically.

The woman timidly gave way to let him past.

"That's not up to you," said Zaitsev sternly. "I'll say which order I want to see you in."

The peasant looked around, took off his cap and smoothed his coarse grey hair down with his palm. He had something about him of the proletarian writer Maxim Gorky. Zaitsev had a burning desire to peel the huge tobacco-stained moustache off his face. The woman raised her weary eyes. She had a tormented air—like most Leningrad women. Zaitsev turned to her with an amiable look.

"Comrade, have you come about the baby?"

"Yes," the woman answered.

"About our neighbour," answered the man at the same time. He carried on, afraid they would interrupt him. "The baby isn't mine. But I've something to say. One of the neighbours. In our apartment. Natasha. Natalya Petrovna Shapkina. A Komsomol member, supposedly," he stressed, meaningfully. "There she was going around with a bump. Always trying to hide it. As if the neighbours couldn't see! Then all of a sudden—the bump's gone! And no baby! What do you think of that, then?"

"We'll get to the bottom of it, comrade," said Samoilov gloomily.

"It's not for my own sake," said Maxim Gorky, thumping himself in the chest. "That Natasha should be moved out of her room. She's a whore. She's no Komsomol member. She's taking up a good room. A disgrace to the community. Casts a shadow. Time to get her out. From her job, from the Komsomol and from the accommodation. Decent people ought to be given her room."

The bearded Maxim Gorky clearly had himself in mind. The housing question had corrupted many a Leningrader.

Zaitsev could hardly blame the man. He, his wife, the kids and probably the parents would all be squeezed into one room, taking it in turns to sleep.

"And you?" he asked, turning back to the woman.

"Yes, I've written it all in the statement," she said wearily.

"Marya Gerasimova," Samoilov answered for her. "Yesterday, her baby was taken right out of the pram. A boy. Left outside the bakery. On International Prospekt."

The woman couldn't hold back and burst into tears.

"Do you have a photograph?"

The woman shook her head, blowing her nose.

"How could I? Didn't even have time to christen him. Pretty as an angel. Golden hair."

"You're a Soviet woman," Zaitsev rebuked her gently. "What's with all the 'christening' and 'angel'? How old is your baby?"

"He was born at St Peter's Fast."

Samoilov grunted. "Best to give up on all that priestly talk, citizen."

Zaitsev worked it out; the age would be about right.

Who knows, Zaitsev thought. For some women, to fall pregnant was a disaster, while others were desperate for a baby. They'd try everything, going from doctor to priest, wise woman to charlatan. This seemed to be a prime example. A bonny blonde baby. Lifted straight out of the pram, blanket and all. International Prospekt, a bustling street. Straight on the tram and you're off. A female citizen carrying a crying bundle would hardly raise any suspicions.

Samoilov had taken Gerasimova to the maternity clinic, where the foundling was being treated for pneumonia.

Maxim Gorky carefully wrote his statement in pencil, biting his tongue in concentration.

Zaitsev looked out of the window. He felt bad for this Komsomol member, Shapkina. There'd been a brief Komsomol romance—on the dance floor, strolls around the park, sitting on a park bench. Now the lover was long gone. And she was hardly going to manage on her own with a baby. Zaitsev could already hear her story: how she'd fallen, lifted something heavy, overstrained herself. Then she'd crack and confess, sobbing and sniffing. What if they expelled her from the Komsomol, sacked her from her job—who would that benefit? How would that be socialist justice?

"There. Finished," said Gorky.

Zaitsev quickly ran his eyes over the illiterate scribble.

"We'll look into it right away, Citizen…"—Zaitsev hurriedly checked over the sheet, then carefully folded it—"… Sapozhnikov. We'll get to the bottom of it. Thank you for your contribution to the investigation."

"The neighbours'll back me up. First she was going around with a bump. Then just like that! No more bump." Sapozhnikov carried on prattling away, twisting like a hunting dog hankering to be let loose. Like any tyrant who lords it over the workers' dormitory or communal apartment, he cowered before his superiors.

Zaitsev opened the door for him. And he immediately felt the onslaught of the many booming voices. Young women, not so young, elderly, some students, by the look of it, some pale and powdered, tidily dressed, some plain and unprepossessing, workers in headscarves, office workers with a six-month perm—the reception was teeming with women.

At the sight of Zaitsev they all fell silent. As if on command they all stared at the investigator, each with a desperate question in her eyes. Their heart-rending hope surged towards Zaitsev like an ocean wave.

II

The evidence lay on a long table lit by electric lamps.

With any dead body, there was always something that distracted even the experienced investigator. Zaitsev knew himself that in order to really take in the crime scene, he needed to scrutinize the photographs, the victims' clothes—sunken, flat, no longer filled by the corpse.

The American Communist's orange shirt glowed like an autumn bonfire. Demov leant in so close he was almost exploring it with his nose.

Zaitsev felt how, like shy young lovers, they avoided any contact, avoided any mention of their nocturnal visit to Smolny.

"Strange outfits," said Zaitsev aloud. "What do you think, Demov?"

"Remember that dive on Kronverksky?" he answered with a question. "I wonder if we're back in the realm of sexual perversions."

Zaitsev saw there was something Demov wanted to add, but he stopped himself.

"Is Martynov back from Kamennoostrovsky yet?"

That was the street where the American Communist, Newton, was registered at a two-room apartment. A separate apartment would have seemed an unthinkable luxury to most Leningraders. A shame, Zaitsev realized: in a communal apartment, his private life wouldn't have been very private, what with the prying neighbours. But this separate apartment didn't give him much hope of finding a witness. But on the other hand, there was the promise of evidence: behind closed doors, those lucky enough to reside in a separate living space tended to feel safe enough to leave things lying around, things that in a communal apartment people would anxiously hide away.

Demov shook his head.

"Interesting," said Zaitsev. "Well, Martynov will tell us if you're right."

"I'm not sure that I'm right. I'm just offering an interpretation of events," Demov added, as if backtracking.

Zaitsev was offended for a moment. But then something caught his eye: a large, bulky necklace.

"*In a sheltered bay, a green oak stands; / A golden chain hangs in its bough…*" he muttered, quoting from Pushkin's *Ruslan and Lyudmila*, as he flicked through the pictures from the scene of the crime, tossing them onto the table until he got to the one he wanted.

Zaitsev looked closely at the photo. It was as he remembered: the necklace was on the blonde, her body slumped against the bushes so it seemed like she was standing and looking at the old woman, Newton and the baby. It crossed the woman's body almost like a military cross belt.

"It's all top-quality fabrics. Silk, batiste," said Demov. "All clean. Smell it."

"Former NEP men?"

Zaitsev also leant over the table. A dense, heady smell.

"What is it?"

"Some kind of aromatic oil."

Beside these clothes, the necklace seemed coarse and clumsy.

"This isn't metal," said Zaitsev, showing him the necklace.

"What did you expect? Gold?" said Demov, raising a faintly ironic eyebrow. "These days a gold chain like that would have been pawned long ago. Glad to see the back of it. Not the sort of thing an honest Soviet citizen has."

"No, hold it and see: it's not copper, not gilt, not brass."

With a handkerchief covering his hand, Demov carefully weighed the chain in his palm. Although it had long been checked for prints, it was an instinctive habit.

Demov paused, either thinking or not wanting to speak at all.

But its lightness spoke for itself.

Zaitsev picked up the phone.

"Put me through to a theatre. Which one?" He turned to Demov. "Just a minute," he added, before covering the receiver with his palm. "Where's got something historical on at the moment?"

The pause dragged on.

"Damn it, Demov, we're going to look like a bunch of philistines," muttered Zaitsev.

"Who's got time to go running around the theatres?" grumbled Demov.

"We'll call you back," said Zaitsev into the receiver before he hung up. He dialled a number.

"Serafimov? No, that's fine, finish that. Then make a list of theatres. Take a photo of something with you, Demov will show you. Head off as soon as you can, take the Ford. Perhaps someone will recognize one of their props."

The opulent golden necklace inlaid with gemstones was clearly a fake.

III

The Fords, so generously issued by Comrade Kirov, set off on their various assignments. Zaitsev took a tram from the dilapidated yet grandiose city centre to the Vyborg Side, Leningrad's industrial district. At times the tram hurtled along, strumming away, at times it crawled along, grinding its wheels. It wasn't a short hop and Zaitsev could well understand how disgruntled the workers were at having to travel so far to work. The Soviet government had decided to share everything equally and had relocated workers to the grand apartments in the city centre, stuffing one family into each room. To put them on a par with the former bourgeoisie. But now they had to cross the entire city to commute to work every day, and for that pleasure they had to get up even before the crack of dawn, storming the trams with their cursing and swearing.

It was already full when he got on. Zaitsev first hung on the footboard, then squeezed himself inside. It smelt of tar, unwashed bodies, damp fur. Passengers started up lackadaisical altercations but, after one or two barks, they fell silent. Fatigue was written on their yellowish-grey faces. Even those who had recently been villagers, who had been lured en masse into the city or transferred by force to the factories by the authorities, quickly took on this unhealthy local colour. It wasn't long before you could no longer tell who was from here and who was a newcomer. "Oi, what are you staring at?" an old woman hissed. "Giving me the evil eye!"

Zaitsev looked away and, following Demov's example, tried to look out of the window. The sky over the Neva was also yellowish-grey. The water looked like crumpled lead. Brick chimneys rose up on the other bank. The smog hung low, gradually turning into the heavy, low Leningrad clouds. The Vyborg Side was a manufacturing district on the city's outskirts, home to many factories and the Red Triangle rubber plant. The American, Newton, worked at the former Nobel factory, now Russian Diesel.

As soon as the tram had crossed the bridge over the Neva, Zaitsev slowly began to make his way towards the doors; the curses of passengers rippled behind him like a churned-up wake. He jumped off when they reached the smouldering red bulk of the factory. Zaitsev looked up. It needed no decoration: this enormous brick building was impressive in its own way. It spoke of power.

At the site entrance, a girl in a secretarial blouse and tie tottered on the spot on her high-heel hooves. She was hugging herself to keep warm. Her red nose and her red lipstick were equally eye-catching. Seeing Zaitsev, she hesitantly raised her hand: should she wave or not?

"Are you from the police?" she asked uncertainly.

Apparently, she had pictured the CID investigator to be more like Nat Pinkerton from the paperback detective series. But in his cap and tattered old coat, Zaitsev could have passed for one of the Diesel workers. Except for the shoes, he thought, following the girl's gaze.

"You could have waited inside," he said softly. "Why stand out here in the cold?"

He saw how, in the blink of an eye, the girl went through the complex, subtle calculations by which Leningrad women could place any male into a taxonomic system, the highest category being "marriage material". But from the secretary's expression, he realized that he hadn't quite made it into that category. He simply never would. Just as plankton would never be filed among the large predators or the even-toed ungulates.

He almost regretted throwing the *gepeushnik*'s sturdy coat out of the window. This one he had bought at the flea market was of a more proletarian stock.

"Our director's very strict," the secretary said drily.

There was a sentry at the porter's lodge. This was no surprise to Zaitsev. After all, Russian Diesel worked on defence commissions. Carefully comparing Zaitsev's face with his police ID, the guard began to write out a pass. He dipped his pen in the inkwell with an important air and glanced at Zaitsev after every word, as though afraid he might suddenly change his appearance. The defence profile clearly made the locals a little jittery.

Only the secretary glanced around, bored.

With a pass in his pocket, Zaitsev was led into the building, to the director's office.

At first it looked like three people were sitting in conference in the spacious office. However, the third turned out to be a huge Lenin: in his portrait, the leader was sitting at a desk that stood flush with the desks of the other two. But these other men were of flesh and blood. One had a thoroughly proletarian face, but with a look in his eyes that reminded Zaitsev of the famous poster "Papa, don't drink!" The man stood up and quickly muttered something politically appropriate. His shrewd eyes suggested he had no faith in what he uttered. He was the so-called "Red director".

"Thank you, Lena," he nodded to the secretary.

The second man, about forty in appearance, had a smooth-shaven skull that gleamed. His lack of hair on top was well compensated by well-defined black eyebrows and a thick moustache.

"Firsov," he said quietly by way of introduction. A blinding white cuff appeared from his sleeve as he held out his hand. "Afanasy Osipovich Firsov."

His bright brown eyes gave him away as a native of the southern provinces. A bright mind sparkled in those eyes. He was the de facto director, no matter what they called him.

His suit was English.

"Zaitsev."

They shook hands. Firsov's hand was soft, intellectual. This one arm with its white cuff was enough for Zaitsev to concoct his entire life story: rich Russian merchant family, university abroad, career in engineering, stayed after the Revolution to serve his country. The only reason he hadn't fallen in the Red Terror was that a giant like Russian Diesel couldn't be managed by class consciousness alone. Only Firsov could command this dragon—new leadership couldn't manage without him. Meanwhile, the Red director had been selected from the loudmouths at the local rally.

The Red director tugged at his jacket to straighten it. Under his jacket he was wearing a traditional *kosovorotka*.

"Must dash. It's time for the Political Information session on the shop floor," said the weaselly Red director. "I'd be glad to help you, but work is work: time waits for no man. Rushed off my feet. Comrade Firsov here will answer your questions. The loss of Comrade Newton is a grave shock to our hearts. Capitalism has reached its claws into the very heart of Leningrad."

The Red director stopped himself, realizing he had perhaps overdone it. His earthy instincts told him to be cautious— after all, it wasn't yet clear why this copper was prowling about, or what this American had been getting up to before he kicked the bucket. "We should never have got involved with that foreigner," said the expression that flashed across his face. And he skittered out of the office.

"How can I help, Comrade Zaitsev?" asked Firsov, linking his hands in front of him on his desk. "Have a seat. Would you like some tea?"

"I won't keep you long."

"Thank you," Firsov said honestly. He gave the impression he knew he was indispensable—such confidence lent him a formidable presence. Not like most representatives of the obsolete classes who hadn't fled the country in time or had hoped in vain that the chaos of 1917 would soon blow over. And now they were deprived of all rights: the "disenfranchised". They tried their best to slip into the background, to avoid being seen or heard. Firsov clearly wasn't troubled by this anxiety. He was content to be seen and heard. He felt shielded by his education, his experience, his knowledge. And perhaps even by advocates at the very top of the party.

"And I'd ask you, Comrade Firsov, not to take too much of my time either. Tell me about Newton."

Zaitsev got up from his chair and began to pace the study pensively, examining the shelves, lingering in front of the portraits and posters. He glanced out of the window. Directors were usually caught off guard by this kind of shift in the *mise en scène*—an effect Zaitsev was counting on.

"I'd be glad to. What would you like to know?" Firsov asked Zaitsev's back.

"Was he popular at the factory?"

The engineer thought, looking at his own hands.

"He wasn't *un*popular," he answered. "The workers liked that he was black. He smiled. He was inquisitive, good-natured. He tried to learn Russian..."—Firsov was silent for a moment, selecting his words—"and that also amused them. They cut him a lot of slack," he added, following Zaitsev's gaze.

"What was he working on?" Zaitsev asked, standing at the window. He then sat down on the windowsill.

"He was down as an engineer," said Firsov, explicitly not answering the question. He crossed his legs and moved his clasped hands onto his knee.

"He didn't get in the way of others working?" Zaitsev asked head-on.

"Not those who wanted to work, no," he snapped.

"But he wasn't much help, either. Is that what you mean?" Zaitsev went over to the desk itself, put his hands on it and leant in. Firsov didn't change his position even a fraction. He made no attempt to move away. Zaitsev caught the smell of his eau de cologne.

"I'm not sure what this has to do with me." Firsov raised a sharp, dark eyebrow. "Comrade Newton didn't have much in the way of educational baggage."

"How do you mean?"

"Well, how do you imagine the situation is in the United States with regard to the rights of black people, Comrade Zaitsev? They're not allowed to attend school or university; they would be shot for trying. Comrade Newton isn't to blame for his lack of education. As for our workers—well, I assure you, the majority are much more archaic in their attitudes than this unfortunate American."

Firsov couldn't stand Zaitsev's proximity and he banged his chair as he moved back.

"But Newton received an engineer's salary and ration cards."

Firsov shrugged. "The party wanted to set an example of a different attitude towards black people. Especially black Communists."

Zaitsev sat down on the table. He somehow needed to unsettle Firsov, tease him, anything to stir him out of his impassivity. To push him to say more than he meant to.

"And how did people feel about it at the factory?"

But Firsov didn't raise an eyebrow.

"You see, nobody treated Newton like a regular Russian Vanka. He was a curiosity, exotic even. But his salary didn't seem exceptional."

"Friends? Did he have any girlfriends?"

"You'll need to ask the factory's Komsomol. He was under their jurisdiction."

Firsov clearly didn't like the question.

"He couldn't make friends on his own?"

"He could hardly speak Russian. But he was a decent, kind man. I am very sorry that such a fate befell him."

From this Zaitsev concluded that Firsov himself spoke excellent English.

"Did you study in America?"

The engineer's brown eyes bore into him.

"Do you need to know for the case?"

There's no messing around with this one, thought Zaitsev.

"Just curious," Zaitsev admitted sincerely.

Firsov softened a little. "In Germany. And it isn't a secret from our party organization, if that's what you mean."

"Come now, Comrade Firsov. I'm a police detective, not a *gepeushnik*. I catch killers and bandits, not spies and class enemies. Did Newton have a family?"

"N-no. No. He lived alone."

"Why are you not so sure?" Zaitsev threw out carelessly, while inside he was ready to pounce.

"I'm quite sure," the engineer muttered. "It's just... I think he wasn't very happy. You know, he was a pleasant, cheerful, sociable guy. Young, with a wonderful open smile..."

There was a pause again. Zaitsev didn't break it.

Firsov tried the same approach again. "But he could hardly speak Russian. And then... this isn't America, of course. Attitudes towards Newton were laudable, but..."

He was clearly hesitant. Zaitsev could see he was embarrassed.

"All the same... Please understand, our Komsomol members tried their best. But our corps of workers... In recent years, there have been a lot coming here from the villages. For them, a black man..."

Firsov fell silent again.

But Zaitsev understood. To those who have recently come to the city from the villages, poor Newton seemed like some wild savage. He was only amusing while he was busy at the workbench, hilariously mangling Russian words with a beaming smile. But the workers would quickly turn nasty if the black foreigner approached the girls. Or if the girls approached him, given his engineer's salary and his separate apartment.

They got into fights and murdered for less on the Vyborg Side. Especially after a drink or two. And most indulged every day without fail.

Zaitsev stood up. "Thank you, Comrade Firsov."

"Sorry I couldn't be more useful to you," said the de facto director of Russian Diesel with a shrug. He gave Zaitsev a firm handshake. "Do you think the poor chap was killed by his comrades on the shop floor? Ah, sorry, that must be a secret of the investigation."

Zaitsev didn't think so.

"You got it," he said with a smile. He added, "Thank you."

Zaitsev knew that if Newton had been killed by a boozy worker, he would have been knocked out by a fist, a rock or a bottle. Or stabbed.

He was lonely and black. Very little Russian. No friends or family, or even a lover. Oliver Newton was easy prey. He would have been easy to lure anywhere by affection alone. Even if it was only purchased affection.

The trail of the black American Communist was taking Zaitsev away from the Vyborg Side, but it wasn't clear where it would lead instead.

Affection. And at least the slightest ability to communicate in English. So far that was all he had.

IV

The following day, Zaitsev asked Samoilov to go to the Intourist office with a photograph of Newton. The Intourist guides were responsible for all foreign visitors. From the day they arrived in Leningrad to the day they left, an Intourist guide accompanied them everywhere, to tell them about the sights and the Soviet life, but mostly to prevent them seeing, hearing or figuring out anything they shouldn't.

"Yeah, I would if—" Samoilov started, but then stopped himself.

"What? Take one of the Fords. No need to run about," added Zaitsev.

Martynov, Demov, Samoilov and Serafimov all froze, in silence, but Zaitsev clearly felt a wave running between them—that avoided him.

"Well, I'm not going to argue with the investigation's party line," Samoilov quipped, raising his open palms. But he didn't catch Zaitsev's eye.

"What the fuck, Samoilov?" replied Zaitsev, unable to hold back his astonishment. He wanted to shout, "Samoilov, it's me!" But instead his voice hardened. "What are you implying?"

"What? I don't know what instructions came from the comrades at Smolny." Samoilov turned his head. Everyone silently looked at Zaitsev. As if Demov hadn't gone there with him that evening.

"As long as we're sure that Newton is the main lead here," Demov said in a conciliatory tone. And he looked at the others, as if inviting them to agree.

"I think we need to shake down the whores," said Martynov. He had come back with nothing from the archives.

"Exactly! They pounced on the American, rubbing their hands with glee, thinking he was a foreign tourist. But he turned out to be a Soviet worker. The girls got in too deep."

"If they were even whores," said Zaitsev.

"Nobody seems to have noticed they're missing," retorted Serafimov.

"Good point," Zaitsev agreed.

Every resident of the city had a network of family ties. Everyone had friends and colleagues. Everyone had someone who would look for them if they went missing.

"They've got to be whores," Martynov insisted.

"You said there was nothing on them in the files," Serafimov suddenly objected.

"Yes," Martynov agreed. "But all that means is they hadn't come to the attention of the Soviet authorities."

Zaitsev recalled the meeting at the factory: the recent boom in workers coming into the city from the villages.

"Or the girls are just from out of town? They recently moved from the country to work at the factory. And nobody's noticed they're missing. Their families are still in the villages, and at the factory they've assumed they've quit and run off with a guy. And the girls at their dorms will just be glad of the spare bed."

He saw that they were listening to him without enthusiasm. Outside the window was dank, chilly darkness; now and then the wind crashed into the glass at full pelt. The light hanging from the ceiling seemed dimmer and yellower. Serafimov suppressed a yawn.

"Great. Samoilov, you swing by Intourist tomorrow. Show them the photograph of the American. See what they say. How many Americans were in the city that day? What did they do? And you, Martynov, show our girls to the Tarnovsky Venereology Clinic. Maybe they've showed up there before if they're in the business. And call in at the clinic on Bolshaya Podyacheskaya, too. Maybe they'll recognize them."

He noticed how they casually exchanged glances.

What's going on? he asked himself.

"All right, guys," said Zaitsev. "See you tomorrow. Here in the morning, fresh and ready to go."

Everyone got up in silence.

"Are you coming, Demov?" asked Samoilov on the way out of the room.

Zaitsev heard Demov's voice in the corridor. Serafimov answered. Martynov sniggered. Zaitsev caught the word beer.

They were all chatting away, heading for a drink on 3rd July Street on the way home.

Everyone except him. He was emphatically not invited.

Zaitsev glanced into the corridor.

He listened to their voices as they receded. The stairwell amplified the echo, but also blended the sounds so he couldn't make out anything else.

The voices were gone.

Zaitsev could hardly believe what had just happened.

There was a light from the opposite office—the door was ajar. Nefyodov was sitting surrounded by catalogue drawers, his nose down as he diligently scribbled away, dipping his cheap fountain pen in the inkwell. Zaitsev tried to remember what assignment he had given Nefyodov. His agitated thoughts swirled around, whipping up bitter silt. He couldn't remember and quit trying. Right now he didn't care.

"Is your report ready, Nefyodov?" he enquired cheerfully, as though he'd been waiting for it all day.

Nefyodov jumped up to stand to attention, turning his little owl's face to Zaitsev. He looked at him without mockery, without malice or frostiness. But also without sympathy.

"Welcome to the club," said his eyes.

Chapter 6

"I'll have a bag of spuds," said Serafimov, handing him the banknotes rolled into a tube. "And if not, then beets. And if not, then—"

"All right, my turn!"

"Comrades, not all at once!" Martynov yelled in a light-hearted way.

He nudged them all out of the way and sat on the edge of the table. He pulled out a blank sheet of paper from the typewriter and began to write down their names with a pencil. Beside each name, the amount. Everyone surrounded the table and a heap of crumpled notes had appeared in front of Martynov.

Samoilov laid three spools of thread on top.

The others stared at him, perplexed.

"Nina gave me them. To swap for flour."

"What? You think I'm going to hang around the market all day?" replied Martynov.

"But, Martynov, you can't get thread like that for love nor money—the kolkhoz farmers are crying out for it. Nina says—"

"Just hold on with your thread," Serafimov interrupted. "Have you written mine down? If not spuds, then beets."

"You see, the petty bourgeois swamp sucks everything in. We told you, Serafimov, don't get married."

This was the scene Zaitsev encountered when he came in.

"You're married?" he couldn't help asking. "Since when?"

"Yes," Serafimov replied, hesitantly.

And from the awkward silence all around, Zaitsev realized: Serafimov got hitched when he, Zaitsev, was in prison at Shpalernaya.

Martynov flicked through the notes, his lips moving as he totted up the total.

"What's all this? NEP men expecting a visit from the tax inspector?" asked Zaitsev, changing the subject.

"Expenses for the trip," Samoilov answered on behalf of the others.

"I don't understand."

"Why would you drive such a distance with an empty vehicle?" explained Samoilov. "May as well chuck a couple of bags in the back seat for our comrades. Make the most of using the Ford."

"Er, I don't follow. Martynov, would you explain to me? Perhaps I'm being a little dense. Yesterday we spoke about a trip to the venereal-disease clinic," said Zaitsev, sitting on the edge of the table beside him. He turned to the list. "Now you're off on a shopping spree?"

"Their idea." Martynov drew back with a disingenuous grin. "Who am I to argue?"

Zaitsev didn't like their general tone at all. But he understood that an altercation was best avoided. For as long as possible.

The same thought had apparently occurred to his comrades. They were trying to behave as if nothing had happened. As far as possible.

"The clinic isn't at Bolshaya Podyacheskaya Street any more," explained Samoilov. "It's been moved out of the city to Lodeynoye Polye. And it's not just a clinic now, it's a high-security venereal hospital. In the former monastery."

There was a flutter of smirks.

"A mere 250 kilometres from Leningrad."

"So the idea is to swing by a few friendly kolkhoz farms on the way," explained Serafimov.

"And why?"

"To feed the city's residents," Martynov explained good-naturedly.

"My wife chucked the thread in—she says they'll swap it for food. Better than standing around here in the queues, not to mention saving your ration cards."

But Zaitsev was now interested in something else. "When was it moved?"

"In the summer," Demov answered curtly. Which was to say, while you were behind bars.

Zaitsev grunted.

"Fine, Martynov. Don't forget to sign for your expenses. You'll have to spend the night with the comrades in Lodeynoye Polye."

"No, I'll try to drive back before night."

"Don't rush." He looked at them each in turn. "But don't spend all day haggling at the markets, either. Have a good chat to the locals. Show them the photos of the girls too: maybe someone will remember their girlfriends."

"Those whores would say it's their own mother for you if they thought that was what you wanted to hear," said Martynov contemptuously.

"Not whores, Martynov, but individuals in receipt of unsanctioned income who have embarked on the path of correction," said Zaitsev angrily.

"Whatever you say."

Hesitantly, they walked away from the table. Demov lingered a moment beside Zaitsev, thick smoke rising from the cigarette in his hand. His lips stretched into an ironic smile.

"It's all right for you, Vasya, you're a single man. Like Diogenes. But we're all family people. You see, even Serafimov threw in the towel." He took a drag on his cigarette, blew out the smoke. He added quietly, in a serious tone this time, "Don't judge them. They'd go to the ends of the earth for their work. But back home, they've got the wife nagging, get this, get that, get a sack of potatoes. Try to understand…"

"Comrade Zaitsev, they're waiting for us at the theatre," Serafimov reminded him.

"Serafimov, take it easy—what's the rush? *We all love the theatre, we rush there every evening*," Samoilov sang tunelessly, quoting the operetta. "What are you going to see?"

"Ah, piss off. Not going to a play. To the costume department," Serafimov replied.

"Still a cultural outing."

"Serafimov, you get ready," said Zaitsev. "I'm just coming. Demov, come with me a moment. I've got something to show you."

They went out into the corridor.

"In here," said Zaitsev, opening a door.

Demov glanced inside. Zaitsev gave him an unceremonious shove.

"Come on, spit it out. What the hell's going on? What are you all playing at?"

Demov pushed away his hands.

"Hands off me. Don't you dare touch me."

"Are you threatening me?"

"What? Comrade Zaitsev, are you mad? I'm a Soviet person. How would I threaten my own comrade? I'm just letting you know."

"That's what I mean, Demov. I've noticed your little comedy act. Just seems a little one-sided, that's all. As I recall, I wasn't the only one who went to meet Comrade Kirov."

Demov shrugged.

"Comrade Zaitsev, I haven't got time for a heart-to-heart. I need to get around the markets and second-hand shops. On your orders, remember?"

"What are you getting at?"

"I fear you're stopping me from doing my job with all this chat and then you'll pin the blame on me for sabotage."

Zaitsev was speechless for a moment.

"What's all this about, Demov?" he said through gritted teeth. "Well?"

With a frown, Demov stepped away.

"There's no point in this."

He turned away. He took out a box of Nord and pulled a cigarette out with his teeth.

Zaitsev tore the cigarette from his mouth, threw it on the floor and stamped on it.

"What am I supposed to do? Are you telling me to resign?"

"None of my business."

"It is very much your business. All of you. How am I supposed to work with my own team looking at me like I'm an enemy."

"'Resign'! As if they would let you go now," Demov said wearily, lighting another cigarette.

Zaitsev waited. But Demov wasn't going to talk.

"They let me out because I hadn't done anything," said Zaitsev. "They got to the bottom of it… and they let me out."

Demov's cheeks collapsed as he inhaled on his cigarette. He nodded as if to say, "Fine, whatever you say, just leave me alone."

"I'm not a rat," said Zaitsev, loud and clear. He seemed to have guessed the question correctly, because Demov immediately looked up at him. Zaitsev didn't look away.

He knew that a lot was hanging on this conversation now.

"Demov, if I can't prove it to the guys then I've got no hope here in the department," he said slowly. "They're afraid to utter a single word to me more than they have to. Help me convince them."

"Listen, Vasya, I'm not blaming you. I know that anyone can be cornered. Anyone. Including me. And you'll sing like a good boy."

"I'm not a rat, Demov," Zaitsev repeated, quietly and seriously.

"But they did let you out."

"What am I supposed to do? Go and beg to go back to jail?"

Demov shrugged again and for a moment he closed his eyes.

"But you're not afraid of me, are you, Demov?"

"I've lived through enough myself. I got through the Revolution and the Red Terror, didn't I? I've already had ten extra years. The guys are too young to know all that. And by the way, why were you arrested?"

"Why didn't they finish you off in 1920?"

Demov laughed.

"You're a sly one, Vasya! Only, please, don't involve me in any anti-Soviet conversations," said Demov with a venomous smile. "I understand where you're coming from, but don't take the piss."

"I'm telling it to you like it is. I'm straight-up, you know I am."

"You are, are you?" grinned Demov.

Zaitsev chose not to carry on with that line of argument.

"It didn't occur to you, Demov, that maybe it was Kopteltsev who got me released from OGPU in view of the extraordinary crime on Yelagin Island?"

"Did he tell you that?" asked Demov quickly. "OK, Vasya, fine. We've had it with that fucker Nefyodov. And you're not helping with your Turgenev heart-to-hearts. If you're asking whether the guys will work attentively, conscientiously, under you, then the answer is yes. They will." He gripped the door handle. "But don't ask for more than that."

"Demov—"

"Don't."

"I know how to rip out Nefyodov's sting. And I'll do it, too. I take it upon myself."

Demov left without answering. But Zaitsev saw: his last words had made an impression.

Zaitsev followed him out.

Serafimov was standing in the corridor, barely awake, his coat on. Cap in hand.

"Serafimov! Quickly—go and join Martynov! We'll sort out your paperwork when you get back. Don't leave a whore unturned! He can ask about the girls and you can do the old woman. People tend to know who the madams are. And you can help load up the potatoes," he added cheerfully. He slapped Serafimov on the shoulder.

He pulled a few wrinkled banknotes out of his breast pocket.

"Here you go. Grab me some grub, too. If circumstances allow. If it's not enough, I'll give you the rest later." He handed Serafimov the cash.

"But we're—"

"Nefyodov will come with me to the theatre. Nefyodov!" shouted Zaitsev, his voice echoing in the hallway.

The owl's face appeared at the door.

"Get your coat! Cultural outing."

Demov turned around. Surprise flashed in his eyes. And he pulled away his gaze like you'd jerk away your hand.

II

They recognized the gemstone necklace at the State Academic Theatre of Opera and Ballet, the Mariinsky.

The theatre was set back from the once grandiose main streets of the imperial capital: this was a district populated by poor widows, students and pensioners. In the block between the Mariinsky Theatre, Nevsky Prospekt and the Morskaya Streets was the infamous Sennaya Square, the cesspit of the city with its network of grubby back lanes.

They went on foot. Zaitsev wasn't in the mood for talking. And Nefyodov didn't try. Zaitsev noticed: he wasn't trying to get him to open up. Neither was he trying any shortcuts to getting to know him. What was this rat playing at? He was either an idiot or else a sly bastard. Zaitsev felt nauseous, as if he were trapped in a jar with a wasp. Running out of air.

They turned into Sennaya Square.

In Soviet Leningrad, the difference between the city's grandiose frontages and its underworld had somehow been ironed out. The once-grand streets were shabby and frayed; the Kolomna district had sunk into decrepitude. And Sennaya Square and the surrounding back streets were the teeming, putrid slums they ever were. Vyazemskaya Lavra still loomed large and grim: the long, three-storey building looked like an apartment block, but was in fact the hangout of criminals of all stripes. At all times of day and night, a din of comings and goings hung over Sennaya Square like fog: shouting, singing, cursing, touting for business. Second-hand goods peddled, stolen goods hawked. In the middle of the day, the pavements were littered with loitering drunkards. Beggars and cripples, the destitute and the desperate, latching on to any passer-by. The dark, crumbling frontages reeked of damp and urine. The dismal houses looked out through long-unwashed windows—or perhaps they had never been washed. Passers-by trod hurriedly through the perpetual grime. Everything was embossed with the stamp of poverty, squalor and crime.

It was a dismal enough crowd on Nevsky Prospekt, or 25th October Prospekt, or whatever it was supposed to be called, but at least there was the occasional ruddy face, beaver-skin hat or fine coat from overseas. Here on Sennaya, everything was grey, worn out and beyond hope.

Zaitsev craned his neck at the sound of hammering and boards crashing. They were putting scaffolding up on the former Vyazemskaya Lavra building. Workers scurried about on the roof. They were building extra floors to meet the demand for housing. Leningrad had a catastrophic lack of accommodation.

"What are you gawping at?" someone snarled as they brushed past. At Sennaya Square, you kept your head down and didn't stop.

The rumble of voices was cut through with a sudden female screech.

"My bag! My bag!"

From the seething movement through the crowds, you could see which way the thief had run, shoving aside those who hadn't already seen him coming and stepped aside. The shriek of a policeman's whistle pierced the air.

A woman laden with bags lost her balance and crashed into Zaitsev. His elbow felt the pistol under his coat. He just managed to catch what was happening from the corner of his eye. Someone dived past them. An elusive hand movement from Nefyodov and before anyone knew what had happened, the thief's legs kicked up as he landed flat on his back.

Nefyodov's face was as sleepy as ever. But his hand had already seized the wrist of the man on the ground.

Zaitsev ran over and threw his arms around the thief as though in an embrace.

"Nefyodov, don't let him out of your sight! Keep your eye on the bag!"

A dense ring of onlookers quickly formed around them. Two policemen in uniform and helmets came pushing their way through the crowd. One of them, the younger one, had cheeks like two rosy apples. Workers streaming in from the villages, thought Zaitsev.

"We're CID," hissed Zaitsev. The thief squirmed in his arms like a fish, spewing obscene curses. "Caught red-handed, with the bag. He's all yours."

Nefyodov flashed his ID. The policemen pinned the thief's hands to his back and led him to the station. The woman who had been robbed tottered along after them.

"Well done, Nefyodov. Excellent reactions," said Zaitsev, straightening his coat. "Did you pick that up in the army?" he added, carrying on the act of not knowing where Nefyodov had served before.

Nefyodov blushed. Come on, mate, time to come clean, thought Zaitsev with disdain.

"In the circus."

"In the circus?"

"I ran away from home as a kid. I was a crafty little one."

"And what did you do there? In the circus? And don't tell me it was French wrestling."

"No, no," said Nefyodov, turning a deeper red. "I was in an act called 'Icarus and Sons'. Maybe you remember it? Acrobatics. I was one of the 'sons'. Just don't tell anyone."

"Oh, wow. The guys'll be impressed. We haven't had any circus artists yet."

"Really, don't tell. The way they are with me… it's not great."

Zaitsev grunted. Perhaps Nefyodov hadn't been an acrobat in the past, and was just a decent actor in the present, but his artless tone seemed sincere to Zaitsev.

"You're imagining it, mate. The way they are with you, I mean. It's CID, not a social club. No one gives a shit about feelings here. No one gets any special treatment."

Nefyodov didn't answer.

They walked past a pawnshop towards a wooden humpback bridge. The bare poplars had shed their last brown leaves into the Kryukov Canal. The litter was slapping against the granite bank.

"Alexei!" came a shout from behind him.

Zaitsev stepped onto the bridge. He immediately turned around when he sensed someone breathing up close behind him.

"Alexei!"

Before them stood a man. Judging by his looks, he could have been anything from twenty to thirty: his face was young but tired, as if drained from within. His plaid coat had clearly known better times. But his clothes were clean. He was slightly out of breath from running. Steam escaped from his mouth in the cold October air. His coat was unbuttoned.

In his hand he was still holding his receipt from the pawnshop.

"Well, well." A stunned smile swam across the man's face. Nefyodov was aloof as he studied the stranger. "I saw you through the window! I ran straight out to catch you."

"I think you're mistaken, comrade. I'm not Alexei," said Zaitsev as the stranger's smile drooped and faded away. "And I don't recognize you, either. Well, it happens."

He turned and carried on walking across the bridge

"Wait!" called the plaid coat. "I'm sorry to bother you! It's just you reminded me of someone. Perhaps you're his relative?"

"Comrade"—Zaitsev turned around with his whole body, losing patience—"everyone has relatives. But who you mean, I do not know. And to tell you the truth, I don't have time to find out."

"Wait a minute," said the man with the receipt, grabbing him by the sleeve.

Zaitsev saw how Nefyodov's gaze was coloured with dangerous curiosity. Again that feeling of being trapped in a glass jar.

"Citizen," Zaitsev barked. "I'm not out for a stroll, I'm on duty, and you're holding me up. If you want to talk, then come with me to the department and we can talk there."

The plaid-coat man shrank back.

"Excuse me, comrade," he muttered. "My mistake. I took you for someone else."

On the other side of the bridge, Zaitsev glanced back across the canal from the corner of his eye. But the man in the coat was gone, already washed away into the crowd on Sennaya Square.

"What kind of a moron was he? What was all that about relatives?" muttered Zaitsev, loud enough that Nefyodov would hear. But Nefyodov's face wasn't giving anything away.

"Are you not from Peter, then, Comrade Zaitsev?" asked Nefyodov.

"I am indeed," Zaitsev answered energetically. "But the only family I have is the orphanage. It didn't occur to me to join the circus, you see, so I was homeless. If the Soviet state hadn't picked me up and fed me, Nefyodov, I don't know where I would have ended up. Or rather, I know full well."

III

The squat, low-pitched ceiling of the porch seemed to belong not to the theatre but to some provincial factory. This was the service entrance, tucked around the side of the building. A long, narrow, windowless corridor took them deep inside.

The turnstile gave off a dull gleam.

Zaitsev showed the porter his ID.

"So, Nefyodov, are you hoping to see Ulanova?" asked Zaitsev as the porter called someone on an internal line.

The porter answered for Nefyodov, his voice stern with a haughty air.

"Galina Sergeevna Ulanova's already gone in for the morning session."

Zaitsev pulled a face at Nefyodov, as if to say, "Ah, you see?"

But this temple of art was not a place for jokes. Zaitsev's ID was returned to him through the small round window, along with a square cardboard pass.

"They'll come down for you," the porter growled.

"Comrades, are you for the costume department?"

A corpulent middle-aged woman stood in the corridor. Her greying hair was cut fashionably short and the hem of a tight skirt peeked out from under her blue work dress. She was wearing slippers. Zaitsev pushed his way through the turnstile. Nefyodov followed, knocking his knees on the iron frame of the revolving part.

"Are you from the police?" she asked sternly. In the theatre, apparently, everyone else was considered an outsider and given the cold shoulder.

"Zaitsev. And this is Comrade Nefyodov."

"Kukushkina," the woman forced herself to say, her hands firmly in the pockets of her work dress. "Let's go." She headed down the corridor without a glance back, confident they were following her.

"You've made quite a commotion here with your chain," said the woman, in the tone of a head teacher scolding her senior pupils.

"Excuse me, madam," said Zaitsev, putting her in her place. "The chain's not ours. It went missing from *this* theatre. And we want to find out how."

Kukushkina's nostrils fluttered.

"I'm quite sure there's been a misunderstanding," she said, bristling.

"No doubt we'll get to the bottom of it," said Zaitsev, stopping her in her tracks.

The costume department smelt of ironing and starch. Layered tutus lay stacked one on top of the other in fluffy heaps. The dressmaker, her mouth full of pins, was kneeling before a mannequin clothed in a black camisole with a white bosom. Another woman was leaning low over the table, cutting with scissors that crunched as she snipped. Zaitsev could make out only a thin back in a knitted cardigan and elbows. The slippery silk slithered off the table.

Kukushkina tapped her glasses down to the tip of her nose. She pulled out a drawer tightly packed with cards. Her nails were long, but yellowish, birdlike. Zaitsev watched in disgust as she flicked through the cards with her talons.

A sweet, surprisingly young face appeared at the door.

"Allochka!" she called, almost singing. "I've come for the fitting for the pastorale in *The Queen of Spades*."

"Quiet please, people are working here," Kukushkina reminded her.

"Pastorale," Nefyodov repeated to himself, with the uncertainty of someone trying to learn a foreign word.

Kukushkina gave him a look you might direct at a cockroach.

"The interlude in Act Three," she explained, enunciating clearly. "'The Sincerity of the Shepherdess'."

The girl gave a sonorous laugh, turned her toes out, then quickly fluttered past. Her straight back, narrow shoulders and muscular legs left no doubt that she belonged in a ballet troupe. The seamstress at the table put down her scissors and threw the dress over her arm, before following the ballerina.

Finally, Kukushkina pulled out the card she had been looking for.

"Here. Necklace," read Kukushkina. "Men's suit. *Ivan Susanin*. Ball."

"When was it last seen here?"

Kukushkina shrugged. "When was *Susanin* last performed? I'd need to see the poster. I don't remember exactly."

"Are you sure?"

"About the show? Of course! All costumes and props are listed and put away after every performance."

"And where was the necklace kept?"

"In the wardrobe," snapped the termagant. "Where else?"

"Who has access to the wardrobe?"

"I do," she said, again flaring her nostrils. "The wardrobe mistresses. The artists."

"So anyone could come and borrow it. Do I understand you correctly?"

"No." Kukushkina jumped in. "No one is allowed in without a pass."

Zaitsev smiled kindly.

"Well, yes, but I meant: anyone from the theatre personnel. Is that right?"

"That's right." Kukushkina pursed her lips. "You don't suspect a member of staff of stealing a piece of costume jewellery and taking it to a pawnshop, do you?" she asked with venom. "Believe me, they would see perfectly well that it's not real."

"How many dressers and seamstresses do you have?"

"Today there are two: Bochkina and Petrova."

"Comrade Nefyodov, would you speak to the citizen?" Zaitsev nodded towards the woman with the pins in her mouth. She looked at them in dismay as she held a pin up to a camisole. Carefully taking the pins from her mouth, she stood up.

"Bochkina," she said, introducing herself.

She and Nefyodov sat down at the table where the cut silk lay. It shone in the lamplight. Zaitsev recalled the lustrous shirt the murdered American had been wearing. He knocked on the fitting-room door.

"Come in!" came the ballerina's sing-song voice.

Zaitsev opened the door halfway.

The dancer stood in front of the mirror in a delicate dress covered in roses, the very picture of a cream cake.

Zaitsev's heart started pounding: before him he saw something that he didn't quite understand. All he knew was that it was very important.

"Comrade, who are you after?" asked the dresser, holding a tape measure extended along the hem.

"Comrade Petrova?" He remembered her name, forgetting it again in an instant.

His head was spinning, creamy roses circling around him, as if he were running around a spiral maze, at the centre of which was something very important. Something he needed to remember. What was it?

The dresser looked at him in the mirror. She seemed very young. Bright eyes under neat black eyebrows, black curly hair pinned back. Either she was frightened or she was of the type they called an "English rose", or perhaps it was the effect of the black velvet curtain behind her, but her face seemed dazzlingly white.

Zaitsev stared at her, this silken rose. The spiralling maze was closing in. There he was, that evening at the ballet. That's right. The suprematist ballet, whatever it was called. Never mind what it was called. *The Nutcracker*, yes. "The Dance of the Shepherds". The pastorale from *The Queen of Spades*, "The Sincerity of the Shepherdess". "*My dear friend, gracious shepherdess,*" sang in his head. "The shepherd…" He heard Nefyodov's voice in his head. "Write up the report, Nefyodov," he had said, "and leave it on my desk." And Nefyodov had said…

"Sorry, I was hoping to have a little chat with you." He heard his own voice as though from afar.

"I'll just—"

He almost had it.

"That's fine, Allochka!" the ballerina exclaimed cheerfully. "You go and talk to the comrade. We're done!" And with extraordinary speed she ran her fingers along the hooks and pulled off the dress, revealing her flat, bare torso.

Zaitsev dashed from the fitting room, almost tripping himself over as his feet got in a tangle with the curtains that served as the door.

He saw Nefyodov soundlessly opening his mouth, with the costume designer Bochkina looking on. He saw Kukushkina; he saw the coals smouldering orange in the black iron. He saw everything at once and at the same time he couldn't see or hear anything, because now only one detail mattered.

"Comrade! What's going on?"

Zaitsev didn't answer.

The shepherd and the shepherdess. The faithful porcelain couple. Forever separated in the room of Faina Baranova.

And now reunited in the Leningrad CID evidence room. But as evidence in two completely different cases.

Chapter 7

Zaitsev had often heard that men feel frightened and lost when a woman cries.

But Olga Zabotkina's tears made not the slightest impression on him. Her large, damp body seemed to exude moisture effortlessly. She took off her glasses as if they were in the way. Zaitsev waited patiently for her to blow her nose.

"Sorry," she said, her nose still blocked. She raised her pink rabbit eyes to him—without the glasses they seemed unusually small. "It's just that everything connected with Fainochka is so awful... so awful..."

Her chest began to rise again in anticipation of another round of sobbing. The woollen shawl slid from her rounded shoulder; she tugged it back into place without looking.

"And you're absolutely sure that this is the same figurine that disappeared from your neighbour's room?"

Zabotkina peered at the photograph and nodded.

"Where did you find it?"

Zaitsev didn't answer.

Then Zabotkina spoke again. "She bought them as a pair. I told your comrade. The one who came."

She looked suddenly worried she might have said the wrong thing to the wrong "comrade".

"He showed his ID. The one who looks like a Finn or an Estonian. Only with a Russian surname. Didn't he tell you?" asked Zabotkina, alarmed.

"It's all fine. I just wanted to make sure," Zaitsev reassured her gently. Naturally, he didn't mention that he hadn't learnt of this since he had been in prison at the time.

"Is it not possible your neighbour might have given it away, for example? Or sold it? Without your knowing?"

"She didn't tell me everything, of course." Zabotkina began to fumble with the end of her knitted scarf. "But I don't think so. No."

"And you're sure that she bought them? You remember that?"

"Of course. At an auction. What was the place called again?... A... A... Apollo? Ah, no, *Apollo* was the magazine, wasn't it? Antiquity? Antikvariat? Or was it Apollo, after all?" Zabotkina looked at him with her watery eyes through her thick glasses.

"Ah," said Zaitsev enthusiastically, "so you and your friend are art lovers. Are you regular visitors to this auction?"

Zaitsev recalled how, seven or eight years ago, auction houses were often selling off trinkets and paintings from palaces, mansions and wealthy apartments. Whatever hadn't been destroyed during the Revolution, and hadn't yet made its way into proletarian museums. Then the supply dried up a little. But the flow didn't stop completely. Auctions were still attracting a lot of collectors, as well as those who simply wanted to ogle at the hitherto closed-off world of the nobility and the rich and famous. Commoners. Amateurs. Bloody philistines, as experienced antique dealers called them.

Zaitsev pictured the two old maids, Zabotkina and Baranova: two ridiculous figures in little pot hats. Sentimentally peering at the dregs of someone else's elegant life. Gazing on longingly as objects were carried away. And all the while, the auction girls keep bringing out more and more items, tags waving in the air. Faina Baranova raises a gloved hand, darned here and there on the fingertips. The hammer falls. She's in luck! The porcelain pair goes to the lady in the gloves.

Zabotkina slightly blushed.

"Do you also love beautiful things?" she asked with feeling.

Zaitsev nodded. "I do. Have you often been to these auctions?"

"Well, I only went to accompany her. Music is more my thing," she added quietly. The end of the sentence seemed to contain an implicit question, as if to ask, "And you?"

Zaitsev looked at her attentively. Zabotkina's earlobes blushed red.

"Was Faina in contact with any foreign citizens?"

"What are you implying? No, not at all," cried Zabotkina, recoiling and pressing her chubby white hand to her chest. Horror flashed in her eyes. Contacts between Soviet citizens and foreigners had already begun to attract the disapproving attention of the party, the Soviet press and, most importantly, OGPU.

"Why would she have relatives abroad?" gasped a startled Zabotkina. "She only had a sister in Kiev."

Perhaps Faina Baranova, a lonely, sentimental middle-aged woman, didn't tell her unattractive yet sensitive friend and neighbour everything about her life. The shepherd couple suggested that Faina Baranova still harboured a glimmer of hope.

Zaitsev nodded.

"Yes, I don't doubt it. Have a look at these photos, Comrade Zabotkina."

Zaitsev placed the photos of the women from Yelagin Park on the table beside them.

Zabotkina bent down low. Then she straightened up.

"Are they sick?" she asked.

It was true that the retoucher, who had "opened" the corpses' eyes, hadn't completely succeeded in lending vitality to their faces. Zaitsev couldn't disagree with Zabotkina's observation.

"Are any of them familiar to you?"

Her nose crept slowly from one photograph to another. She straightened up again.

"No. I've never seen them. And if I have, then only very briefly, because I don't recognize them. Might be best to ask at the co-operative where Fainochka worked. Maybe they were on the same line."

Zabotkina wasn't stupid. Zaitsev thought for a moment how unfair life was, putting her in this plump, clammy body. Who was going to care about Olga Zabotkina's mind and soul if her lips were the same shade of greyish pink as raw meat?

He tried to be kinder than most people would be and to smile at her. But he couldn't bring himself to.

"Thank you, Comrade Zabotkina," he said, getting up.

There was nothing more to talk about with her. He had already been to the co-operative where Baranova worked and no one had recognized the Yelagin victims.

In his head, he was already referring to the murdered Faina Baranova as the Shepherdess.

Now he needed more on the Shepherd.

II

In the October drizzle, the Russian Diesel building looked sullen, squatting heavily by the road like an ailing ogre.

The yellow electric light inside was harsh on the eyes.

"Citizen," said Zaitsev assertively, holding open his ID. "You're probably not thinking straight. Do you think I've come here to fill out some invoices or something? The Criminal Investigation Department wants to speak with your director. And the investigation has no time to wait. Get the director here right away."

The secretary squinted a little at the ID with a twitch of her lips, made up with oily-looking lipstick, and her fashionably plucked eyebrows. The words "investigation" and "criminal" left a frosty silence in the reception. The visitors pressed their briefcases closer to their chests, a mixture of curiosity and apprehension on their faces.

"Wait a moment, comrade," said the secretary, smoothing her skirt as she moved to stand up. "I'll ask the director."

Zaitsev didn't even wait until she was out of her wooden office chair, trying not to catch her silk stockings on any splinters. He walked quickly around her desk and pushed the door to the already familiar office.

"Comrade, what's this? Have you got an appointment?" the Red director spluttered angrily in his proletarian accent, looking up from his newspaper with his large forehead.

The desk next to him was vacant.

"I need to speak to Comrade Firsov."

Behind him came the staccato tapping of high heels.

"Lenochka, it's OK. I'll see the comrade," the Red director shouted over Zaitsev's shoulder.

In the time since Zaitsev had last seen him, he seemed to have lost his sheen. He no longer trundled along like the jolly little Kolobok from the Sovkino cartoon.

He went over to the door and listened. He quietly turned the key in the lock and turned to Zaitsev.

"Who's interested in him?" he asked quietly.

"Criminal Investigation."

"You see... he's... uh... not here."

Zaitsev was beginning to lose patience.

"Kindly go and look for him, then. Tell him the detective is waiting in his office."

"He's... uh... gone."

"On a business trip? Where? How can I contact him?"

The Red director stared at him in surprise.

"Surely you'd know best," he said.

He lowered his voice to a whisper and answered the next question before Zaitsev had even had time to ask it.

"Comrade Firsov was arrested this morning." His face said, "Surely you knew?"

Zaitsev felt like he'd been caught napping. Suspicion was already spreading on the director's face.

This morning—while he was talking to the witness Zabotkina.

"May I use your phone?" asked Zaitsev.

"Go ahead, comrade investigator. Is it confidicial?" He grasped the door handle obligingly, showing he was ready to leave his visitor alone with the telephone, poised on the vast desk like a black-lacquered frog.

Zaitsev gestured as if to say, "No need, it's not confidential"— assuming that was what he meant. He picked up the receiver.

"Duty officer?" asked Zaitsev. "It's about the arrest of Firsov..." He didn't remember his first name. He covered the mouthpiece with his palm and looked up at the Red director.

"Name and patronymic? Afanasy Osipovich."

"Afanasy Osipovich," repeated Zaitsev.

"They showed their ID. All by the book." The Red director carried on chatting away, as though more afraid of silence than of a police visit.

"Thank you for your assistance, comrade," interrupted Zaitsev.

He listened to the duty officer's reply. He hung up. And then, forgetting to take leave of the Red director, he departed, escorted by the grim silence of the secretary and the visitors in the reception.

The duty officer had reported that no detainee of that name had been brought into the Criminal Investigation Department that day.

Zaitsev walked quickly, as if trying to catch up with his own thoughts, and they were off at full pelt.

Their IDs, he thought. What IDs? No Firsovs had been brought into CID. Were they in disguise, then, these mysterious people with IDs who had dragged Comrade Firsov away this morning from right under his nose?

But what if these IDs held the key to how the victims had ended up on Yelagin Island—to that ill-omened clearing, far from the paths and onlookers' eyes? But how? Had they walked there themselves? Without protest, without resistance. Paralysed by fear and bewilderment. Perhaps, stunned by the words "You're under arrest".

III

The tram careered through the industrial outskirts, then slackened to a slower pace. It was barely crawling by the time it reached the centre, close to bursting with the passengers' vexed impatience. With no release for the growing pressure, the tram exploded with bickering and cursing.

Zaitsev loved such moments of forced idleness. And the background noise usually helped him concentrate. But not today.

If he was right, then he needed to look for gangsters with fake ID cards.

And they were unlikely to have restricted themselves to Russian Diesel. A Soviet man cannot stop himself once he's tasted the power bestowed by a document with a stamp. In this sense, Zaitsev had no class prejudices: in his eyes, even racketeers and hustlers were still Soviet citizens first and foremost.

The tram ground along the rails, spitting orange sparks where the wires met. It lingered at the stops, the bell helplessly dinging, as crowds of foul-mouthed passengers forced their way off or on, squirming into its already stuffed belly; no one paid the slightest attention to the departure signal.

Zaitsev was fuming. In the end, he couldn't stand it, and as the tram started to drag itself away from the stop, as if gasping for its final breath, he jumped down and set off on foot. He almost broke into a run.

Fortunately, Leningrad pedestrians are always alert to others sharing the pavement, eager to avoid collisions or even to brush against a passer-by. Zaitsev quickly manoeuvred his way through the crowd on Volodarsky Prospekt. He sprinted past the benches, trays and fold-out tables where second-hand booksellers hawked their wares, surrounded by book lovers leafing through a volume that had caught their eye.

And what if it hadn't been a mistake? he thought as he hotfooted his way across the city. What if he found out the command came from Gorokhovaya Street, from CID?

In that case, Firsov's arrest was a bad sign. If Firsov was arrested by CID, then he, Zaitsev, was in the dark about it. Who would have given the order over his head? Surely not Demov? Or Samoilov? Who could have sanctioned it? The head of CID, Kopteltsev himself? Who else?

It all stank to high heaven.

Zaitsev reminded himself not to run ahead, not to jump to any conclusions before he had the facts. First he needed to find out precisely what was going on.

He made himself slow down. But he didn't manage it for long. His legs carried themselves. He was walking so fast he had a metallic taste in his mouth. He stormed in through the doors to CID. The duty officer stared at him in surprise: what's the rush?

"Hi," said Zaitsev, leaning across the counter towards the duty officer. "Tell me, was a man brought in this morning?

Shaved head. About so tall, well dressed. In a suit that's clearly foreign. Ring any bells?"

The duty officer shrugged. "Nope."

"Sure? And without the suit?"

He shook his head. "What is there to remember? No one's been brought in."

"Hmm, I see," muttered Zaitsev. The duty officer's words were reassuring in a way. So it wasn't CID that arrested him.

Fraudsters, then.

Zaitsev decided to rule out that last possibility.

"Listen"—he turned back to the officer on duty—"what's the closest police station to Russian Diesel? Can you put me through?"

"Do you want me to transfer the call to your office?" asked the duty officer, intently running his finger down the list of city police departments.

"I'll wait here."

Without thinking, Zaitsev tapped his pockets, but then remembered he didn't have any cigarettes. He glanced around for someone to ask for one, when he stopped himself: no, giving up means giving up.

The duty officer was repeating the personal data over the phone. Zaitsev, leaning his elbow on the counter, made as if he were studying the portrait of the leader framed by red ribbons that hung on the wall behind the duty officer. Then his gaze shifted to the dusty ficus tree in the corner. The duty officer hung up.

"No one by that name, they say. Not by that name or that description."

"I see. Thanks."

So, fraudsters. As he expected.

"Will you do me another favour? Put me through to Russian Diesel. Director's office."

The duty officer handed him the receiver.

"Zaitsev," he introduced himself curtly in the slightly crackling silence. "About Firsov again. How many were there?"

"Two."

"What did they look like?"

The Red director murmured, "Like normal."

"Uniform? Plain clothes?"

"Coats. You know. Caps."

"What kind?"

"Normal kind of coats. Grey. Like half of Leningrad wear." Zaitsev could hear his accent in how he pronounced "coats" and "wear".

Zaitsev hung up.

On the stairs it dawned on him: the secretary. He remembered her gaze giving him a fleeting appraisal. No two-legged male escapes that fate. She'd be able to give him a comprehensive description. She's the one to ask. She'd be able to describe the criminals in detail, in more detail than would ever occur to the men themselves.

His hand on the banister, he turned to the duty officer and asked, as if on the off chance, "And is Kopteltsev in?"

The duty officer nodded. "I don't think he left."

Zaitsev nodded in turn and quickly ran up the stairs. So someone is posing as a police officer...

This, Zaitsev reasoned, might answer the question of how. How did the killers make their victims go to Yelagin?

But what about why? What for? Could it really have been for the sake of fur coats and handbags?

This was the classic question, ancient and foolproof: why?

In other words, the motive was still unclear.

"Zaitsev!" came an echo up the stairwell. Zaitsev leant over the railing and looked down: the duty officer stood in the square of light, looking up.

"It's Russian Diesel again. Shall I put it through to your office or will you come down?"

Zaitsev quickly calculated: he was closer to the office now.

"Put it through."

In a few bounds he had covered the remaining steps.

"Zaitsev," he said into the receiver. He heard a click: the duty officer had disconnected.

"'Allo? 'Allo? That you, comrade policeman?" Zaitsev recognized the Red director's way of speaking.

"Yes?" he asked tersely, somewhat annoyed. How did Firsov manage to work alongside such a buffoon?

"I'm, er… This… Maybe it's important, maybe not. But so we don't have any misunderstandings…"

Zaitsev was silent, which seemed to make him even more nervous. Best to give him space to say more than he meant to.

"The… er, the comrades who took Firsov away," said the Red director, suddenly lowering his voice. The sound turned into a kind of tickle in his ear.

"I can't hear you," snapped Zaitsev.

"So that's how things turned out," the Red director said, louder. "I'm calling to say: I had my suspicions, yes. Those suits he wore. An expert in the old regime, you know. He went to the Americas, and whatnot, studied in the what-have-you, Englands and Germanies. Yes, yes. I gave the necessary tip-off."

Zaitsev suppressed his irritation and made his tone sparkle with admiration. "Is that right? Good man, good man. So your suspicions were confirmed?"

His approach worked.

"Well, yes!" The Red director was almost gleeful. "Since the OGPU comrades came for him, that must mean for sure that he's vermin."

"OGPU? You're sure it was OGPU? Not the police?"

"I didn't manage to tell you. But yes. Clear as day. IDs, all by the book. Political administration. That's why I'm calling. Tipping you off. I don't know what kind of trouble he's been cooking up for you, but just so you know, comrade policeman, this Firsov is no mere troublemaker. He's vermin. A lurking enemy."

Zaitsev flew into an instant rage. "Why didn't you say so right away?"

"Well, like... You didn't ask."

Zaitsev thanked him for the valuable information and hung up.

He sat down. In his head he cursed the stupid party puppet with every expletive imaginable. But now what to do?

OGPU had its own agenda.

And he had his. For him, Firsov was a valuable witness in a case in which Comrade Kirov himself had a personal interest in the investigation. In which Zaitsev's freedom was on the line.

Kirov's name opened doors.

Zaitsev decided. There was no point in discussing this with Demov. He'd see it as a provocation.

There was only one person he could possibly speak to.

IV

Kopteltsev didn't lose his head. He didn't flare up. He just took out his handkerchief and dabbed his forehead. He looked like he was unwell. His big greasy face seemed to be clinging for dear life on to its black, close-set eyebrows and its jutting, knobbly chin. He lowered his body into a chair, in silence. Today his plumpness didn't seem so ruddy; instead he seemed wan, short of breath and sweaty.

"Right," he said, writing down Firsov's full name, year of

birth and place of work in his notebook. Zaitsev gave him quick answers, while carefully watching Kopteltsev.

"Right," he repeated. And he closed his eyes for a moment, as though pierced by pain.

What's the matter with him? wondered Zaitsev.

Kopteltsev opened his eyes.

"If it's OGPU, then he's either at Shpalernaya... er, I mean Voinova"—he immediately corrected himself, glancing quickly at Zaitsev. Had he noticed his slip of the tongue, using the pre-revolutionary, non-Soviet street name?

In his eyes flashed... apprehension? No, it was something else.

Kopteltsev carried on: "...or Kresty. Or Peresylnaya. Vasya. Whichever prison it is, we'll find him. I'll find out."

"Listen, Alexander Alexeyich," said Zaitsev. Kopteltsev's tone and quick actions dispelled his fears, even encouraged him. I'm not an enemy, he wanted to tell him. But instead, he said: "There's one more thing."

And he told him about the murder of Faina Baranova. That there could be a connection between the cases.

Kopteltsev sat with his hands clasped on the table in front of him. He paused, staring at his thumbs, as if not quite recognizing them.

"What do you say?" Zaitsev couldn't help but ask.

"Vasya, don't spread yourself too thin."

"What do you mean by that?..."

"I mean exactly that! Comrade Kirov is extremely interested in the swift and successful investigation of the murders in Yelagin Park. He's interested in answers. He's not at all interested in the nuances and the delights of your intellectual sophistication. He wants accurate and clear answers!"

"But these, as you say, nuances—"

"Bullshit!" Kopteltsev hit the table with his podgy palms. "We've been allocated exceptional resources. How am I going to report back to Smolny? Hurrah, comrades, we've uncovered the murder of some bookkeeper, and even better it's one long since consigned to the archives? So can you just wait for news on Yelagin, if you please? Wait while our friend Zaitsev weaves his cerebral lace."

"Why's the bookkeeper less worthy?" Zaitsev asked provocatively. "Isn't Soviet law the same for everyone?"

Kopteltsev sighed like a seal. "Seriously, Zaitsev, were you born yesterday?"

Zaitsev was about to object. But since Kopteltsev's response was a suspicious glare, his eyes alert and ready for battle, he fell silent. He waved a hand.

"All settled?" asked Kopteltsev, applying pressure.

"OK."

"Well, fine. Off you go, Vasya. I'm waiting for the Intourist report, by the way."

V

Laughter rang out in the corridor. The sound of voices. Something falling. Something being dragged along the floor.

People started to peep round their doors to see what the noise was.

It looked like Martynov and Serafimov were dragging along a drunkard. It was a big, grey, lumpy sack of potatoes. Zaitsev raised an eyebrow.

"Come and get 'em, guys!" came Serafimov's joyful cry.

"Come in list order, lads," called out Martynov as he bumped open the office door with his backside and dragged the sack in by the neck. "Who's first? Well, what're you standing there for, ladies!" he shouted by way of greeting. "Servants were abolished in 1917, don't you know. Along with exploitation of one man by another. The car's outside—go and help yourselves to whatever you ordered."

Zaitsev rolled his eyes.

Martynov let go of the neck of the sack. He straightened up.

"Oof, my back! I'm going to need a new one at this rate."

"What's in the sack? Beetroot?" Demov turned to him animatedly. And straight away the entire team gathered around the sack, as if on command. Crouching, Serafimov fumbled with the twine, trying to untie the knot.

A police helmet appeared from behind Serafimov's back.

"Zaitsev, there's a visitor downstairs for you. Shall I send her up?"

"Is she pretty?" Samoilov quickly asked, winking at Zaitsev.

In front of outsiders, the team came across as friendly and perfectly content, Zaitsev observed.

"Well, er…" said the officer.

Zaitsev somehow immediately realized that it was Zabotkina. That old windbag, he thought angrily. If she had any experience of the opposite sex it was purely literary.

"Vasya, don't mess this up!" Demov encouraged him. "Could be your last chance!"

Zaitsev walked around them and went out into the corridor without glancing back.

"What are you grinning for, Demov?" he heard behind him. "You can stomp down and fetch your grub yourself!"

"Well, out of respect for my service and experience…" Demov rattled.

"Ha ha, right, old man. You could still pull a plough!"

"I'm telling you, the produce in the country is on another level. Nothing like what you get in the co-op. Isn't that right, Serafimov?"

Martynov began to paint a picture of their trip, embellishing with such exaggerated and spurious details that he soon had everyone in tears.

"And what about the whores, Martynov?" Samoilov reminded him. "Could anyone identify the photos?"

Martynov didn't even manage to open his mouth before Serafimov barged in.

"Wait, let me tell you about it!"

VI

Zaitsev walked quickly through the lobby. He decided to give Zabotkina a piece of his mind there in the reception, in front of the duty officers.

But the woman who stood up to meet him wasn't Zabotkina.

"Comrade officer…"

Against the grubby walls painted with state-issued paint, against the shabby furniture, her face shone. And the dull, tired faces of the policemen and visitors around her straight away seemed not to be faces, but the snouts and muzzles of beasts.

She stared at Zaitsev. There could be no mistake: she was the one who wanted to talk to him. It was the dressmaker from the theatre. He could hardly forget a face like hers. But what was her name again?

"How can I help, citizen?" Zaitsev asked. And then he remembered: Allochka. Alla.

"Petrova. Alla Petrova. From the theatre," she reminded him. She looked flustered. Odd. Such a banal surname—for someone of such beauty. Zaitsev always imagined that beautiful women were never downcast or dejected, but held their chins up high and carried themselves through life with pride, letting others scurry around removing obstacles from their regal path. But Alla Petrova clearly felt awkward.

Zaitsev was struck by the haste with which she reminded him who she was. As though she were used to being forgotten about.

"And you're?…"

"I'm here on business. Personal," she said hesitantly, snapping the clasp of her purse and glancing back at the sullen visitors sitting opposite the counter, and at the helmets of the officers on duty.

"Shall we go in?" Zaitsev suggested, letting her through the door first.

In the lobby, she started speaking again right away.

"You see, I wanted to… Sorry."

"What for?" he asked, surprised.

"Forgive me… I just… I saw that you… When you came to the theatre… You see, they're just like that. She didn't mean to. She didn't want to embarrass you or give you a fright. When she…" Alla mimed unfastening an invisible outfit. "Ballerinas. They don't understand what it means to be naked. When they're muscle all over. Practically athletes. I didn't want you to think…"

Zaitsev realized he wasn't listening to Alla, just looking at her. He cursed himself. Concentrate!

"I see, Comrade Petrova. Embarrass? Why? This is Criminal Investigation, not the Institute for Noble Maidens." He added, more gently this time, "If you really want to know, we get a lot worse here from certain female citizens with their, er, parasitic lifestyle. If only you knew what they got up to. Well then, good day to you!"

He gripped the banister, making it clear that the conversation was over.

"I just wanted to…" Alla began fiddling with the clasp on her purse again.

"Did you remember something about the fake necklace?"

"Yes. Well, no. I don't know…"

At that moment, the front door swung open. Samoilov and Demov came in from the street dragging a heavy sack that smelt faintly of dry soil. They set it down on the floor.

"That's it, I've ruptured something," rattled Demov.

"Comrade Zaitsev, you can go and get your own provisions out of the car," Samoilov invited him in an edifying tone, his eye on Alla Petrova.

"What provisions?" grunted Zaitsev. He saw that familiar spark of glee in Demov's eyes. Whether Zaitsev was a stool pigeon, an agent provocateur planted by OGPU, or their same old faithful comrade, was of no consequence now: Demov simply couldn't miss this opportunity.

"Comrade Zaitsev observed in communication with other human beings," he said with delight.

Zaitsev's witty response was bursting to get out, but first he needed to remove Alla Petrova from the line of fire.

Samoilov also assumed that one plus one equalled a couple. He was clearly impressed by Petrova's looks. But he took a more gallant approach.

"You just ignore him, miss. We're old comrades-in-arms of this old hermit. We're just happy for him. These are the potatoes we bought at the kolkhoz. He probably didn't tell you. This is it: modern romance. You got a string bag on you? A net? What? You left your net bag at home? How are you going to carry them home? They're grubby, these spuds."

Alla Petrova looked at him, stunned. She opened her mouth without knowing what to say.

"I… We… We're not…"

Samoilov realized. But kept up with the act regardless. "You know what? I'll leave your sack here. Vasya can bring it round this evening. That right, Vasya? That'll be all right, won't it?"

"That'd be great," Alla muttered, looking helplessly at Zaitsev.

"Zaitsev? Is that the best thing?" said Samoilov, determined not to let it drop.

"Yes, yes," muttered Zaitsev irritably.

"I'd better go. I have to go." Alla grabbed the door handle.

"He could even chuck the potatoes in the car and bring them round," continued Samoilov. "If the car's free."

"Do come by again soon!" Demov called as she left. The door slammed.

"*Merci*. Thanks a bunch," said Zaitsev, destroying Samoilov with his stare. "You never fucking give up, do you?"

"You what?"

Demov got it and laughed. He stepped over the sack and began to climb the stairs.

But Samoilov was completely absorbed by the mysterious stranger.

"Well, have you got another lady lined up for the potatoes?" pestered Samoilov.

"She's not a lady, Samoilov, she's a witness. Here about a case."

Zaitsev picked up the sack. It felt like it was full of scrap iron.

"Still, quite a looker."

"Don't forget to drop off her spuds, Zaitsev!" Demov shouted down the stairwell.

"Yeah, yeah. Help me shove this out of the way, then."

"Where to?"

"Samoilov," Demov called from the stairs. Samoilov just turned his head towards the sound.

"Where do you want it, Vasya? Under the stairs? Won't be there later," Samoilov confidently declared. "Leave it at reception at least."

They carried the sack over together.

"She's not bad, anyway," Samoilov repeated again, out of breath. "But far too good for our Vasya, of course. Ladies like

169

that—they want an artist, or a wealthy NEP man, or a director. Not the likes of us."

"Samoilov!"

"What?"

VII

Kopteltsev knocked cautiously. He opened the door a crack. As he thought—no one there. The laboratory had been transferred to the basement. Lines ran from wall to wall. Pegged to them with ordinary clothes pegs were drying photographs—mugshots, yet another punch-up in the industrial outskirts. In the black-and-white prints, the blood looked like spilt ink.

Kopteltsev quickly darted to the archives. Demov organized everything with clinical exactitude. The negatives were arranged by date. Kopteltsev quickly flicked through until he found May. What was the date? He didn't remember the date. Leningrad homicide. That was all he knew.

His palms were sweating. Why was he sweating so much? It's not summer, he thought. Yet Zinka was always nagging him to go to the doctor. Like hell he would.

Finally he found the right one. On the negative, the curtain looked light grey. And the woman looked black. That damned black Communist—as if there wasn't enough of a headache for everyone without him.

Kopteltsev found a negative with the overview of the room. He slipped it into his pocket. He checked the rest of the negatives, holding them up to the light, looking for any showing the cursed bookcase. Here was one: the figurine was clearly visible, the shepherdess with flowers on her skirt, her china hand raised coquettishly. And the conspicuously empty space next to her.

Kopteltsev slipped this one in his pocket, too. He quickly pushed the drawer back.

And he walked out calmly, adopting an imposing gait. Only those who have something to hide run. What did he have to be afraid of?

Chapter 8

∎

Everything had already gone awry on the steamer, the vessel that was supposedly carrying six young American Communists towards a brighter future in the country that had defeated class and racial prejudices.

Or so Oliver Newton had thought. But the other five had been less convinced.

Samoilov checked his notebook: Amanda Green, Katherine Barrow, Michael Brown, Patrick O'Neill and Martin McDonagh.

"Is their current location known?" Zaitsev was quick to ask.

Samoilov nodded.

"And where's Martynov got to?" Zaitsev interrupted.

Demov shrugged.

"Went for a shit and vanished into thin air," Serafimov answered with his usual flair for words.

"Hmm. What else have you got, Samoilov?"

He continued.

...Or rather, they themselves did not really know what awaited them: the future was blurred in a rainbow fog. In any case, as it turned out, they were in no hurry to shake off their racial prejudice, along with the New York dust.

The phone rang.

"Yes?" shouted Zaitsev.

"They've brought the prostitute in."

"Great," Zaitsev muttered and hung up.

"Well, Samoilov. Is that what they told you?" Zaitsev was sceptical.

"That's what she said. Amanda Green."

"Interesting. So to her that was just how things were. Nothing secret about it, then. No hesitation, she just came out with it all openly." Zaitsev stood in front of the window. But before him he saw a ship, the ocean. The dead face of the black man.

"The American way," summed up Samoilov.

"By the way, comrades, I read in the press that black people are still getting lynched in America," Serafimov said. He, as always, occupied the settee. And as always, he never missed a Komsomol meeting.

Amanda Green was now a student at Leningrad University. The other Americans had travelled on from Leningrad to Moscow. Intourist gave Samoilov the address of Comrade Green, who turned out to be a thoroughly Russian-looking girl with short hair. Only her quality knitted suit was clearly not Soviet. And her accent, of course. That aside, Comrade Green spoke Russian pretty fluently.

But Oliver Newton didn't, Zaitsev noted to himself.

"Did she learn Russian here?"

The phone let out a trill again. Zaitsev picked up the receiver and dropped it straight back down.

"She says she learnt back in New York. The city's full of Jews who fled from the pogroms under the tsar. She learnt from them. When she was working for Communism."

"So what happened on the ship?" Zaitsev steered them back.

Oliver Newton had, apparently, decided that his bright future had already come. There on the steamer. He invited a lady to dance. She was white.

His fellow Communists called him aside.

"Gave his snout a clean, you mean?" specified Zaitsev.

"No, they didn't touch any snouts yet. Just gave him a warning."

From that very first evening, it wasn't so much that relations between the Americans were strained, exactly. But Newton felt like he was now sailing on his own, and the other five were on their own.

"Such lack of consciousness. And supposedly Communists, as well," said Serafimov.

"Americans," Demov shrugged. "You can't wipe out two hundred years of prejudice in an instant."

These "situations", as Amanda Green called them, continued in Leningrad. Signals through the party line. White American prejudices began to spread throughout the student body, as Samoilov diplomatically called it. Soviet students— yesterday's children of workers—were more susceptible to backward ideas than to progressive ones. And in the end, the Communist International had intervened—the organization advocating for Communism globally. However, it continued to take an idyllic view of the working class as a source of progress rather than prejudice. And who would let them see things as anything other than idyllic? Who would risk rocking the boat?

They had a gentle discussion with the students, introducing them to the situation of black people in the United States.

Four Americans were transferred to Moscow, out of harm's way.

And they put Newton in Russian Diesel. Which only made matters worse. Amanda was studying at the university, while Newton was only nominally registered there. They tried to extinguish these "situations". But now they were smouldering below the surface, like Leningrad peat bogs. Until one day the fire broke through to the surface.

Zaitsev realized that Amanda Green wasn't telling Samoilov everything. Or did she just not know everything?

"Right then," said Zaitsev. "Samoilov, get ready for Moscow."

"Why me?"

"Why you? Since you're developing this line, you'd best go and talk to the rest of the Americans."

The phone rang.

"What?" Zaitsev shouted angrily into the receiver.

It was Kopteltsev. "Where are you all? Why is only Martynov here?"

"Oh shit," said Zaitsev.

"Oh shit. Oh shit. Oh shit," said Demov, Serafimov and Samoilov.

"We're on our way," Zaitsev promised down the line.

II

The first thing that Zaitsev saw when he entered Kopteltsev's office was her backside. A plump behind squeezed into a blinding fuchsia skirt. The way she was dressed suggested both poverty and vulgarity. She was leaning over the desk.

Kopteltsev and Martynov stood at the desk, looking down at where she was pointing.

"What's up? Have you started already?" Samoilov asked from behind Zaitsev.

The woman straightened up and turned around. This was Agent Savina. She was the "prostitute" who the duty officer said had been brought in. Savina worked undercover, infiltrating the scene at Ligovsky Prospekt. The only way they could talk to her without breaking her cover was to arrest her. Her detention was very believable. The left sleeve of her jacket had a fresh rip. Savina's left eye had begun to swell.

Zaitsev greeted her. She just nodded and leant back over the desk, thrusting out her backside.

Zaitsev walked over to the desk. Laid out on it was a map of the city. Savina's hands lay on it like two cuttlefish, covered in cheap little rings. Kopteltsev sat behind the desk.

With a pencil, he marked the place where Savina rested her finger. Her fingernail was dirty.

"And here. Here. And here," she quickly pointed to one location after another.

Her finger drove along the map, like a divining stick.

"Here. And here. Here."

"Mokhovaya Street?" asked Kopteltsev, stretching out his short fat neck.

"Pestelya."

"I see." Kopteltsev scribbled himself a note on a piece of paper. "Send four to each venue? What do you think?"

Savina shook her head.

"Here, perhaps," she tapped her dirty fingernail on somewhere near Nevsky, that is, 25th October. "That's where you find the posher ones. Two'll cover it—one at the front door, one at the back. Two to question them. They'll give in straight away, won't give you any trouble. You'll get by with four. But here"—she transferred her grubby finger across the Neva to the Vyborg Side—"you'll need a dozen at least. That's where the workers are. Mainly young 'uns. That'll break out into a fight, no doubt."

Zaitsev realized they were talking about clandestine brothels.

This was a city-wide operation. Yes, every resource was being thrown into the case of the murder on Yelagin, as Comrade Kirov had promised.

The three murdered women, presumed to be parasites on the working classes, had not yet been identified.

"Listen, wouldn't it be quicker to pull these whores in separately for a chat?" Zaitsev asked across the map.

"Whores?" Savina smirked. Zaitsev expected a long, colourful and unprintable tirade by Agent Savina: her virtuoso command of profanity was paramount among her professional skills. "Comrade Zaitsev, prostitution has been stamped out in Leningrad," she pronounced sternly, as if reading from a lecture sheet at a political session.

She's at it too, thought Zaitsev with a grimace inside. Agent Savina had been brought into CID no more than an hour ago, and she was already behaving like everyone else. She had already been enlightened. And she had already drawn an impassable line between herself and Zaitsev.

With the speed that could be a matter of life or death in her business, Savina read Zaitsev's face, or simply guessed what he was thinking. Her eyebrows softened a little.

"The fact is," she started in her normal, calm tone, "that prostitution in the usual sense has really almost disappeared. Or is completely under control. But there are also prostitutes, so to speak, under cover. In the daytime, they're ordinary workers—office clerks, housewives. And outside work, they indulge in, so to speak, unsanctioned earnings. No tattoos. No clique. You'd never know."

"Get it now, Zaitsev?" Martynov winked triumphantly.

"Sounds like our girls," said Demov.

"Yes, perhaps. Seems possible," Zaitsev agreed, looking at the numerous crosses that Kopteltsev had marked on the map.

There were a lot of them. An awful lot. The city map looked like a cemetery.

Zaitsev recalled: the dispensary from Bolshaya Podyacheskaya had been transferred to Lodeynoye Polye. Away from Leningrad. And turned into a maximum-security hospital. The women had recognized this new trend right away, and had adapted to it with impressive speed. While he, Zaitsev, was sitting in a cell at Shpalernaya, the picture in the city had completely changed. Yes, you could say that prostitution had been eradicated. Now it was no longer allowed to take root. But instead it had spread on the surface, stretching far and wide. From the brothels on Ligovsky Prospekt and around Sennaya to ordinary apartments, rooms, outbuildings. The scale of the operation was impressive. The number of police officers involved, too.

It was decided not to talk about the purpose of the operation to those on the ground. The murder on Yelagin Island had been kept out of the newspapers. The witnesses had all signed a non-disclosure form and it was hoped that no one in the city really knew about it.

What Comrade Kirov feared most were rumours, gossip, panic, and in the long run damage to the reputation of his brainchild, the workers' park. Zaitsev understood very well: in Leningrad, a bad reputation tended to linger. If Yelagin got a reputation as a wilderness, it would soon become one, a magnet for all kinds of trash and hooligans, the scum of society, and not the proletarian mothers with prams and smiling workers Kirov hoped to attract.

Kopteltsev's eyes scanned the crosses.

He's lost for words! Zaitsev realized.

"If you think about it logically," reasoned Samoilov, as though nothing had happened, "a man goes to a whore most often on his day off. Firstly. Secondly, everyone has a six-day working week, which means that everyone's day off is a different day. Why not fan out across the city? One day in one area, next day in another."

Again, everyone hovered over the map. Zaitsev knew Demov too well, and he could see that he was deliberately stalling: he didn't want to be considered a smart alec. But when no one spoke for a while, Demov opened his lips.

"If we go straight in for the chase, we'll scare half of them off," Demov continued. "Best to hit one area, then lie low for a bit, give it some time, let them settle back down. After a while they'll resurface. Then we strike," he suggested.

To Zaitsev, all this sounded like fishing with a hole in your net.

The crosses seemed to him to form a pattern. Some kind of logic. He just couldn't quite see what it was.

"Saturday," Savina suggested resolutely. And she explained, "Six-day week or not, old habits die hard. People still like to knock back a few on a Sunday, day off or not. And if they're thinking of popping by for a bit of action, most likely they'll go on Saturday."

"I think…" Zaitsev said as he bent over the map. He wanted to show the others what he could see.

"Oh yes, Saturday isn't going to work for you, is it?" Kopteltsev interrupted good-naturedly. And everyone else looked as though they had been waiting a long time for Kopteltsev to say this.

Ah, the same old crap. Not such a new broom after all, Zaitsev thought venomously.

"Meaning?…"

Kopteltsev pulled out a desk drawer and tossed a stiff cardboard ticket over to Zaitsev.

"Rejoice: you'll ride in comfort. Like a bourgeois. Soft sleeper carriage."

Zaitsev looked at Samoilov. He was studying the map.

The soft sleeper carriages were mainly used by celebrities, foreign tourists, senior officials and workers heading to Moscow for business.

"What for?" Zaitsev took the train ticket. It was for a first-class compartment.

"Meaning?…" Kopteltsev said, as though mimicking him. "To interrogate the American Communists. You're leading the case, aren't you?"

But what Kopteltsev was really saying was something else entirely: that he himself had taken over the reins.

"They're important witnesses. Who better than you?"

"And the second ticket?" asked Zaitsev.

"Ooh, you've got some cheek lately, Zaitsev," Kopteltsev laughed. "Second ticket? The only people who book the entire compartment are NEP men the Soviet regime hasn't yet finished off. Even the writer Comrade Alexei Tolstoy travels on one ticket."

"I doubt that," Demov muttered quietly.

"Nefyodov can come with me," Zaitsev answered with a challenge. He looked around at them. Yes, he intended to adhere to the rules of camaraderie. Even if they were all ready to turn their backs on him. Had already turned their backs.

"Quite unnecessary," Kopteltsev answered unexpectedly, looking Zaitsev in the eye.

They all looked Zaitsev in the eye.

"I've transferred Comrade Nefyodov to the archives," he said. He added expressively, "He's indispensable there."

"Guys, enough talking." Savina broke the long silence. She was clearly starting to feel like an actress in someone else's play.

"Yes, it's time for Comrade Savina to get back to the street, back to her primary assignment," Kopteltsev agreed. He nodded to Martynov.

Savina swerved away. "Come on, then, Martynov... Samoilov, let's get it over and done with!"

She jutted out her chin, shielding her eyes.

Samoilov readied his fist, but hesitated.

"What?" Savina opened her eyes.

Samoilov looked at the others for support.

Savina had no time for his pussyfooting around. This was work. "Oh, come on. Get on with it."

Samoilov steeled himself and with full force thwacked his fist in her face. The rest barely had time to grab the screaming Savina.

Zaitsev silently took the ticket, turned and left.

III

He walked back to his office. He locked the door. He turned the dial on the safe. The file with Faina Baranova's case lay where he left it yesterday.

Zaitsev slapped it onto the table, on top of the rest of the papers. He began to flick through the pages, quickly scanning through in search of the report he was after.

Odd.

He was sure that Nefyodov's report had been filed.

He took the photographs from the crime scene—from Baranova's room. He began to deal them onto the desk one by one. Sometimes he gazed intently at a whitish speck, bringing the picture closer to his eyes. But he discarded each in turn.

To no avail. Not a single spot turned out to be the porcelain figurine. But Demov had definitely photographed the overview of the crime scene. In every minute detail. Including the bookcase.

Neither the report nor the photographs he needed were now in Faina Baranova's file.

Zaitsev's palms went cold.

He sat down on his chair, staring blankly at the sprawled-out pages and scattered photographs. His hand reached for the telephone. He dropped it again.

What was the use? What would he say? Comrades, who's taken files from the case and hidden them?

He had nothing to prove that they had ever been in Baranova's file at all.

But who could it have been? Demov? Samoilov? It could have been anyone.

It was clear that their friend Kirov was truly quaking with his ardent Communist desire to get straight answers. And pronto.

Zaitsev realized that none of them trusted him. They no longer believed in him professionally. They must have thought Zaitsev was dragging the investigation aside. Into a dead end. Letting the squad down. He realized that if he failed, Comrade Kirov wouldn't be satisfied with blaming just Zaitsev. Everyone remembered the Pyotr-Jacques case. Heads would roll again. They knew it. What did someone like Zaitsev have to lose? He was already as good as dead. But Kopteltsev, the new director of CID? They'd say he had messed up, failed, hadn't got things in order, that he hadn't justified the trust they had placed in him. Kopteltsev was clearly not ready to lose his post. And losing his job was the least he could expect. Comrade Kirov didn't tend to stand on ceremony with enemies of the state.

Kopteltsev could have very easily come in and taken those items from the file. Zaitsev suddenly realized this.

He felt sick.

He picked up the photograph of the murdered woman. Faina Baranova in her armchair: the flower, the duster, the weary, eternally calm face. No one particularly cared about her during her life, and no one was any more interested in her after her tragic, brutal death. The poor woman.

A porcelain shepherd had disappeared from her room—that was a fact.

But it was the only fact.

Who had brought the little shepherd to Yelagin Island?

Faina Baranova's killer?

The black Communist Oliver Newton?

But what if Oliver Newton was Baranova's killer? A Soviet Othello.

Then who had killed Newton?

He needed to talk to Firsov, no matter what. He was the only one at Russian Diesel who could speak English, which means he must have talked to the American.

185

Mary had a little lamb—the words suddenly sprang into his head. Zaitsev for a moment saw some lips painstakingly pronouncing the words. Lips and hair all piled up like women used to do a long time ago...

Zaitsev sat at his desk, twirling a pencil in his hands. He tried to concentrate, to peer more closely into the fog, to see where the diverging roads of the various theories led.

But he couldn't. All that went round his head was an English nursery rhyme about Mary and her lamb, repeating like a jammed record.

He was now the only one who cared about Faina Baranova's case. Zaitsev felt he owed it to her. And the English words kept surfacing like an itch.

"Why does the lamb love Mary so?"
The eager children cry.
"Oh, Mary loves the lamb, you know,"
The teacher did reply.

IV

"So when are you going to take your spuds, Comrade Zaitsev? They're already putting down roots."

The damp, dark city in the door frame seemed particularly unenticing. Rain dripped from people's hats, gushed from their umbrellas. The asphalt glistened like oil; cars rustled past; orange windows affectionately called out to those who were not yet at home. For those who had no one waiting for them at home, the lights in the windows aggravated their loneliness.

Zaitsev stood at the door.

"I will, I will, Sviridov," he reassured the duty officer.

He quickly ran up the stairs to his office. He found the right page in his notebook, the right address, hastily pulled it out and shoved it in his pocket. As he passed Kopteltsev's office, he heard noisy voices inside. Tobacco smoke drifted out from beneath the door. The city-wide operation was being planned on a grand scale, drawing in ever more participants.

"There's your sack in the corner." The duty officer nodded to the place where it had been awaiting its owner. It had clearly lost a little weight in the course of the week—it no longer looked so full to the brim. The duty officer noticed Zaitsev's expression and read his thoughts.

"Might have borrowed one or two for dinner," he confessed.

"What are you talking about, Sviridov?" Zaitsev exclaimed amiably. "Just take some more!"

The duty officer didn't hang about. He plunged both hands into the sack, piling up an armful of potatoes that he pressed to his stomach.

"Get a move on," Zaitsev ordered. "I've got to get going!"

The duty officer pulled out a drawer and stashed the folders and newspapers right on the floor. The potatoes bumped as he sprinkled them into the empty drawer.

"Go on, go on. I can't carry the whole sack on my own anyway."

The duty officer laughed. "Bye, Vasya. *Merci*. Ta for the spuds."

"See you later, Sviridov."

Zaitsev threw the emaciated sack over his shoulder and went out.

The rain immediately set to work on him. The bag dripped mud and bits of sacking. There was no way he could take it on a crowded tram.

The bag gradually filled with heaviness, his palms burned. He wanted to tear the sodden cap off his head and throw it away.

At Morskaya, Zaitsev grabbed the sack with one hand and with the other fished the piece of paper out of his pocket. He checked the number of the house and apartment. The apartment was on the top floor. Zaitsev pressed the button several times. The lift didn't respond. The janitor had probably shut it off, tired of cleaning up after the new proletarian inhabitants of the house, who treated the lift like a toilet. Zaitsev stomped upstairs to the fifth floor. The doors of the apartments stared at him with their many mailboxes and signs shouting the names of the tenants: at least a dozen on each door.

Finally, Zaitsev threw down the sack from his aching back. He found the sign with the right name. It was cardboard. Written in ink was how to ring: "Three short". Like every *kommunalka* door, it was littered with the nameplates that made up a Morse code of call signs in every conceivable combination: three short; one long, two long; short, long.

Zaitsev briefly pressed the copper buzzer three times. He listened. Quiet. Perhaps she wasn't home. You idiot, he thought to himself. He was about to leave when suddenly the door clicked and opened. The chain flashed.

A face shone in the darkness.

"It's you!" said a surprised Alla Petrova. She was obviously trying to remember his name. But couldn't.

"I promised you some potatoes."

Chapter 9

I

Leningrad Station in Moscow was an almost exact replica of
Moscow Station in Leningrad, so for a few minutes you could
easily be convinced you hadn't gone anywhere, and had spent
the night amid the knocking of wheels and the snoring of your
travelling companion for nothing.

The air on the platform reeked of burning, but it was a
refreshing change to Zaitsev after a night in a hot, stuffy
couchette. Weary passengers poured out of the carriages,
their faces wrinkled. Zaitsev remembered the clinking of
glasses and the drunken chatter on the other side of the
thin wall of his compartment. Obviously, most passengers
were making the most of the start of a business trip for a
gruelling night of "letting their hair down". Fortunately, it
had turned out that he would be sharing the compartment
with a large, taciturn fellow who hung his coat and hat on
the hook, shoved his institutional pigskin briefcase in the
space below, and shot a suspicious glance at Zaitsev, whose
only luggage was an old canvas army satchel—he was clearly
wondering if he should tuck his wallet under his pillow just
to be on the safe side.

"Comrade, don't worry—I'm a cop," Zaitsev said indifferently, feeling the varnished coolness of the cabin wall on the
back of his head. He closed his eyes again.

Embarrassed, the fat man muttered something apologetic.
He quickly changed into flannel pyjamas and fell asleep.

Zaitsev woke up several times in the night from the heat.
Black telegraph poles flitted by. In the blue light, with the stiff,

starched sheet pulled up over his head, the fat man looked like an iceberg. Zaitsev was pestered by thoughts. They were dark, swift and formless, like the shadows that fell obliquely on the walls of the compartment. Eventually he was lulled to sleep by the knocking and pitching motion. Zaitsev woke up when the clatter of the wheels stopped.

The fat man was already sparkling, his hair washed and slicked back. He smelt strongly of soap and mint-flavoured tooth powder. Without a glance at Zaitsev and his modest, patched clothes, he silently donned the armour of a Soviet executive before heading out to blend into the crowd on the platform—almost everyone getting off the Leningrad train was wearing a hat and carrying a briefcase. This stream of passengers was almost exclusively men the age and portliness of Gogol's Chichikov.

As Zaitsev left the station, there could be no doubt: this was Moscow.

The huge bowl-shaped square surrounded by the three railway terminals was teeming with the most colourful people. In Leningrad, everyone walked slowly: even factory workers sauntered along, in pace with the common rhythm. In Moscow, they sprinted. Zaitsev was quickly snatched up by the crowd, carried along a few metres before he managed to step aside and escape from the stream. He walked right up against the very wall of the station.

The passengers from the Leningrad train—unmistakably identifiable by their briefcases, hats and preoccupied frowns—meanwhile rushed to the Moscow taxis, and the Willys and Packards of their various departments. Zaitsev began to look for someone in the crowd to ask the way to Lubyanka. On foot, of course. He didn't know the Moscow tram routes, and in any case he was curious to see the city on the way.

But then two men in blue-topped caps approached him. It was so reminiscent of his arrest that for a moment Zaitsev felt a cold fist in the pit of his stomach. Both saluted.

"Comrade Zaitsev?" asked the more senior in rank. In response to Zaitsev's nod, he just said, "Follow us."

Wondering whether this was perhaps how they arrested you in Moscow, Zaitsev walked with them. Passers-by stole quick glances at him, immediately averting their eyes. A man in modest civvies flanked by two sturdy *gepeushniks* could hardly be anything but under arrest. Zaitsev got into the black car. The door slammed. The disquiet still lingered somewhere in the pit of his stomach.

The car flew along the wide metropolitan street. Both men were affably silent, ready to fire with an explanation at any point. In the meantime, they merely looked at him kindly. Their complexion wasn't the Leningrad hue—both were ruddy, healthy.

The car sped to Lubyanka.

"He's for Uglov. The comrade from Leningrad," the young man told the sentry, instead of showing a pass at the window. The guard nodded. The iron gates parted. The car rolled through.

The first thing they did was take Zaitsev to breakfast. The canteen was also brand new, welcoming. And the breakfast was very, very satisfying. The two men also ate, to keep him company, exchanging jokes and flirting with the handsome waitresses in bonnets.

Then they led him on a long walk along corridors lined with soft carpets. It was a sunny, orange-tinged autumn day in Moscow. And Zaitsev couldn't shake off the sense that he wasn't in the main bastion of OGPU, but in a sanatorium out in the sticks. After the unsettled night on the train, the hearty breakfast had a soporific effect. Zaitsev had the feeling that if he told his companions he needed a nap, he'd be whisked off directly to the luxurious sleeping quarters. He wouldn't be surprised.

They walked past the reception, through soundproofed double doors. Standing tall to receive them was the former revolutionary sailor and Petrograd Chekist of the early post-revolutionary years, Uglov.

"Zaitsev!" he exclaimed joyfully. "What are you staring at? Like we've never met before!"

The young men silently disappeared, the well-oiled doors closing behind them just as discreetly.

"I'm checking you haven't grown a second eye," said Zaitsev, giving him a hug.

Both slapped each other on the back. Uglov was still as skinny as anyone in Leningrad. To the same degree that Kopteltsev resembled some kind of accountant, Uglov conformed to all the stereotypes of an investigator: he was as svelte and energetic as a hunting dog.

Uglov lifted his round, black leather eyepatch to show that his eye socket was still empty.

"Listen, have you come straight from the train?" he asked in a cheerful shout. "Have my lads dragged you in starving? Let's get you some breakfast!" And he picked up the phone.

Zaitsev assured him that his lads had already fed him.

Uglov pressed the switch to hang up, but he didn't put the handset back on the hook.

"You've got that look, Zaitsev. Peter chic. Looks like you're about to be planted in some brothel. Let's fix you up."

And he began to turn the dial.

"I'm so glad you've… Hello? It's Uglov. I've a man here, you need to get him fitted out. Yep, the full works. Athletic build, height…" He glanced at Zaitsev. "About a metre eighty-five." He covered the mouthpiece with his palm and asked, "What shoe size?"

Zaitsev showed him the red American boots he had thanks to Comrade Kirov.

"What are you doing in those dancing shoes?" asked Uglov, surprised. "Winter's on its way. Yes, ordinary boots. He doesn't know what size. You'll figure it out."

He crashed the handset down on the cradle.

"Come on, then. Let's go."

The phone let out a trill.

"Uglov speaking. OK, on our way."

He saw that Zaitsev was looking at him sceptically.

"The car's waiting. We'll be there and back in no time."

In the car, Uglov chatted incessantly. His voice was so enthusiastic, so upbeat, that it seemed forced. Zaitsev could barely get a word in edgeways. But Uglov either didn't notice or didn't want to notice.

"I love the Arbat," he said. "So unlike Peter. Twisting lanes and dead ends. Lovely, lovely. Just a bit too far from HQ. Well, with a car that doesn't matter. But anyway! The Arbat was built a long time ago. You need to know that. There are new buildings though, built especially for the workers. Central heating, parquet floors in all the rooms, a bathroom, hot water—all the mod cons."

Again, Zaitsev could hardly get a word in.

"Cars, oh yes. We've got used to cars here. This isn't Peter, where you go everywhere on foot. Here the distances are something else. On another scale. It's the capital, after all!"

And again, Zaitsev couldn't get a word in.

"Supplies are good. We've got rations. Restaurants are opening again. Food Corps deliveries. Not like in Peter. Here, you know, you can eat properly, like a Russian. And is there a Madame Zaitsev on the scene?" he quickly asked and laughed immediately.

Zaitsev shook his head.

"A shame. The family and moral character of employees is of great importance."

"And is there a Madame Uglov?" As far as Zaitsev remembered, this ascetic soldier of the Revolution simply didn't have the time or the mental space to think about his enduring legacy. For Uglov, personal and family life were petty bourgeois.

Instead of an answer, Uglov laughed.

What's he laughing at the whole time? Zaitsev thought, disgruntled. In the past, in their Peter years, it was a rare thing to see Uglov smile. And when he did, it was usually a venomous, malicious snarl directed at the defeated enemies of the working people and the Soviet state.

"What do you know, there is."

Before Zaitsev could even open his mouth, Uglov was off again.

"Oh, the ham at Eliseevsky!" he exclaimed, nodding his chin at the window. Tverskaya Street flitted past with its shops. Moscow's answer to Nevsky Prospekt. The NEP era had also worn off in Moscow, but whereas in Leningrad it had been replaced with only poverty and dilapidation, here in Moscow it was clear people were comfortable, well fed. Straight away, Zaitsev hated Tverskaya.

Finally, they arrived. Uglov rang the bell at a door that was quite inconspicuous and unremarkable. They were let in, and it was only inside that Zaitsev saw a neat little sign: "Supplier". It was not intended for mere mortals. There were no queues here and orders were taken effortlessly, like paying for a meal in an expensive restaurant—as though not wanting to offend important customers. A woman stood with her back to a mirror, glancing back at her reflection with a sour expression. A black fox hung from her shoulder. Two employees patiently awaited her verdict. The director quickly approached the woman and whispered something to her. She turned around arrogantly. But at the sight of a lean, one-eyed man in an OGPU uniform complete with insignia that spoke of his high rank and standing she was somewhat deflated. The workers, who just a moment before had been fawning on the lady, sensed a change in magnetic attraction and deftly and firmly nudged her somewhere behind the curtains.

"Who are we dressing?" A bald man came up to them, a measuring tape draped around his neck. He looked kindly from Uglov to Zaitsev. Both were tall, both were of an "athletic build".

"Guess, Arkasha," answered Uglov with a smile.

"One moment," he said, clicking his fingers.

Zaitsev was suddenly surrounded. The measuring tape nuzzled him here, hugged him there. Then out came the suits, shirts, jumpers. In the dressing room, Zaitsev was ashamed of his worn-out skivvies, so many times washed and mended by Pasha. Peter chic—he recalled Uglov's scornful words. Since when was Uglov a dandy? And married? The new underwear was pleasantly cool against his body.

"Well, there you are! A handsome groom ready for a bride!" exclaimed Uglov with a clap of his hands when Zaitsev came out of the fitting room.

"Are you satisfied, comrade?" asked the measuring tape, twisting ingratiatingly. "English cloth, top grade."

Zaitsev nodded. He wasn't comfortable. The new suit felt stiff, like a double-doored wardrobe.

"I love an athletic build," sang Arkasha, smoothing the fabric, picking off invisible dust particles. "Everything sits right. No fussing about. Not like those office comrades—sometimes you have to work a bit harder to get it right."

The young lady had her coat ready. Another woman was holding a scarf and a matching woollen cap.

"He'll also need a winter coat. And boots. And a winter hat. And gloves," Uglov ordered.

The measuring-tape man nodded. "Nothing but the best."

Two bundles wrapped in austere paper were soon laid at Uglov's feet. One larger, one smaller.

"And what's that?" asked Uglov, poking the smaller with the toe of his boot. Zaitsev noticed for the first time that his boots were brand new, dazzlingly shiny.

"That's the old coat, sir," the measuring-tape man explained, as if apologizing.

"Are you kidding?" said Uglov. "Burn it."

Zaitsev was still full from breakfast so he turned down Uglov's offer of a "second breakfast".

"We'll have a coffee, though," Uglov insisted. "I always have coffee at the Metropol at eleven, I'm afraid—even the end of the world wouldn't come between me and my morning coffee." And he directed the driver: "To the Metropol."

The Metropol had been a luxury hotel before the Revolution and after the Revolution it had become a hostel with a canteen. Now, Zaitsev was amazed to see, it had begun to regain its former status.

The middle-aged waiter, who seemed to have sat out the turbulent times, had the dull sheen of old-regime, pre-revolutionary manners. He placed a silver tray with a coffee pot onto the tablecloth, which was a bluish off-white from the starch. The fine-china cups were so delicate the sunlight shone through them. There was cognac in a crystal decanter, gleaming like amber. Steam rose from the coffee. Through the window you could see the Bolshoi Theatre. Uglov noticed Zaitsev's gaze.

"We'll go to the Bolshoi this evening! We'll have a box," he said as he raised his glass. He tipped it back, showing a slim Adam's apple.

It's a bit too much—this Moscow hospitality, thought Zaitsev. But he was so glad that at least one of his former comrades wasn't shying away, clamming up or avoiding eye contact in his presence that he answered Uglov with a broad smile.

"Great! We all need cultural development. But first—"

"Oof, what a bore you are!" sighed Uglov as he leant back in his chair and lit a cigarette. The tobacco was fragrant, obviously from abroad. Uglov read Zaitsev's look in his own way.

"Want one? It's not like smoking that hay you get in Peter."

"I've given up."

Why's he going on and on about Petersburg? thought Zaitsev.

"Really?"

"Well, I still have to chase around after bandits. You know, Uglov, I need my lungs to be in a fit state."

"Ah, that's an unsubtle hint at the subtle circumstance that I've let myself go now I'm ensconced in my office," said Uglov, narrowing his only eye through the bluish smoke. Then suddenly he added, "By the way, do you know that Peter's own Semenova is dancing at the Bolshoi now? Whenever you're feeling homesick, missing the swamps, you just head to the theatre. Seeing her makes you feel better!"

And Zaitsev understood: Uglov was intentionally laying out an appetizing spread of Moscow's delicacies. He was going out of his way to show off the bounties of his new department. He had summoned Zaitsev to Moscow. To his office, at OGPU. Did he know then that his department had a file on Zaitsev?

"What are you goggling at?" asked Uglov.

He poured the coffee.

"In general, you know, you shouldn't judge too quickly. Moscow isn't as bad as it seems to some comrades from Leningrad," he added with unexpected tenderness. "You need to get to know it. Take a closer look."

Zaitsev hastily averted his eyes.

"Uglov, I just need to close this case. It's not about getting a dead-end case packed off into the archive. It's about catching whoever killed Baranova. I just have to."

Uglov paused. Zaitsev knew: he got it.

"Is this Baranova... an acquaintance?" asked Uglov, formulating his question delicately.

Zaitsev shook his head. "I just need to."

"Need to for whom?" Uglov asked. An unnecessary question.

"For myself," answered Zaitsev, although he knew no answer was required. He knew: Uglov understood.

"This is the last thing I need to do," Zaitsev promised him. Indeed, what was there keeping him in Leningrad?

II

Uglov wasn't best pleased about it, but he was also particularly keen for Zaitsev to be transferred to Moscow as soon as possible. He turned some kind of administrative stopcock. The OGPU car braked, then spun around to head in the opposite direction.

Zaitsev knew the cogs' teeth were turning as he returned to Leningrad, so this time he got quite a good night's sleep on the way.

In the morning gloom, Zaitsev eagerly jumped down to the platform. The dark shadows of passengers flitted past. The air was warm and humid: suddenly, out of nowhere, a mild Atlantic breeze was blowing through Leningrad. His new winter coat now seemed clumsy and cumbersome, and the winter boots were heavy and hot. The business passengers streamed off the train: more pigskin briefcases, more pale, puffy faces after a late night "relaxing". Zaitsev moved in the vapour trail of their breath.

As a group, the American students he had spoken to in Moscow came across like the proverbial Buddhist monkeys: they saw no evil, heard no evil, spoke no evil.

They all described Amanda Green as "a girl with a big imagination". All three of them emphasized how much the Soviet Union had changed their perspective. Nevertheless, it was clear from the things that were omitted that Amanda Green had been telling the truth.

"I see," was all Zaitsev said in response. It wouldn't have been difficult to get any of them to talk. But they simply didn't interest him. In the tragedy of Oliver Newton, they were just a clutch of malevolent extras. He was looking forward to interrogating Firsov again.

It was for his sake that Uglov had made several calls.

"Comrade Zaitsev!" A woman's voice cried out, then seemed to break off.

Zaitsev turned around. Alla was walking towards him, stepping carefully on the wet platform in her light slip-on shoes. Her arms were laden with something.

"It's suddenly warmed up here. So I thought…" She hesitated. She timidly held out the thing she had in her hands.

"It was winter when you left," she said. "So I thought…" She faltered again. She couldn't help but notice Zaitsev's expensive new overcoat. And in Alla's hands was an old but sturdy mackintosh, with an English checked lining.

"Good thinking!" exclaimed Zaitsev. "I'm baking in this box."

Like any ordinary Leningrad couple, they addressed each other in public using the formal "you".

He was only too glad to take off the bulky new coat. He shoved his arms into the cool sleeves of the mackintosh. Alla quickly and deftly folded up the coat: a movement familiar to her from work, where after each performance she would have to put away dozens of costumes.

"Zaitsev! There you are! Your carriage awaits!"

Zaitsev saw Serafimov in the distance, at the start of the platform.

Alla seemed to freeze.

"It's OK," Zaitsev tried to reassure her.

Alla didn't even offer him her hand. She turned on her heel and silently walked along the platform, like a stranger, like someone he didn't know, back towards the station building whence flowed streams of people, breathing out light and a slightly pungent warmth.

Serafimov waved, assuming Zaitsev hadn't spotted him. Zaitsev waved back.

He could only presume that Alla was somehow extremely shy. But what was the point of talking if they were going to meet that evening? All the same, Zaitsev felt a little wounded.

III

"Have a seat, comrade," the duty officer suggested kindly. "Need to look after your legs. Not going to get new ones on the state, are you?"

"It's fine," shrugged Zaitsev.

The walls were painted ochre to waist height. Nothing fancy—any administrative opulence remained behind closed doors in the offices. The metal mesh over the ceiling lamps made the light seem even yellower, the ceiling even lower. Zaitsev felt the din of the blood pulsing in his temples.

"Where's the detainee?" he asked the duty officer impatiently.

"They're fetching him. Shall I get you some tea?"

Zaitsev didn't answer.

The blue top of the duty officer's cap bent over the papers again.

This was strange. It was just a few months ago that he himself had entered this very building with his hands behind his back.

"Comrade Zaitsev?" With new boots creaking at every step, an OGPU officer entered the reception. "Come with me."

Zaitsev had already seen this hunchback with dandruff on the shoulders of his new tunic. He wasn't the kind you'd forget. The hunchback affably waved a slender, ape-like hand. Zaitsev followed. He smelt of cologne. Zaitsev couldn't remember his last name: Investigator... Investigator... No, it was gone. At any rate, he was the lead investigator on the Firsov case.

They went up and down stairs, along corridors, yet more stairs.

"We're a bit crowded here. But we're moving to a new building soon. On Volodarsky Prospekt." The hunchback chatted away sociably.

More corridors. Unnervingly familiar. It seemed to Zaitsev that with every step the walls were getting closer. Fortunately, they stopped; the hunchback was already unlocking the iron door.

"Some tea, maybe?" he asked.

"No thanks," said Zaitsev. Eating or drinking in these walls seemed unthinkable. The man's last name came back to him. "Thank you, Comrade Aprelsky."

A man sat hunched up on a stool in the middle of the room, his back to the door.

"A quarter of an hour and not a minute more," the hunchback reminded Zaitsev as he followed him into the room. Apparently, Uglov's magic only stretched as far as tea.

Zaitsev didn't like it. Not one bit.

"I am interrogating Comrade Firsov in the context of a criminal case," he reminded the hunchback. "OGPU..."

At the sound of a voice, Firsov's head jerked, but he didn't turn.

"If you want to talk—talk. Don't like it—the door's there," said the hunchback, and he licked his flaky lips. He walked to the desk and sat down, pulling the chair in close. Zaitsev stood behind Firsov. There were no more chairs.

Zaitsev walked around Firsov, who slowly raised his chin. Zaitsev was dumbfounded. Firsov had a fresh abrasion on his face. His nose was smashed. His lip too. Firsov sat, carefully holding up his own body. Like a man whose insides were bruised. With the one eye that wasn't swollen, he looked at Zaitsev. There was a flicker of recognition. His burst lips quivered.

"Comrade Firsov," Zaitsev began.

"Citizen. Citizen Firsov," the hunchback corrected him.

"I want to talk to you about Oliver Newton. Remember him? Bear in mind that this is an official conversation. It's called a witness testimony."

Firsov was silent. Zaitsev saw his gaze gradually come into focus, harden.

"Why are you not saying anything?" interrupted the hunchback.

Firsov cleared his throat.

"I killed Oliver Newton," he snapped.

The hunchback's eyes darted back and forth. For a second, he and Zaitsev looked at each other. Each, it seemed, was as amazed as the other.

"I killed Oliver Newton! That's right!" Firsov tried to scream, but all that emerged from his throat was a croak. "Out of jealousy. I've signed everything. I'll sign it again. I killed him!"

The hunchback slowly began to pour a glass of water from the pitcher.

"Citizen Firsov," Zaitsev began patiently.

"You don't believe me? It was me! I did it!"

"Tell me how you killed him. All your actions, in order."

"It was me! First him! Then her! Then him! All of them!"

The hunchback quickly splashed the water from the glass into Firsov's face. His screaming broke off.

"They can still shoot you, you son of a bitch. There's a whole folder on your sabotage and vermin activity," Aprelsky remarked calmly. "The comrade from the police is interviewing you. Don't play your games here." He nodded to Zaitsev. "Carry on, comrade."

"No," Zaitsev interrupted him firmly. "We'll continue this conversation at CID."

IV

Comrade Aprelsky absolutely did not like that idea. One call to Kopteltsev. A quarter of an hour's wait. And then Comrade Aprelsky received word directly from Smolny about what level of assistance they expected him to provide the Criminal Investigation Department.

Comrade Aprelsky's ears were crimson by the time he hung up.

The arrival of the witness from Shpalernaya at Gorokhovaya alarmed everyone at CID. Or rather, not witness but now suspect.

Firsov himself sat upright on a chair and looked straight ahead with determined eyes. In them, Zaitsev again saw that purpose, that composure, that strength of mind that he noticed in him at their first meeting. These qualities seemed to return to Firsov with every sip of the hot tea he had been given before the interrogation. The tip of his nose turned red; a translucent drop began to collect on it; Firsov wiped it away with his sleeve. He straightened up again.

Kopteltsev wanted to be present at the interrogation. It was a breakthrough in the case—everyone saw that. Zaitsev could still feel the cold wall between himself and the team. But now, for the first time, warm trickles were breaking through. As if the wall were starting to thaw. Yes, they were still wary of him, keeping a distance like you might from a rabid dog. But the dog had come back with prey in its teeth—they couldn't deny that.

If not friendship, he had at least regained some respect.

Firsov gave his name, his year of birth. You could hear the rustle of pencil on paper—Serafimov was taking notes. Demov had a cigarette in his mouth, which he hadn't yet lit. Samoilov looked on from under his brow. Kopteltsev looked as though he had nothing to do with it. Firsov responded to them all with a cold and crisp stare. Zaitsev didn't like this look one bit.

"I killed Newton. What is there to talk about?"

"We'll get to that," muttered Zaitsev. He took a sheet of paper from the file. "When and how did you meet Citizen Newton?"

"I don't know," Firsov answered irritably. "I don't remember when."

"How do you not remember?" Samoilov interrupted.

"I just don't. I didn't attach any importance to it. 'When?' I don't remember. He arrived at the factory. He got to work. Or rather, he was put to work. Then I met him. It's all documented. In the personnel department. Why would I need to remember?"

Zaitsev saw that Demov had taken the cigarette out of his mouth and was playing with it in his fingers. He was observing Firsov attentively. Zaitsev looked probingly at the old investigator: he was obviously absorbed in his train of thought. *A penny for your thoughts*—a familiar, long-forgotten English voice from the past suddenly echoed loudly in Zaitsev's head. He looked away from Demov, forcing himself to turn his attention back to Firsov.

"So perhaps you don't remember the women?" Kopteltsev couldn't resist butting in.

Zaitsev wanted to smash the ashtray down on his head. To shove this piece of paper in his mouth.

Too late. That much was clear.

Firsov understood, too. Zaitsev could practically see the engineer's experienced mind quickly calculating the new scenario.

Firsov nodded.

"I don't remember. I killed the women, but don't remember how. It's all a haze, like smoke. Like fog."

It was like a wave rippled through the room.

Something stabbed Zaitsev inside.

"I killed them. That's all there is to say."

"Right," said Kopteltsev, stretching out the syllable. His big puffy face was sweaty.

In the blink of an eye, Firsov had gone from being a suspect to being the accused.

The interrogation proceeded according to the protocol. Kopteltsev had by now seized control and was leading, asking the questions. Firsov answered. The pencil rustled.

Firsov talked, and talked, and talked, rounding off his elaborate digressions and reining them into structures fenced in by commas, dashes, colons and semicolons, giving everyone in the room the feeling that their heads were being filled with sand.

"Can you be more specific, Citizen Firsov?" Kopteltsev couldn't help but ask.

Firsov raised his dark eyes to look at him. He nodded.

And again the mass of words flowed like concrete.

He spoke eagerly and at length, but all the while Zaitsev had the feeling that Firsov was weaving a net of elegant words while slipping like an eel between the holes.

Zaitsev stared intently at Demov. He was silent, fiddling with the cigarette. Firsov talked about his relationship with the American Communist, about Newton's escapades, his visits to prostitutes, and about a drunken quarrel, but with every word Zaitsev had an increasingly strong sense that everything that was happening was somehow irreparably wrong. The more Firsov said, the deeper he propelled himself into this bloody affair, the less Zaitsev believed him. And the more enthusiastically Kopteltsev nodded along.

"But why? Why?" he demanded, interrupting Firsov impatiently.

"He, this black man of yours, tried to attack me. Sexually."

Time seemed to freeze in the room. Even the smoke seemed to stop rising from the cigarette butts in the ashtray.

"In what sense?" Kopteltsev broke the silence.

"In the deviant sense," Firsov said clearly and distinctly, looking directly at the CID chief.

Demov's cigarette crumbled in his fingers.

"You want more specific detail on that, too?" Firsov asked.

Kopteltsev grunted. "That won't be necessary."

V

Firsov was taken to a cell. The shorthand notes were sent to be typed up.

From the very moment that Firsov mentioned "prostitutes", Zaitsev knew exactly, not through instinct but for a fact, that the suspect was lying. It looked like Firsov wanted to be arrested by Leningrad CID at all costs. But why?

Kopteltsev and Demov were talking quietly at the table. Zaitsev didn't come any closer.

"He's trying to protect someone. As clear as day," he heard Demov say. He couldn't make out Kopteltsev's reply.

"We can't arrest him," Zaitsev couldn't help but say.

Kopteltsev suddenly looked past him.

"It's all bullshit."

"Lying to pin a few murders on himself? An interesting theory," Kopteltsev answered coldly.

"He's just fucking around with us. Playing for time."

"Let's say he is. Playing for time. For what?"

"We can't arrest him," repeated Zaitsev.

"We absolutely can," said Demov. "There's a confession right there."

Firsov had signed the transcript of the interrogation without reading it.

"But there's no evidence backing up—"

"There's none to the contrary."

That was true. They simply didn't have any evidence. No fingerprints, no hair, no envelopes with addresses, no notes. Nothing. Only this heap of words piled up by Firsov.

Zaitsev wanted to tell them that Firsov had in fact learnt about the "prostitutes" at Yelagin from him, Zaitsev. During their first conversation in the office, at the factory.

But he didn't.

VI

It was raining as if to say, "Do you think I'm going to stop? I'm not stopping." The damp air from the Neva cut right through you. The rain made the light from the street lamps seem shaggy.

Zaitsev walked without knowing where he was going. He paid no attention to the rain drenching him through. It dripped from his cap. Mentally, he tried to compose his upcoming conversation with Uglov. Uglov expected him to move to Moscow. And Zaitsev knew that he didn't have the

209

answer Uglov wanted to hear. He kept thinking about life in Moscow as a black abyss that Uglov seemed determined to fill with trivialities: ham and boots, new clothes and cars, theatre tickets, caviar from Eliseevsky and food boxes from the OGPU supplier, even the room of his choice (when no one else in Moscow got to choose where they lived). And now he was trying to shoehorn a wife into it. But Uglov was slipping into the abyss all the same, and that was the only reason he was trying to grab hold of his hand—Zaitsev's hand. But Zaitsev now realized that he couldn't help him. More likely, Uglov himself would drag him down.

And what about this Comrade Aprelsky? What an odd name… As if they weren't allowed to have normal human names there. Or maybe they could—and that was the most disturbing thing about it.

Zaitsev didn't know what he would tell Uglov, or how. All he knew was that no matter how difficult things were here, he would never move to Moscow—he would never get a transfer to OGPU. He rehearsed the various ways he could respond: by being frank, straight to the point, or veiled, deprecatory, critical, apologetic?

Firsov was lying. During interrogations, almost everyone lies. They're trying to protect someone. Themselves, for example. Trying to avert suspicion. Trying to say less than they know.

But Firsov didn't know anything. He wasn't protecting anyone and he wasn't averting anything.

He had been badly beaten there. He could hardly breathe from his broken ribs. He had been holding out his sprained fingers, trying not to touch anything. He had had teeth knocked out. Zaitsev should know what happens there. Only Zaitsev had used to think that that was just him, that his circumstances had been exceptional. Now he was seeing it with Firsov. There, at Shpalernaya, the lump of flesh sitting before Zaitsev was so utterly different from Firsov, the director of Russian Diesel, the former Firsov, who had been elegant, arrogant and invulnerable.

This new Firsov was ready to do anything just to get out of that OGPU cell, even if just for a while. Better to be locked away pending trial for murder. Just for a break. After the interrogations at OGPU, it would be a relief to be downgraded to a "mere" homicide suspect.

What had Comrade Aprelsky been muttering about there? Vermin, saboteur?

The idea that Firsov was to blame for saboteur activity like espionage as well as for murdering Newton struck Zaitsev as being utterly implausible. He even stopped in his tracks.

What was Firsov guilty of? Was it really just his family background and his Berlin diploma? The way he spoke and the quality of his suits?

What was Zaitsev supposed to do?

If they locked up an innocent person, then Comrade Kirov might praise them for their speed, efficiency and precision. And the killer would remain at large.

But what could he do about it?

He suddenly realized he had walked to the wrong place. He suddenly noticed the rain, the wind and the cold, all cutting through to the bone. Alla lived in completely the opposite direction.

Chapter 10

I

Zaitsev vaguely remembered the beginning of winter. The city was smothered with snow, and the very next day it seemed that it had always been that way and always would be. He vaguely remembered how they had seen in the New Year: a pinkish stain of spilt wine on a tablecloth, a mosaic of a salad, a wheezing gramophone and a lamp draped over with a shawl to make it cosier.

But he couldn't say precisely how it was that he had been taken off the Yelagin Island homicide investigation. Subtly but firmly dropped from the case. He had barged his way back in once or twice, but he couldn't be bothered a third time. Sometimes the team retired to Kopteltsev's office and then Zaitsev knew: they were discussing the Yelagin case. Judging by the fact that they still slammed the door shut in his face, the case was ongoing. Strange. Had Comrade Firsov kept to his vivid account, his colourful version of events? Had he come up with any more names?

Zaitsev responded to call-outs. To crammed communal apartments in the centre and workers' barracks on the outskirts. He inhaled the damp smell of dog on the police bus when they brought Ace of Clubs with them. He usually dozed on the way, his hands tucked under his armpits, while the others all snapped at each other. He interrogated suspects, inspected crime scenes. He blinked whenever Demov accidentally caught him with the magnesium flash. He picked up empty bottles with a handkerchief over his fingers (they were an indispensable part of almost every Leningrad murder). He wrote up transcripts and reports.

And now there was Alla. Where it was going and what their "relationship" was were two questions Zaitsev didn't really ask himself. They both had a tacit understanding that they wouldn't follow the generally accepted code: sign the marriage register, move in together, buy a sprung mattress, then… Zaitsev didn't even think about the "then", and Alla didn't say anything. They both scurried between their rooms—his and hers. Alla never complained about him working late; she was busy herself at the theatre in the evenings, working until her back ached, shifting piles of costumes, ironing, hemming, putting them away.

When they finally had a moment together, the apartment would already be full of nocturnal silence. And it would seem not only that they were alone in the room, but that they had the entire apartment to themselves. They would sit by the stove and watch the coal fire, where they baked potatoes. Alla would roll the hot potatoes out of the silvery grey ashes with a fork. They ate their supper sitting on the floor. Zaitsev preferred to think that both of them were content. Pasha also silently accepted the new order of things. Or rather, she acted as though there were no Alla. And Alla only once asked who Pasha was. Zaitsev replied, "Pasha, a neighbour." That was the end of the matter. Alla had no burning desire to pick up Zaitsev's life by two corners and give it a good shake. And Zaitsev was secretly grateful to her for that.

So they drifted on, led by the stream. Winter was already beginning to thaw at the edges, the snow was getting greyer day by day. It was getting warmer and damper. The wind blew through every nook and cranny of the city.

There had been a murder on the Petrograd Side.

Zaitsev joined his colleagues on the bus to the crime scene. When the bus drove up to the bridge, it suddenly started to snow: large, bulky snowflakes. The sky seemed suddenly to drop lower, drawn to the earth by soggy ropes.

"Look at the palace OGPU are building themselves," said the driver, nodding with his chin as they stopped at the junction. Zaitsev turned to look. Through the veil of snow, he could just make out the gigantic construction site on Volodarsky Prospekt, which the locals still called Liteyny. Zaitsev wanted to respond, to say… He turned around and saw that everyone's faces had glazed over, shut off. Only Ace of Clubs looked up in response to the movement and looked Zaitsev in the eye. Zaitsev didn't say anything and went back to looking out of the window.

On the bridge, it looked like earth and sky had both collapsed and the bus was bumping along through a greyish, flickering space, where neither up nor down existed. A tram passed like a dark ghost. The Leningrad February was up to its old tricks.

In the damp blizzard, Zaitsev couldn't see where they were going or where they had turned. Finally, the bus stopped; the engine cut out. Ace of Clubs jumped up and had a joyful stretch after a jolty ride lying on the floor. The dog pulled on its leash. Serafimov and Samoilov jumped out, the snow slurping under their feet. Demov messed about getting through the door with all his equipment. Zaitsev was last to get off.

Involuntarily he glanced at the expressive sculptures that framed the top corners of the house's front porch. Petrograd Side had been a fashionable district before the Revolution. Here, as in the city centre, Zaitsev was always struck by the contrast between the shapely elegance of the pre-revolutionary houses and the life that lurked behind their grand but dilapidated facades: the impoverished, cramped, fetid post-revolutionary life, crammed in with all the noise and cooking smells of the communal flat.

The house manager was stamping about by the front porch in a hastily pulled-on, half-length fur coat. The janitor stood nearby with a wooden shovel and looked grimly at the dog.

"Look, the mutt's a copper, too."

"This way, comrades," said the house manager as he dashed over to the front door to open up. The defunct caged-in lift shaft. The boarded-up service entrance. The smell of cats, stale food and urine. Everything was as it was in the hallways of thousands of Leningrad houses, once so well-to-do until the Soviet authorities handed them over to the common people. They quickly stomped upstairs. Ace of Clubs poked his nose here and there, left and right, his tail pressed against the soiled steps. The bronze rivets stood as a reminder that before the Revolution there was a carpet.

The door to the apartment was wide open. The neighbours, alarmed by the incident, peered out onto the landing. It seemed to Zaitsev that he was yet again watching the same old scene he had seen played to death—as though it were always the same old neighbours. "Sit, dog." At the handler's command, the dog sat, its tail wrapped around its body, its pink tongue dangling.

They walked down a long corridor cluttered with old things. Again, Zaitsev had the feeling that every time they were called out it was always to the same communal apartment. All they had done was to remove a tall mirror from the hallway, for example, and replace it with a broken wardrobe. The washtub might be strung up differently, or the old bicycle might be hung on another wall. There might be fewer boxes, or more. But the smell was always the same.

The house manager led them to the room. Demov quickly examined the lock.

"No sign of it being forced open. Well, let's have a look."

He entered the room. In went Serafimov and Samoilov behind him. The room was large, spacious and full of light—as much as was possible in Leningrad with its eternally murky sky. Zaitsev stepped into the room. And stopped in his tracks.

It was as though all extraneous noise were muted. A ghostly Demov silently set up the tripod. Soundlessly, the spectres of the team flitted past, their mouths open.

The deceased was dressed in a scarlet silk robe with broad sleeves. The corpse sat up straight in an armchair, only the head drooping slightly as if under the weight of the pearl beads draped around the forehead; the ends disappeared somewhere into her hair. Her white hands, clenched into fists, seemed waxy against the silk. They lay one on top of the other. A flower poked out from the right hand. A bright vermilion against the scarlet robe.

"Carnation," said Demov, suddenly acquiring a voice again. He bent over, waved his palm several times over the flower and—adhering to all the safety regulations—wafted the air into his nostrils, rather than breathing in directly. He added, "And it's alive. Unlike the citizen."

"In February?" replied Samoilov, banging the drawers of the cabinet. "Unusual."

"Here you are. Her ID'll be in here," said Serafimov, pointing to a patent-leather ladies' handbag. He flicked the clasp. He took out the hard-covered identification booklet and read aloud, casting a quick glance at the murdered woman, then at the photograph.

"Karaseva, Elena Petrovna."

The house manager confirmed the victim's identity. The camera flash doused the dead woman in light.

Elena Petrovna Karaseva, a pharmacy worker.

Serafimov and Samoilov went to talk to the neighbours.

Zaitsev carefully scanned the room.

Everything today was like déjà vu. Why did he feel like he had seen all this before?

Zaitsev looked at the murdered woman's pale face, with its tired eyelids that looked rusted up. This chair. This strange hairstyle. These large, undoubtedly fake pearls. This maddeningly alive carnation—or rather dead, of course, as it was cut, but still fresh. It glowed like a flame over the cold, dead fist.

Zaitsev used all his might to shove this thought out of his mind. I'm tired, he told himself. I haven't had enough sleep, I'm walking around in a daze today. But try as he might, he gave up and had to admit that this murdered Karaseva reminded him in a strange way of Faina Baranova. And both of them reminded him of the oddly dressed women killed on Yelagin Island.

Or were they killed—and then dressed up?

"Demov," he called.

But then a stretcher was brought in and laid on the floor. It took some effort to shift Karaseva's body, frozen in rigor mortis, from the chair. The corpse was awkward to get hold of, but finally the orderlies managed to pick her up and move her out. They covered her with a sheet. It rose up like some grotesque mountain.

II

Zaitsev finished the report. The dreary, monotonous drudgery of life gave rise to the same dreary, monotonous crimes. Perpetrators were either caught red-handed (because, as a rule, they were lying right there, drunk, or because they were dim enough to try to sell what they'd stolen right away), or the cases were filed away as a dead loss, adding to the mounting statistics of unsolved crimes that would never be solved because the investigation had fizzled out and been called off. Citizen Vyatkin, after partaking of liquor, smashed a bottle on the head of Citizen Bashmakov. Citizen Spitsyna, registered as a prostitute, was visited by a certain Citizen Svechkin, and after partaking of liquor together…

Zaitsev stretched and yawned. He pulled the report out of the typewriter.

"Vasya, are you busy?" Demov came in without asking permission to enter. Without even making eye contact with Zaitsev.

"Of course I'm busy. Stupid question."

Demov didn't react to his tone. "Here's some more. Have fun."

He dropped four folders onto the desk. Even one glance at them immediately made Zaitsev's head fill with sand.

"And the meeting?" he asked Demov's back.

"What meeting?" he asked, sourly, not turning round. But he did stop at least.

"About Karaseva—the homicide in Petrograd Side. With the flower."

"Flowers, schmowers—"

"Demov, please. Someone's been killed." Zaitsev was genuinely taken aback.

Demov turned around. "The fact is there's a more important project as far as Soviet citizens are concerned."

Ah, that means Yelagin, Zaitsev realized.

"When you've closed it, take it down to the archive. Got it?"

"Yes, OK, OK."

Demov left the room.

Zaitsev told himself: no, it's not worth getting offended over. This thought didn't give him much comfort, but he didn't have anything better up his sleeve. He pulled folders towards him. So it's a dead end, then. Without interest, just to occupy his hands and assuage his anger, he opened, closed and tossed aside file after file. Guess what, yet another citizen attacking another one after partaking of liquor... The investigation has been aborted. The investigation has been aborted. The investigation has been aborted. And then he froze. The penultimate folder turned out to be the homicide case: Karaseva. The woman with the carnation in her hand.

III

The archive smelt of old paper dust. There wasn't even the usual musty basement smell, drowned out as it was by the unique aroma of old, low-grade paper. In the 1920s, when there was famine in Petrograd, and afterwards all you could get was the bare essentials, the paper was worse than ever. Now it was slowly decomposing, crushed in the card files. The faded yellow of the pages echoed the dull yellow of the dim light bulb. Wooden shelves, densely packed with files, stretched far back into the depths, barely visible in the semi-darkness. There was no one at the wooden counter, polished by thousands of impatient or bored elbows.

Zaitsev rang the bell. He was wrong: there was someone there. An owl face emerged from behind the counter.

Nefyodov eyed him in silence.

"And where's Ovechkin?"

"We're on shifts."

Zaitsev looked for the words for what to say next.

"Were you asleep down there?"

"Reading."

Nefyodov had, apparently, still not yet exhausted his capacity to surprise. Reading. Well, how about that.

"Well, anyway—hi, Nefyodov." It dawned on Zaitsev that Nefyodov had been exiled to the archives as part of the same cold, unanimous, unspoken conspiracy that kept Zaitsev as an outsider within his own team. But at least in Nefyodov's case it was justified.

"Hello."

"This one's a dud."

222

The only strange thing was how Nefyodov seemed to be toiling away in the CID archive, when surely he could have got himself transferred back to OGPU. I would have, in his place, thought Zaitsev. But Nefyodov's face reflected nothing, like a sleepwalker, asleep with his eyes open. Was Nefyodov's mind really as blank as he looked? Or was he perhaps about as interested in Zaitsev as in a bug crawling along an old file?

He was fast approaching the point of no return. And at this precise moment Zaitsev knew that this was exactly what he intended to do. He lowered his hands, clutching the Karaseva case file.

It couldn't get any worse. He would deal with Nefyodov, if it came to it. He had dealt with far worse than him in the past.

"So, Nefyodov, can you keep your mouth shut?"

A spark in his clouded, sleepy eyes.

Zaitsev began to explain.

Out of nowhere, an inkwell, a pen and a sheet of paper appeared on the counter. Nefyodov carefully dipped the pen in the inkwell before painstakingly forming some purple letters, carefully following the line. His thin neck diligently stretched out from his frayed collar. Zaitsev realized Nefyodov had learnt to read and write as an adult. Could he even read fluently? he wondered. Because if he couldn't, then there was no way he could read through as many cases as he needed.

"I mean, in general…" Zaitsev stopped him. "You don't need to write this down. I can't even really say exactly what to look for. Just something… anything out of the ordinary. Anything that stands out as odd. It could be the clothes. The position of the body. Even the…"

Zaitsev twisted his arms around his head, as if demonstrating an intricate ladies' hairstyle.

"Or objects in the victim's hands. Not a bottle, or a scrap of fabric torn from the killer's clothes. But anything strange. Like what? Goodness only knows. Anything. Do you understand?"

Nefyodov didn't nod.

"Imagine during the civil war," Zaitsev went on, leaning his belly against the counter, "and the strange clothes they wore back then. Fashion wasn't on the agenda. Our janitor used to go around in his old chamberlain's uniform. Waste not, want not, he'd say. Anyway, I don't mean go back that far. Have a look in the recent cases, will you, but just the homicides. Got it?"

"Just Leningrad or in the province too?"

"Just Leningrad. For now."

Nefyodov nodded slowly, belatedly answering Zaitsev's question. He carefully studied what he had written. Then, without bending down, he pulled out from somewhere a tin plate that reeked of old cigarette ash. Some matches. And before Zaitsev had time to be surprised, the flame was already licking the page he had just written.

"You said keep your mouth shut," Nefyodov explained with the same sleepy expression on his face, and Zaitsev thought that if he had just made a mistake by drawing Nefyodov into it, then it could be a much more serious mistake than he had imagined. Nefyodov was certainly not dim-witted or careless. "When do you need all this?"

Zaitsev raised his arms, still holding the Karaseva file in one hand.

"Yesterday."

Who else did he have to ask?

IV

From the corridor, Zaitsev picked up the smell of fresh coffee emanating from his room: the rich, bitter aroma seemed to exist separately from the usual fog of cooking smells, the soapy steam of laundry boiling on the stove, the odour of unclean bodies and of old junk in the corridor.

Zaitsev smiled. Alla must be in his room making coffee. His head throbbed and he realized how desperate he was for a cup of coffee.

"Comrade Zaitsev." Pasha poked her head out of the kitchen. "I've been sitting here waiting for you."

"Hi, Pasha. How are you?"

"Come here. Where it's light."

Zaitsev followed her in. He only went in the shared kitchen in the mornings. And now he was amazed at the great crush of people, the din of all the cutlery. It was the time of day when everyone tried to cobble some dinner together. The neighbours greeted him.

Pasha led him over to the kerosene lamp on the table and turned it on.

"Have a look. And then tell me I've ruined it."

"Pasha, you know I don't care. I could walk about in a sack and not notice," he said, trying to laugh it off.

"No, Comrade Zaitsev, have a look. But I'm saying so you don't hold it against me after."

Pasha laid his mackintosh out on the table. The one he had worn twice at most.

"And? What?"

She turned it over to reveal the hem.

"Here, look. I decided to give your old raincoat a wash ready for spring."

She pointed with a finger at the lining, where some inked letters floated, clear to see. *Nikolai Viren*, Zaitsev read.

"Come on, Pasha. It's from a flea market, it could have been anyone's." Zaitsev tried to give his voice an air of nonchalance. "Just a little spot. No big deal."

"Well, I don't know," said Pasha, voicing her concern out loud. But in her eyes Zaitsev could see that wasn't all. Pasha placed a small square of card on the table. Zaitsev quickly covered it with his palm.

"It was sewn into the hem at the bottom."

None of the neighbours noticed anything. Fortunately, you could rely on Pasha: in her role as janitor, she was as diplomatic and cautious as a foreign minister.

"I see," said Zaitsev casually, tucking the photograph into his pocket. "*Merci*, very much."

In the hallway he had a look.

He went into his room. He took off his coat. Hung it up. Unwound his scarf. Hung it up.

"Well, hello. What's up?" asked Alla with a smile, walking over to meet him. "You haven't caught a cold, have you? I'm going to have to get going for the performance."

Instead of answering, Zaitsev threw the crumpled mackintosh onto the table. The cups shook, hit one another and rang out.

He grabbed Alla by the elbow, aware that he was hurting her. She screamed. He pushed her into a chair.

"What's come over you?"

He slammed the photo down on top of the mackintosh. A tsarist admiral decked with medals. And a little girl on his knee.

Alla looked at the photograph as if it were a venomous snake.

"How do you explain this? Who's Viren?"

All the colour drained from her face. Even her eyebrows seemed to become anaemic.

She answered quietly, or perhaps simply sighed.

"What? I can't hear you!"

Alla was breathing heavily. Zaitsev even felt sorry for her.

Barely audibly, she whispered again. "Viren—that's me."

Chapter 11

I

A week passed and there was no word from Nefyodov, who had been tasked to search for anything "odd".

Zaitsev began to fear that there was probably nothing the former circus acrobat would consider odd.

Zaitsev tried to recall if he had ever seen Nefyodov look surprised. No, never. And then there was his zealously outstretched neck. If Nefyodov had learnt to read and write late in life, then he would take until the Second Coming to read through the archives. Zaitsev regretted asking him. He should have realized he needed to do everything himself.

On the tenth day, the anxiety had passed and had given way to anger. He's ratted on me, the bastard, Zaitsev told himself. He was convinced. The notorious organizational measures just hadn't been implemented yet. But they were coming.

On that same day, Nefyodov turned up at his office. He stood with a somewhat stooped posture, bent under the weight of a dense stack of loose, yellowing files that he carried with both hands, his chin pressed down on top. He danced a little *pas de valse*, closing the door behind him with his foot.

The tilt of his body changed. And then the landslide hit Zaitsev's desk. It smelt of old dust and old paper.

"Odd," he announced quietly, not saying hello.

Nefyodov had picked up on a lot more than Zaitsev had expected.

"Wow, Nefyodov…" Zaitsev began. But then the phone rang. "Zaitsev speaking. Can't hear you!"

"I'm calling from the theatre," Alla whispered a little louder.

He didn't ask why. From that evening on, Alla Viren called him from work in the middle of the day. For no reason. But Zaitsev understood why. She was, as it were, checking the safety cable, to see if it was broken. She had been stunned by his direct question that evening. But she had been quite open with him. Alla's secret was now in his hands. Like a live bird being thrust into his hands: hold it safe, don't let it go. "And where did you get the paperwork for the name of Petrova?" Alla shrugged. "A guy." Zaitsev didn't need to ask. The lawless years after the Revolution were so wild you could get your hands on any official paperwork for next to nothing. The cheapest were the deeds to houses and shops. Later they were completely worthless. Everything became publicly owned, taken over by the state.

Alla Viren's family left the country after the Revolution. Alla remained, blithely ignoring the risks. "And if anyone recognized you?" The daughter of an admiral. With such striking looks.

Alla just shrugged. She never went anywhere. Just from home to work, at the theatre, then back again. Like some kind of nocturnal animal.

Alla's voice rustled on the phone: she was talking some kind of nonsense. Zaitsev was hesitant under Nefyodov's attentive gaze.

"OK, bye," he said, hanging up.

And he nodded to Nefyodov. "Sit down. Sit down," he repeated, almost as a question.

Nefyodov didn't sit down. But he didn't leave either. The tiered, twisted mountain of yellowing paper gave off that familiar bitter smell of decay. One of them had to be the first to speak. To break cover.

Nefyodov was clearly waiting for an explanation. He couldn't just turn him round and send him away.

"I don't remember if you had already started with us or not," Zaitsev began, launching straight into a lie. He remembered everything perfectly well. He immediately felt annoyed. Thoroughly sick of this whole quadrille. Of needing to dodge. Opening up another front of lies. And Alla on top of it all… Reality was doubled, tripled, swimming about before his eyes.

"Comrade Zaitsev," Nefyodov called out.

"What?"

"When? You weren't sure if I had already started with you or not. When?"

Zaitsev stepped into the conversation as if onto ice.

"So anyway, it was a call-out. A murder. On the corner of Nevsky and Sadovaya."

He even forgot to refer to these two old city streets by their Soviet names, 3rd July and 25th October. To hell with that! he told himself.

"The victim was Faina Baranova."

Nefyodov nodded. The sleepy owl's face grew brighter.

Zaitsev pulled out the Baranova case file from a drawer of his desk. He found a photograph of the corpse: in the black-and-white picture, the scarlet curtain looked grey and the figure in black was no longer quite so theatrical. She didn't even particularly look like she was dead, sitting in her chair with the feather duster in her hand.

He turned over a photo to show Nefyodov. "So Nefyodov, what the hell is a single, middle-aged Soviet worker doing dressing up like this?"

"A roommate? A lover?" Nefyodov quickly batted back.

Zaitsev shrugged. He didn't mention Yelagin Island—it wasn't safe.

"We talked with the neighbours in the *kommunalka*. No one mentioned a roommate or a feller."

231

"I know," Nefyodov answered, in a way that was almost brash. "I spoke to them."

"Ah, right. So, you were already with us," Zaitsev pretended. "It's strange."

"I wrote the report."

"Did you?"

Zaitsev flicked through the Baranova case file for show.

"It doesn't look like your report is here, for some reason. Never mind, it doesn't matter, not to worry. You spoke with the neighbours, and the others also had some conversations. At the end of the day, it's clear there wasn't a feller or a room-mate in the picture."

Nefyodov looked at him somewhat sceptically.

He seemed reluctant to emerge from his hideout. But Zaitsev could see he had that impatient instinct which meant he couldn't sit still. The same instinct that drove Zaitsev on. That instinct that made you throw caution to the wind. That made you forget about everything that wasn't connected to the matter in hand. That instinct that shouted: here's a lead!

"In general, Nefyodov, it's very odd. Her entire get-up. And all this stuff in her hands. It's all very skilful. The neighbours didn't see or hear a thing…"

"Or they're lying," Nefyodov said quietly.

"Or they're lying," agreed Zaitsev. "But there's no finger-prints or any other clues. He's a crafty one, it seems, very skilful. The bastard. Or bastards. Such skill only comes with experience. Don't you think?"

Nefyodov nodded.

For a moment he seemed to be weighing something up. Then, without saying a word, he got up and went over to the pile of folders. And he quickly began to sift through, casting a quick glance at the cover of each case file, immediately dropping them onto the floor one by one.

Apparently, he had decided to reconsider his selection.

He threw a file onto the moleskin settee. Again he slapped some of the files onto the floor. The smell of dust and ageing paper was unbearable. Zaitsev could feel it in his nostrils, and for a moment he even sympathized with Nefyodov. What must it be like to sit like this for days on end in the archives?

Another folder flew onto the sofa. Nefyodov's hands flickered back and forth, pale and flabby. Did he make up the story about being an acrobat? It somehow seemed implausible that these little white cuttlefish could hold, pull, throw and twist an entire body on the trapeze. Zaitsev remembered how deftly Nefyodov had stopped the thief on Sennaya Square.

A third folder fell onto the settee.

Nefyodov nodded at the desolate remains on the table and on the floor. "Not those."

Zaitsev was amazed. By his reckoning, there were dozens of files. And Nefyodov seemed to know their contents so well that he could sift through them with nothing more than a glance at their covers.

"Nefyodov, were mind tricks your speciality in the circus?" Zaitsev couldn't resist asking.

A frown was his reply.

Oh yeah, we're not into jokes, are we? thought Zaitsev.

Zaitsev picked up the three folders tossed onto the sofa.

"Go on, sit down," he said. "We've got a way to go yet."

Neither noticed that this was their first conversation where they had slipped into using "we".

II

Three cases lay before him.

Zaitsev pulled out the crime-scene photographs and laid them out along with the dates.

14th April 1929.
Murder victim: Olga Karpova, b.1912, student at the Technological Institute.
Murder victim: Peter Nedremov, b.1912, student at the Technological Institute.

Bodies found in a room of a communal apartment on International Prospekt. The room belonged to Nedremov. The lack of evidence of the lock being picked and the fact that both were students on the same course led to the conclusion that Nedremov and Karpova were in a relationship. An empty bottle of sleeping pills was found. The case was categorized as double suicide and closed.

1st January 1930.
Murder victim: Leonid Fokin, b.1899, musician in a folk ensemble.

Body found on a bench in the Summer Garden. The high blood alcohol concentration and the date (Soviet citizens still clung to the vestiges of pre-revolutionary traditions and liked to celebrate the New Year in style) both pointed to an accidental death. In essence, a very ordinary Russian story. Citizen Fokin had enthusiastically seen off the old year and welcomed in the new. He had set off for home drunk, sat down on the bench, fallen asleep and frozen to death.

30th August 1930.
Murder victim: Natalia Sirotenko, b.1894, worker.
Murder victim: Tarja Rohkimainen, b.1910, worker in an artel collective, part-time job as a nanny.

Bodies found inside a disused church. The case couldn't be solved from the evidence found. The investigation didn't result in any specific conclusions. And then, as Zaitsev understood it, there was the murder on Yelagin Island, and the case was dropped in priority; they'd had to strip back their case-load, and to clear the decks this one was quickly closed and archived (Zaitsev recognized Samoilov's flamboyant signature dashed off in a hurry).

Zaitsev remembered the two students. Definitely. Even then, at the call-out, at the first inspection of the crime scene, something seemed odd about it. For a moment, but then it was forgotten. You saw a lot of strange things in Leningrad, after all. "I'm strange; but who isn't strange?" Who said that? Griboyedov? Or was it Hamlet? The Danish prince didn't know about the Revolution, the civil war, military Communism and the New Economic Policy—when each and every time the contours of life changed beyond recognition, when "norms" became a word with little relation to real life; and now the NEP had been cancelled, and in its place was something else new, something unprecedented.

Zaitsev didn't remember the third case at all. He looked again at the date. True, how could he? That was when he was in the OGPU cell.

Between the second and third pictures, Zaitsev placed the photograph from the case of Faina Baranova, May 1930.

The last to fall on the table was the picture of the murder victim, Elena Karaseva, February 1931.

Five in total.

No, six, if the murder on Yelagin, October 1930, was also somehow related. But what evidence did he have? A pair of porcelain figurines from Faina Baranova's room and a vague whisper of intuition. Let's leave that one aside for now, he decided, and perhaps come back to it.

Five murders, seven victims. The dead: men and women, some single, some married with a family, some young and some not so, white-collar and blue-collar workers, educated and illiterate, party members and not, Russian, Finnish, Jewish. Nevertheless, they were all somehow connected, and the thread that linked them all could lead to the culprit. Or culprits.

"Nefyodov," he called, "have a look. What do you see?"

After all, why did Nefyodov instantly fish out precisely these files from the pile? Nefyodov leant his flat face over the table with expressionless eyes.

The phone trilled.

"Zaitsev speaking."

"Your carriage awaits," said the duty officer. "It's by the entrance."

Another trip squelching through the wet snow and cold, damp streets in unfriendly silence. Again, someone had been deprived of their life, their difficult, grubby, not particularly joyful and not at all sober life—just like those of most Leningrad residents.

Zaitsev grabbed his cap.

"Nefyodov," he asked. "Fancy going to the movies tonight?"

Nefyodov's face flashed with something that might be described as surprise.

"No," he answered.

"Excellent. Come round to mine after work. What? I can offer you a first-class spread: black bread, yellow butter, brown tea. Moika, eighty-four."

Unless Nefyodov had family and a hot dinner waiting for him at home—who knows? It was difficult to imagine him as a family man. However, picturing him as a circus acrobat wasn't much easier.

Down on the street outside, the engine growled and coughed impatiently as though hurrying the operatives along.

Zaitsev scooped up the files, heaped them into a pile and straightened out the edges. He handed them to Nefyodov.

"Bring these with you. But discreetly. Some extracurricular reading in a small friendly circle."

He saw Nefyodov out, locking the door after them. Out of habit. Not that he was trusted with any official secrets these days.

"At home you mean?" It seemed Nefyodov couldn't quite take it in.

"No, Nefyodov, at the Astoria Hotel restaurant."

Their police salary would hardly have stretched to dinner for one. And even if it were enough, the burly doorman would never let them past the thick velvet rope barrier in their shabby suits. Unless you waved a warrant under the bastard's nose.

"Oh, and bring some grub," shouted Zaitsev, already on the stairs. "If bread and butter doesn't sound like enough."

III

Nefyodov came. And it was only at that moment that Zaitsev realized he hadn't at all expected him to accept the invitation.

Nefyodov stood in the middle of his room like a penguin on an ice floe.

Zaitsev took out the cups. A knife, some spoons. And he stealthily watched his guest. Nefyodov looked around. Zaitsev knew this professional gaze, quickly and tenaciously taking it all in, drawing up a plan of action in case of a future arrest and search: entry point, exit point, layout, possible leads, hiding places. At the same time, Nefyodov looked just as he always did: as though someone had lifted him out of his bed but forgotten to wake him up. Having completed his inspection, the guest dropped his battered canvas rucksack from his shoulders, untied his scarf from his throat and, as if keen to pay his way, handed Zaitsev a half-circle of dark sausage.

Zaitsev wasn't going to stand on ceremony: he'd had nothing since lunch, and lunch had been pasta with meatballs, where the meat content was restricted mainly to the name.

"Ooh, proper fancy," he teased amiably, breaking the sausage into two. "How do you find the time to run around shopping? Or is it your wife?"

"Tatar rag-and-bone man. *Khalat*," Nefyodov answered, stirring the tea with a serious look, as though he feared there was hydrochloric acid in the teapot.

Khalat was the nickname since pre-revolutionary times for the Tatar rag-and-bone men who did the rounds of the backyards buying old trash for a pittance. And stolen goods.

Zaitsev stopped. The aroma of sausage was no longer quite so appealing.

"Horsemeat, then? If it's Tatar."

Nefyodov shrugged. "Protein and calories—it's all there."

"True."

The sausage disappeared in a matter of minutes; the tea didn't even have time to cool. Zaitsev moved the empty but still warm teapot onto the floor. He laid the files out on the table.

"Come on then, Nefyodov. I'll all ears. I won't interrupt."

Nefyodov laid out the photographs in the same order that Zaitsev had put them in earlier, in the office. Good memory, then.

"First of all, the clothes," he said. "Very odd outfits. And who knows what that is on her head."

"I'm with you there."

He started with the students. They didn't look in the slightest bit like would-be Soviet engineers, never mind that they were students at the Tech Institute.

First, it wasn't immediately clear which was him and which was her. Both had long hair, parted in the middle. Similar faces. Second, the clothes. Both were wearing some kind of long, baggy shirt, all floppy folds of fabric.

"Why would ordinary Soviet people wear this bizarre get-up?"

"Poverty," suggested Nefyodov. "They find it, they wear it."

"Students, maybe. But Faina Baranova had a job. And Elena Karaseva. Might not have been much. But Baranova had a fairly ordinary ladies' wardrobe: light blouses, dark skirts, knitted cardigans."

"Maybe it's a sect," suggested Nefyodov.

"Worshipping what, do you think?"

"People get all kinds of things into their heads."

"True enough. And on their heads, too, by the looks of it."

They couldn't help noticing the corpses' intricate hair-styles.

"Nefyodov, no one has long hair these days, even the Chinese. And look at this."

Zaitsev picked up the photograph of the murdered bala-laika player.

Froze to death while drunk. It seemed logical. His striped suit with short breeches and flamboyant white collar could be explained as a costume for a New Year's Eve party. And the guitar, it seemed, had stayed in his hands even after he had fallen into a drunken slumber, which would prove lethal. But what was that on his head? It was as if he were pulling off a sweater, had twisted it and got his head stuck in the neck, and left it like that—except he had tossed the sleeves back so they didn't get in the way of his eyes.

"Unless we assume that someone dressed them once they were dead."

"And did their hair?"

He took a photograph of the most bizarrely dressed of them all: the two women found in the locked church.

"By the way, Nefyodov. What did it say in the scene report? Was the church locked from the inside or outside?"

Nefyodov rifled through the case notes.

The Finnish woman was wearing a jagged crown and her shoulders were covered with a colourful rug. Sirotenko, the office clerk, was dressed in an opulent garment, like a robe but not a robe. The only bit that made sense was the thin waistband; everything else looked like a mound of curtains. Two braids fell to the sides of her face, and a third snaked about her forehead.

Next to these two, Faina Baranova, and even Karaseva with her pearls, looked austere and sensibly dressed.

"From the outside," Nefyodov finally answered.

Someone had locked them in.

Rohkimainen's lifeless fingers were wrapped around what looked like either a wand or a carved chair leg, as if she were about to write something on the floor with the tip. Spread out before Sirotenko was an open book. Zaitsev brought the photograph up to his eyes: what was the book? he wondered. But however hard he looked, he couldn't make out any text. But he saw something else. The horsemeat sausage suddenly resurfaced; Zaitsev swallowed down the bitter taste. His face contorted.

"What?" Nefyodov edged in.

"Take a look."

"Fuck me. What is that?"

Six taut strings stretched up from Sirotenko's head: the ends were fixed to her complicatedly braided hair, which explained the tight intricacy of the hairstyle. They converged above—where they were attached to the frame of the high church window. The dim Petersburg daylight flowed in from the window, casting a beam that highlighted the full length of the strings.

Someone had put the corpse in a kneeling position. And fixed it in place.

"He's really made an effort here, the bastard."

Zaitsev turned his attention to the photograph of the murdered students. Now he had no doubt: this was no suicide. He compared it with the picture of Faina Baranova. He showed it to Nefyodov.

Two red curtains.

He well remembered the scarlet curtain in Baranova's room, like some kind of evil red grin overlooking the sitting corpse. In the photograph, they looked grey. The same shade as a piece of cloth on the wall in the room with the students, and even a pillow. It was definitely the same fabric. The rest of the students' room was spartan and bare.

"*Faina wasn't one for anything flashy,*" Zaitsev remembered her neighbour saying.

In both cases, someone had brought in the fabric and hung it up.

The killer. Or killers.

"And look at how they're sitting."

"This one's sitting quite naturally," Nefyodov disagreed. "He flopped down on a bench, fell asleep and froze to death."

"Yes, but look at the women especially."

The victims were all in peculiarly mannered poses.

They were all either sitting or kneeling.

The murdered student looked like he was wagging a finger at his girlfriend threateningly. And she was raising her hands. In exactly the same gesture as Sirotenko, the office clerk who was found in the church.

It was just about possible to imagine this was a suicide pact: two lovers waiting for death in this posture, kneeling, their heads bowed. The rest was down to balance; their centres of gravity stopped both corpses from falling. But the others?

"And none of them have empty hands," Nefyodov noticed.

"Exactly."

"And all this fake jewellery on them."

Zaitsev looked Nefyodov in the eye. There could be no doubt that the five murders were somehow related.

Nefyodov looked at him and replied, as if reading his thoughts, "I won't be able to get anything on the Yelagin case."

Chapter 12

I

"Na-na-na-na!" came the baby's joyful cry as he squirmed about, kicking his chubby legs. His little body was wrapped and tied to the back of the chair by two wide strips of cloth so there was no danger that the energetic child would fall off. Zaitsev couldn't help but smile in response to his toothless grin.

"He misses his nanny," said the mother. She sniffed and looked away.

"Don't worry, citizen," said Zaitsev. "You can cry. Don't be shy."

"Na-na! Na-na! Na-na-na-na!" shouted the baby in frustration. He clearly wanted to talk about his missing nanny, Tarja Rohkimainen, but, unfortunately, he didn't know how.

"He's got some lungs on him," commented Zaitsev. "A future opera singer, no doubt."

"God forbid," the mother replied earnestly. "What kind of profession is that?"

"Citizen, don't fret. I don't care if your nanny was a collective farmer, if she left the kolkhoz legally or not. I also don't care if she lived with you without registering with the housing committee."

The woman blushed to her ears.

"The thing is—" she began.

"I understand," interrupted Zaitsev. "But the Criminal Investigation Department really isn't interested. What we investigate is murders. And what I want to do is catch whoever took the life of your employee. That's all."

At the word "murder", the mother hurriedly pulled the baby out of its seated captivity and moved him over to the cot. As if she were afraid he might hear too much. Forced too early to abandon his wordless paradise.

"Forgive me, comrade policeman. I've forgotten everything you said—it's all fuzzy. Remind me again…"

"It's all right, I know. The circumstances have changed."

She brought her chair closer to Zaitsev, sat down, wiped her eyes with the back of her hand, dabbed them with the corner of her sleeve.

"What do you need to know?"

II

Zaitsev placed his palms to his eyes and pressed. He moved his hands away. Then looked at the pictures again.

The more witnesses he and Nefyodov interviewed, the more they spent their days off and evenings on it, the more he found out about the victims—and the stranger the photographs seemed.

There seemed to be no link whatsoever between the lives of the victims and their deaths. That was Zaitsev's main concern.

Here were the photographs—it was all there in front of him.

The same raised hand gesture—in at least two. Red curtains—in two. Weirdly flamboyant clothes—in all of them. Strangely intricate hairstyles—in all of them. Items in their hands. Strange poses. It seemed to him that the photographs were trying to tell him something. There was undoubtedly an intention behind them all: to sit them like this, dress them like this, do their hair like that, position certain objects in their hands.

Dressing them up, doing their hair, setting them in poses— to say what?

246

Through the wall came the sound of the neighbours' radio blaring away. A lively folk ensemble. Zaitsev let out a groan, as if from toothache, pressed his temples with the heels of his palm. As if he could squeeze the answer out of his recalcitrant, sluggish, weary head.

On the other side of the wall, it now sounded like they were rushing about the room, clapping like some whip cracking, on top of the music, the whistling and squeals. Boyish zeal and girlish exuberance, so to speak.

Zaitsev jumped up from his chair. Impossible! He scooped up the photographs from the table. He rustled in a drawer of the sideboard and found a roll of sticking plaster.

"Will you give it a rest, for fuck's sake?" Zaitsev heard from the next room. Clearly not everyone in the apartment was a fan of folk ensembles. But instead of quiet came an eruption of balalaikas—the neighbour had apparently turned the volume dial all the way. He must have had a drink or two for payday. The apartment was never normally this noisy. Time for the Soviet police to intervene, Zaitsev thought irritably. But he didn't need to: at that moment he heard several furious blows to the door. "All right, quit your banging!" retorted the neighbour. The radio suddenly went quiet. The residents of the *kommunalka* tried not to cross the line in their quarrels.

As was wise.

Zaitsev went to the kitchen and borrowed some scissors from a neighbour. The stale-food smell reminded him that he hadn't eaten for a long time. He soon forgot again.

Back in his room, he began to stick the photos up on the wall, the scissors clattering and bits of plaster clinging to his fingers. By date of murder. The earliest. Then later ones, then later still. The latest. He stepped back. The wall now looked like a factory girl's shrine of celebrity cards. Sometimes, when you can't see the wood for the trees, you need to step back and look from afar.

This was exactly one of those times. He felt that he was prowling about, right up close. And he just couldn't see the main thing that was right in front of his nose.

Zaitsev stepped back. He considered the pictures from a distance.

Once again he was struck by the naturalness of the corpses' positions. From afar, without looking closely, they could be mistaken for living people.

He pushed the battered armchair into the middle of the room and sat down. He still had the feeling that before him were pictures of living people.

"Comrade Zaitsev!" came a neighbour's voice from the corridor. Great. Seriously?

"What?"

"The phone!"

"I'm coming!" Zaitsev called back. He slipped out so that his neighbour didn't have time to stick her curious nose into his room.

"Did you win the lottery?" she asked.

"Where'd you get that idea, Nyusha?"

"Always holed up in your room. What have you got hidden away in there? Have you come into some money? Must have had some luck come your way!"

"What's come my way, Nyusha, is work up to my ears. Come in and have a look around if you're so curious."

"What for? To see your bugs and cockroaches, eh?" she sneered as she drifted along to the kitchen.

Zaitsev picked up the phone.

"Hello?"

It was Alla.

"What are you up to?"

This simple question was difficult to answer. Zaitsev didn't like to lie unnecessarily. But now he was having to lie constantly to Alla.

"I'm a bit busy." He stopped himself. "I'm reading."

"Anything interesting?"

"Very. Are you calling from the theatre?"

"Yes. So is our date off today?"

Oh, curses.

"Er, no, Alla. It's just today's a bit—"

"It's just today's looking a bit busy, right? See, I'm getting the hang of it."

He heard a smile on the other end of the wire, but neither she nor her affectionate intonation deceived him. It was obvious Alla was offended.

"What is it, Alla?"

Alla was silent for a moment.

"It's just we're meeting less and less, that's all."

Zaitsev knew that this was true: he was meeting Nefyodov much more often than Alla these days. His evenings and his days off were being sucked up by this investigation.

"Let me see what I can do, OK?" asked Zaitsev.

"OK."

Then the beeps. Alla had hung up. Zaitsev was annoyed. With himself first and foremost. As luck would have it, they had started meeting less and less often precisely after the event with the ill-fated mackintosh. By now, there could be no doubt that Alla saw him as a wimp and a coward; as far as she was concerned, he'd found out that his girlfriend had origins in the enemy class and had assumed someone else's identity—and he had run for the hills.

Walking along the corridor, Zaitsev promised to himself that he would sort things out with her.

Then, as soon as he entered his room, where the photos

of the dead stared at him from their rectangular windows, he immediately forgot all about it.

Zaitsev leant back on the rickety, creaking chair. He closed his eyes. The yellow light from the bulb. The feeling of sand under his eyelids. Zaitsev opened his eyes wider. He stared at the photos. All together they contained some kind of meaning. Oh, if only he could get his hands on those from Yelagin Island. Maybe it would be clearer with one more piece of the puzzle?

He stared. The passage of time gradually began to slow down. And soon it completely stopped. In the ink-black window stood the dank Leningrad night. And the dimly lit room, with Zaitsev sitting in his braces, was reflected in it to the smallest detail. Zaitsev glanced at the reflection and shuddered: in his chair, he himself looked like a carefully simulated portrait of a living person.

His memory opened up before him like curtains parting.

He pictures a theatre curtain, a blanket draped over a string. His older sister Tanya shouts to him, "Alyosha, watch your step!" She tugs at the blanket with both hands and it slides across, folding in pleats like an accordion. The other children are holding one end of the string and the other end is tied to an upturned table, its four legs sticking up helplessly.

"The children prepared their *tableau vivant* in secret. They've set up the entire scene by themselves," Mama whispers in Russian. "Miss Jones only—"

"My first syllable!" shouts Tanya, facing them with a stern expression.

Their parents, a godmother, an aunt and uncle, the governess Miss Jones, a grandmother, a great-aunt, Papa's brother and his wife, other faces… His memory is trying to focus, but nothing happens: it's as though the screw thread has worn down on the wheel of the binoculars.

Children drag out some kind of tedious song. They take a few steps. The table skids along heavily behind them.

"Our Tanya's the stage director," Mama is quick to add in a whisper. She receives an indignant glare from Tanya and puts a finger to her lips, as if to say, "Sorry, not another word from me." Mama has her hair curled up in a loose bun.

Alyosha doesn't sit with the grown-ups. Nor does he join in with the children acting out their paintings behind the "curtain", with the costumes, hats and even wigs they had found in an out-of-the-way cupboard. His sister, brother and cousins—you can't tell who's who in their silly costumes. They're growling and squeaking in horrible voices and pretending they're not themselves at all. But they won't let him play with them. He's trying to make sense of the rules of this game. What does *tableau vivant* mean? And what about the "charades" bit? How do they think up the ideas? And how are you supposed to work it out? He clearly visualizes his hand, white and chubby. The hand is holding down a sheet of paper, and next to it are some coloured pencils and porcelain ramekins with his watercolours. He's supposed to sit quietly at the table, out of the way, and keep himself busy. Drawing, for example. He's the "little one". Little ones aren't allowed to join in the big ones' games of charades.

"Wonderful!" Mama whispers in English, turning to Miss Jones with a smile. Miss Jones, straight as a stick, blushes, but doesn't take her eyes off the "stage". The children freeze in their acted-out scene. Katya pulls the curtains open, revealing a world of activity.

The adults are throwing syllables about like balls.

One of the uncles gets it right; his pink, bald head glistens.

"My second syllable!" Tanya announces, again lifting up one hem of the bedspread.

Alyosha doesn't understand a thing. He's painting a beautiful

Aunt Alice in a blue velvet dress. The water in the cup immediately turns blue. He's so engrossed he doesn't notice when the game of charades is over. Dad lights a cigar.

"Huh, what's that supposed to be? An octopus?" Tanya asks in a mocking tone. "Why blue? Give it here."

He pulls the sheet towards himself, shoving out an elbow defensively.

"Agh!" cries Tanya.

The cup is knocked over, splashing her dress. The blue water spills across the table, heading straight for his painting. Furious, he lashes out, roars at his sister. The water turns red. The adults scream, Dad drops his cigar. On the table, where there was blue painty water, there's a red stain spreading. Alyosha smells that sweet, ferrous aroma—the smell of blood.

Zaitsev flinched. The chair gave a loud creak and he woke up.

It was dark outside, but he could hear a shovel scraping on the pavement. Pasha was already at work: it was morning. Zaitsev's body was numb. He stood up.

The photos stared at him like little eyes, contrasting darkly against the wall, which was blue in the half-light.

And, finally, Zaitsev could see them for what they were.

III

"Where?" Samoilov asked again. And in surprise, he looked Zaitsev in the eye for the first time in a long time.

"To the museum."

"To the museum!" confirmed traffic controller Rozanova, the CID's resident Komsomol activist. Rozanova forcefully pushed Zaitsev aside. She didn't like Samoilov's tone.

"I, as representative of the Komsomol organization—" she began energetically and loudly.

"*Female* representative," Demov corrected wearily from his corner.

Rozanova gave him a fierce glare.

"You're another conversation entirely. Our party unit has been keeping an eye on you for a while now."

"You flatter me, Comrade Rozanova," Demov sighed, before fencing himself off with his newspaper. "Anyway, I can't stick around. It's time for Political Information."

Zaitsev saw that Demov was deliberately winding Rozanova up: he was holding the newspaper upside down.

Zaitsev himself had nothing against her. She was vociferous, guileless, but he actually quite liked her.

"What's going on here?" asked a surprised Serafimov, looking in at the door. "Is this a meeting?"

"They're dragging us to a museum."

"The tempestuous Komsomol is building up to a frenzy," added Demov. Rozanova didn't miss the thinly veiled snipe at her, and seemed rather pleased with herself for spotting it.

Serafimov looked with interest from Demov to Rozanova. It seemed like a skirmish was afoot.

"Another wisecrack on its way?" She turned to Demov, her nostrils flaring.

"God, *she's not human!*" he retorted, again calling on his repertoire of literary quotations.

"How dare you insult me to my face—" she began.

"Comrade Demov isn't insulting you!" Zaitsev interrupted in a conciliatory tone. "He means you're more than merely human, you're a Komsomol member," he added, steering a dangerous conversation towards safer waters. Was Demov quoting from Ilf and Petrov? Or perhaps it was another writer. Well, either way, Rozanova wouldn't have got the reference— what did she read besides the grey party pamphlets?

"Comrade Rozanova has a point," Zaitsev went on, turning

to flattery to appease her. "I have to say, our police force is a bit lacking in terms of culture. We should set an example to Leningrad youth. We're going to the Hermitage."

Naturally, Zaitsev didn't mention that he was the one who had hinted about it to Rozanova in the first place. He framed it this way so she would immediately get on the phone ("Hello, comrade, is that the State Hermitage?") and—as always— leap out of her little red corner, bursting with energy, utterly convinced that she had thought of the inspired idea herself. It was high time Leningrad's police were acquainted with Leningrad's museums!

"No, we're going to the State Russian Museum," Rozanova corrected him. "The Hermitage couldn't set aside the man-hours for us."

"Fine, the Russian," Zaitsev shrugged. "I'm in favour."

No one even looked at him. Rozanova didn't like the others' silence.

"And you, comrade?" she said, launching an attack on Samoilov. "When was the last time you went to a museum? Or the theatre? Or the philharmonic? You should be ashamed of yourself! Now, when the Soviet government opens up the doors to the treasures of world culture—"

"If there's a robbery at the museum, we'll be there on the double, my dear girl," said Samoilov.

"How dare you! I'm not a *girl*!"

"More's the pity," Demov whispered softly.

"What?!" Rozanova was furious now.

"What what?" he asked, feigning innocence. Demov hated Rozanova with the hatred of a man whose youth came at a time when ladies still wore large hats and lace-up boots.

"Your moral and ideological appearance has long raised questions," Rozanova said menacingly.

"For whom?" asked Demov in genuine surprise.

"In general, let's say. You can stir up all the demagoguery you like, but tomorrow at eleven hundred hours you'll be at the State Russian Museum for an excursion. We'll meet in the lobby! Attendance is *not* optional."

Spinning on her heels, she stormed out of the room, almost knocking over Serafimov.

"You just summon up some crooks, get them ready for action," Samoilov muttered after her. "And, sure, at eleven hundred hours we'll be there. What do you want, Serafimov?"

"We've got a call-out. The bank clerk robbery on Vyborg."

"And I can't, I've got a ticket for the ballet," cheeped Samoilov.

"What do you think, Samoilov? If Rozanova wasn't such a beast, but some scythe-wielding maiden out of Turgenev, would we have taken a kinder view of the Komsomol schemes?" Demov asked in a melancholy tone, as he picked up his scarf and pulled on his coat.

"Yeah, obviously. If my granny had a dick, she'd be a grandad," Samoilov was quick to add.

But Demov had already changed his tone as he turned to Serafimov.

"So, the Vyborg Side robbery. Good haul, then?"

IV

At eleven hundred hours in the lobby of the State Russian Museum, Zaitsev quickly spotted Rozanova and Nefyodov. The impatience was palpable on Rozanova's face. Her desperation to prostrate herself before culture. Nefyodov, as usual, looked like he had just got up but still wasn't quite awake.

"Hello," said Rozanova with a nod to Zaitsev. Glancing around, she pressed her handbag to her side with her elbow. "The other comrades are late."

Groups of visitors gathered and went in. A thin, middle-aged man in a black suit hovered nearby; the collar of his shirt was crisp white. Zaitsev noticed he kept glancing their way, gradually narrowing his orbit. Zaitsev caught his eye. At that point the man in the suit walked straight over.

"Comrades, I'm meeting a delegation of policemen," he said, almost as a question.

"That's us," Zaitsev replied.

Nefyodov's gaze floated up the walls. Rozanova, somewhat embarrassed, spoke up.

"The enthusiasm of the masses is still slow to kindle. It was me you spoke to, comrade. Rozanova." She quickly grabbed his hand and shook it by way of greeting.

The man in the suit looked surprised, but said nothing.

"So far, the cultural consciousness of police workers lags somewhat behind their class consciousness," Rozanova explained.

The man in the suit smiled affably. "Well, the quantity is no doubt compensated for by quality." He introduced himself: "Nikolai Semyonovich."

"Zaitsev."

"Nefyodov."

"Well, comrades. If you please, let's begin."

He held out a slender hand, one that had clearly never known physical labour, inviting them to follow. And with a steady gait and the posture of a host, he walked towards the marble staircase with its raspberry-red carpet. All three followed along behind him. Light streamed in through the huge windows. Rozanova looked down at her feet.

"So this is how the tsars lived, huh?" said Zaitsev, trying to strike up a conversation with her. "I suppose they needed a colossus like this for, what, six or seven people?"

Rozanova squinted at him.

"Petty-bourgeois thinking, Comrade Zaitsev. The tsars didn't live here. This is where they kept these cultural treasures out of reach of the working people," she said, sounding out of breath. Climbing the stairs while performing a tirade was no easy task.

Zaitsev paused for breath.

"Never mind. The main thing is that you're trying. You're stretching yourself," Rozanova encouraged him. Zaitsev saw Nikolai Semyonovich raise an ironic eyebrow.

He's going to go back and tell everyone how he showed around some idiotic coppers, Zaitsev thought with distaste. Then he almost walked right into him—their guide had suddenly stopped. He turned to face them.

"What do you want to see today? Perhaps some humorous sketches from rural life?"

Zaitsev didn't miss the politely veiled mockery in his voice. Or maybe it was a sincere desire to find a way to occupy his sudden guests at an appropriate intellectual and cultural level.

Be that as it may, humorous sketches were certainly not part of his plan.

"Humorous sketches sound all right," Nefyodov shrugged.

"We're not schoolchildren, you know," Zaitsev interjected. "It's not all fun and games. If you want to know, catching criminals often requires intelligence and calculation. It's hardly our fault that the Soviet Republic called us up and we didn't have time for studying or university. Or even to read books. Or that many of us didn't even manage to finish school."

"I didn't say…" muttered Nikolai Semyonovich, but it was clear that that was, in essence, precisely what he had said, and that he now felt rather awkward. As a man of culture and integrity, the last thing he wanted was to offend someone. It hadn't crossed his mind to offend these three badly dressed, weary-looking policemen who had gathered at the museum.

"What would you like to see?" he asked again. But his eyes were softer, more lively.

"I'd like to see some folk art," said Rozanova. "Where we see the high spirit of the Russian individual. Only without the religious opiates."

Nikolai Semyonovich was clearly giving it some thought.

"You're perhaps thinking of Bryullov?" he asked courteously. Although it was immediately clear to everyone that Rozanova was hearing the name Bryullov for the first time, Nikolai Semyonovich's tone was so serious and compelling that she nodded.

"Indeed."

"An excellent idea! Follow me, comrades."

They ambled through the halls. Across smooth and bright parquet floors. Past people in portraits—all face and opulent, stiff outfits, as if they were encased in wooden planks.

Nefyodov suddenly nudged Zaitsev with his elbow. He slowed his step. Nikolai Semyonovich carried on at his pace, Rozanova hurrying after him. Nefyodov waited until they had some distance between them.

"So why are we here?" he asked Zaitsev.

"Cultural development for good Komsomol members. Are you a Komsomolets, Nefyodov? Time to up your game."

He pretended to be engrossed in some portrait of a woman with heavy make-up: beetroot cheeks on a white chalky face. Now he was sure that Rozanova wouldn't hear them. Nefyodov stood next to him.

"You see, museums have one annoying feature: they tend to be closed at night."

Nefyodov stared at the portrait.

"Are you going into hibernation or something, Nefyodov?" Zaitsev bristled. "Winding down your mental faculties? How else would we get here during working hours? They'd never give us the day off to come here—not you or me. I had to let Rozanova loose on them."

He pulled out the photographs.

"Look properly. The victims. They're all depicting some kind of living picture. The parts in a game of charades. But what kind of picture it might be is a question for an investigator with high cultural awareness. So let's go and get some culture. Come on. We've got an hour or two to learn what we can."

Zaitsev sensed that the attendant's face had turned in their direction. Just in case, he quickly tucked the photos into the first pocket he came to.

"Pictures? Charades?"

"Well, yes. It was a game people used to play."

"Somehow I don't remember a game like that."

"No, not you and me, Nefyodov. Not for the likes of us. It was a game rich kids played. The bourgeoisie. In the days of tsarism. First they'd think up a word or phrase. Then dress up and act out a scene. And everyone else had to guess what it was. You get the first syllable from the first scene, the second syllable from the second scene, and so on."

"You think someone went and killed a dozen people for the sake of a word game?" Nefyodov was incredulous. "So we would run about trying to solve a puzzle?"

"You think I'm wrong?"

"Fuck knows." Nefyodov looked at the beetroot beauty from under his swollen eyelids. "But why? I can understand bumping people off to steal their stuff. But to kill people for no reason—"

"But there could well be a reason. Only, to find out what it is, we first need to understand what he is trying to tell us."

"*Us?*" Nefyodov grunted.

"It's like a letter in a bottle, Nefyodov. Addressed to whoever finds it. And since corpses are usually found by CID, then yes, Nefyodov—*us.*"

"A Petrovian-era portrait of an unknown subject," came a friendly voice behind them. Both almost jumped in fear: they hadn't heard the attendant approaching. It was written on her face that she wasn't going to let them go without a full-blown lecture about portraiture in the reign of Peter the Great.

"Comrade Zaitsev! Comrade Nefyodov!" came Rozanova's trumpet voice. She had finally noticed that half their group was missing and had her head down, charging towards them like a young bull. "There you are. We've been looking for you." She cast a belligerent look at the attendant, as if to say, "What do you want?" "Come on, then. Keep up!"

"That picture's one of striking beauty, Comrade Rozanova! A feast for the eyes! We couldn't tear ourselves away!" Zaitsev shouted to her. "We're indebted to the Komsomol unit for this cultural input. We're soaking it all up. Very enlightening."

"We're developing culturally," Nefyodov explained to the attendant for some reason. She immediately looked suspicious: she scanned Nefyodov from top to bottom, especially his pockets, as if worried if he had somehow, mysteriously, stolen a picture from the wall.

"Come on, Nefyodov. Time to get more enlightened."

Zaitsev gave the attendant a broad smile (which left her feeling even more anxious), nudged Nefyodov to hurry him along, and dashed off to catch up with Rozanova.

V

The trip to the Russian Museum, however, was fruitless.

"There was a lot I liked," Nefyodov said shyly, once they had squeezed themselves onto the tram. "Especially the one with the earthquake."

"That's it, Bryullov can rest in peace: 'Phew, Nefyodov approved!'" Zaitsev tried to joke, but his mood had soured.

Outside the tram windows, the air swiftly filled with dusk blue. The evening twilight had an aftertaste of missed opportunities; the day had ended to no avail.

"There are a lot of museums in Leningrad. We'll find it somewhere."

The passengers' faces were weary. The tram was lit up with electric light. The faces turned a shade of green.

"You bet," Zaitsev answered drowsily.

He hated to think that his idea could be wrong. It couldn't be. But Nefyodov was right: there were a lot of museums in Leningrad.

"Have you heard, Nefyodov? They say if you go to the State Hermitage and spend at least a few seconds looking at each picture, then even without stopping to sleep, eat or relieve yourself, it would take five years. No? You should know. It's a fact."

"Well, we've checked the Russian Museum."

"You, Nefyodov, are an optimist."

Nefyodov got off at his stop, raising a hand in parting.

"See you tomorrow," said Zaitsev, although Nefyodov didn't hear: the doors had already closed. The tram trundled on down 3rd July Street, which the locals still stubbornly called by its old name, Sadovaya. The dark masses of houses flashed past. Here and there, windows were already glowing orange squares. The tram steered around St Nicholas Naval Cathedral. Zaitsev jumped off.

As he walked, he thought about Faina Baranova. The image she conveyed was a portrait, a painting—but not of herself. Likewise with the Karaseva case. But he hadn't seen any portraits like that in the Russian Museum—with a feather duster or a carnation. Were they somewhere else? Were these even real portraits he might find in a museum? Or were they thought up in the deranged mind of a sick killer? Was he sick?

Perhaps he was an ordinary mobster. Gang rituals sometimes looked brutally meaningless, but behind them lay their own indestructible logic. The form they took seemed savage, but the goal was crystal clear. Maybe this was some new gangster tradition? A new gang from out of town. Did it have some significance? Or not?

Or perhaps the killer was a lone wolf, utterly deranged, who was improvising some kind of portrait?

But the rest of the victims were clearly also telling stories of some kind. But where to find them?

Out of habit, as Zaitsev walked he fiddled with the sharp corners of the photographs in his pocket—by now, he always had them on him. An automatic movement, like a card sharp smoothing the deck. It helped him think. Only, for some reason, nothing seemed to help.

But then what were the victims on Yelagin Island depicting? That group was the most complex, and, of course, if he had been able to get to the bottom of it, it might have shed light on something in the other murders. Or perhaps not?

No matter how Zaitsev turned the jigsaw pieces about in his mind—the syllables, the portrait—no matter how he flicked at the corners in his pocket, nothing good came of it.

Maybe he had just forgotten how to play charades?

"Need an extra ticket?" A voice brought him round.

"What?"

A citizen loomed before him, both hands in his pockets. Fragments of melodies burst out from a few open windows and floated in the air: the Conservatory was humming like a beehive. The lanterns of the theatre opposite gave off a milky light; a crowd was pouring into the illuminated entrance.

It was a ticket tout.

"No," said Zaitsev.

"Have you got a spare?" asked a citizen in a beret who had run up to the tout. "Yes, please. How many have you got? Are they awfully dear?"

But she was already pulling her purse out of her handbag. The citizens of Leningrad were ballet-mad. In this city, people always had money for the ballet. Especially now, when there was an existential question at stake: who was better, Ulanova or Dudinskaya?

"Got any more?" asked a citizen in a cap.

Zaitsev turned to face the service entrance. Alla would be finishing before the performance today: they had finally hired another wardrobe assistant. Zaitsev already knew the theatre routine. The artists had long since gone to their dressing rooms. Alla had already handed them their costumes. The musicians dashed into the building, their lacquered instrument cases glinting. Zaitsev was once again struck by their ordinary faces, their completely ordinary features. If it weren't for the cases, he would never have imagined mugs like that might be associated with music, that those fingers could tease out a harmony. The guard also knew Zaitsev by now and no longer bothered him with questions about which of the dancers or singers he was hanging around waiting for. Finally, at the end of the low corridor, Alla appeared in her coat. In her hand was a small piece of paper. And her face looked somewhat anxious: her gaze was focused beyond Zaitsev. She pushed the turnstile and came out.

"Listen, I have to wait for someone," she said instead of a greeting, and held out a square piece of paper: her pass.

"Well, hello anyway," said Zaitsev. "A lot of ballet fans hanging around here today," he remarked. It certainly wasn't the first time they had had to "wait for someone".

"It's not us. It's the artists who invite people. I'm only passing it on."

"And bankrupting the theatre while you're at it."

"You don't understand, these are people of culture. For them ballet is like—"

"Oh, I get it. I see alcoholics every day."

Alla didn't have time to answer. She waved eagerly to someone behind him. Zaitsev turned around to see a rotund, nattily dressed man hurrying towards them.

"Alexei Alexandrovich!" exclaimed Alla.

"Allochka, hello," he said, kissing her hand and casting a good-natured glance at Zaitsev. "Is this your friend? The one who works at a school?"

Zaitsev shot her a surprised look. Alla blushed right to her ears.

"Yes."

"A pleasure to meet you," he said, examining Zaitsev with the curiosity of an old matchmaker.

"Likewise." Zaitsev shook his hand.

"You teach history, if I recall correctly?" the rotund natty dresser continued.

"That's right," Zaitsev confirmed without a blink. "And you?"

The natty dresser smiled. "I work in a museum."

"I was asked to give you…" Alla finally managed to interrupt and held out the theatre pass. At that moment, yet another orchestra musician flashed past them. The natty dresser's hand made such a quick grab for his prey, and his elbow collided with the musician's case with such force, that he lost his balance and would have fallen over had he not snatched at Zaitsev's sleeve. He yanked Zaitsev so hard, pulling him with his entire body weight, that as Zaitsev freed his hands from his pockets to steady himself the photographs fluttered out onto the ground.

"Ah, I'm so sorry!"

Swearing to himself silently, Zaitsev crouched down and hurriedly began gathering up the pictures. But the cursed rotund smart alec rushed to help even faster. He was holding the photograph of the women in the church. He was already peering closely at the image.

Now he'll get a fright. He'll turn pale. His mouth will twist in horror.

But nothing of the kind happened.

The blue eyes were just as calm as before. His large pink forehead and soft cheeks carried on radiating bonhomie.

"Is this one of your pupils?" Alexei Alexandrovich asked quite innocently. "An attempt at a reproduction of *The Annunciation*?"

Zaitsev thanked the heavens for the terrible print quality: the natty dresser hadn't noticed anything suspicious. The female corpses did look a bit like clumsily painted figures of living subjects. Zaitsev nodded. He took the picture. And, even before he understood or could explain to himself what he was doing, he replied, "That's right. Only I can't for the life of me think of the artist."

"Van Eyck," the natty dresser answered calmly. "It's Van Eyck's *Annunciation*."

"That's the one!"

"We've got it—in the Hermitage," Alexei Alexandrovich added proudly. "Well done, your student. Not a great talent, by the looks of it, but he's trying. It's not entirely successful, but a valiant attempt. And that's the main thing. How old is he or she? Which years do you teach?"

Alla's ears turned red again.

"Alexei Alexandrovich, you'll be late for the performance!" she reminded him. And she grabbed Zaitsev's arm to pull him away. Zaitsev felt sorry for her from the bottom of his heart.

But he wasn't going to help. The natty dresser was already pushing the revolving door.

"And can I see this picture?" he asked, thinking on his feet.

"Well, of course! Art, as they say, belongs to the people."

Like a locomotive, Alla pulled him away.

"And bring the student!" shouted Alexei Alexandrovich. "I'll leave a pass for you at the service entrance."

Alla pulled away and, letting go of Zaitsev's hand, she walked off. Without looking back, she began to run to the tram stop. He paused for a moment, then ran after her.

"Alla, stop!"

He tried to catch her hand.

"Alla, wait!"

The crowd at the tram stop was watching them. Flustered, she slowed down. Zaitsev caught up with her.

"Alla, it's fine. I even found it funny. History teacher. I really didn't mind!"

"Sorry."

"Honestly, I'm not offended! Come on."

Deep inside, he was of course offended. This was how Alla saw him, then: she was ashamed to be going out with a copper. For Alla's friends and acquaintances, a policeman was on a par with a soldier or a fireman, the sort of man who would go out with a cook, a nanny or a laundress. Never mind that the Revolution had turned everything upside down. It had and it hadn't. After all, in the new Soviet society, Alla was just a dressmaker in a theatre costume department. But she still felt like an upper-class young lady who had managed to fit into the new society as best she could, without sacrificing too much of her principles. As though she were outside society. Because, although it was officially called the State Academic Theatre, it was still reserved for the Mariinsky types. They had never stopped calling it the Mariinsky, after all. And the same ballet lovers, or almost the same ones who had marvelled at Karsavina, the prima ballerina in the time of the tsar, now found an escape from Soviet reality by coming to admire Ulanova. *The Queen of Spades* was still *The Queen of Spades*, whether it was under the Soviet system or the tsar.

Alla stopped. Behind the fence, St Nicholas Naval Cathedral was a soft blue in the darkness. The light from the street lamps didn't reach the asphalt.

"Sorry," she repeated again.

"Absolutely no need to apologize." What else could he say?

"I just don't want them to think you're... Because you're not like that."

"And I just don't want you to be upset because of this," Zaitsev said. "It's nothing."

She looked at him incredulously.

"Really. Sticks and stones may break my bones, but being called a history teacher will never hurt me—as the wise saying goes. Seriously. I don't mind."

She thought for a moment: did she believe him or not?

She sighed. "Fine. Come on, then."

He hesitated.

"What?"

"You know... I'd probably best get back."

He said "I", not "we", she noticed. Alla pursed her lips slightly. The distinction didn't pass her by.

"You're not..."

"It's just been a long day today. You'd better tell me which classes I teach at least? Or we'll dig ourselves into a hole. Best stick to the official version."

Alla smiled a little. "Are you seriously going to visit Alexei Alexandrovich?"

"Why not?"

267

"What was the picture, anyway?" she suddenly remembered. "That one. Whose is it?"

"Oh, yes—it was Nefyodov, can you imagine?" said Zaitsev, turning to get going.

"Nefyodov?"

"Self-taught. A diamond in the rough, so to say."

This is how we live, he thought. She's lying and so am I.

Alla shook her head. She clearly believed him.

"You teach middle grade," she answered.

A tram appeared from around the corner.

"It's yours," said Zaitsev, glancing at the three coloured lights up on the front of the tram.

They kissed goodbye.

Perhaps she wasn't entirely convinced that he wasn't offended. Anyway, never mind, Zaitsev thought, as he walked along the dark and deserted Moika embankment. Only the lights in the windows of the houses lit up the way. The inky black water splashed. Van Eyck! So it really did exist! And if this was a genuine picture, then the others must be too. Whether this knowledge added anything to the investigation or not, and, if so, what, Zaitsev couldn't yet say. He only felt that the trail, which had gone stone cold, was warming up again. There was definitely something there. And everything else that wasn't connected to this was pushed out of his mind. At a moment like this, he simply needed to be alone.

Chapter 13

I

The palm which he pressed against the sheet of cigarette paper ached with cold. The windowpane seemed to be carved out of ice. The wind occasionally punched against the window like a fist of air. Snow flew up and down, then to the side, then obliquely, now upwards again. It seemed to pour from everywhere: from the heavens, from the earth, out of the walls. There was no earth, no sky, no Fontanka, no buildings— everything was a blur, spinning in a grey-white haze. February in Leningrad was a cruel test.

Zaitsev compared the photograph and his drawing from it. The layout of a crime in its purest form. But you still wouldn't recognize the seated woman with the carnation.

He no longer wanted to take any risks.

Glancing briefly and in the dim light outside the theatre, Alexei Alexandrovich could still mistake a crime scene for a photograph of an inept student painting. But that was unlikely to happen if someone looked through the photos slowly in the light of day. He had got away with it once. He wouldn't be so lucky again.

He still needed to call Rozanova—"to unleash the Komsomoltsi", as Demov had put it. Zaitsev picked up the phone. Then hung up again. He suddenly realized that no one would notice his absence. And if they did, so what? Would he be dismissed? But he wasn't skipping work. He was going to question an expert in the case of the murder of Citizen Karaseva, "the woman with the carnation"—not that anyone gave a damn about her, either.

These days, Zaitsev barely saw Serafimov, Samoilov, Demov and Kopteltsev—just briefly in the corridors or on the stairs. He was still officially part of the team and they sat together in the canteen, looking outwardly like a model happy family. But in Zaitsev's presence, the team now only talked about trivialities: cinema, operettas, girls. And never about what they always used to talk about before. About cases. About *the* case.

Where had their investigation led? he wondered. An unthinkable number of people and cars were being thrown at it. It was growing. Branching out. But where to? He could only judge by their gloomy faces—and concluded that the case was hard going.

Outside, the wind was so fierce and everything was so immediately covered with snow that Zaitsev could barely see where he was going. Passers-by were walking in the same blindness. To avoid falling under a tram or cart, Zaitsev decided to follow the Fontanka as far as the Neva, and then head towards the Hermitage. On the Neva embankment, he immediately regretted it. The freezing, damp wind ripped the last vestiges of heat from his body. The other shore, with the golden spire of the Peter and Paul Fortress, was nowhere to be seen: the bridges seemed to break off into a white nothingness. Snow clung to his eyelashes. Zaitsev pressed on, leaning forward, cowering from the wind and snow. He almost missed the awning over the door and the copper plate marking the service entrance of the State Hermitage.

Alla wasn't at all delighted when Zaitsev reminded her of his date with Alexei Alexandrovich.

"What do you want to meet him for?"

She was still embarrassed by the "history teacher" incident. And, Zaitsev realized, she was reluctant to combine the two areas of her life: him and the theatre.

"If you want to go to the Hermitage, why don't we go by ourselves?" she suggested. "We'll buy tickets and..."

"He seems like an interesting person, your Alexei Alexandrovich."

"Firstly, he's not mine!—"

"Fine, not yours. But interesting."

"He's not at all interesting. He's a grey hamster from the heraldry department."

"He's not just ancillary staff. He can tell us something about the paintings."

"Sign up for a guided tour!"

"I don't want to go around with a group. Wouldn't that be annoying? Everyone pushing and shoving, creeping along at a snail's pace. And all you hear is them banging on about the tsars..."

"Then we could go on our own," Alla insisted. But she did eventually give him Alexei Alexandrovich's telephone number.

"And where's the boy?" Alexei Alexandrovich asked at once, as Zaitsev knocked his hat down onto the bench, shaking off the snow that was melting in the warmth. He stomped his boots.

"Tonsillitis," he lied on the spot. Nefyodov had gone to interview Karaseva's neighbours. All known friends, acquaintances, colleagues—anyone who had at least some kind of contact with the victims; they were all down on one big chart, in the hope it might show up some crossovers. But so far the chart had only grown and swollen, but revealed nothing new.

Maybe they were mistaken in linking these killings into one series? Not they. He.

His hands and face began tingling from the heat in the lobby.

"Oh, what a shame," said Alexei Alexandrovich. "Well, we can do it another time. When he's better?"

Zaitsev didn't have time to answer.

"But we can't have you coming here in a blizzard for nothing!" Alexei Alexandrovich enthusiastically inserted on his behalf. He waited politely until Zaitsev pulled on the huge felt shoe covers required for the sake of the precious parquet floor. "Ready?"

And off they went.

Alexei Alexandrovich, the grey hamster, chatted incessantly. Apparently, he wasn't often treated to new faces in the heraldry department. And he must have been tired of the old ones. Not married, Zaitsev concluded.

He left a couple of sentries on guard on the surface of his consciousness, in case Alexei Alexandrovich surprised him with a direct question. But he focused his attention squarely on the paintings that flickered past. The rectangular frames on the walls seemed like windows, and the Hermitage itself was a building intricately turned inside out, its inhabitants gazing out, oblivious to passers-by like him, Zaitsev. They went about their business: embracing, comforting babies, writing, reading or simply displaying dishes of food, apparently on the windowsill.

In his felt slipper boots, he sailed silently past faces: brown like bark or glistening pink like pearls. Past landscapes and group portraits. And the further they went, the more strongly Zaitsev felt an ache below his stomach: he felt sure that he was on the right track. In the poses, the robes, the hairstyles, in that elusive quality that relates to the style and spirit of art, he saw a resemblance to the photographs which he had stuck up on the wall of his room. This feeling was like falling into an abyss. You float on and on—and you don't know when you'll hit the bottom.

"Comrade Zaitsev!" the hamster called again, loudly.

"What?… I was looking around," said Zaitsev, acting confused.

"I see. Well, here we have something to see."

"Sorry. What did you say?"

"I said: we're here. This is Dutch art of the fifteenth and sixteenth centuries," said Alexei Alexandrovich, widely gesticulating. "Here is your Van Eyck."

And Zaitsev, once again a little envious of someone else's education, held his hands behind his back and began carefully to examine the tall, broad and abundant canvases. At the very bottom, velvet armchairs and little settees jutted out into the room, like coquettishly pouting lips.

They went around the collection, then again, and then they each did a figure of eight. They met in the middle. Alexei Alexandrovich was clearly confused and dismayed.

"Never mind, we'll find it. Shall we go on to the next hall?" suggested Zaitsev encouragingly. Perhaps Alexei Alexandrovich didn't leave his heraldry department very often and he had managed to forget where everything was in the museum itself.

"This is all of them," he insisted.

"Well, not all, it turns out."

Alexei Alexandrovich jerked his head.

"All the paintings are grouped by country, school, era," Alexei Alexandrovich explained. "The entire Dutch collection is here. It's either here or it's nowhere."

"Might they have swapped them around?"

Alexei Alexandrovich looked away. "Absurd. This is a museum, not a living room!"

"So you're saying that if *The Annunciation* isn't here in this hall, then there's no other hall where it could be? Right?"

"If it's Van Eyck's work, then this is where it would be!"

His little hamster cheeks drooped.

"And was it perhaps not Van Eyck?"

"No, it is definitely Van Eyck," Alexei Alexandrovich insisted.

"You couldn't have confused it with another?" Zaitsev prompted him gently.

"When did your student paint this reproduction?" asked Alexei Alexandrovich, evidently pursuing some thought of his own.

Before Zaitsev could answer, a group of sightseers shuffled into the hall, muttering, their felt slippers softly rustling: a dark, bumpy caterpillar, covered in tufts with faces. The female guide—in a tight skirt—patiently waited for her tail to retract. Only then did she start speaking. The hamster sat down on a scarlet settee. He was clearly trying to remember something.

"No one can know everything," said Zaitsev, trying to console him again. "Such a huge museum. Paintings here, there and everywhere."

"Are you mad?" squealed Alexei Alexandrovich. "This painting is not one you can confuse with another. Do you understand what a masterpiece is?"

My goodness, thought Zaitsev, what passion! He decided to give Alexei Alexandrovich a moment to calm down and pull himself together. He began watching the tour group. They followed the guide like calves following their mother.

Alexei Alexandrovich pulled out a handkerchief and wiped his forehead, as though this might help the thought process under his skull.

"Excuse me, citizen!" Zaitsev leapt to his feet, waving. The guide turned around and glared. "May I ask a question?"

"Are you with the group?" she asked sternly.

"I'm not, no."

"Well, I'm afraid you're interrupting us," she snapped before turning back to her flock. "The period of the emergence of capitalist relations in the Netherlands…"

Zaitsev knew how to handle people like her.

"Does that mean I'm not a Soviet person, then? That I have no right to access knowledge? We don't live under tsarism, in case you haven't noticed."

The vixen grimaced. "Let the comrade ask!"; "Shame not to let him"; "Maybe it'll be interesting for everyone"—there was a dissonant murmur of support from the group. They looked like students: broad faces, quite rustic-looking. Zaitsev felt kindly towards them.

"Tell me, do you know an artist called Van Eyck?"

A cold stare. Of course.

"How can I find his *Annunciation*? A famous painting. I'm very interested in seeing this masterpiece."

And then something amazing happened. It seemed to Zaitsev that for a moment her icy face cracked, as if struck from the inside with a hammer. Shattered to smithereens. But the next second the guide gathered herself. Her face turned cold again, just with two scarlet patches on her cheeks. And a third began to rise treacherously from under the high collar of her white blouse.

It seems her transformation didn't go unnoticed by the group.

"Don't you know?" came the voice of a comrade who sounded like it wasn't the first time he had pestered his guide with questions.

"Of course. I know. This. Painting," the vixen rapped out, turning her face to Zaitsev. "And you. Comrade. Are holding up. This. Group."

The group muttered their displeasure. Suddenly everyone wanted to see *The Annunciation*. And precisely this Van Eyck, about whom no one had cared a second ago.

"We'll go through to the next room!" the guide shouted in the piercing cry of a Neva seagull. And she shuffled through the open doorway in her clumsy shoe covers. The group grumbled, but after a moment of confusion they trundled after her—nobody wanted to miss what they had paid for, after all.

Zaitsev walked over to Alexei Alexandrovich.

"Well, it's just absurd." His cornflower-blue eyes looked up over his Chekhov spectacles. "I promised you *The Annunciation*, but it turns out it's not here." After a moment, he went on. "It's a good job the boy has tonsillitis. Youth doesn't take disappointment well."

Zaitsev almost asked, "What boy?" But he realized in time and gave a sympathetic nod.

"Alexei Alexandrovich," he said softly, sitting down beside him.

Again the cornflower-blue stare.

What the hell, Zaitsev thought to himself. And he pulled out the sheets of cigarette paper.

"Take a look at these."

Alexei Alexandrovich flipped through the sheets one by one. Faina Baranova. Karaseva. The two students. Again the women found in the church. Again Faina Baranova.

"You're not a teacher, are you?" asked Alexei Alexandrovich.

"No, I'm not a teacher."

II

"Alexei Alexandrovich, have another look. Are you sure?"

"Of course I'm sure!"

"I suppose you're based in the numismatics department—"

"Heraldry!" he cried out, as if he had been pinched. Zaitsev cursed himself silently. But the hamster had already seen red. "I see that for you, comrade, heraldry and numismatics are two equally unnecessary disciplines that serve only to overburden your minuscule brain!"

His spectacles flashed angrily.

Ah, the eloquence has awoken, thought Zaitsev. He waited out the explosion with his hands in the pockets of his cheap jacket.

"That's right," he agreed meekly. "That's why I decided to ask you as a man of education and culture."

It worked. Alexei Alexandrovich gave another irate puff, but then, it seemed, his anger subsided.

"Excuse me," he said. "I had no right to say that."

"Don't worry. I'm not easily offended," Zaitsev assured him.

But Alexei Alexandrovich wasn't convinced. "You see, for me the Hermitage is… This is my life. I knew straight away that my place was here, when I was still a student. Studying law. I could walk through this museum with my eyes closed and know where I was. There was no way the Imperial Hermitage would give me a job, so I came here as a volunteer."

Of comfortable means, then, thought Zaitsev. If he could work here without a salary.

Apparently, Alexei Alexandrovich guessed his thoughts exactly.

"I know what you're thinking," he said with a frown. "The parasitic classes."

"I didn't think anything of the sort," interrupted Zaitsev.

"Of course you did," Alexei Alexandrovich insisted, returning to a more affectionate tone. "You're a young man of a completely different era. And I'll tell you: the era has nothing to do with it. Young people's dreams are always forged from the same material. Regardless of the political system. For me, the Imperial Hermitage was like your… your Osoaviakhim? Did I pronounce it correctly? You probably show up to do your bit—unpaid, naturally."

His eyes were damp. He looked into the distance. Or more likely into the depths of time; somewhere in the distance he saw himself, the young lawyer.

Zaitsev held the sheets up closer.

"Is this also in the Hermitage?" he asked, bringing Alexei Alexandrovich back down to earth.

"Yes, this one is, too. It's… it's…" said Alexei Alexandrovich, jabbing a finger at the top of the sheet, almost breaking through the paper. "It's Dirk Bouts, *The Annunciation.*"

The students: Zaitsev made a mental note. Alexei Alexandrovich whisked this sheet behind the others.

"And this," he poked frantically at the pitiful figure of Fokin, the drunk who had frozen to death, his arms outstretched. "Watteau, *Mezzetino.*"

"And the painting's called?…" Zaitsev asked, marvelling at the artist's complicated name.

"*Mezzetino.*"

"Ah, great."

"Painted by. Antoine. Watteau."

"Also in the Hermitage?"

A withering look. "Yes. Everyone ought to know Watteau."

"OK. And the next one?"

Alexei Alexandrovich peered closely at the drawing of the photograph of the murdered corpse of Karaseva.

"What's that in her hand? A flower?"

"A carnation."

"This is Rembrandt," Alexei Alexandrovich answered, his voice suddenly dull, stifled. "*Woman with a Pink.*"

"A pink what? Who?"

A pause. His rounded shoulders rose and fell.

"Comrade Zaitsev, you could write a doctorate on this painting alone," he said sadly. And again fell silent.

"Also in the Hermitage?"

His silence could be taken for a yes.

"And this, Alexei Alexandrovich? Have a look: recognize it?"

Faina Baranova with the flower and her—or someone else's?—feather duster.

Alexei Alexandrovich seemed to have calmed down a little; his voice still sounded sad, but the words poured out of him again without any effort, like water from a tap. Zaitsev tried to engrave every word into his memory; he didn't know yet what detail might shed light on the murder of Faina Baranova, or how.

"This is Isabella Brandt. Better known as the first wife of Rubens. This portrait is by Van Dyck, a famous portraitist, extremely fashionable, very successful and renowned. Rubens himself painted several portraits of Isabella. But this one is from the Hermitage collection. Isabella died quite young by our standards, of the plague."

"Did they have children?" Zaitsev asked, just in case. Perhaps Faina Baranova only seemed to those around her like an old maid with no personal life, but in reality...

"Three."

Alexei Alexandrovich's astonishing memory was a delight to Zaitsev.

"Can I see them? Not the children, obviously. These paintings. Here in the Hermitage."

"Now?"

"Yes, now. If I may."

"The museum's closing soon. Visitors will be asked to leave." Alexei Alexandrovich glanced back at the darkening windows—he was clearly keen to get rid of this wearisome man with his endless questions.

"I didn't buy a ticket. That means I'm not a visitor. Lead on!"

"Where to?" Alexei Alexandrovich was confused.

"What do you mean where? You said all the paintings were kept together in their own halls."

"We've already been to the Dutch old masters."

"We didn't know that we also wanted to see these paintings."

"We went through those halls. They're not there."

"How do you know?"

281

"Young man!" His voice again broke into the shrill notes. "Your ignorance—"

"Oh, yes, my ignorance, I know"—Zaitsev raised his palms reassuringly. "I'm not arguing with you. So why do you think they are not there?"

"Because they are not there!"

Zaitsev was familiar with suspects breaking into "hysterics": seasoned criminals resorting to screaming and fighting, showering everyone and everything with abuse. But, apparently, this happened to the intelligentsia, too—in their own manner, naturally.

"I'm sure that for you," Alexei Alexandrovich said with caustic emphasis, "all these paintings are much of a muchness, but for other people, they are all unique, like the faces of loved ones. You would presumably notice if your beloved was not at home?"

"Yes, I'd say so," Zaitsev nodded. Can't say for sure, though, he thought with regret.

Zaitsev tried to answer quickly and concisely, so as not to rile his rather touchy interlocutor.

Alexei Alexandrovich shook his head with a sigh.

"OK then, let's go."

"Just one more question," said Zaitsev, leaning in so close that he could smell talcum powder from under the arms of the anxiously sweating Alexei Alexandrovich through his old but good-quality jacket. "If I described a picture to you, would you recognize it?"

"It depends on your literary prowess."

"That's to say, you could?"

"That's to say, I doubt it," Alexei Alexandrovich retorted. What a load of bull about fat people being good-natured. Alexei Alexandrovich was toxic.

"I'll try anyway," said Zaitsev, refusing to back down. A

caretaker passed through the empty room, questioning them with her eyes alone.

"We're leaving now!" Alexei Alexandrovich called to her in his most honeyed tone.

"Won't be a minute!" added Zaitsev. The caretaker glanced suspiciously at them both, but said nothing.

"So…" Zaitsev strained his memory. It plunged him straight into the dank morning twilight. Yelagin Park slept—a vast mass, darkly golden, like old brocade. His cold, sodden feet: he had trudged across the grass to the scene of the murder in the same canvas shoes he had on when he was arrested in June. The bushes. A yellowing tree. The dawn sky was gradually turning blue. The bridge was visible at a distance. The orange shirt of the black American Communist blazed like fire, immediately drawing his eye. The centre of the group wasn't the black man, though, but a woman in costume jewellery. The corpse of the old woman was on her knees, her arms outspread: a sheet was thrown over them. Another murdered woman, also on her knees, younger. A cry. A baby! In the arms of the murdered woman. As if the old woman had just been handed him, the only one among them still alive, by the other corpse.

Zaitsev fell silent.

Alexei Alexandrovich looked down at the rounded snouts of his felt slippers. Shit. He doesn't seem to recognize it…

"I could try to sketch it on a piece of paper? Here, on the back." Zaitsev began to fuss. Shit. Have I cocked it up?

Alexei Alexandrovich finally parted his lips.

"Judging by your description, it's *The Finding of Moses*. Paolo Veronese," he said. And then a malicious spark flashed in his eyes. "Moses is the baby depicted in the picture. Veronese is the artist who painted it," he explained scornfully.

Zaitsev's heart started racing.

"Will you show me?"

Alexei Alexandrovich already understood that there was only one way to get rid of his guest, and he stood up from the scarlet settee.

"Why not. Come on."

Alexei Alexandrovich walked as if deflated. It was obvious that he was tired. A caretaker with a grey moustache was already shutting the doors labelled with a brass plaque reading "Venice Sixteenth Century". But he recognized Alexei Alexandrovich.

"You're rather late."

"We'll only be a second." Alexei Alexandrovich had again turned into the lovable chubby hamster he was the first time Zaitsev met him at the entrance to the Mariinsky Theatre. "There's a Veronese I'd like to show my friend. We've been arguing about the dating. There's a beer at stake, by the way."

Well, he made light work of that—lying like a pro, thought Zaitsev.

"It's a deal." The caretaker smiled, with one hand opening the door to let them in, and flicking the light switch on with the other. The lamps immediately glowed with a yellow light.

"And you'll be owing me that beer!" Zaitsev called out cheerfully and loudly.

But there was nothing cheerful about this. It was eerie. As if something was behind the heavy curtains of blue silk, watching them (but with a knife at the ready). Alexei Alexandrovich scanned the walls, the paintings, making ridiculous circuits of the room, as if he was demonstrating a waltz without a partner.

In this entire blue hall, there was no Moses.

III

Zaitsev strode to Konyushennaya Square. Or at least, that's the direction he presumed he was going in. The winter haze had already rendered the houses identical. The wind was trying to tear the globe-shaped bulbs from the street lamps. The snow whipped at you like wet ropes. Zaitsev could only lift his face occasionally before receiving another icy slap in the face and immediately nestling his chin back down into his scarf. A few rare pedestrians hurried past, bent over and peering up from under their brows. Zaitsev's thoughts carried him far away. For the last hour he had been wandering without thinking. It was only when he suddenly came round that he peered ahead at someone familiar and thought: definitely! It wasn't so much a face that he recognized, or a silhouette, but a gait.

"Alla!" he called out.

But at that moment a tram in the square, filled with light and silhouettes, noisily made a turn and—amid all the rattling and grinding—Alla, if it was her, didn't seem to hear him. Her figure quickly receded, leaning into the wind. Zaitsev picked up his pace, but he kept his distance, though he wasn't entirely sure why. Probably because she said they had an opera today, and the costumes assistant was ill, and she would have to stay at work until long after the performance had finished—she couldn't leave until she had put away all the costumes.

Zaitsev hurried on in pursuit, suppressing the voice inside that kept telling him it was pointless and he shouldn't run after her.

Alla turned into the gateway of a reddish house. Zaitsev looked around: it was Baskov Lane. He watched carefully. Clutching her handbag under her arm, Alla walked diagonally across the inner courtyard to the only entrance. The door issued a cloud of vapour and banged shut behind her. Zaitsev quickly noted all the windows with lights on. First floor. Third on the left. Fourth. Fifth. How long did Alla need to walk upstairs? He mentally climbed each flight with her. Now she was on the second floor. The little landing. Then up another flight. The third floor. Suddenly, a male silhouette stood at one of the windows. Someone had obviously knocked on the door. Not a communal flat, then. The man then disappeared back into the room. Had he gone to open the door? Then there were two people in the room. A female silhouette. The man went to the window, drew the curtain.

Zaitsev didn't feel jealousy or anger. Just surprise. The jealousy clearly hadn't yet reached his consciousness. He ought to wait here, by the entrance or under the arch. What do jealous lovers do when they've been deceived? Or maybe he wasn't jealous because he had no right to be? Zaitsev glanced again at the thick curtains. Or was he perhaps jealous after all?

"Right. Well," he said aloud.

What to do now? Should he do anything at all? What?

Suppose he waited for her here. Caught her red-handed? Then what? Have an argument? What were you supposed to do in these circumstances?

The seconds ticked by, crept by like ants that had started scouting out his body. He shuddered. To hell with this! He couldn't hang around here waiting for her. Back on Gorokhovaya Street, all the windows on their floor would be lit, thick grey smoke swirling from several cigarettes; the team would be rattling through their end-of-the-day catch-up on the Yelagin Island murder investigation. Wouldn't they all be surprised when he!...

Zaitsev stepped out from the arch.

When he got to Gorokhovaya, the snow on his coat and hat had become a thick, icy crust. He was so cold that at first he didn't feel the heat in the lobby. The green lamp glowed on the desk by the attendant. The cleaning lady pushed a rag up the stairs, her backside swaying. Zaitsev ran up beside her, dripping chunks of ice.

"For crying out loud! I've just scrubbed that!"

He quickly pushed the door to the office: empty. The entire building: all the lights were off. Kopteltsev's office: locked. He darted back down the wet stairs.

"Where's Demov? Samoilov? Where is everyone?"

The duty officer stared at Zaitsev, perplexed. In violation of the rules, he took off his helmet and stood it on the table like an outlandish paperweight. It was from this gesture that Zaitsev realized that neither Kopteltsev, Demov nor Samoilov was in the department—no one who might have had something to say about it.

"At the pub," the duty officer finally answered.

"At the pub? How come?"

"Celebrating."

"Which pub?"

"The usual."

Zaitsev didn't stay to hear any more, but dashed back out into the snowstorm. There was only one bar that could be "the usual": the one on the Fontanka embankment. The steps led down to a basement and a sign saying "Tea room", but that didn't fool anyone. He himself had celebrated many successful operations here with his comrades—when they were still comrades in the usual, rather than the Communist, sense of the word. Back in a time that now seemed mythical to Zaitsev.

He guessed right.

"Vasya!" came a joyful yell from Samoilov as he raised his bulky tankard. Faces turned towards him. Cigarette smoke floated beneath the low ceiling, and around the dim bulbs gathered a halo of human exhalation. Their faces were all radiant.

"Hey, Vasya!"

"Come and join us!"

For a moment, it almost seemed as though none of it had happened: the new director, Zaitsev's arrest, the summer in the OGPU prison, the strange return straight onto the Yelagin Island homicide case, and the even stranger boycott that squeezed him off the case again. Kopteltsev's collar was unbuttoned, his fat chin spilling out of the top. Serafimov was ruddy. Demov's eyes had a sentimental sparkle. Everyone had already managed to put away a few.

"Well, have a seat then!" Kopteltsev waved his fat hand.

"Waitress!" shouted Samoilov. "Another large over here!"

"And snacks!" Demov raised his empty plate.

"And snacks!"

Zaitsev sat down. He suddenly felt as light as a traveller returning home from a dangerous expedition.

"Why are you beaming like a bridegroom?" asked Kopteltsev, mocking him amiably.

"He's dug something up, that's why. Do you think I don't know him?" muttered Demov, tipping the bottle; the clear liquid glugged into his glass. "What you having? Double or a triple?" he asked, holding up the bottle by its neck.

"Come on then. Out with it. Before you burst." Samoilov slapped him on the shoulder. "What have you got?"

Zaitsev gestured to show "Just a small one". Demov nodded, slammed the bottle down on the table and handed him a glass.

"Wait, wait—the boss has got something to say."

Kopteltsev stood up, clutching his tankard.

"Comrades. Speaking officially."

"Look at him," mocked Serafimov. "All official now, are we?"

"Serafimov, shut up! Or he'll lose his train of thought!"

"Officially," said Kopteltsev, raising a glass. "Our investigation has been a colossal success."

"Colossal cesspit, more like," Samoilov interposed with a drunken slur.

Kopteltsev didn't seem to hear.

"We did a great job."

"Which investigation?" Zaitsev leant towards Samoilov with a smile.

"You know, the black man from what's it—Yelagin. Remember?"

"Oh yeah?" Zaitsev felt his face go numb, as if a dentist had injected him with novocaine.

"...a nest woven from threads that ensnared the leadership of the Leningrad factory..." Kopteltsev's voice seemed to come from under a pillow. Zaitsev caught the name Firsov, the words "vermin" and "sabotage".

"Nest?" Zaitsev couldn't believe his ears.

"Yeah, they bumped off the black man, remember? Enemies," Samoilov confided. He was bleary-eyed, with a reckless glint.

"The American Communist, that is," Demov corrected him. "Casting a shadow on the Soviet people," he explained while chewing, his Adam's apple bobbing up and down. Kopteltsev was still droning on. "And this Firsov—turns out he was a German spy."

He pointed to Kopteltsev, as if to say, "Listen to him." Still he droned on with his radio broadcast.

"...comrades from OGPU, to whom we at CID owe sincere thanks."

"They twisted our arms, Vasya! Oh, they did," Samoilov sandwiched in, without any connection. "You just listen, I..."

Demov appeared to have kicked something under the table, accidentally; it tumbled with a clatter and rolled. Samoilov let out a brief, jovial expletive before diving with one arm under the table to catch the empty bottles and line them up.

"What did you want to say, Vasya?" Demov leant over sympathetically, his elbow missing the table and almost sending the remaining snacks flying. "You rushed in at the speed of light."

And Zaitsev suddenly realized that the relaxed, friendly expressions on their faces had nothing at all to do with him. It wasn't friendliness. It was that fuzziness that softens the sharp corners of the world that you only get from the hard stuff. There wasn't anything to celebrate at all.

"Me? Oh, nothing. I was just frozen like a dog, so I ran to warm up my insides a little."

"Ah, very wise." Samoilov either believed him or pretended to.

A middle-aged waitress in a grubby apron slammed down a bowl of salted peas in front of Zaitsev. Then a plate of roughly chopped herring. Onion rings. Last of all, a slightly misty bottle of vodka. Which Samoilov immediately reached for.

It occurred to Zaitsev that, actually, it was precisely what he needed right now.

"Go on then, Samoilov."

Alla quickly shook off her drowsiness. She unfastened the chain, opened the door.

"Come in, then. I thought you said you weren't coming today."

"It isn't today, it's tomorrow. Or rather, that was yesterday, and now it's today."

She started to brush the snow off his coat.

"No, don't. You'll catch a cold. I'll do it."

He swayed from side to side. His breath told the rest of the story.

"You've been drinking?"

He waved his hand as if to say, "Huh, so what?" He suddenly felt exhausted and ravenous, but more exhausted. He sat straight down on the rack where the neighbours' galoshes stood in a row.

"With the comrades. Alla, where have you been?"

"Me? At work." Her tone was completely natural. "Shall I make some tea? I won't be long."

"At work?"

"Well, yes. How strange you are. Three acts, as usual. The costumes girl was ill. Didn't I say? I think I said."

"I think you did," Zaitsev answered peaceably.

"What?"

"What what?"

"Why are you looking at me like that?"

Her face seemed bluish in the low lighting. And very, very honest. An ordinary face. Beautiful. As always.

"Nothing. Let's just go to sleep."

Chapter 14

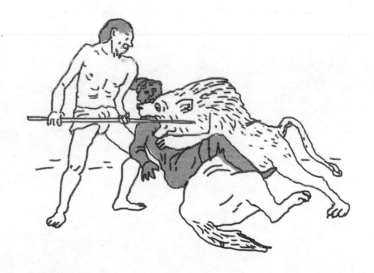

I

This was a place where time came to a standstill. Huge shelves lined every wall, stretching up to the high ceiling. The tempests of history, raging outside, collided with these racks and ebbed away with a whimper. But spring, sun, youth, all ebbed away, too. Branches covered with the first delicate, sticky April buds tapped on the window in vain. The smell of antiquity was ever present here, under the aegis of books: old wood, old paper—not cheap, dusty, decaying paper, but aged, mature and yellowing nobly. The daylight tried fruitlessly to break in through the windows. It was always early evening here, cosily marked out by the light of the table lamps with their green shades that were a balsam for the eyes. The public library forged its passage through time like a colossal, sturdy ship.

Zaitsev had at first thought of trying Alexei Alexandrovich again. "He's off sick," came a squeaking tenor down the line. Zaitsev didn't have time to ask anything else before the short beeps hit his ear: they had already hung up. It seemed to Zaitsev that it might have been Alexei Alexandrovich himself who had answered.

He tried again to get through, but no one would pick up. He asked the operator to put him through to the research department ("Say it's CID"). The line crackled as the receiver was placed on the table. Then the receding click of high heels walking away. Then approaching again.

Again the crackle. Then the same answer, but this time in a female voice: "He's off sick."

Zaitsev quickly tracked down Alexei Alexandrovich's home address, on the former Grechesky Prospekt. But the room was locked, the neighbours shrugged, and Zaitsev had no warrant to break in. He bashed his fist into the door jamb. He couldn't deny he'd messed up. He had scared him off with the phone calls. Alexei Alexandrovich, the grey hamster, had run away. As a representative of the obsolete class, he can't have been comfortable with the close attention of the law-enforcement agencies.

And so Zaitsev had become the owner of a library card and had come here to browse.

At first, Zaitsev felt like his footsteps were making an unthinkable, shameful noise. Trying to step as lightly as possible, he tiptoed to an empty table, carefully lowered onto it a stack of books he had ordered and switched on one of the soothing green lamps. He silently sank into a chair and, quietly, as if even his eyes could disturb the peace, glanced around the room. There were several rows of tables. In the cones of light from the table lamps shone the inclined bald patches of venerable researchers and the bare elbows of female students. Male students too, of course, but they weren't so interesting. Zaitsev especially liked the look of one student: with lush, unruly hair, she almost seemed to be writing with her nose, bending right down to the table with her beautiful myopic eyes. A Jewish princess, no less. Pages were turned quietly; pencils scribbled away quietly. A young man in a long Tolstoy shirt, slumped onto the table: closed eyelids behind thick glasses. Zaitsev suppressed a yawn, took the first slim book from the top of the heap and opened it up.

The image of the murdered students hit him square in the eyes. It was only after a second that Zaitsev realized it wasn't the corpses before him—not a picture taken at the scene of the crime, but a young woman in a gown heeding the words of a sharp-winged angel. *The Annunciation*, he read.

Wherever Alexei Alexandrovich had disappeared to, it hardly mattered: Zaitsev no longer needed him.

Zaitsev's fingers didn't tremble as he leafed through page by page. His thoughts were not muddled. His head was light and clear. Only his heart pounded in his ribcage.

He found all the pictures relatively quickly in the book.

Zaitsev peered at the black-and-white photographs of these paintings that were strangely familiar to him—and yet he was seeing them for the first time. It was eerie to see them in their true form, albeit as illustrations in a guidebook. And not through the distorted mirror of a crime scene.

It was eerie and strange. Zaitsev was particularly struck by the multi-figured and magnificent *The Finding of Moses*. He gave this reproduction a long examination. The women, the black man, the baby. Even the path and the trees. But nevertheless, this was the picture that the killer (or killers) had reproduced with the least insistence on accuracy: there were fewer corpses at Yelagin Park than figures in this painting, and for this Zaitsev was deeply grateful.

He tore himself away from the page to take a breather. Again he directed a stealthy glance at the Jewish princess, diligently scribbling a summary of the large book she was holding open at the top; her hand seemed especially pale, young and beautiful against the background of the old, yellowing pages. Zaitsev looked around. Profiles of readers hunched over. And in front of him a nape, another and another. Zaitsev flinched: one face was turned towards him. Zaitsev ducked straight back down to his book. He had a feeling it was the old bat who had given the guided tour at the Hermitage: "the period of the emergence of capitalist relations in the Netherlands…" Her hair was twisted into two plaited snakes diverging from the middle of her forehead. He cautiously peered up again. But she had already turned her back.

II

"Vladilen Tractorov." Nefyodov stepped back to admire his handiwork. He had attached a few more sheets to their chart, from top to bottom.

"Tractorov?" Zaitsev was somewhat surprised by the eccentric name.

"The name they gave him in the detention centre. Vladimir Lenin—Vladilen. A hint at a new, more Soviet life."

The boy's former lifestyle had been opaquely anti-Soviet. A street kid who dealt cocaine in working districts, mercilessly cut with chalk, flour and aspirin. He had been detained several times by CID.

"We've got his prints here."

No documents, no relatives. He was eventually put in a juvenile detention centre, from which he didn't manage to escape. Then he was transferred to a vocational college for an apprenticeship. From there, he disappeared. Only to be picked up again by CID. But this time as a victim. The corpse was sitting at a table. The tabletop was scattered with playing cards.

Nefyodov gave his address.

"Why do you think this new case is one of ours, Nefyodov? That apartment has long been known to CID."

Leningrad's casinos and gambling halls had recently been shut down: they were a token of the NEP, the New Economic Policy that had since been revoked. But the gamblers hadn't gone anywhere. Neither had the hustlers or the card sharps. They had just gone underground.

"There's big money at stake," continued Zaitsev. "Mainly

business travellers they rip off. They find them through the hotels—the Astoria and Hotel Europe. Anywhere where the customers are on the larger size. They've got a place where you can have some fun while you make a pretty penny. At first they let them win little by little; they lead them on, then clean them out."

"So they usually go for the larger customer, but this time... an apprentice? He had nothing to take. Nothing but the shirt on his back."

"Perhaps this bright young thing," suggested Zaitsev, "decided to try his luck for something better. But he got in too deep and the sharpies did away with him."

"And how do you explain the house of cards?"

"House?" asked Zaitsev, turning to face him. "I can't see any house in the picture."

Nefyodov put his hands together in the shape of a roof.

"Yes, Nefyodov, I know what a house of cards is. And?"

"Well, the table got knocked before they took the picture. The cards went everywhere."

"Oh. A house, you say..."

Zaitsev hesitated. It was certainly odd. If this was a message from the card sharps, a kind of warning, then he had to admit that he hadn't seen anything like it before.

"We need to have a word with our friend Misha. Maybe they've changed their old MO down there, while we've been chasing drunkards and thieves in Okhta."

"But look at his hair. And the weird coat."

It was true Tractorov's hairstyle really was unusual for an apprentice. He was dressed in a long frock coat. His hair had been curled and combed into a neat parting.

"OK, let's say you're right. Go on." Zaitsev nodded.

Nefyodov turned to the chart with a pencil in his hand. And he began to read out the names in the Tractorov case, which he had already written in the columns. His roommates in the student dorms. The other students. His teachers.

"Any crossovers?" asked Zaitsev.

"None."

"That's it, Nefyodov. That's it."

There were no crossovers on the entire chart. They had already had to glue on several additional sheets. The chart had taken on a life of its own. But in no way had it brought them any closer to solving the riddle. There were still no intersections or mutual acquaintances among the victims from any of the paintings.

"A bloody waste of time," Nefyodov summed up. He threw his pencil like a small spear and it landed perfectly in the glass on the table.

"Wait a minute," muttered Zaitsev thoughtfully, peering at the columns of names. "Nefyodov, have you ever heard of the theory that everyone in the world is linked by just six handshakes?"

"What do you mean?"

"Supposedly everyone is connected with everyone else at a remove of no more than six people. I know someone who knows someone who knows someone who knows you."

"Seems unlikely." Nefyodov didn't have much faith in the gigantic chart, even though he worked on it with the zeal of a bureaucrat. "It'll stretch as far as the corridor soon, but what's the point?"

Trying to roll it up, Zaitsev struggled with the unwieldy sheet as though it were a sail.

"We don't have a lot to go on, true. Patience, my friend, patience."

"Patience," he repeated to him back in the office on Gorokhovaya Street.

His desk was already piled high with a mountain of files. The typewriter stared at him with a grimace. The day ahead looked as tedious as usual.

Nefyodov dragged himself down to the basement, to the depths of the archives. Nobody tended to notice him much; he had already become something of a shaggy underground gnome, except without a beard.

Zaitsev didn't rush to open up the files. He stood at the window and looked down at the Fontanka. But what if Nefyodov was right? That Tractorov was one of theirs. What painting should he look out for? Let's say he struck lucky and stumbled upon it in the Hermitage after only three weeks of searching. He could start with a guidebook, of course, in the hope that this painting was large and famous enough to be considered of interest to art lovers. But what if it was small and not well known? Or if it wasn't in the Hermitage at all this time? And what if it wasn't a painting at all, and Tractorov just got bumped off by a hustler, and the house of cards was nothing but an eccentric, yet meaningless detail? Gangster chic, and nothing more to it?

In any case, it would be five days before he could start digging around: he couldn't do anything until the weekend, when his time belonged to him alone. In the meantime... Zaitsev sighed, overcame his loathing and loaded the first sheet of the day into the typewriter.

III

But he only held out until lunchtime. The canteen was a cacophony of fumes and clatter, but there was no sign of Squad 2. An aroma of cabbage spiralled from the huge vats: cabbage soup. He was starving.

Five more days, then it was his day off. Five whole days!

Zaitsev resolutely left the queue (it immediately closed up to take his space). He'd get by without.

Outside, there had been a sudden thaw. His shoes squelched in the icy slush. The sky was reflected in the dove-grey puddles, with crumbs of ice. Zaitsev thought of the bakery at the junction of Nevsky and Liteyny. Maybe there was one closer; he couldn't remember. He crossed Nevsky under the very nose of a tram, narrowly missed a black Ford, a horse and cart. Leningrad was the former capital of the empire, even now the second-largest city in the USSR. But pedestrians behaved like it was a village, crossing the street wherever they wanted, whenever they wanted, cutting straight across, diagonally, or even wandering along the carriageway, listlessly dodging the few cars. Most of them had recently been villagers, after all, who poured into the city in search of work. They still had their provincial habits, never mind that they were lethal with the city traffic.

Zaitsev followed the tram tracks. On the other side, the view opened up where Liteyny Prospekt heads for the River Neva. That is, Volodarsky Prospekt, of course. Zaitsev saw a cluster of people crowded together, their backs facing outwards. Of course! A second-hand bookstall! That was even better than a library. He forgot all about the bakery, quickly ran across the intersection, oblivious to the cursing and car horns flying about behind him. He quickly edged his way in, nudging elbows with an intelligent-looking kind of clientele, to get to the books laid out in fans and terraces.

Here was every kind of book imaginable. Creamy paperbacks: poetry collections. Hardbacks with spines embossed with lustreless golden lettering: collected works, printed with the obsolete letters ѣ and ъ. Volumes of magazines shouted for attention, bound in covers with marbled patterns.

The second-hand bookseller gave him an aloof glance.

Must be my face, Zaitsev noted, because the second-hand bookseller couldn't have objected to his poor, shabby clothes: the other browsers looked like perfect beggars. Moving along the stall, Zaitsev stepped on a few more toes.

"The comrade'll have Nat Pinkerton and the pamphlet on Communist sexual hygiene," came a snide comment from behind him. Zaitsev ignored him; he didn't turn around. He finally managed to catch the eye of the second-hand bookseller.

"Have you got a guide to the Hermitage?"

No response. He hadn't heard, presumably. He calmly handed another customer three books, with squares and triangles on the cover. He took the customer's money. Then he ducked under the table. Zaitsev was seized with irritation. Typical Leningrad snobbery. The bookseller surfaced with a stack of books, handed someone a volume. And then he suddenly shoved a small book towards Zaitsev. Again without looking at him. And then he started having a cordial conversation with another customer—a regular. Oh well, what difference did it make? It was a guide to the Hermitage. Zaitsev began to turn pages.

"Have you come to buy or to read? It's not a library," one of the browsers reminded him coldly.

Zaitsev ignored him. "How much?" he shouted to the stallholder, who was facing away.

He named the price.

Zaitsev had no idea if it was expensive or cheap, if you were supposed to haggle here or not. He didn't have much hope of asking anyone. He handed over the money. The stallholder shoved it in his pocket without counting it. Zaitsev worked his way back out through the crowd. He tucked the small, thick book into his coat pocket. Then he changed his mind and transferred it to his inside pocket. And then he couldn't wait any longer, so he stepped away from the scurrying stream of passers-by and eagerly opened it.

IV

In the dim light of the corridor, Zaitsev straight away noticed the strip of yellow light coming from under his door. Someone was in his room. His immediate thought was of certain uninvited guests. Zaitsev stopped. He held his breath. Silently retreat? Quietly leave the apartment and get away before it was too late? Or was it already too late? His hand quietly found the cold grip of his pistol. Zaitsev hid his hand and the gun in his pocket. Of course, it wouldn't come to shooting: that lot were wimps, they wouldn't risk getting shot at. And he had no intention of firing. It would only be to make them leave. To force a retreat. And get the envelope. If it wasn't already too late. He silently gripped the handle and pushed the door open.

Alla was sitting at the table. She looked at him, moved her gaze to his hands.

"The Hermitage?" asked a surprised Alla. "It's that where you've been?"

He realized that he was still holding the small guidebook in his other hand: an impromptu shield in case of a knife attack.

"Well, I'm a history teacher, now. Got to look the part," he answered with a frown.

Alla's face froze. But then she went back to normal, her eyebrows softened. "Is that why you don't call any more, you don't visit?"

Instinctively, Zaitsev glanced behind the door. All clear. Hard as it was to believe. He walked into the room. He put the guidebook on the table.

"Will you have some dinner?" Alla asked in a deliberately casual tone.

"Alla…"

"Listen, I know." She laid her hands on his shoulders. For a moment, he placed his hands on top of hers. He felt their soft warmth. He took them off.

"And I know that it would be better if we took a short technical break," he said firmly. It's not worth getting upset about, he reminded himself—but of course he was. He couldn't help it.

"Technical?" Alla shrank back. "Technical?"

"So you don't object to the word 'break'?"

Alla picked up the saucepan from the table and took off the lid. The fragrant steam escaped. She ran to the window, turned the latch, opened the window and tipped out the contents of the pan. And then threw the pan down too.

"I should have known I had this coming!" she cried with tears in her voice.

"Alla!"

She grabbed her coat and hurried out of the room.

"*Eugene could never bear tragic manifestations, girlish faints or tearful lamentations,*" muttered Zaitsev, thinking of Pushkin's *Onegin.* He was furious with himself.

Should he run down the corridor after her? Was it too late?

He threw open the window. A figure flitted out of the front door.

"Alla! Wait!"

She didn't even turn around.

But Pasha turned and looked up from where she was scraping the snow with her prickly broom.

Zaitsev saw a crow hurl itself from a tree onto the discarded dinner below. It was a banquet down there. At least someone would enjoy it.

How could he make it up to her now? What did people do in situations like this? Zaitsev walked to the table, racking his brains. But he stood there and couldn't find a single thought in his head.

Behind him came a delicate knock. Oh, thank goodness! He rushed to open the door.

But it was Pasha. Zaitsev felt a pang of disappointment, to his surprise.

"Ah, Pasha. Hello."

She was holding the saucepan.

"I shouldn't have let her in, should I?" Pasha seemed surprisingly wrongfooted. "Never can tell with you. You Komsomoltsi these days, you never get married." She grumbled on, hamming it up. "You never can tell these days what's going on: are they living together or not? Is it all over between you, then? Or not? Well, I'm sorry. But next time just say: should I let her in or not? Are you going to have something to eat?"

"I don't know, Pasha," came his irritated answer to at least one of her questions. "Maybe best not stick your nose in where it doesn't belong."

But nothing could cast a shadow over Pasha's joy. And nothing could distract Zaitsev from what was of most interest to him at that moment.

Still in his coat, he sat down at the table and opened the guidebook on the page he had bookmarked. The painting was called *The House of Cards*.

V

The Hermitage was exhausting. Huge broad staircases, echoing halls, mighty columns, and gold, gold, gold: all intended for people with plenty of time and nowhere to rush off to. Designed for leisurely processions and promenades. And certainly not for anyone who needed to dash through almost at a trot.

In vain, Zaitsev flicked through the pages whose corners he had turned over. No matter how many halls he tried, he couldn't find any of the paintings he wanted to see.

The guide was old, from before the Revolution. It was probably out of date. Zaitsev decided to give in and ask.

"Excuse me, but how can I see this picture?" Zaitsev approached a man with the look of a professor. It was obvious from his brisk, no-nonsense gait that he wasn't a tourist.

"Sorry, I don't work here!" he responded, not pausing or slowing down.

"What are you after, comrade?" asked an attendant, appearing out of nowhere. Had she been hiding behind the curtain or something?

The guidebook, its spine softened by use, fell open on the right page. The attendant slowly clicked open her spectacles case and mounted them on her nose. She looked at the illustration.

"Chardin's *The House of Cards*," she read. In a perfectly ordinary tone of voice. But it made Zaitsev jump to hear the name pronounced out loud.

"You'll need the French paintings. Go straight on—"

"I know," interrupted Zaitsev. "I've just come from there. But the thing is, citizen, the picture isn't there."

"You probably didn't notice it," she quickly explained.

"Perhaps. But then your colleague also didn't notice it?"

"So you've ask—"

"Yes, I asked," Zaitsev interrupted.

"…asked? And?"

"It wasn't there."

"Well, that means it doesn't belong to the Hermitage."

"It says here that it does." Zaitsev whipped out the guidebook, flicked through and showed her the cover. The attendant examined it incredulously.

"That's from before the Revolution. The exhibition might have been reviewed. It's sure to have been reviewed."

"And what does that mean?" Zaitsev decided to stick to the role of the good-natured fool. "They've swapped them around or something?"

"They might have been moved. If it's not considered of great artistic value it might have been archived."

"Put in a storeroom, you mean?"

A nod.

"I see. And if they're in the storeroom, can I go and see them?"

"What? Are you out of your mind?" She looked at him as if he were about to take his trousers down. But suddenly Zaitsev's attention shifted: he saw that they were being watched. Two twisted snakes on her head, the narrow skirt, narrow lips. The old bat. Not only had she noticed him, but she also recognized him. Or did it just seem that way? That all of a sudden everyone was interested in him and these paintings?

"Well, yes, that's what I thought." He brought the conversation to a swift end. Aren't they good at creeping up on you in their felt shoe covers? "Thank you," he added and made a swift move for the door.

Behind him he caught a quiet but distinct voice, sensing it in his spine more than in his ears.

"What was he looking for?"

"*The House of Cards.*"

But Zaitsev couldn't stop. And that was all he heard.

VI

Zaitsev's legs were buzzing. He only had to close his eyes and all he could see under his eyelids were frames, frames,

frames—like you get after a whole day fishing, when all you can picture is the float bobbing about before you. A negative result is still a result, he reminded himself.

Zaitsev had really walked around all the halls he had book-marked in the guidebook. And he hadn't found a single one of the pictures he was looking for.

The two *Annunciations* by Bouts and Van Eyck weren't there.

The portrait of Isabella Brandt wasn't there.

The Woman with a Pink by Rembrandt wasn't there.

Veronese's *The Finding of Moses* wasn't there, either.

Nor was Watteau's *Mezzetino*.

And *The House of Cards*, depicted by the poor murdered Tractorov: that wasn't there, either.

These were major paintings in all respects. Both the size of the canvas and the stature of the masters who painted them. Objects of considerable value. As far as Zaitsev could judge from what he had read, of course.

Perhaps the guidebook he had bought from the second-hand bookseller really was out of date. But if the book could be believed, then Alexei Alexandrovich was not mistaken. The paintings had simply disappeared from the museum.

"Bloody hell," said Nefyodov when Zaitsev told him about his findings. Or rather about what he hadn't found. They were standing in a pub. A poster on the wall was just visible through the cigarette smoke: "When I eat, I am deaf and mute." Slowly their untouched beer warmed up and the head settled.

"So, what you're saying is, it's like chucking out the *Bronze Horseman*?" Nefyodov clarified. Rembrandt and the other names were all new to him.

"Yeah, not far off," said Zaitsev, throwing a salty cracker into his mouth. "And the Academic Theatre, Kazan Cathedral and St Isaac's while you're at it."

The waitress brought their sausages and cabbage. She pushed Nefyodov's cap out of the way and put down the plates. Nefyodov shoved his cap in his pocket.

"But why?" The obvious question.

Zaitsev stuck his fork into a grey sausage; juice sprayed out.

For a while both chewed vigorously, as if choosing to follow the recommendations of the poster to the letter. In fact, they simply had no answer to that question.

Instead all they had was a downpour of questions.

Theft? It could be. Burglars were everywhere, museums were no exception. But to pilfer a massive canvas in a heavy frame? And why would the State Hermitage Museum have kept it a secret? Why wouldn't they have reported it to the police?

Zaitsev felt like a bloodhound rushing about following a trail that had split in two. It had diverged. And it wasn't clear now which one to run after.

"So, what have we got, Nefyodov? On the one hand, someone's killed almost a dozen citizens, right? On the other hand, someone's stolen paintings from the State Hermitage. All paintings of considerable value. Or perhaps they weren't stolen. Perhaps they were just put into storage."

"What difference does it make if they're of considerable value?" Nefyodov sipped his beer.

"Because they're not of ideological value," suggested Zaitsev. "Not in harmony with the Soviet system."

Nefyodov nodded.

But Zaitsev himself didn't feel the answer was convincing.

How many times had it happened that they hadn't found what they were looking for. They had been looking for a missing husband and instead had uncovered embezzlement at a bank. They had been looking for whoever had bumped off a prostitute, and ended up discovering a cocaine den. Now he had a similar feeling. But what was the connection between the victims? And what did the paintings have to do with it?

Zaitsev was faced with a heap of information.

Well, let it grow, he decided. They had to keep going. They needed to keep collecting clues, evidence, strange cases, seemingly unrelated facts, motley detritus, unremarkable and insignificant information, trivia, minutiae. Let the heap grow and grow. It would reach a critical mass, and then it would fall. Like an avalanche down a hill. It would rush down, sweeping away all the disproven theories, leaving behind just one: the right answer.

"These sausages—not bad," he said, his mouth full. He skewered another piece on his fork and nodded to Nefyodov with his chin.

VII

In fact, he wasn't even sure that they were faced with two directions.

Perhaps the paintings were in fact just a smokescreen, one that the criminal hoped would disgust, scare, confuse and distract from what actually connected all these murders. That is, the true connection that could ultimately lead to the killer: that was where they needed to dig.

Perhaps the paintings themselves were lying in crates in the museum's warehouse. Zaitsev was aware that even something as big as a theatre or a museum was in fact much larger than what was visible to the general public. There was the world backstage—the engine rooms, warehouses and workshops—and it all ticked over twenty-four hours a day, not just when they let in ticketed visitors. If that was the case, there was no conundrum.

311

And perhaps, in the case of the group murder on Yelagin Island, they had long ago found the evidence that explained it all. It wasn't for nothing that they had worked for almost half a year, with reinforcements, at a relentless pace.

This was how Zaitsev reasoned as he stared at the white sheet of paper sticking out of the typewriter.

It was all possible.

Zaitsev had very few rules in his own little rule book. But one of them was, if something was ringing alarm bells, then there was definitely something to it.

Zaitsev puffed out his cheeks, exhaled and yanked the unfinished report from the typewriter. He quickly inserted a clean piece of paper and bashed at the keys, sprinkling a row of letters onto the page.

In another folder, he easily found Kopteltsev's signature. At first he went over it with pencil, pressing down onto a sheet below—the file was headed for the archive, anyway. He then went over the imprint carefully in ink. Then he compared the result with the original.

He let it dry. For a moment he felt a pang of conscience. In principle, Nefyodov personally hadn't caused him any harm. And yet, said another, more cynical voice. Yes, the risk still remained. Not only might Nefyodov be transferred to a remote northern garrison as some kind of security guard, he might even be brought before the purge committee. But, perhaps that was for the best—otherwise, how would he ever get rid of Nefyodov, his attentive owl eyes?... Zaitsev's conscience spoke up again, the same nagging voice: Nefyodov hadn't himself done anything to harm him; if he had wanted to, he would have done so long ago. Never mind—Zaitsev quickly silenced the inner voice. Your GPU mates will get you out somehow.

He folded the sheet in half.

With the files under his arm, he quickly ran downstairs to the basement, to the archive. The dim yellow light was on as always. Nefyodov's shaggy head emerged from behind the counter.

Zaitsev had already opened his mouth when he heard someone's footsteps. Someone was approaching.

"Nefyodov, it's a while since you've been out to see if it's night or day! How can you tell down here without any windows?" His tone was aloof.

"Not at all, Comrade Zaitsev," Nefyodov answered, his reply not fitting the question.

"Anyway, well done." Zaitsev gave him a wink. He slammed the files onto the counter and went out.

Nefyodov picked up the files and took them over to the table.

"Hey, is there anyone here? Come and take this evidence." The voice was at the counter; an impatient palm hit the button of the bell a couple of times.

"Coming," replied Nefyodov sullenly.

Then he went back to the table and pushed the folders aside; he would have time to register them in a minute. Instead, he unfolded the sheet Zaitsev had left and carefully studied its contents.

Chapter 15

I

Leningrad's criminals weren't the smartest bunch. And as a result, the city's detectives weren't always particularly astute, either. Kopteltsev put important casework away in his safe. But he didn't always keep a close eye on the key.

That was what Zaitsev was counting on, in any case.

Kopteltsev was already on his way out. He was standing in the lobby, leaning against the duty officer's counter, his backside slightly protruding, while he signed himself out in the register. The staircase was damp and gleaming; it was so late that the evening cleaning lady had already finished.

Zaitsev flew down the last few steps.

The pen scratched the paper as Kopteltsev was knocked off balance, grabbing at the counter with both hands to right himself. He might have fallen had Zaitsev not caught him in an embrace. His boss was on the large side.

"Zaitsev! Are you drunk or something?"

Zaitsev released him from his embrace, feeling like he had pulled a muscle. Kopteltsev turned out to be heavier than he had expected.

"Jeez. Almost smashed my noggin there."

Kopteltsev smoothed down his tunic and got his breath back.

"Can you not look where you're going?"

"What the fuck was that that I slipped on?" Zaitsev pretended to fumble about, confused, with something under his feet. Meanwhile, he quietly transferred the key he had extracted from Kopteltsev's pocket into his own.

The duty officer leant out from behind the counter, craning his neck. "Did the cleaning lady leave her rag on the floor again? She's always doing that."

"Can't you get a brighter lamp in here? We're stumbling about in the dark," Zaitsev interrupted irritably.

"Look at that mess in the register now." Kopteltsev shoved the thick tome over to the duty officer.

"First we'll need a blotter," said the duty officer, fussing about.

"All right, Zaitsev," Kopteltsev grunted, calmer now. He gripped the door handle. "See you tomorrow."

"See you tomorrow!" Zaitsev called after him. He patted his pockets. And quietly, but distinctly, he said in the duty officer's direction: "I've left my cap upstairs."

"Ooh, watch it or your bald patch'll catch a chill," the duty officer chuckled, terribly pleased with his joke.

Zaitsev grabbed hold of the railing and leapt up the stairs.

In Kopteltsev's office, his eyes quickly adjusted to the twilight. The night expanse above the Fontanka seemed bright in the large windows.

His hands moved swiftly and deftly. His breathing slowed, as though he were asleep. At the same time, somewhere at the far end of his consciousness, Zaitsev continued to follow a parallel chain of events—head back to his office, unlock the door—aware that he couldn't spend longer in Kopteltsev's office than he would fetching his cap. Duty officers had an exceptional sense of time and an uncommonly tenacious memory for those who enter and exit, especially at such a late hour. The phantom, parallel Zaitsev began fumbling about blindly, looking for his cap in his office.

The real Zaitsev refrained from any unnecessary movements. He took an imprint of Kopteltsev's wax seal—could be useful. Then put the stamp back. He carefully examined the safe door for any intentionally positioned slivers of wood veneer, feathers or hairs whose absence would alert its owner of an unexpected visit. No, Kopteltsev was clearly not afraid of anything. The key turned smoothly and firmly. Zaitsev opened the safe door.

Not just one file. Heaps of files. Yes, CID had been working with reinforced powers. A vigorous six months on this investigation. The evidence was all there. But he couldn't really make anything out in the dark belly of the safe. What if Kopteltsev's paranoia was focused inside the safe? His hands began to sweat in their gloves. It was time to speed up.

Zaitsev made sure that the safe door covered him in such a way that any light in the office wouldn't be visible from the street. Then he switched on his torch. Checked for any hairs or anything else laid out as a trap. No, none here either. Zaitsev clamped the torch between his teeth. That was better. Silently, with one movement he pulled out the entire stack of folders at once, pressing tightly down so that no leaf accidentally flew out. He sat down on the floor. And quickly began to sift through.

Words jumped out from the pages: *terror, terrorist group, anti-Soviet, sabotage, vermin, German spies.* He even double-checked the cover. No, this was definitely Yelagin Park. With a firm hand, Kopteltsev had been steering the investigation into some anti-Soviet conspiracy. And lists of surnames, surnames, surnames. And the surname Firsov. Many times. Everywhere. That explained their strange grins and even stranger toasts that time in the pub–tea room. Or rather, it still didn't make sense. What conspiracy? It couldn't be.

He heard a strange noise. He froze. The noise didn't stop. Oh, it's my breath, Zaitsev realized. He forced himself to calm his breathing. He wiped his forehead with the back of his hand. His time was up.

"Ha, that's the old thing you were looking for, was it?" Back downstairs, the duty officer at the front counter looked up and winked at him. Zaitsev nudged his "old thing" further back on his head.

"You can talk, Kondratyev! All right, goodnight."

"Adieu. Oh, Zaitsev, wait a sec!"

Another of his idiotic witticisms, thought Zaitsev. "Yes? What is it?"

"Here, this came with the evening mail. I thought I'd pop it round to you later. But take it now if you want."

He held out a plump brown office envelope.

Zaitsev wasn't expecting anything in the post, but he didn't let his face show that. He signed out in the register.

The door slammed, letting Zaitsev out and the night cold in.

II

"Here, comrade, it's for you."

Nefyodov put the receiver to his ear. There was a rumble down the line. With his half-closed eyes, Nefyodov's face looked as sleepy as ever.

"That's right," he answered.

He hung up.

"So I suppose the incident is, as they say, dissolved?" asked the portly, clean-shaven comrade in a fine Cheviot-tweed suit, as he leant back smugly in his chair. The arms of the chair ended in gilded lion heads. A museum piece, Nefyodov noted. But his face gave nothing away.

"Comrade…"

"Prostak," the clean-shaven comrade reminded him.

"Comrade Prostak," Nefyodov repeated. He liked to give the impression of being slow: it was a quick way to put people off talking to him.

"And next time..." Comrade Prostak raised a chubby finger. "Comrade... er..." He leant over his belly towards the table to read the bold signature forged by Zaitsev. "Comrade Kopteltsev can contact me directly."

Nefyodov reached out for the warrant. But Comrade Prostak was spry and got there first.

"Yep!" He waved the piece of paper theatrically. "And I'll have this as a keepsake."

"Comrade Prostak, it's Moscow on the line." His secretary's feline snout appeared around the door. "The People's Commissariat of Trade for you."

But Prostak had no intention of lowering his hand. The sly bastard, thought Nefyodov.

"Put me through, Lyusenka. And take the comrade here to the exit, if you would."

Nefyodov weighed up the options. Should he twist his arm for it? Was it worth it? He glanced out of the window behind him. First floor, a tree.

"Come with me, comrade," said Lyusenka. With the same expressionless face, Nefyodov followed her out.

III

Zaitsev jolted upright. He sat on his bed and listened. Quiet. On the floor was just a greyish rectangle of light—from the street lamp.

Clatter. Another bump on the window.

Zaitsev pulled his pistol out from under his pillow. He silently walked over to the side window. He peered out carefully. Nefyodov was standing in the light of the street lamp, looking up and making no effort to hide.

Zaitsev waved as if to say, "Come up."

He put the pistol on the table, quickly pulled on his trousers, quietly walked down the corridor. Trying not to let it click, he unlocked and opened the door. He didn't hear any footsteps either on the stairs or on the landing. But suddenly a hand appeared in the gap—and Nefyodov entered.

In his room, Zaitsev lit a kerosene lamp.

Nefyodov glanced at the pistol. "Hey," he whispered. "How's it going?"

"What happened to you? Get attacked by a bear on the way or something?"

There was a hefty rip in the shoulder of Nefyodov's jacket. Nefyodov shrugged, raising the shoulder with the rip.

"A drainpipe."

Zaitsev didn't know what to say. Of course. A drainpipe.

"Did you get locked in the museum for the night?" he mocked.

Nefyodov didn't keep up the jocular tone. He pulled a piece of paper out of his pocket and dropped it onto the table. Zaitsev recognized the memorandum he had forged.

"The little bastard kept the warrant. He was about to kick up a fuss," explained Nefyodov. "Started to ring Smolny. I had to wait until it got dark."

It gets dark very reluctantly in April in Leningrad. Nefyodov had to climb through a window late at night to rescue that bit of paper from being kept hostage.

"Jeez, Nefyodov." Zaitsev couldn't hide his surprise. He glanced at the alarm clock: he had barely slept at all. "Circus kid. You could have climbed in here easily enough. Bit more personal. What's with the stones? Trying to smash the window?"

"Your tree's too far," Nefyodov muttered. "From the window. Didn't think I could jump it."

"Aha, so you did consider it. Good lad."

Zaitsev didn't know if Nefyodov was joking or if he was serious.

Nefyodov suddenly sat down without being invited. He laid his hands on the table. Under his jacket, his back was skinny, boyish. How old is he? Zaitsev wondered for the first time. He could have a look in his personal file later. Out loud he asked, "You hungry?"

Nefyodov looked up at him. Surprise. Nefyodov was clearly touched.

"What? Why are you staring?" Zaitsev was embarrassed by this impulse: did he have a fatherly instinct after all? God forbid.

"Go on then, tell me from the beginning. And I'll rustle up some fat and carbs."

He remembered that there was some bread in the drawer. Possibly also some sugar.

"So does this sod have a name?"

"Prostak."

"What?"

"That's his surname."

"Prostak? Simpleton?" Zaitsev laughed. "Must be a party pseudonym. Poor chap. Anyway, go back to the beginning. You went to the Hermitage, and—"

But Nefyodov didn't exactly *go* to the Hermitage, he broke in.

"What do you mean, Nefyodov?"

"Through a little *fortochka* window. I had a look and saw the way the cats creep in and out. So, I figure, if there are cats, there must be some kind of storeroom. And if there's a storeroom, then I want to have a look for myself."

"Is that, so, Nefyodov?" Zaitsev set the coarsely sliced bread on the table. "Not particularly Soviet methods, if you want to know. Not very Komsomol methods either, for that matter."

"Well, Soviet methods only scare them off. By the time we show up again, they've already covered their tracks."

Zaitsev thought of how Alexei Alexandrovich had scarpered.

"Experts, curators—doesn't matter how educated they are. The way I see it, Nefyodov, you have no prejudices," said Zaitsev. "As far as you're concerned, they're all crooks. Think about it while I boil the kettle."

Zaitsev went out with the teapot into the dark corridor. He stopped. "Be careful," he reminded himself. "Careful."

Nefyodov was still sitting in the same position when he returned with the hot teapot. Two cups hung from his thumb.

Zaitsev poured the tea. Nefyodov eagerly watched the stream of hot liquid. He even stopped chewing.

"So what about those crooks?" Zaitsev said, bringing up the topic with feigned nonchalance.

"Yes. So. None of our paintings are in storage at the Hermitage."

"Not ours—the people's," Zaitsev corrected him. "But why are you so sure? Did you go through them all box by box?"

"No," answered Nefyodov, shifting the bread behind his cheek. "Everything they've got there is listed in their catalogues. The paintings *were* in the store. But then they were transferred to some enterprise called—"

"Antikvariat," Zaitsev answered.

Nefyodov stared at him. "That's the one. Antikvariat. How did you know?…"

Zaitsev dropped the thick brown envelope onto the table.

"What's this?" Nefyodov put his unfinished bread back on the plate and reached out for the package.

"It came today with the mail."

Nefyodov studied the ink lettering: the address of the Criminal Investigation Department, Zaitsev's name written in full. He turned it over: nothing on the back. Anonymous.

"Exactly. Judging by the stamp, it was sent from Leningrad, from the Main Post Office. Inside there's a letter. A detailed description of the scheme by which paintings of considerable value are being transferred from the State Hermitage to this Antikvariat, whose Leningrad representative is a Comrade—"

"Prostak," Nefyodov broke in. "I went to him with a warrant. After the Hermitage. That is, I had a dig around at the Hermitage first. Then I headed there, to Antikvariat. But what's it got to do with us? They're just transferring, well, pictures."

"That's right, Nefyodov. I don't know yet. But I sense it's got something to do with us."

Zaitsev suddenly remembered: Faina Baranova.

"Do you remember Baranova's neighbour? Zabotkina. She mentioned in her statement that her friend Baranova loved auctions. That was the name she couldn't remember. She remembered it as either Apollo, or Antiquity, or Antikvariat. It was where she bought the shepherd and shepherdess figurines. And we know that one of those figurines then turned up precisely at the crime scene on Yelagin Island."

The trail, which had long gone cold, suddenly seemed to fill with warmth. But it still wasn't clear where it was leading.

Zaitsev picked up the tube standing on its end in the corner: the rolled-up chart had managed to gather dust since it had ceased to be useful for anything else. He unrolled it on the table, holding down the corners and edges with plates, cups and the table lamp. A sea of futile rectangles filled in with names. And now the first had come to life. It would be followed by more and more. Logic would prevail. He stared hungrily at these names.

Somewhere beyond the wall, the neighbours' clock wheezed. There was a dong, another, a third. Zaitsev came to his senses. It was three in the morning.

He looked at Nefyodov.

"Tell you what, Nefyodov. I'll put the mattress on the floor. Sleep here and in the morning, before work, head straight to the Main Post Office with this package. Ask them nicely. Maybe they'll remember who sent it. It's not every day that citizens strike up a correspondence with the police."

Zaitsev picked up his alarm clock, thought for a moment and, suppressing a yawn, set it for two hours earlier than usual.

IV

"Vasya, finally," Demov greeted him. "Judging by the bags under your eyes, I see your personal life is working out well."

These days, their conversation consisted entirely of jokes like this. Demov placed some files on his desk.

Zaitsev waited for him to leave the room. He pulled the phone over to him. His hand froze on the receiver. Was it dangerous to call directly from here?

He laid the sheet out in front of him. Surnames. Descriptors. Arrows. Sleep really hadn't worked out that night. The truth seemed to be lingering so close. And Zaitsev felt himself propelled by the same instinct that drives a cat to chase a mouse, a bow on a string or a fly. He simply couldn't sit still.

Whether Nefyodov was asleep on his mattress or just pretending, Zaitsev didn't care. He sat up the rest of the night, studying the documents from the brown envelope under the yellow cone of light from his lamp. And then the unnecessary alarm clock started clattering away on the floor. Zaitsev realized that the entire night had passed.

Handwritten lists. Typewritten copies of official documents, with seals and signatures. This was more than enough evidence against Comrade Prostak. Antikvariat had been tirelessly removing paintings, furniture, porcelain and coins from the State Hermitage. But while the furniture, porcelain and coins could still find buyers like Faina Baranova, who would turn up and buy an almost three-metre canvas? Zaitsev just couldn't make sense of it. And if they did, where was a Soviet citizen going to hang their new painting? In the factory barracks? In their communal apartment? Supposing an institution bought one for the lobby or a meeting room. But they were hardly going to choose *The Annunciation*.

"Religion is the opium of the people," Nefyodov agreed, quickly slurping his morning tea at Zaitsev's.

"Yes, indeed. But I tell you, this Prostak, it seems like he's just your ordinary common hustler, only in a completely new guise. Pushing stolen goods. Which he himself steals. And he passes his theft off as performing official duties."

But how did the murder victims fit into all this? What could the artel worker have bought, say, or the nanny Rohkimainen? Tractorov, the apprentice? Or the black Communist Newton? Fokin, the musician in the ensemble of folk instruments? Art like this would be completely out of their league.

"I can't imagine having anything so bulky in my room," mused Nefyodov, speaking with the voice of the people. "What would you do with it? Partition your room?"

"Maybe not you, circus kid."

"You're no better," he muttered.

"No, I'm no better," Zaitsev agreed. "They somehow forgot to tell me about Rembrandt when I was out on the street. Or Veronese, for example. But, you know, Leningrad is full of connoisseurs who will gladly hand over their cash to this Prostak for one of these paintings. Maybe this Comrade 'Simpleton' is just a nobody like you and me. Perhaps, with his thick skull, he has no idea what state treasures he's squandering. Worse for him if he does know."

"I just don't get it. We know Baranova bought the figurines. This Fokin might have bought a coin to make himself a gold tooth. The other woman—what's she going to take? A tablecloth? I mean, what were they all killed for?"

"It's not proven, Nefyodov, that there's a connection between them and this whole Antikvariat business. But if, for example, you're investigating Citizen X for murdering his wife and along the way you find out that X also embezzled money to take his lover to Sochi, are you really not going to report the embezzlement to the corresponding police department?"

"What?" was all Nefyodov asked.

"OK, eat up. And don't forget your filthy socks when you go."

"My socks are already on me," Nefyodov innocently reassured him.

"I'm glad to hear it."

Nefyodov stomped over to the post office, which was relatively close to Zaitsev's place. And Zaitsev headed straight to Gorokhovaya.

They had already piled the routine tasks on him. He pushed everything aside. And dragged the phone over. After a moment's reflection he stayed sitting. He thought it through. What did he in fact want to ask Uglov?

In front of him lay the crib sheet he had compiled that night. The box with Comrade Prostak's name bristled with arrows; there were also the names of the signatories to the various documents. Stamps from the Moscow branch of Antikvariat. So, their Moscow comrades. Various arrows pointed up to the capital.

Zaitsev made his decision. He reached for the telephone.

They put him through surprisingly quickly.

"Hello, Vasya! So, have you booked your ticket to Moscow?" Uglov's joyful voice rumbled down the line.

"Yeah, nearly. Listen, do me a favour, would you?" asked Zaitsev. "I need to get a sense of some Moscow comrades: who they are, what kind of people and so on. And most importantly,

I want to know what kind of relationship or acquaintance they had with a certain Comrade Prostak."

"What?"

"That's his name."

"Good Lord."

"Indeed."

"Prostak? Simpleton? Is that a nickname or something?"

"A party alias, I think."

"What is he, a party leader?"

"Think so. On the trade side of things. You come across him?"

"No, of course not. Go on then, I've got a pen."

"Uglov, you're a legend! You —"

"Yeah, piss off. I can see you're hardly going to show up down here until you get out of that shitty mess up there."

"I really… I just need to close this case and that's it. I will fly to you on the wings of love."

"Fuck you. Go on, then."

Zaitsev began to dictate the names.

V

Nefyodov had never had occasion to visit the Main Post Office—once the central postal sorting office for the entire Russian Empire, back when there was still an empire. He looked around with interest at the enormous hall with its echoing tiles and high glass roof. The space was huge; you could imagine it teeming with postal carriages and their horses.

"Citizen, are you sending a telegram?" asked a woman in a uniform jacket who was heading in his direction. Apparently, they didn't like people standing around gawping.

"A parcel."

"In the province? In the city? In the Union?"

"In the city."

"Window number six."

Nefyodov took off his cap to come across more gently. But then he changed his mind and put it back on.

He leant over the counter to peer through the window. On a table, he saw a pot of pungent, molten, brownish-red liquid, with a stick standing up in it. A bald man with black over-sleeves reached up to the window as if to receive something.

"Dispatch," he said.

"Sorry, what?" asked Nefyodov.

"Give me whatever you're sending."

Nefyodov handed him his ID.

The little man put on his glasses. He studied it carefully. He looked up at Nefyodov's face in the window, then again at the photograph.

"Dasha!" he shouted into the depths of the room, where Nefyodov could see a heap of stuffed canvas post sacks. "Dasha, I knew that parcel to CID was going to be trouble. Come and deal with this comrade now. Please," he concluded in the triumphant tone of a man whose worst expectations had been fulfilled, as always. And Nefyodov was glad that he didn't seem to need to refresh anyone's memory.

Dasha turned out to be a skinny, fishy-looking woman with a grey plait curved into a wreath and piercing scarlet lips, which turned into a sceptical pout when she saw Nefyodov.

"You're the policeman?" she asked, looking slightly disappointed. Goodness knows what she imagined. "Yes, well, come in then. Don't be shy." The fishy lady unlocked the door to usher him in. "Come on. Or they'll start queuing behind you."

The next in line, an auntie in a beret, straight away appeared in the window. She held out a neat little bundle. The man in the oversleeves tossed it onto the scales. He pointed at the parcel with a pencil, giving firm instructions.

"It needs a return address. I can't accept it without."

The auntie quickly scribbled the required information with the pencil. He stirred the stick in the pot which gave off that sharp but not unpleasant smell. He dabbed some brownish blobs on the seams of the parcel, then stamped them with the seal.

"Comrade, are you falling asleep there?" called the fishy lady. Nefyodov turned away with regret: he loved the smell of molten wax. He took out his notebook and pencil.

"Citizen, first state your full name."

"My name is Pankratova. Daria Alekseevna," she said, already peeking at his notebook to see what he was writing there. Nefyodov tilted it so she couldn't see.

"Daria Alekseevna. I hear you received a suspicious package. Is that right?"

"Well, I say! It wasn't suspicious. It looked perfectly ordinary. It's just we saw it said 'Criminal Investigation Department'. Seemed unpleasant somehow. And Stepan Fedorovich—he sits over there—well, right away he said, 'Open it up, show us what's inside. For all we know there's a severed head in there.' Well, not a head, of course, that wouldn't fit in an envelope. But a knife? Or something bloody."

Daria Alekseevna was clearly an aficionado of the paperback adventures of Pinkerton.

"And what was in it?"

"Papers, documents," she said with a shrug of her bony shoulders.

It sounded like the very package Zaitsev had received.

"And how was it, comrade postal worker, that a parcel was sent without a return address? As I understand it, you shouldn't accept a parcel without one."

"What?" Then an ear-piercing yell. "Stepan Fedorovich! Stepan Fedorovich, come here a minute!"

331

The man with the oversleeves approached.

"Listen here, this comrade from the police has insinuations to make." And she made an inviting gesture, as if to say, "Can you believe it?"

"What insinuations?" He corrected his glasses, as if wanting to get a better look at Nefyodov.

"That a parcel was sent without a return address on it. Comrade, what if there'd been dynamite in there? Or poison?"

"How can it not have had a return address?" Stepan Fedorovich frowned. "That can't be right."

He turned away, looking towards the sacks. As if an excess of visual impressions had distracted his mind's eye.

"Someone brings a parcel. I show them: write the return address here. And they say they've got a note with the address on. And left their glasses at home. Could I just stick the address label on. So I do. I glue it. And I do the sealing wax and the stamp. I weigh it and accept the payment accordingly. And they say, 'Oh, no, the house number is wrong, let me fix it.' So I give it back."

Nefyodov seemed to visualize what Stepan Fedorovich saw in his memory at that moment. He passes the package back to the window. He waits. Takes it back. Tosses it into one of the sacks without another glance.

While he had been waiting, they must have simply ripped the address label off.

"And you didn't notice. What did the label say? Perhaps the name of the street?"

Stepan Fedorovich shrugged.

"Sorry. Who knew a woman could be such a lowlife."

"It was a woman?"

"Well, yes." Pankratova perked up. "And a very sophisticated one too, by the look of her. Goodness me! Honestly, these days you can't tell!"

"And what did she look like? Can you describe her?"

"Oh no, I'm no writer. Just looked like a woman. Yes, she seemed decent enough, that's right."

"Young? Old? Grey hair? Blonde? Red? Fat? Thin? Tall? Short?"

Stepan Fedorovich thought hard.

"She had a hat on."

And Pankratova's eyes lit up. And then her whole face, densely sprinkled with powder.

"Youthful," she declared with snide emphasis.

VI

One thing was perfectly clear and could no longer be ignored: the engineer Firsov had nothing at all to do with the murder on Yelagin Island.

"This isn't just a dubious connection. Without a shadow of a doubt there is no connection."

Kopteltsev suddenly stood up. He slid towards the door quietly—surprisingly quietly for someone of his stature. He jerked it open. He was reassured: there was no one in the corridor. He closed the door again and, thinking to himself, locked it. Zaitsev silently watched this whole charade. Kopteltsev slowly lowered his rear into his chair. He clasped his hands in front of him, as usual peering at his own thumbs as if he had just discovered them.

"Hmm, well," Kopteltsev finally said.

"Please. If you don't want to get involved—don't. The others don't need to get involved. Just give me some time. I'll bear the responsibility alone."

Kopteltsev put a cigarette in his mouth, arching over a little in his chair as he fumbled for a lighter in his trouser pocket. A click and he took a puff. A longer drag. He's taking his time, thought Zaitsev. Giving it some thought. Kopteltsev blew two fangs of smoke out through his nose. And a second later the muzzle of his pistol was staring straight at Zaitsev.

"It's too late," said Kopteltsev. "The train's left the station."

In Kopteltsev's chubby fist, his pistol seemed diminutive. Zaitsev froze for a split second against the back of the chair. There was still half a moment to jump up.

But Kopteltsev placed the gun flat and slid it across the table to Zaitsev.

Zaitsev caught it reflexively.

"Read it," ordered Kopteltsev.

Zaitsev turned the pistol over in his hands. A weighty little German model, engraved with a dedication to Kopteltsev. This was no mere pistol, but a premium weapon.

Zaitsev returned the gun with the hilt facing forwards.

"Did you read it?"

"I did."

"Well done."

Zaitsev was silent.

"Do you know what?" Kopteltsev narrowed his eyes amid the cloud of smoke. "I can see you're finding things hard at the moment. Clearly a sign you're overworked. Let me give you some time off. A couple of days. Have a rest. You've earned it. Three days, let's say. What do you say?"

He flicked the ash from his cigarette.

"Are you content with the situation?"

Zaitsev stood up. He went to the door. He gripped the handle.

"No, I'm not," he said. And he went out.

"Where are you off to?" asked the duty officer in the lobby, looking up as Zaitsev passed.

"Three days' leave," said Zaitsev. "Boss's orders."

"Lucky you."

On Nevsky Prospekt, Zaitsev hailed a cab. He quickly came to an agreement with the driver. He hopped into the battered old carriage. Zaitsev's eyes swam indifferently over the shabby equipment; it occurred to him that the rattletrap was older than he was.

"Old man, you sure your charabanc isn't going to fall apart halfway?"

"You'll fall apart first," answered the cabbie.

"Harsh words."

"Don't like it, get out."

"Why are you in such a filthy mood?"

The cabbie began to curse the financial inspectors and the new tax, which threatened to shut down his company once and for all. His and tens of thousands like his.

"You sound like a NEP man. And you know what they do with NEP men now," Zaitsev explained. "It's time to cross over to the Soviet rails."

"Who you calling a NEP man? Me?"

"I didn't come up with it. I'm just setting out the political situation in the country."

"Ooh, check you out. Where you from then?"

Zaitsev needed some time with his thoughts. But this chatterbox was distracting him.

"CID."

They drove to Yelagin Park in complete silence.

"Wait, don't slow down yet."

"What?"

"Drive around, I say."

"Comrade policeman, don't get me mixed up in your work."

"I'm not mixing you up in anything. Just keep going."

Hooves clattered on the dead earth smoothed down by trucks. Construction was in full swing in Yelagin Park.

"Hey there," Zaitsev called out to a man with a shovel over his shoulder.

"Yeah?"

"Are they building a hospital here?"

"No," he said. "This is the park. Where the hospital is I don't know."

"Park? But the park is right there."

"This is a new park. Culture and recreation, they call it."

"No way!"

"Yeah. That's what I've heard. Some saboteurs have been exposed."

Ah, so much for a secret investigation, Zaitsev said to himself, not without mockery. And the man carried on, evidently in the mood to chat; it was a break from his tedious work, after all.

"Construction couldn't get started because of them. But once they exposed them, they let the vehicles in. We're working day and night now to catch up."

Too late, Kopteltsev had said. The train's left the station. Now Zaitsev saw why with his own eyes. In the distance, a Ferris wheel was already going up.

"Where can I find the hospital?"

"Fuck knows."

"OK. Thanks for that."

Zaitsev leant back in his seat.

A few minutes later, the cabbie couldn't take it any longer—he turned around.

"What are we doing? Saunter along the embankment?"

"Take me back to Nevsky," Zaitsev said after a pause.

"You'll pay both ways," warned the cabbie.

"Of course."

Zaitsev was thinking about the engraved inscription on Kopteltsev's pistol: Comrade Kirov had personally given the

engraved weapon to the head of the department, in gratitude
for the successful resolution of the case.

VII

Zaitsev saw Nefyodov right away. A figure loomed tall on the
corner of Fonarny Bridge and the Moika, as they had agreed.
Leaning over the fence, Nefyodov was clearly staring at the
water, watching the ducks that bobbed along like sunflower
seed-husks. Zaitsev was just about to call out to him when
alongside him he heard something—not so much a noise,
but a noise stopping. The flash of a varnished black flank. A
car pulled up, and with it the reflections of houses and the
bright spring sky came to a standstill. Zaitsev kept on walking.

"Comrade Zaitsev!"

A big, sturdy man jumped out of the car. A cap in his hand.
He was holding it tightly.

"Comrade Zaitsev."

Zaitsev froze as the man approached. He probably
shouldn't look in Nefyodov's direction. He was presumably
watching from afar, keeping an eye on the operation, so to
speak. Zaitsev considered his options. Punch the big man
in the guts and run for it, shake him off in the linked-up
courtyards? There was only the driver in the car, and he
could lose Nefyodov. He wouldn't start running in time. Or
should he give himself up? He could finally stop looking
over his shoulder. Zaitsev knew that sudden calm felt by
convicts once they're behind bars: they might have lost the
game, but at least it's all over.

The big man approached.

"Comrade Zaitsev, just a little chat."

"Excellent," answered Zaitsev, inappropriately. This weary
relief poured down on him like a dream.

"So shall we get in the car?" the big man suggested hospitably. "It's not far."

Meanwhile, the car had rolled closer and was waiting; the motor hummed. A passer-by dashed by without even a glance. There weren't many people on the bridge. They had waited, the bastards, until he had turned off the noisy and crowded Sadovaya Street. They didn't want any fuss.

The door swung open as if by itself.

"Get in," said the man in the same good-natured tone. "We don't need any fuss, right?"

Zaitsev climbed inside. The big man flopped down onto the seat next to him, grabbed the leather loop with one hand, and gently tapped the driver on the back with the other: off you go. A nauseatingly familiar *mise en scène*. Fonarny Lane wavered and swam back and forth. The car poked its nose into an archway, backed out, turned around and taxied back to Sadovaya.

All right, Zaitsev told himself. It's all right. There were at least two major junctions before Shpalernaya. If not three. They would definitely have to slow down. That was his chance. Pull the handle, jump out of the car—and run. He knew the courtyards here better than these little shits knew their own rooms. Now you see him, now you don't. Sadovaya Street flashed by: carts, trams, people, people, people. His muscles tensed.

The first junction: the traffic controller held up his baton to show "drive on". No luck there. The car turned into Nevsky. Not to worry. There was a crossroads ahead with Liteyny, even better: those large tenement houses built in the 1860s and 1870s were strung together with passages from one courtyard to another, criss-crossing entire blocks. Zaitsev squinted at the big man: he remained silent all the way, calmly looking straight through the windscreen ahead. Zaitsev steeled himself for his move. He felt the coldness of the metal door handle. He rested his feet on the trembling floor.

But the car rolled past the wide river at Vladimirsky Prospekt, on the other side turning into Liteyny. Zaitsev stole a stealthy glance at his companion. He sat there like a tree stump, staring straight ahead with his pewter eyes. Finally, the car turned off onto Nekrasov Street. And then again, into Baskov Lane.

"We're here," the big man announced. "There's the front door. Go up to the first floor. The apartment's on the left. It's open."

But he himself didn't move. Keeping a low profile, perhaps. They were waiting for him in the apartment. Zaitsev opened the door. The big man touched his sleeve.

"No funny business, please."

Zaitsev jumped out onto the pavement.

And then he felt an unbearable nausea. He recognized this house, once covered with reddish stucco, now flaking and peeling off. The lattice on the gate. The front door. The window. This was where he had seen Alla

Chapter 16

I

Zaitsev passed the money through the kiosk window.

But instead of cigarettes, the seller's hand returned cupped like a bowl.

"Another ruble."

Zaitsev grabbed the notes from his pocket and put in the required amount. He took the flat card packet.

"Comrade, have you got a light?" he asked the man behind him in the queue. "Much obliged."

He bent down with the cigarette to the burning match. And inhaled.

The vile, musty smell of the dirty apartment in Baskov Lane still seemed to linger in his nose. He once again ran through the entire conversation in his head, stopping on comments he wasn't sure about. Had he slipped up somewhere? Had he missed something?

"...I don't understand. Am I arrested?"

"Not at all. Why would you be? It's just a conversation. A friendly chat."

"It's just I'm on duty at the moment and while we're talking I'm supposed to be out catching criminals!"

"Of course, that's true. And we're not stopping you. You need to catch criminals. And by helping us, you help the common cause: catching, as you say, criminals."

His speech twisted in smooth slippery loops.

"...Saboteurs and opponents of the Soviet regime, hidden class enemies. To say the least."

343

Zaitsev spotted the sheet of paper under the man's elbow. He was constantly checking it. It was handwritten.

"What enemies? I'm in Criminal Investigation. We've just had our purges."

Zaitsev tried to steal a glance at the sheet in such a way that it wasn't obvious where he was looking. His eyes darted there, then looked away. As luck would have it, the man kept moving his hand along the piece of paper, always covering over one part or another.

"Comrade Zaitsev, purges are a sound measure, as experience has shown, but they're not enough. The enemies are in disguise. An enemy might recruit someone who, yesterday, seemed to be the perfect Komsomol member."

"If I suspect anyone, then, of course, I'll be sure to let you know," Zaitsev assured him peaceably. His eyes flitted down to the paper and up as if by chance.

"Agent Chrysanthemum"—he couldn't help noticing these last two words.

"Oh, no. It will be better if you just tell us everything. And we'll decide what is suspicious and what is not. Comrade Zaitsev, stop wasting our time and start thinking what you're going to tell us, or else I'll start to feel bad about keeping an investigator from his duties at the height of the working day."

"I never have time for chit-chat. I've got call-outs to respond to. Reports to write. I don't stand around chinwagging," he persevered. "Unless it's related to a case."

It was like some kind of awkward dance. One advanced. The other retreated. And so for a while they circled one another, trying not to stand on the other's toes, until the man passed the sheet of paper to Zaitsev.

"Sign here, here and here." He pointed. He had dirt under his fingernail. Zaitsev began to read.

The man grinned. "It's a statement of non-disclosure."

Zaitsev signed.

"After all, you've already been arrested once, Comrade Zaitsev," his interlocutor reminded him as if in passing.

"They let me go."

"They gave you a chance," he corrected. "Make the most of it." And quickly softening his tone, he added, "Think about what I've said."

"I will do."

The sheet of paper disappeared into his pigskin briefcase. Zaitsev looked at the dreary wallpaper: brownish-red, the pattern half rubbed off. The old settee, its cushions squashed flat. The curtains again. This apartment was a kind of safehouse, then, where they met their informants. So as not to blow their cover with a visit to OGPU.

He calmly and firmly looked his interlocutor in the eye.

"'Til we meet again, Comrade Zaitsev." But the man with the pigskin briefcase wasn't stupid—he didn't offer a farewell handshake. "And all the best to you."

Interesting, thought Zaitsev. Chrysanthemum, then. Eminently suitable. Chrysanthemum it is. A fragile and refined blossom.

The chrysanthemums... have long since faded... he remembered Pasha's crooning. She never did like Alla. Well, well.

But he liked her.

What a fool he'd been.

The cigarette was hot and bitter, the smoke tore at his throat: either they had got worse since he had quit, or he was out of the habit. He threw it away, unfinished. He went into the telephone booth. Fortunately, he found some kopecks in his pocket.

It was a long wait to be connected. In the silence, something clicked and crackled.

"No, no messages for you," the attendant answered.

"Any calls from Moscow?" asked Zaitsev impatiently.

"Nothing from Moscow."

Uglov still hadn't called back.

It was OK; there was still time.

Zaitsev left the booth. He saw a passer-by—a nondescript, grey Soviet man, respectably dressed, unassuming—reach down and deftly pick up the cigarette that Zaitsev had tossed away, barely started. Zaitsev pulled out the pack, gave it a squeeze and threw away the whole thing. He looked at his spread fingers. They didn't tremble. He wondered, how would an ordinary grey Soviet man feel in his shoes right now? Would he be afraid? Would he run away to his second cousin in Kursk or down to Rostov? Or do they not come for the ordinary ones?

He remembered the files he had seen in Kopteltsev's safe, marked with the words *subversion, sabotage.*

And Kopteltsev? Was he playing along? Since when? After all, he had left GPU to lead CID. Or was there no such thing as a *former gepeushnik*?

"Comrade, wake up! Go home if you want to sleep!" hissed a woman in a cloak, waving her basket at him. Passers-by manoeuvred past him as he stood like a rock in the middle of a stream. Zaitsev started walking. Neither slowly nor quickly. The same as everyone else. Not standing out or attracting attention. You only run when you're chasing someone. Or someone's chasing you.

And he was neither one nor the other.

His nerves were a wreck by the time he reached his apartment. He almost ran past the kitchen, not greeting the neighbours. He batted from his face someone's sheets that were hanging in the hallway.

Chrysanthemum, then.

His key didn't fit in the lock. It was only after a second, one that lasted an eternity, that Zaitsev realized that he was shoving the key in upside down. He smiled. No need to panic, ladies, he thought. He turned the key again. Now the lock crunched obediently.

Zaitsev's heart sank. A pause. Then it went again.

Straight away he saw that the table was empty. He went over to it, as if hoping that he was mistaken, that it was just the way the shadow fell, deceiving him. But he wasn't mistaken. The chart wasn't there. Zaitsev glanced in a corner: maybe he had forgotten that he had rolled it up and left it there? But the corner was empty.

The dresser was empty. He banged and slammed as he pulled out each drawer one by one. In the dim hope that he had tidied everything away without thinking. There was nothing there.

He quickly crouched down to the floor and peered under the dresser. Under the table. Under the bed.

If he thought he had already known the taste of horror, he was wrong.

Everything was gone: the chart, the files with the old, long-closed and archived cases—he had had no right to take them out of the building. Now they were gone. The photos had disappeared. The opened package with the anonymous letter and the documents from the Hermitage had disappeared, too. Even the guidebook was gone—probably taken just in case, along with the rest of the papers. Zaitsev felt his chest being squeezed. Without thinking about the curtains, without even locking the door to his room, he rushed over to the dresser, grabbed the corner and yanked it away from the wall. The dresser stood like a cruiser, almost in the middle of the room. The back of the dresser: empty. Zaitsev fell to his knees, running his hands over it, as if he didn't trust his own eyes.

It was empty. He turned around to lean his back against the wall. His heart thumped so hard it was difficult to breathe.

He thought they had nothing on him.

But they had everything on him.

He himself had given them everything.

No need to panic, he told himself. It's not too late. Think, he forced himself. Think. If they had already got their hands on the documents, they would have spoken to him, er, differently. More curtly even than last summer, when they had broken his ribs in prison on Shpalernaya Street.

He got up and left.

II

"Comrades, who requested a call to Moscow?" A girl with brightly painted lips rose from behind a wooden partition. "You?" she asked Zaitsev. "Booth number three, please."

He closed the door behind him. The telegraph booth was like an elevator box with its wooden panels. A plush bench tried in vain to tempt him to sit down.

Zaitsev picked up the phone.

"Hello?"

"Yes, go ahead."

He recognized the voice of the secretary. Or so he thought, anyway.

"Zaitsev speaking. I need to speak to Comrade Uglov."

"He's at a meeting."

"I'm calling from Leningrad CID."

"He's at a meeting," she repeated with kindly persistence.

"It's urgent. When can I reach him? I'm calling from Leningrad."

"Call back in an hour."

Zaitsev hung up. He returned to the counter and paid. He glanced at his watch; the two black hands speared the paunchy numbers around its face. "One more call to Moscow."

He named the time. The girl shrugged under her silk blouse.

"It's important," Zaitsev said for some reason.

"What do I care? It's your money, not mine." She handed him his receipt with the new time on.

The theatre was empty.

"This is a surprise," Alla said with a smile.

Zaitsev gazed intently into her face: not even a hint of emotion.

"I..." he began, and stopped short. A flock of thin women approached the service entrance. Without make-up, the dancers seemed very young. "We need to talk."

His tone clearly seemed strange to her. Zaitsev now saw a question on her face.

"Is there somewhere quiet we can go?" He stuck his hands in his pockets.

"Let's go."

The injunctions on the bulletin board fluttered in the through draught. They walked up narrow staircases and along low corridors that didn't tally with the spacious elegance of the theatre's front of house. From somewhere came the strangled howls and sighs of a grand piano: someone was rehearsing. It smelt of powder, sweat, rosin. The dressing rooms. Barely stopping, Zaitsev pushed open a door: a row of empty trifold mirrors stared straight at him. There was no one in here. He pulled Alla by the hand. Pushed her in. Slammed the door behind them.

Alla was stunned. "What on earth?!"

He noticed how she shouted at him—in a whisper.

On the way from the telegraph office, he had tried to imagine this conversation—rehearsing his lines. He pictured how he would get to the crux of it. Without giving anything away. Deliver the main question in a knockout blow that she doesn't see coming. The same way he always got suspects to talk. Criminals. Enemies. Alla was an enemy.

But when he saw her in front of him—this clean forehead, this pure look, this face—his expertise became meaningless, his words vanished. All he could squeeze out was:

"What's at Baskov Lane?"

"Baskov Lane?"

Alla instantly realized that it was pointless to deny it. Her cheeks burned, became deeply flushed.

"A seamstress," she shrugged. "Private. A little extra work. Made to measure. Various clients. Even people from the theatre. To supplement my income… My God"—she pressed her thin fingers against her temples. "I can't even imagine… But why did you follow me? You could have just asked! You know how badly they pay at the theatre… And there we… quietly… so the tax inspector doesn't…"

She piled one lie on top of another. Zaitsev admired how natural she looked.

"A seamstress, you say. Perhaps suggest that she shave off her moustache," he muttered. "The seamstress."

Alla stared at him for a second, stunned. But only a second. Apparently, a new approach was born in her head.

"It isn't what you think…"

"For goodness' sake, Alla." Zaitsev couldn't help himself. "Stop it."

"All right. It's not a seamstress." Her voice suddenly ablaze with defiance. "I'm seeing someone else."

No matter how obvious the lie, Zaitsev felt it like a stab. To some extent, Alla was telling the truth: it was still betrayal. Your girlfriend is cheating on you with OGPU. You think she's your girlfriend, but in fact she's on duty. She has a task to fulfil.

350

Alla continued to develop her melodramatic version of events.

"I'm sorry. It's all such a muddle. There's no reason. It's nobody's fault. It just happened."

Zaitsev didn't say anything.

She looked at him shyly, plaintively. Checking—Zaitsev saw—whether he had fallen for it or not. He almost admired the courage and abandon with which she lied. Like a small dangerous animal dashing about, looking for a way out.

"...I didn't want to. I just didn't know how I felt. What feelings I had for you and for him. I still don't know."

It was already starting to seem like this was true.

"Wait, Alla. Wait a minute. This is all detail I don't need."

Her beautiful eyes looked so genuine. Alla must have noticed the way he had paused. She made a sudden dash, slipping from his hand, and made a grab for the door. He managed to pull her away, sent her flying. She bumped into a table, setting the perfume bottles tinkling, wobbling the mirror. Zaitsev pulled out his pistol.

"Freeze," he said softly. He repeated it, more quietly this time. "Freeze."

Suddenly, it was as though all the cavities of the building were filled with sound. The orchestra was starting its rehearsal. Bursts of music rumbled and crashed.

So much the better, Zaitsev thought. He couldn't make out at first what Alla was saying. Her voice was trembling this time.

"You know how they pull you in. First an arrest. Then it's: you can help us. And they let you go. You know what it's like. Don't you?"

"No."

"It's easy for you to say," she interrupted. "You're a Soviet citizen. You don't know what it's like to run and hide, to have to hide who you are. All I want is to live! I just want to live. It's how it is. It's not my fault—I didn't choose who to be born as."

He wanted to ask, had this been a job since the very beginning? And if not, at what point was she tasked with it?

He forced himself to swallow these questions.

"Alla," said Zaitsev calmly. "None of this is of interest to me right now."

"No? I'm doing what I need to survive. Don't tell me you're not too?"

Alla flinched at the click of the safety catch. She froze. Her eyes looked down the barrel of the gun, into the black eye of death.

"Of course I am," Zaitsev agreed. He came very close to her, the muzzle of the gun almost buried in her stomach. "Don't move. And don't do anything stupid. You and I are going to leave now, calmly. And you're going to give me back everything you took. And then you can live however you like."

III

The girl with the perm frowned, looking at the receipt.

"Comrade, this call has expired."

"I know." Zaitsev smiled. "It's my fault. What am I supposed to do? Book a new one?"

"Wait," she sighed.

Zaitsev didn't even make it to the bench where others dutifully waited their turn, before the girl waved to him.

"Booth number three."

Zaitsev picked up the phone. "Hello?"

"Go ahead." The voice was that of the same secretary. The same benevolent tone. Zaitsev introduced himself.

"Comrade Uglov is busy. Call back in five minutes."

Zaitsev hung up. Five minutes means what exactly? Five minutes? Or half an hour? Or tomorrow? Or never?

He stepped out of the booth. Should he wait here? Without thinking, he sat on the bench. Should he book a new conversation? Or go straight to the station, to the ticket office and get a one-way ticket to Kursk? Rostov? Orel? The Urals? No need for a return. Was he wasting precious minutes right now?

"Comrade. Comrade," said the old man in the hat beside him. He spoke gingerly, even apprehensively. His large freckled hand rested on his cane. "Comrade, are you feeling all right?"

"What?" Zaitsev didn't understand.

"You've got blood on you."

"Ah," said Zaitsev, pulling his jacket around him. "It's nothing. Recent operation. Appendicitis. Nothing serious."

"You need to be careful with the stitches."

The old man was waiting in the queue, and was obviously bored and delighted to have found someone to talk to.

"When you're young, you have no thought of poor health," he mused. "Nor do you feel young when your health is poor…" He was clearly in the game for a long conversation.

"That's true." Zaitsev stood up with a smile and added, more to himself: "I need to do everything more slowly now; rushing definitely won't help."

He paid for the short conversation with Moscow and left the telegraph office.

By the time he reached CID, his thoughts had returned to some order. At least, it seemed that way. Stop, he told himself. Problems are either real and demonstrable, or they're imagined: there are those that are knocking on the door, and those that so far exist only in the mind. Don't overestimate your ability to calculate everything in advance, he told himself; sometimes it turns into just paranoia. It makes it difficult to think.

First of all, he needed to stock up on bullets. The arsenal was closely guarded, certainly—but from strangers. Not from insiders. All the better. But he needed to act quickly.

"Comrade Zaitsev!" The voice splintered into an echo in the stairwell.

Zaitsev pretended not to hear. But Nefyodov quickly caught up with him.

"Comrade Zaitsev!"

The last thing he needed. Nefyodov was also dangerous, he reminded himself. Zaitsev tried to behave just as he would at any other time.

"Hi, Nefyodov. What have you been doing? Poking your finger in where it's not wanted?"

Nefyodov's hand had a stiff, white chrysalis in place of a finger. The bandage criss-crossed his palm. But he had already managed to get it dirty.

"Comrade Zaitsev, a question."

But he looked more like he had an answer. Something urgent. The light from the desk lamp that was always on glinted on the duty officer's helmet. Zaitsev understood.

"Well, let's go to the office, then, if you have a question."

In the office, Zaitsev came over all hot. The April sun beamed through the glass, heating the room like a greenhouse. And he couldn't take his jacket off.

"So, what's up with your finger?" he asked cheerfully.

"Dislocated. It's nothing. Look at this." He held out a brown piece of paper: parcel paper.

What Nefyodov was showing him resembled a child's drawing.

"I don't get it."

"This was drawn by an employee at the Post Office. They couldn't describe her in words. They weren't writers, they said."

Zaitsev took the piece of paper. A pancake face. A dash for a nose with two circles of nostrils. Thin lips. Slits for eyes.

"Yeah," Nefyodov continued. "Not artists, either, sadly."

But somehow, the drawing managed to express an arrogant expression: pursed lips, narrowed eyes, nostrils flared in proud indignation. It was clearly drawn by a woman—the hairstyle was conveyed with particular care.

"I know who this is." Zaitsev tossed the drawing onto the table.

"Who?"

Zaitsev thought for a moment. How to say who? His memory stubbornly resisted adding any sound. He remembered the attendant referring to her, yes, by her surname. But the sound of it quivered in a blur.

"I can't remember. Something beginning with L? Or Avilova, maybe?"

Nefyodov bent at the waist and dived under the table.

"Let's have a look. Maybe there's a connection somewhere."

He hoisted out the roll of paper and began to stretch it out. It kept disobeying him and wanting to roll back up.

Zaitsev staggered, as though the floor were tugged out from under his feet. And Nefyodov muttered to himself under his breath.

"Maybe one of the dead knew an Avilova. Or something beginning with L."

He pressed one corner of the chart down with an ashtray full of charred black flakes. He held the other side down with the desk calendar.

Zaitsev looked at it like a ghost.

Nefyodov met his gaze.

"I jumped, by the way," he explained, as if slightly surprised at his own words. "Just one dislocated finger." He raised his bandaged hand. "And your windowsill, Comrade Zaitsev—best get it fixed before it falls and lands on someone's head."

Zaitsev was silent, and Nefyodov interpreted this in his own way.

"I saw you being bundled into the car," he explained. "When I was waiting for you on the corner."

That's right, Zaitsev remembered. He had seen Nefyodov on the embankment.

"I hid everything," Nefyodov explained. He spread his hands over the table. "The chart, the files, your ration cards, the bundle of papers."

"The chart?…"

"What? If stopped, I would have said it was a roll of paper for the wall newspaper we're making," he said, fudging an excuse on the spot. "Don't worry. I got it in the building, I'll get it out again."

His sleepy eyelids didn't rise once. His expression was as calm and blank as ever. Zaitsev wanted to pounce on him, shake him, slap him round the head and get out an answer to the most important question.

"And I burned your envelope," Nefyodov added in the same voice, as if it were the simplest thing in the world. He nodded to the ashtray. He had understood. And Zaitsev understood. He picked up the ashtray. The corner of the chart immediately curled up, just waiting to be let loose.

Zaitsev looked at the fragile black flakes. One scrap hadn't burnt out completely: old photographic card burned poorly. You could just make out the flourish of the final golden letter from the name of the studio.

Now all he had left was his memory. Only what he remembered himself.

Zaitsev smoothed out the chart again and reset the ashtray at an angle. Was Nefyodov sticking his nose in? Probably yes.

Burning and ripping everything to shreds. Anyone in his place would do the same.

Zaitsev felt heavy, as if he were now chained to Nefyodov. Like the imperial penal colonies he had read about where prisoners were fettered in pairs.

The sleepy eyelids fluttered. Nefyodov looked at him firmly and clearly.

"Don't try to keep secrets, Comrade Zaitsev. Nothing you keep hold of will ever remain secret for long."

He bent over the chart.

"So, Avilova, then. Avilova…"

IV

"What do you mean, Comrade Zaitsev?" Nefyodov became worried. "Forgive the expression, but are you mad? Do I look like a museum worker? In case you can't tell from looking at me—I didn't go to any university."

"Oh no, you can tell," Zaitsev assured him. "But we've only got three days. Two," he corrected himself. "Don't fret, Nefyodov. Any institution of art and culture needs people to wash the floors, clean the fireplaces, pack crates and so on. In the theatre, for example…" He stopped short. He hadn't just turned the page on Alla—the page was ripped out, crumpled up and thrown away. "Museums also have porters, chimney sweeps, cleaners. You look great. Better than the real deal. Go on, off you go."

Nefyodov took off his cap. He thought for a moment, then took off his jacket, too. He unfastened his holster. He shoved it all into Zaitsev's arms. With the light gait of a thief, he rounded the corner of the building and disappeared. But Zaitsev imagined he could still see him in his mind's eye. Nefyodov had found a little *fortochka* window that cats used to slip in and out. He sneaked down into the basement of the Hermitage, in the service building. The first thing he needed to find was a fire-escape plan, so he could memorize every staircase. He then had to find the personnel department. Or bookkeeping. Or estate management. He didn't need to steal anything. He just had to look the fool. And find out who this Avilova was. If, of course, it was Avilova.

Zaitsev wrapped Nefyodov's holster up in his jacket and squeezed it all into a tighter bundle. The blue-eyed windows peered at him from all sides; it was a beautiful day; the sky was clear. He was surrounded by nothing but stone and water. Hanging around like that only attracted attention. Zaitsev pictured himself dreamily loitering, admiring the view of the Swan Canal, set in granite, and the Neva, just visible through the arch. A perfectly natural occupation in Leningrad.

"Citizen!"

Zaitsev turned around. A bearded face. A janitor.

"Citizen, if you're planning on taking a leak here, don't even think about it."

He put a whistle in his mouth, indicating that he was serious.

"All right, no need to be so vulgar," answered Zaitsev. "For your information, I'm admiring our beautiful city."

"Admiring my arse!... I don't want any trouble, I'm warning you," the janitor threatened. And he began waving his prickly broom about. The embankment was already perfectly clean. The janitor was just keeping an eye on the stranger.

Time to move on, Zaitsev thought with frustration. Where should he go? Especially as he was carrying Nefyodov's pistol wrapped in its cocoon.

Zaitsev ought not show up near the Hermitage itself, and certainly not inside—too risky. If Avilova was the one he was thinking of, then he would simply scare her away. She would remember him. It would be hopeless, a wild goose chase. Like Alexei Alexandrovich—it was a good job it wasn't him they needed to speak to, otherwise where would they find him now? Maybe teaching somewhere in Torzhok. Or maybe not Torzhok. This was a big country.

A citizen turned off the embankment, a patent-leather handbag swaying and glinting on her elbow. Zaitsev squinted against the sun, then turned towards the water; the glare danced there too.

"Comrade! It's you."

That was a conversation starter Zaitsev was never comfortable with. He looked up. In front of him was that dragon from the Hermitage. Her hair parted at the front into two twisting snakes. Her narrow eyes and mouth like a slit cut by a blade. He wasn't mistaken.

His only mistake was how his memory had rearranged the sounds in her name.

"Lilovaya," she introduced herself. "Tatyana Lvovna Lilovaya."

"Zaitsev," he shook her narrow, dry hand. He was in no hurry to speak—let her lead the conversation.

Tatyana Lvovna, apparently, interpreted this as confusion and, as an educated, well-brought-up person she immediately rushed to his rescue.

"I saw a young man in breeches in the service building. Not one of ours."

"Do you remember all the young men in breeches who work for you?"

"The Hermitage is a large and complex family, but a family nonetheless."

Zaitsev had heard that before somewhere. Yes, that's right—in the *kommunalka* where the murdered Faina Baranova lived. A family that guards its secrets jealously from strangers.

"I thought to myself, if he's a thief, what's he doing calmly walking about in broad daylight? And if not one of ours and not a thief, then he's one of yours. And since he's not wearing a cap or a jacket, that means he's probably got a comrade waiting for him outside."

"Tatyana Lvovna, you'd be quite an asset to CID." Zaitsev could not resist.

To his surprise, she nodded.

"It had also crossed my mind. The work of an academic is akin to the work of a detective. Gathering evidence, analysing the facts. You propose a hypothesis, interrogate it, draw conclusions… Look at that janitor staring at us. Poor thing. Shall we let him think we're having an affair like the French—a mature, experienced woman and a passionate young man?"

She deftly linked her arm in Zaitsev's. He bent his elbow.

"How lovely." Tatyana Lvovna smiled.

"Why did you send me the parcel?"

"What? Aren't we going to wait for your comrade?"

V

"Young man, drink your beer while it's still cool," said Tatyana Lvovna softly. She picked up a piece of fish and with her pink nails tore off the dry scaly skin. Nefyodov gawped at her, as though he were faced with a talking horse.

"I thought you were a cultured woman," he couldn't help himself from asking, quite innocently. "But you're eating dried roach?"

Zaitsev grinned. Nefyodov played his own version of Ivan the Fool for appearances; it was amazing how even the smartest people bought it, himself included.

A dignified Tatyana Lvovna tore off the amber flakes from the fish and put it in her mouth. She chewed for a long time; her cheeks quivered beside her closed lips. Zaitsev and Nefyodov paid close attention to the repast. Finally she drank some beer and spoke.

"What's the connection? Incidentally, this is what they call the cultural bar. In the vicinity there's the Philharmonic, a children's publishing house, the Russian Museum: all staffed by—as you deigned to notice—cultured people. They're children's writers over there, for example."

Zaitsev and Nefyodov looked over. Three very ordinary, nondescript-looking citizens—ordinary co-workers—were laughing at a table with large mugs of beer.

"I no longer know where the dividing line is," said Tatyana Lvovna, "between 'cultured' and 'not cultured'. This Prostak... Oh my goodness, 'Comrade Simpleton'—it's as though he chose that surname intentionally! Well, he's done a sum total of two years at a parish elementary school! Do you understand? Two! I know, I made enquiries. This savage, of course, has no idea what he is doing. Never mind Rubens—for him it's a bunch of swans on an oilcloth. Never mind the Hermitage—for him it's just a commission."

She saw that Zaitsev wanted to say something, and she even seemed to guess what it was.

"You, of course, are not professors," she assured them quickly. "But for some reason, you seem to care. Why do you understand the difference? Why is it that you understand that this is a crime? Perhaps intelligence isn't the prerogative of the educated?"

Zaitsev and Nefyodov looked at each other.

"Well, from a technical point of view there is no crime," Zaitsev began cautiously. "Even your documents... the ones you sent to us. It's all above board. The Hermitage handed over such and such items to Antikvariat. Signed and stamped. Even if Antikvariat is selling what belongs to the people—in theory, it's been authorized by the people themselves."

"The Soviet people and the proletariat have yet to grow intellectually before they can access the cultural heritage that they inherited after the Revolution," Tatyana Lvovna continued. "And they will get there! One day," she added, with a degree of uncertainty. It was evident that Tatyana Lvovna didn't expect this happy moment any time soon. "They will realize one day! But then what? It will be too late!"

"Tatyana Lvovna, what do you want from us?"

"Help."

"We're Criminal Investigation. We're not an educational organization. As far as we're concerned, Comrade Prostak and his organization haven't broken any laws."

Tatyana Lvovna drank her beer.

"Then why were you chasing after these pictures?" she asked calmly. "It was you who came to us first. You started asking us about the paintings. It wasn't me asking you."

True.

But Zaitsev wasn't about to tell Tatyana Lvovna that someone was roaming the city, killing Leningrad residents and using their bodies to create hideous still lifes based on the Hermitage paintings.

"Tatyana Lvovna, I'm not saying that you are wrong. You're right. We need to confront it. Confront it! Write a detailed letter to Comrade Kirov. To the very top. Write to the government. The People's Commissariat. Write to everyone."

She looked away.

"There's going to be an auction in Berlin soon," she said wearily. "Lepke Auction House. It's a very well-known house. For wealthy lovers of old masters. If this isn't stopped right now, it will be another catastrophe for the Hermitage collection. Do you understand? It's not the first. But it is irreversible.

Another crushing blow to our collection. Our grandchildren will never see these pictures. They will decorate other people's villas and mansions."

"They will see them because soon there'll be world revolution and all the bourgeois will be kicked out of their villas and mansions," Nefyodov muttered quickly into his tankard. They were surrounded by the dense noise of the bar. But that didn't mean others couldn't hear them.

Tatyana Lvovna stopped short. Did she understand his warning? Zaitsev saw that she was thinking.

But he was mistaken. She understood Nefyodov differently.

"Is that how you see it?" she asked in amazement.

Nefyodov raised his owl's face to look at her.

"Me?"

"The proletariat," she said irritably. "Soviet people. Those who 'haven't been to university', or whatever you call them."

He looked at this middle-aged woman. She was like an old cobra installed by the Indian Raja to guard his fortune: even though the Raja was long gone, the old cobra sat coiled up, defending the abandoned treasure.

"When was the last time you visited the Hermitage?" Tatyana Lvovna asked Nefyodov contemptuously. Nefyodov was gnawing on a dried roach.

"About an hour ago," he answered.

She snorted. She clicked open her handbag and began rummaging for something.

"Here." Tatyana Lvovna threw several photographs onto the table in front of Zaitsev. "The highlights from Lepke's catalogue. I understand these names and titles won't mean much to you," she said, giving Nefyodov a contemptuous glare. "But you"—she looked at Zaitsev—"seem less hopeless than your comrade. Take my word for it. These are first-class works. Priceless. This Prostak may not know what he is doing. But

Lepke's clients, those American and European millionaires, have no illusions about their value."

"And how do these millionaires know what this Prostak has got his hands on?" asked Nefyodov. But Tatyana Lvovna ignored him: he no longer existed as far as she was concerned. Zaitsev flipped mechanically through the pictures: photographs of paintings.

He looked and yet didn't see. He was deep in thought. What if OGPU remembered about him? What if Uglov—Uglov, with whom he had gone through so much—had turned into the sort of manager who "was here just now, but he left five minutes ago"? And if all this wasn't a coincidence? What if it had been precisely after Nefyodov went to see Prostak? No wonder he had been so cocky with him. Antikvariat's activities were being directed from above, from Moscow. The People's Commissariat of Trade, did Tatyana Lvovna say? Commissariat of Trade?

What if Faina Baranova, aficionado of pretty trinkets, had accidentally stuck her silly, curious nose where it wasn't welcome? And the others? No. It couldn't be.

But what if this last idea—this ridiculous idea, worthy of the farcical novel *The Twelve Chairs*—what if it was true?

Suppose all of them—each individually—had bought something for themselves. Broken up the set. Not knowing the great value of the items they were buying. And then what if the killer collected the items back one at a time. But what? Coins? Stamps? Jewellery?

Were there coins in the world whose value exceeded that of human life? Stamps?

Zaitsev had come to believe that perhaps there were. And that there were people who were willing to pay fabulous prices for such things. Those millionaires, as Tatyana Lvovna put it…

But why the fanatical cruelty? The laborious and risky farce with the fancy dress and staged charades?

Zaitsev felt he had all the details in front of him—but still he couldn't see the full picture. He couldn't stand this feeling, of his mind being stuck, not getting anywhere.

"*Allegory of Eternity*. Rubens"—a voice interrupted his thoughts. He looked up. Tatyana Lvovna nodded her chin at the photo at the top of the pile. She was apparently very fond of her job, because she immediately launched into her spiel: "Rubens composed it as a study for a tapestry commissioned by Duchess Isabella for a monastery in Madrid. Cesare Ripa, author of the famous 1593 work *Iconologia*, considered the central female figure to be Eternity. Here"—Tatyana Lvovna pointed at the photograph with a long, pink fingernail—"here you see a snake biting its own tail. A symbol of ceaseless time… the image of Eternity is represented by an old woman… Genius hovers over Eternity. Genius hands down a garland and these cherubs are three putti supporting the garland from below…"

Nefyodov looked on as if Tatyana Lvovna were delivering a sermon in Chinese.

"The picture is incomparable. That it is incomplete only makes it more perfect. Its lightness…" Tatyana Lvovna's lips trembled. Two red patches appeared on her face.

And turning round to where the waitress was serving a fresh round of beer for the writers, she almost squealed:

"Girl! Bring us some vodka!"

Chapter 17

Martynov couldn't stand it; he turned away. Demov clicked the catch in place to set the tripod. Trying not to look at what he had to photograph.

"So," Samoilov began. "The position of the first corpse..."

Zaitsev could see he was deliberately trying to stick to the dry formulae of the protocol. But to describe this crime scene in simple human words seemed impossible. From a distance came the visceral sound of Agent Sundukov vomiting.

The dead had been found by some fishermen. This was a desolate stretch of the bank of the Neva. Nothing but huge granite boulders and trees. A swirling wind wrinkled the river, despite the May sun. The city puffed in the distance with fumes from the factories.

The killer had dragged one corpse onto a granite boulder, chiselled and hewn to the shape of a bollard by nature itself. The corpse lay on its stomach. Golden curls hung down.

Martynov carefully leant a foot on the slope of the granite boulder. He grabbed hold and pulled himself up. He reached out to touch the woman's throat. He turned and shook his head.

"Already stiff."

He jumped down and brushed his hands on his trousers.

"Forensics will confirm more precisely."

"Look at this, for fuck's sake," sighed Demov. "How did the bastard even do this?" He looked away. He could focus on the corpses through the camera viewfinder.

Samoilov and Demov had the same approach to defending their consciousness from what they saw. Zaitsev put up his defences in his own way, with Tatyana Lvovna Lilovaya's voice sounding in his head: "the image of Eternity is represented by an old woman", "a snake biting its own tail", "Genius hands down a garland".

There was a heady scent of roses. Nauseating even, perhaps because of the unfamiliar chemical smell mixed with it.

"Three putti are holding the garland from below." Were the kids a year old? Two? Three? There was still baby fat on the bare, frozen bodies: folds of fat as though pulled into pleats by threads. Zaitsev felt cold with anguish, as though death had embraced him as it brushed past.

"I'd shoot the bastard on the spot," Samoilov swore.

At a distance stood the ambulance with its red cross. But there was no one here to rescue. The old woman, the plump young woman with the golden curls, the three infants—they were all dead.

Samoilov walked over to pass on instructions. The paramedics could come and take away the bodies. They stepped cautiously with their stretcher, keen to avoid damaging the evidence and prints—not that there were any.

They placed the stretcher on the grass. They began to transfer the tiny bodies. "Hold the head, the head," warned the woman in the white coat. She started to cry. Her words left Zaitsev feeling even more queasy and bitter. All three corpses fit side by side. They covered them with a sheet. But that didn't make the horror go away.

"Argh!" one of the agents cried out. He jumped away, swearing, throwing away the snake that was twisted in the garland—for a moment it looked as though the reptile were alive.

II

They drove to Gorokhovaya in complete silence. Each in his own way thought—or tried not to think—about what he had seen. Or simply didn't want to think or speak.

Zaitsev thought about the three children. They certainly couldn't be to blame for anything. They hadn't bought trinkets, stamps or coins from Antikvariat. Someone was murdering Leningraders in a strange connection with the paintings that had left the Hermitage. And whatever that meant, these pictures were now his only clues.

His or theirs? Was it worth forgetting for a while the tangle of lies and suspicion, insults and exclusion?

Zaitsev decided.

"Demov," he said softly. "Demov, listen."

Demov reluctantly turned away from the window. Outside quivered the perfectly straight lines of Leningrad streets. They had already left the outskirts and were driving into the city centre.

Demov unclenched his lips.

"Listen, Vasya, let's talk later. Not in the mood to discuss the criminal remnants of the past in today's society."

And he went back to staring out of the window.

Zaitsev also turned away. Oh well, at least we're clear where we stand, he told himself.

The whole team gathered in Kopteltsev's office for a meeting. A sophisticated homicide, where three of the victims were children: this required urgent measures. They started with the need to establish the identities of the victims. Go around the neighbourhood with their photos.

Zaitsev stood up.

"Excuse me a moment. Bathroom."

"Yes," said Samoilov sullenly, without a trace of irony. "I know how you feel."

Sundukov blushed ever so slightly.

"What's up with you, Sundukov?" Serafimov said sincerely. "The only reason I didn't throw up back there was because I hadn't eaten."

"Comrades." Kopteltsev called for their attention. "Let's express our disgust and anger through our investigative work, not our physiological processes. Go on, Zaitsev."

Zaitsev went out into the corridor. Identify the dead. All perfectly logical—in full accordance with the rules of detective work. It's just this was a crime that defied the rules. Zaitsev thought of his and Nefyodov's chart: how much time and effort had they expended to find out everything about the dead? And for what?

Now, in Kopteltsev's office, for the first time he clearly felt that these crimes had nothing to do with the identity of the victims. Their names, their place of work, their origins, family and party membership, who their colleagues, friends, neighbours were. The very concept of personality. All of this was irrelevant. The paintings and only the paintings were the key to what was going on.

What kind of key? He didn't know. But one thing Zaitsev knew for sure: Comrade Prostak wasn't acting alone. Someone was instructing him from Moscow.

He locked himself in his office. He was done with being cautious. He requested a call to Moscow. "Just a moment."

Zaitsev didn't know where to dig. He was simply digging and hoping that sooner or later he would break through to the light.

Whether it was shaky or reliable, this was his only trail: the paintings. The phone line crackled.

"Go ahead."

How many times had he heard this affable, smug "Go ahead"?

"It's Zaitsev, from the Leningrad Criminal Investigation Department. Put me through to Comrade Uglov. It's urgent."

A clicking sound down the line. It sounded like the secretary was putting him through. Another click. The smug voice returned.

"Comrade Uglov's out of the office. Can I take a message?"

Suddenly, Zaitsev heard the familiar baritone in the background: "Get rid of him somehow." Obviously, the switch hadn't worked, and an invisible Uglov was giving instructions to the secretary. Zaitsev's heart pounded.

"Hello? Comrade Zaitsev? Can I pass on a message?"

"No. Thanks."

And he hung up.

He sat for a moment, not thinking anything. A spasm constricted his breathing. He was shocked, although he had expected this. Then he was seized by rage. Well, no, Uglov, that's not happening. Zaitsev snatched the telephone receiver.

"Put me through to the station controller. For Moscow, yes. It's urgent."

A few seconds' wait.

"Go ahead."

"Criminal Investigation. Detective Zaitsev. I'm heading to Moscow tonight; leave me a ticket."

The controller flapped about, muttering: he would have to check availability, it was a popular train.

"No, comrade, you didn't understand me," Zaitsev barked. "I'm on duty in the Organized Crime Squad, I'm not going to the Bolshoi or the Tretyakov Gallery. The case I'm investigating is of particular urgency. And if you don't understand my words, then I'll come by with the appropriate paperwork."

A few seconds of silence, either in bewilderment or anger.

"A ticket for one?" asked the controller.

"For one. Round trip, returning the following evening," Zaitsev blurted down the line.

III

Anyone who ever used the word "lackey" in the sense of "obsequious" clearly knew nothing about it. The head waiter, burly and handsome, like an admiral, spread his arms out before him. Zaitsev saw the contempt in his eyes and it was not half-hearted. With his shabby suit and his canvas shoes, Zaitsev's provincial look was clearly not one of a man of influence. The maître d's dense whiskers puffed up like a lion's mane.

"There's nowhere to sit… comrade!" He almost spat out the last word. "Comrade" didn't mean much here at the Moscow Metropol. The velvet rope and velvet curtain at the entrance reliably separated the sheep from the goats. Zaitsev poked his ID under the nose of the maître d'.

"Firstly, I'm not your comrade: it's comrade detective to you. Secondly and lastly, Comrade Uglov is sitting over there by the window, waiting for me. He will happily confirm, I'm sure."

The admiral, having doubted at first, relented a little. Zaitsev's first remark didn't impress him, but the mention of Uglov made him flinch for a moment. And a moment was enough. Zaitsev stepped past, threw back the curtain. Indeed, he was not mistaken. Uglov had told him that he had coffee at the Metropol at eleven on the dot every day. And there he was, sitting at his favourite table by the large, clean window, squinting through his smoke rings at springtime Moscow with its leafy-green haze.

Zaitsev slammed a chair down opposite Uglov, and flopped himself in it. Uglov's one eye stared at him. Zaitsev saw he had been taken by surprise. The admiral was hurrying towards them, full steam ahead, holding a bound folder and peering at Uglov's face; he seemed equally ready to cordially open the menu in front of Zaitsev or to throw Zaitsev out. Uglov nodded. The open folder was laid down in front of Zaitsev.

"Coffee," Zaitsev said without looking, eager to send the head waiter away as soon as possible.

"So, you thought you'd catch me off guard," Uglov calmly remarked. He flicked the ash from his cigarette, stubbed it out in the ashtray and leant back in his chair. It was as if he were seeing Zaitsev for the first time. Zaitsev was silent. The game of who'll blink first endured, until Uglov couldn't stand it any longer.

"Vasya, you do realize your provincial Petrograd swagger isn't going to cut it here? I only have to point my finger, and all that'll be left of you will be a damp patch on the chair."

The eye squinted unkindly.

Zaitsev leant towards him across the table.

"Uglov." Zaitsev looked into this one eye, this eye that was burning with anger, and tried to speak as calmly and sincerely as he could. "Uglov. It's me."

He saw how the malevolent twinkle in Uglov's eye lingered, and then went out. His cheekbones softened. Uglov grunted, and moved away.

"That's what I fear," he muttered.

The maître d' returned with a silver coffee pot and a thin, translucent porcelain cup, gently clinking on the saucer as he placed it down in front of Zaitsev.

Uglov waited until the waiter had retreated, majestically carrying his broad back.

"Just tell me—" Zaitsev began.

"I'll tell you," Uglov interrupted. "Drop this thing. I made some enquiries. You're climbing above Kopteltsev's head. Does he even know that you're here?"

"Nobody knows," Zaitsev lied.

"Well, that's good at least," Uglov nodded. "Tell you what, Vasya. Have some coffee. Treat yourself. Go to the Tretyakov Gallery. Have a stroll around Moscow. Then go home, buddy."

"Uglov." Zaitsev spoke in the same Petrograd tone from the 1920s. "Just tell me. And I'll slither away. What did you find?"

"And?"

Zaitsev was silent.

"And then what? Why do you need to know?"

"I want to know," Zaitsev said firmly. "I can't not want to know. You can't. That's what we're like."

"This is trouble. It's bad. Believe me. Very bad. And now completely unnecessary."

"Now?"

"Yes, haven't you heard? Haven't you noticed? The twenties, all that dashing about and derring-do—it's over, Vasya. Things are different now."

"How?"

"Not like the way we were, anyway."

"We", Zaitsev noticed him say—all was not lost, then.

"And you, Vasya," Uglov went on, "you never give up, do you? Like a hunting dog that won't stop chasing the hare, even when your paw's shot to pieces."

"I just need to find out. And leave. I'm giving you my word. I'm not an idiot."

Uglov picked up his cup. He took a sip. He sipped his coffee for a long time, looking out of the window. All Zaitsev saw was the black patch on his eye. It's not working out, he realized.

"The People's Commissariat of Trade, then," Uglov suddenly forced out, as if against his will. "Does the name Angarsky mean anything to you?"

"No."

"Well, never mind him. He's just a cog. Like your Prostak. But he's the Antikvariat contact here in Moscow."

"Did you get something from him?"

Uglov either didn't hear or pretended not to.

"What do you think the People's Commissariat of Trade is doing?"

"To be honest, I don't give a fuck. What?"

"A lamentable political myopia," Uglov murmured. "Are you planning to join the party, Zaitsev?"

"Sure, whatever."

"But there are such simple things you don't know about the Soviet state."

"Fuck off."

"Have some marmalade. It's superb."

"Talk. Come on, talk."

From the side it might have looked like two old comrades enjoying a meal and the view of the Bolshoi Theatre. Yellow Finnish butter was melting in a dish. The bread rolls were covered with a napkin. Here, at the Metropol, Uglov knew full well, almost the entire service staff knew him as their boss—from time to time pretending to be an ordinary visitor. Simply put, a good proportion of the staff at the Metropol were informants. It was at this thought that Uglov allowed himself an especially broad smile. He was a picture of joy in all his might. He fed himself marmalade.

"And you have something—treat yourself," he urged Zaitsev, a bit too loudly and a bit too jovially. "You don't have this in your canteen."

Zaitsev played along. "Oh, I will, don't worry."

"So, your royal ignorance." Uglov lowered his voice. "The Soviet state has extensive trade contacts with foreign industrialists. Promoting, so to speak, the rise of Soviet industry."

"Millionaires?" asked Zaitsev. He suddenly remembered Nefyodov's naive question, which almost made Tatyana Lvovna choke. But it wasn't a stupid question: how were these millionaires aware of what Comrade Prostak was extracting from the Hermitage?

As he listened to Uglov, he couldn't believe his ears.

"...In short, while Gulbenkian was playing hard to get, this Mattison—"

"Wait a minute, who? Gulbenkian? An Armenian?"

"Originally. But he's Parisian. Oil millionaire. Collects paintings and, you know, stuff with a famous name on it. So, Mattison—"

"Also a millionaire?"

"No, he's small fry, a trader. But smart. And he quickly led the comrades from the People's Commissariat of Trade to another big fish. The shark of capitalism, so to speak. Mellon, that's his surname. An American. Andrew Mellon."

"Wait a minute. You mean to say this Mellon and this Armenian—"

"He's not Armenian, he's French—lived in France for a long time."

"Doesn't matter. You mean to say that they're prodding this Prostak and saying, 'I want this picture, and this one, and that one'? And Comrade Prostak brings them out on a silver platter and wraps them in a piece of paper?!"

"Comrade Prostak, I would say, is only packing up the purchases. He's like a clerk."

"Uglov," said Zaitsev. "These paintings are priceless, they're public treasures. We need to—"

Uglov slammed his palm down on the table so hard that everyone in the room turned on them. Zaitsev recalled how Uglov had been shell-shocked twice, leading to lasting nervous problems.

"We don't need to do anything," Uglov croaked. Saliva appeared in the corners of his mouth.

"Uglov," Zaitsev said firmly, "some illiterate crooks are plundering the cultural treasures of the Soviet country for the sake of foreign capital—"

"Shut up!" grated Uglov. "Stop it!... Our Soviet country..." Uglov spoke in a metallic voice, and his entire person—skinny, one-eyed—suddenly seemed old, dry and creaky, the spitting image of Kashchey from the Russian fairy tales. "Our Soviet country is earning hard currency. And by the way, these people you call 'illiterate'... Let it be known to you that Comrade Pyatakov, a member of the Soviet government, the son of a sugar manufacturer, has graduated from university and he knows the value of these paintings. It's just that for Soviet industry certain things are more valuable right now than your Rubenses and Rembrandts!"

Uglov's profile was trembling.

Zaitsev moved to get up.

"Sit," Uglov barked. He jerked him down, no longer worrying what his army of informants would think, those whose gaze was fixed in their direction. "Sit," he almost hissed. "I'm only telling you all this because otherwise, Zaitsev, you'll be like that dog—chasing your prey, limping along on three legs. Until you keel over. But if you're in the mood to die, I can set something up for you like the old friend I am. Much less trouble that way. I'll give you a compassionate shot to the head. Do you understand me?"

"What good marmalade they have," said Zaitsev. He pulled it over and began to eat it straight out of the bowl, spoon by spoon. Spoon by spoon.

The head waiter gave a contemptuous snort and turned to his desk.

Uglov managed, if not to calm down—his eyelid and the

corner of his mouth were still twitching—then at least to pull himself together. He watched Zaitsev, and didn't touch either his coffee or the Moscow pickles on a plate on the starchy tablecloth, strewn with small patches of May sunshine refracted through the crystal vases.

"I knew from the very beginning," he said in his absolutely ordinary voice. "You'll never leave your Finnish swamps. You're a dead loss. No Moscow's going to lure you out of there. You're a fool, Vasya," he added with regret. "Heading back to Peter today?"

Zaitsev nodded.

IV

Zaitsev knew Uglov well and he had known him long. He wasn't afraid of his nervous fits or his facial twitches. But the simple and seemingly innocent question of when he was leaving immediately set him on high alert.

Zaitsev stood in the narrow, carpeted corridor. Passengers pushed past with their briefcases in a hurry to find their compartments. Ignoring the way the train shook, Zaitsev gazed intently at the platform. In Moscow, unlike Leningrad, it was already dark at that time of night. But in the light of the yellow street lamps, Zaitsev saw two rosy fellows in ordinary civilian clothes sidle up to the conductor of the next carriage. They flashed their ID cards. And the conductor made an inviting hand gesture. Zaitsev stepped back from the window. He sat down on the already made-up bed with its comforting smell of starch. The light from under the silk lampshade was reflected in the lacquered panels. The carriages were old and luxurious—from before the Revolution. The guard's whistle. The platform slowly retreated. Zaitsev slipped out of the compartment. The corridor was empty;

all the doors were closed; passengers usually sat quietly for those first few minutes, looking out of the window or laying out their toiletries.

Zaitsev walked quickly down the corridor. He passed the clanging vestibule. Walked through another car. Another vestibule. Carriage. Vestibule. Carriage. Vestibule. The floor rocked and shook more and more—the train was picking up speed. Finally, as he left the last vestibule, he was hit by a waft of bodies, tar, coal: that incomparable railway smell for travellers in the hard carriage. Zaitsev quickly spotted the most likely candidate: a fat man in a panama hat.

"Comrade," said Zaitsev. "I'm in the soft carriage. Was shot twice in the back in the civil war—can't take anything soft. I tried to get comfortable, but it's no good. I'd be better off standing."

He pulled out his ticket. "Do you want it?"

The fat man eyed him suspiciously.

Zaitsev understood. "I don't need anything for it," he said, pulling it out of his pocket. "I was given a ticket for the soft carriage on account of the party. Wounded in action."

The spiel was a success. At the sight of the VIP ticket, the fat man's eyes sparkled greedily; he didn't think to look into Zaitsev's young face and doubt his story about being wounded in the civil war. He eagerly reached under his bunk and pulled out a basket wrapped in fabric and tied at the top. He handed his ticket to Zaitsev.

"Here, thank you, really, thank you," Zaitsev enthused.

"Goodnight, comrade. All the best with your back."

Zaitsev sat for a while, peering at the others in the wagon out of the corner of his eye. It was safer here among people in the open carriage than there, in a locked compartment. But he still didn't feel safe. He could be removed from the train at any stop. "Come along, comrade. No need to kick up a fuss"—and that would be it. It wasn't like he could grab his pistol. And if he did, the rest of the passengers would immediately pile in and hold him down, always eager to do their bit in the name of justice.

Zaitsev jumped up. Again carriage, vestibule, carriage, vestibule. A locked iron door. The mail car. This was where his "defective" childhood came in handy: only street children roamed the country like this, getting on and off trains like rats. Zaitsev went back to the last passenger car. He locked himself in the toilet. He pulled down the sash window. His body remembered every move. How to haul yourself up, where to cling on, where to place your hands, your feet.

Hanging from the roof, Zaitsev smashed in the glass of the next window. He hammered away the sharp shards with his heel. And like a lizard he slipped inside. He fell onto the sacks, a corner of a box jabbing him in the side. Never mind. He settled down comfortably on the mailbags.

Maybe he was imagining it all. Or maybe not. He never liked to be 100 per cent sure of anything. He tucked his hands under his armpits—another proven way to keep warm. And he soon fell asleep.

Meanwhile, the two ruddy fellows did their rounds. They reached the door of the mail car. They pulled the handle. Locked.

"He's given us the slip, the bastard."

"Or this isn't the right train."

"Fuck knows."

Suddenly they both had the same hunch at the same time. They rushed back. Yanked the toilet door: locked.

"Exactly. He's in there, the bastard," one whispered. They stepped aside quietly. One deftly and softly dropped on all fours and peered through the fine mesh grille near the floor.

He gestured as if to say, "Yep, he's in there." The second silently took out his gun, stood ready. Both froze like caryatids.

The first knocked.

"Comrade, you've had your turn. Fallen asleep in there, or what?"

There was a rustle behind the door, movement. The lock clicked. The door swung open. They went in for the grab.

"Hey, what's all this?" squealed a red-haired man in a T-shirt and underpants. One of the men loosened his grip. The toilet window gaped open like a dark jaw: it was a damp night out there. The man rushed to the window, stuck his head out. Looked right, left.

"What? I came out for a smoke. What of it?" muttered the man they had seized. "Even opened the window so as not to cause a nuisance. All above board!"

"Go on, then. Piss off. Quick."

Both waited until they were sure he had gone.

"Can't be the right train," answered the first. They got off at Bologoye.

Knowing Uglov as well as he did, Zaitsev was also confident that, having missed once, he wouldn't take aim for a second throw. It was enough for him to drive the enemy away. Away from Moscow, that is.

On the platform, Zaitsev quickly tucked himself into the throngs of arriving and departing passengers, those meeting or seeing off others, letting the crowd carry him into the city. It was chilly. Nothing strange there: it meant that ice had flowed into the Neva from Lake Ladoga. Zaitsev glanced at the station clock tower; he could do with going home to warm up, but he didn't really have time. He had better go straight to work.

His brisk pace warmed him slightly. Walking along Ligovsky Prospekt, Zaitsev shuddered as he thought about

the capital—that greasy, oily city, with its complex group-
ings, government chess and party intrigues. You just pull a
tiny thread—and in no time at all word reaches all the way
to government member Comrade Pyatakov. A web that Uglov
was entangled in, too.

Even the shabby Ligovsky Prospekt with its shady gangs
felt free and safe in comparison. At least Zaitsev knew how to
deal with ordinary petty criminals.

On the Fontanka embankment, close to the walls of CID,
he saw a horse and cart. The nag stood with its long suede
lips, but the driver was nowhere to be seen. The cheek, Zaitsev
thought.

Zaitsev crossed the road.

"Comrade Zaitsev!" A pleasant voice called out to him. It
seemed familiar.

He turned around. Or rather, he didn't quite. A damp,
pungent rag covered his face, which rapidly became a deep
darkness, devoid of any thoughts or feeling.

The man stretched a canopy over the cart, covering his load.
He jumped up, clicked his tongue and clapped the reins. The
horse shook its mane and set off, briskly clattering along the
street.

V

His body felt like it belonged to someone else. Either from the
cold, or from being motionless for so long. Bushes. The trees
were still covered with buds. His head was heavy. The familiar
sensation of coming round from ether: he knew it from having
had surgery. Swaying, staggering, like he was drunk. Zaitsev
remembered something: Fontanka embankment. He tried to
look around: no, this wasn't Fontanka. Where would you find

a scrap of bare earth in the centre of Leningrad? Everywhere was rock. But he was lying on soil. Gradually, the feeling of it being his own body returned. Zaitsev realized that his hands were tied behind his back. His feet were free. He rolled over and got onto his knees. He was wearing red trousers. A white shirt. His feet were squeezed into some tall boots. Someone had changed his clothes. He could just about make out some open space behind the trees: that must be the Neva or one of its tributaries.

"Good morning, Comrade Zaitsev. How did you sleep? Not too cold, I hope?"

Zaitsev saw a man sitting on a fallen tree and watching him with interest. At a distance, the dancing orange flames of a small bonfire.

Zaitsev watched morosely. Alexei Alexandrovich stood up. He was wearing practical golfing trousers tucked into knee-high socks, English style. Sturdy boots.

"What are you doing, Alexei Alexandrovich?" Zaitsev tried to ask. His mouth was dry; his tongue was like sandpaper. Alexei Alexandrovich walked up to him and lifted his head by the hair; Zaitsev felt water on his lips, and began to drink eagerly. Alexei Alexandrovich then put away his flask, which was emblazoned with a Boy Scout badge.

"How do you feel, Comrade Zaitsev?" he asked sympathetically.

He waited for an answer that didn't come.

"Aha, we're playing who can keep silent the longest," he teased. "Well. Nothing wrong with that. I understand perfectly well what kind of questions you've got in there right now," said Alexei Alexandrovich, jabbing a finger on Zaitsev's forehead.

"Your first question: where am I? The answer: here."

Alexei Alexandrovich stood up, adopting a demonstrative posture with his foot resting on a fallen trunk: the orator about to recite a tale. He pulled out a small book, opened it and read with expression:

"Paulus Potter. *Punishment of a Hunter.*"

He slammed the book shut and tossed it into the fire.

"A brochure for savages like you. You're a savage savant— at least you can read. You even signed up to the library. Commendable."

"So enlighten me then," croaked Zaitsev. "What kind of painting is it? I haven't come across it."

Behind his back, his fingers were living an independent life: they fumbled around, crept along, tugged at the rope. He just had to buy some time. Alexei Alexandrovich was so self-assured and smug, he was bound to be complacent.

"Why not, since you ask. *Punishment of a Hunter.* We're presented with fourteen scenes: twelve small vignettes surrounding two larger scenes. In the smaller scenes, we see a hunter basking in his glory. You bet! Young, capable, athletic, the very picture of a model Komsomolets. Master of his new destiny! Ah, but little does he know!"

Alexei Alexandrovich met his victim's glassy stare and grinned with satisfaction.

But he misunderstood his captive's fishy gaze. Zaitsev wasn't listening at all to his narration—all his attention was focused on the tips of his fingers tugging at the rope.

"And in the two central scenes we see the consequence. The former victims, the animals, collaborate to put their hunter on trial. And then they mete out his punishment. His dogs are strung up from a bough. The huntsman himself is grilled on a spit. Among the fourteen scenes, we see certain mythological tropes... But why am I telling you this? I could go on for hours, telling you about Potter and Holland of the Golden Age... Dr Nicolaes Tulp, who is captured in Rembrandt's famous *Anatomy Lesson... Punishment of a Hunter...* There's so much I could tell you about this small picture. And about the others. Alas, it won't make you any less savage. Or the others. You lot are all the same. I know your second question: why me? Because, Comrade Zaitsev. You could have stopped these savages. But you didn't. I was counting on you. But you don't understand simple words. Beauty has no effect on you, either. I checked! I made sure! But no, neither persuasion nor clarification—nothing seemed to work with you philistines. You don't understand subtle hints. One cannot negotiate with a savage. The likes of you understand only pain!"

"You are the savage," Zaitsev answered. "You're killing people, Alexei Alexandrovich."

"People?" Alexei Alexandrovich squatted in front of him. "Huh?" He cupped his palm behind his ear. "I thought I heard you say 'people'. I must have imagined it. What we're talking about are a bunch of wretched, depraved souls whose entire life consists of nothing but eating, defecating, sleeping and serving the Soviet Union. No one misses them. They were already forgotten by the very next day. Well, OK, by the next week, once I had liberated this beautiful city from those miserable hordes of worthless organisms. But the paintings... Paintings, Comrade Zaitsev, live for centuries. This is what I have been trying to explain to you. What I've been screaming at you! I've been screaming at you from the very beginning. In your very ears!"

"Paintings are more important to you than living people?"

"The paintings in question are masterpieces. The pinnacle of the human spirit. While the individuals you've been harping on about are the precise opposite: the very trough of mankind, the lowest stage of human development. Philistines. Neanderthals. Infusoria. And great works are sacrificed, destroyed, for the sake of some food to throw into their stinking, putrid mouths?"

"Don't lie—you know nobody's going to destroy them, these paintings. They won't be burnt or ripped up. They'll carry on being hung on the wall. Just in another country."

"They belong to this city!" With all his strength, Alexei Alexandrovich kicked Zaitsev, again and again. "They belong here!"

Alexei Alexandrovich took a deep breath, pulled out a handkerchief and dabbed his bald head.

"Why am I trying to explain to you? I won't get through to you. Enough. You're beyond hope."

He shook his head.

"When I met Comrade Prostak, I thought he was the one I needed here. But you're even worse, Comrade Zaitsev. Well, you'll achieve one good thing: your worthless husk may remind other fools of the beautiful picture that, thanks to your negligence, has now been sent to Berlin for auction, and from there, God only knows where to…"

Zaitsev needed at least a few more minutes. The rope was weakening, but the knot still wouldn't yield. Whatever he did, he needed to keep Alexei Alexandrovich talking.

"What are you laughing at?" Alexei Alexandrovich asked in surprise.

"You said fourteen? Fourteen?" asked Zaitsev. "You're going to butcher me into fourteen parts?"

"Well, you are an animal," Alexei Alexandrovich said contemptuously. "You're bidding farewell to life, but even this fact is beyond your imagination. You find it laughable. Well. At first, I thought about choosing the lower of the two central scenes for you. Yes"—he waved his hands around as he spoke—"and the Leningrad Zoological Garden seemed perfect for the occasion. This idiotic Sancho Panza of yours is eminently suitable for the role of the dog hanging by its neck."

"Is Nefyodov here?" Zaitsev was worried.

"But then I thought: the fire would attract attention. And they'd notice the smell of your chargrilled body. So I chose one of the corner vignettes. Ah, a shame the little book's gone bye-byes. Otherwise, I'd show you. Well, then, I shall describe it in my own words. A naked Artemis surrounded by her escort nymphs. A rather common motif. What a gullible lot Soviet women are... Well, you, Comrade Zaitsev... You're the cheerful Komsomolets Actaeon, hunted by his own dogs. Don't worry, Comrade Zaitsev. I know you don't have any four-legged friends. Or two-legged ones, for that matter. Well, I've set you up with a companion."

Alexei Alexandrovich leant over Zaitsev and noticed the loosening rope.

"Tut-tut, you bad boy."

He tightened the knot around his wrists. Then he helped Zaitsev up, lifted him onto his feet. Zaitsev tried to headbutt him, but Alexei Alexandrovich dodged him in time.

"Well, now, no need for that. We're almost done. Take a little walk with me, arm in arm."

He dragged Zaitsev along behind him.

"Here, Comrade Zaitsev. I thought: a large fire, a real bon-fire, would be too noticeable, we would be interrupted. But then I thought: why not have a metaphorical bonfire? I shall grill you, Comrade Zaitsev. Slo-o-o-owly, slowly."

Before them stood a tree with a long, thick bough, looking like an outstretched arm. Or a gallows, Zaitsev realized with horror. Below the bough, on a rickety canvas chair, the kind beloved by fishermen and artists, Nefyodov was teetering on his very tiptoes. Hands tied behind his back, noose around his neck. With his pointed toes, Nefyodov looked as though he were mid dance. His boyish face was mortally pale.

"Your dog," Alexei Alexandrovich said gently. He grabbed Zaitsev by the wrists and fiddled with the knot. And his foot casually knocked the chair out from beneath Nefyodov. He dangled, twitching in the noose.

Zaitsev felt that his hands were free, that Alexei Alexandrovich wasn't holding him. Zaitsev rushed forwards, caught Nefyodov by the legs and raised him up. He clung on. Nefyodov hissed. But he was alive. Zaitsev's arms were quickly going numb from the weight. Nefyodov coughed. He was breathing. Zaitsev's only thought was not to drop him.

Alexei Alexandrovich laughed.

"I wasn't mistaken about you, Comrade Zaitsev. Utterly primitive."

He picked up the chair and folded it up.

"You see, you had a simple choice: to rescue your dog or to catch me. And what did you choose? But today I'm feeling generous. I'll help you learn the error of your ways. And while you're standing here hugging like Easter bunnies, I'll go and bring out the real dogs, my dear Actaeon. German shepherds don't like it when strangers wander around the zoo uninvited. Farewell."

And his footsteps crunched away.

VI

"Push me up," Nefyodov croaked.

"How? Got any more precise instructions?"

"Well, push. No not like that. Push my feet."

Zaitsev, panting, shuffled down and caught Nefyodov by the feet. He almost couldn't feel his hands, every muscle tensed.

"Nefyodov, it wasn't me who was in the circus, remember."

"Get down. Legs out wide. And push me up."

Zaitsev tried to bend his knees. It felt like they were going to snap and he would collapse like a broken lever. He took a deep breath and with a grunt he heaved Nefyodov's body up. It seemed at first that he couldn't do it, but then he did. He let go, and collapsed onto his back.

Nefyodov swore as his stomach hit the bough. And then he added in his ordinary voice, "Well done."

Zaitsev looked up. Nefyodov was hanging from the tree, doubled over the bough on his stomach like a strange caterpillar.

"Comrade Zaitsev, now climb up here."

"OK, now you're teaching the expert."

Zaitsev scrambled up quite quickly, crawling on his stomach to Nefyodov. He clutched the bough with his legs. And with his hands and teeth he worked on the knot. Then he loosened the rope around Nefyodov's throat and threw it away. The colour soon returned to his face. Nefyodov placed his hands on the bough, like a horizontal bar. He pulled himself up handsomely, not forgetting to point his toes, as befits his art. He doubled up, head over heels, and, spinning like a ball in the air, landed with a bump on two bent legs, arms stretched out in front. Then he straightened up and rubbed his neck.

"Nearly suffocated," he summed up. And again he fell into his Nordic calm.

"Congratulations," answered Zaitsev from above. Holding on by his hands, he let himself drop down from the bough.

And then they both heard it: something was approaching, and fast. Flexible and strong, like iron springs. "And now, Nefyodov, we have to run!"

An ordinary dog can run much faster than an ordinary person. But when it comes to picturing an abstract map of the area, dogs are worse off. Zaitsev raced ahead, hardly seeing where he was going, his arms outstretched in case. It was only from hearing him that he knew Nefyodov was there beside him. He ran to the Neva. To the water.

He didn't expect to knock the dogs off their trail. But in the water, the dogs would lose their speed advantage—and their ability to leap straight at the victim's throat.

He straight away saw where the shore ended and the water began; large white chunks of Ladoga ice glided past, drifting to their final resting place in the Gulf of Finland.

"You'll drown, Comrade Zaitsev," begged Nefyodov. "We can't swim. We'll freeze. If the current doesn't get you, the ice will."

The dogs couldn't just smell them, they could see them. Excited barks burst from their throats.

At full speed, Zaitsev ran crashing into the blisteringly cold water.

VII

"Where in the heavens have you been?" Pasha gasped. "You're shaking all over."

Previously, Zaitsev had thought that the expression "his teeth were chattering" was a slight exaggeration. Now he knew that it wasn't: his jaw was chatting away on its own, like machine-gun fire.

Pasha unlocked the apartment with the key from her bundle. The corridor was numb in somnolent silence—the neighbours were asleep.

"In you go, quick. You're dripping puddles. Straight to the bathroom! Everything off. And quiet!"

Zaitsev was sitting on the floor with a blanket around his shoulders, his whole body shivering, when Pasha came in with a steaming bucket in her mighty hands.

"What? Nothing I haven't seen before," she whispered, pointing to the water.

Zaitsev stood barefoot in the bathtub. It felt like his skin was peeling off from the sizzling-hot water. He almost screamed.

Pasha first handed him a towel. Then the blanket again.

Then he went and sat on the bed. He was still shivering furiously.

Pasha returned with a large bottle of something cloudy. It glugged into a glass.

"Drink it. Down in one."

Zaitsev gulped it down, fighting back his revulsion. He waited. He swallowed back the urge to be sick.

Pasha gave him a second.

"One more."

Zaitsev shook his head: no.

"Where the hell have you been?"

"I wanted to drown, Pasha."

She threw up her hands.

"Because of Alla, or what?"

"Because of her."

That was all Pasha needed to know.

"What a fool," said Pasha, drawing out her vowels. "For her? Really? Drink it."

Zaitsev tipped back the second glass. Pasha gently nudged him on the shoulder; he tumbled over onto his side. He felt Pasha pull his legs up and tuck him under the blanket, just like when he was a boy. Images flashed beneath his eyelids: dragging a kicking dog with him underwater, powerful blows from its paws, having no power left to restrain the beast, streams of silver bubbles floating up. Human lungs are larger than dogs', and dogs can't hold their breath...

And Zaitsev died a second time that day.

VIII

"Zaitsev, you look kind of lousy," said Demov to his right, his tone sympathetic.

"Yeah, you look dreadful," confirmed Serafimov on the left. Samoilov turned around.

"Vasya, your breath stinks. I'm getting drunk sitting this close to you. I know you had a day off. Celebrated in style, I see. But for Christ's sake, have a mint or something?"

"Or drink some kefir," prompted Demov.

The hall filled up quickly. Every knock of a chair against the ground and Zaitsev thought his head would explode. His eyes were burning from the murmur of voices. He covered them. All he could see were balls of fire. Streams of bubbles, powerful blows from a strong beast, trained to kill. He opened his eyes; no matter what, he couldn't crash out in front of the others. It felt like a fever.

His body seemed light.

Finally, the presidium filled the seats around the red table-cloth. The chairman rang the bell; Zaitsev nearly howled. Someone poked him in the shoulder, gesturing to him to go. Zaitsev looked up: Kopteltsev was standing in the doorway, beckoning to him.

"Comrade, mind my toes!"

"Sorry."

Zaitsev squirmed his way out of the row of seats, under the disgruntled glares of the presidium.

"Sorry."

He left the room with Kopteltsev.

"Let's go," said Kopteltsev. "We need a word."

"Now?"

"Won't take long."

They headed for the stairwell at the back of the building.

Kopteltsev lit a cigarette. He took a few puffs. "Why did you call the kennels?"

Zaitsev was amazed at how quickly the kennels had reported him.

"Oh yeah. I wanted to ask them. I had a thought. What we could do to work more effectively with sniffer dogs."

He still hoped to find Alexei Alexandrovich. The dogs hadn't touched him, so he must have trained them. He must have learnt somewhere. There weren't many places in Leningrad where they bred guard dogs.

"Mmmm." Kopteltsev looked at him, taking a drag on his cigarette. He exhaled, and added, "Martynov's been purged."

"Martynov?"

"You're surprised?"

"Yes, I'm surprised."

"Not wondering, why not you?"

"I live one day at a time. I don't look far ahead."

"Quite right."

"Why Martynov?"

Kopteltsev frowned, knocked off the ash with a tap of his fingernail.

"So you got left."

"What do you need me for?"

"Makes no fucking difference to me. I don't need you."

"So who needs me then?"

"Better to ask in what way."

"I.e.?"

"A black sheep can be useful."

"And that's me?"

"For when things turn sour. After Pyotr-Jacques, you know, everyone's an expert. Comrade Myedvyed also has an interest."

Comrade Myedvyed was the head of the Leningrad OGPU. Kopteltsev's former boss. A friend of Comrade Kirov. A serious conversation, then.

"Oh, thanks. Black sheep it is, then."

"Look on the bright side. You'll get the pick of the bunch. You'll work independently."

"Oh, thanks."

"You're welcome. Work. Get results. It's all in your hands. Solve a case—great. Fuck up—well, you already were a dead man walking."

"That's not a black sheep. That's a scapegoat."

"You know best, professor."

So now they were going to put him on cases to save others from criticism. Not a bad idea. Well, one thing made him feel more optimistic: at least OGPU had left him alone. And wouldn't be bothering him any more. Never again.

"What am I supposed to do now?"

"Don't make any mistakes."

Kopteltsev put his cigarette out on his sole and flicked the butt through the banister to the bottom of the stairwell.

"Come on, better get back to the meeting. They'll enlighten you, tell the news."

"What news?"

In the corridor, someone called him from an office.

"Ah, Zaitsev, it's you I'm looking for. The Hermitage on the line. They say it's urgent."

"I'll catch you up," he called to Kopteltsev, already a few steps ahead.

"No idle chatter!" Kopteltsev answered, not turning around.

Zaitsev picked up the phone.

"Zaitsev."

"Comrade Zaitsev!" Tatyana Lvovna's voice sounded somehow girlishly loud. She was resounding with joy. Zaitsev immediately felt a throbbing pain behind his left eye. "Comrade Zaitsev! The Lepke auction fell through!"

"Fell where?"

"It was a complete flop!" rejoiced Tatyana Lvovna. "Due to the tense economic situation worldwide," she drilled on in her tour-guide voice, "and especially given how fraught things are in North America, there are very few wealthy buyers. Do you understand?"

"No."

"They didn't manage to sell our paintings! Not all of them," she corrected. "They'll come back to Leningrad. Of course, they sold a few. Alas. But! Many of them will come back. We heard by telegram yesterday."

She began to squeal with joy as she read out the names.

"What did you say?" asked Zaitsev. "*Punishment of a Hunter*?"

"You know that one? Paulus Potter. It's not up there among the greats, but it's a dear little thing. They didn't manage to sell that either. Did you hear me? Comrade Zaitsev?"

"Yes," said Zaitsev, "I know that one. You see, Tatyana Lvovna, the time has come for these foreign millionaires. The world revolution is on its way—soon it will be universal."

Silence reigned at her end. Tatyana Lvovna had hung up.

Zaitsev pushed the door, trying not to let it creak. He quietly slipped into the hall. The speaker was delivering a speech, almost throwing his head back like a nightingale revelling in its song.

Everyone applauded.

They hissed at Zaitsev as he squeezed back to his place amid a sea of applause.

"Why the applause?" he whispered to Demov and Serafimov.

"Everything will be different now. New times," Demov answered.

Exactly the same words as Kopteltsev had just used.

"What?"

"Didn't you hear?"

"And here we were wondering why they transferred Kopteltsev to us from OGPU, rather than sending some

397

big-city copper here to Leningrad," Samoilov began to argue in a whisper, but Demov interrupted him.

"I wasn't wondering. And in general, I don't remember any conversations about it—there were none."

"Oh, yeah, my mistake," agreed Samoilov.

"So what did I miss?" asked Zaitsev, not following.

"They've signed the decree. The police are being merged with OGPU. We're all one department now."

"There is no longer Greek or Jew," Demov explained. "Amen."

"Well, clap then. Clap. Why aren't you clapping?"

So Zaitsev started clapping.

AVAILABLE AND COMING SOON
FROM PUSHKIN VERTIGO

Jonathan Ames

You Were Never Really Here

A Man Named Doll

Olivier Barde-Cabuçon

*The Inspector of Strange and
Unexplained Deaths*

Sarah Blau

The Others

Maxine Mei-Fung Chung

The Eighth Girl

Amy Suiter Clarke

Girl, 11

Candas Jane Dorsey

The Adventures of Isabel

Martin Holmén

Clinch

Down for the Count

Slugger

Elizabeth Little

Pretty as a Picture

Louise Mey

The Second Woman

Joyce Carol Oates (ed.)

Cutting Edge

John Kåre Raake

The Ice

RV Raman

A Will to Kill

Tiffany Tsao

The Majesties

John Vercher

Three-Fifths

Emma Viskic

Resurrection Bay

And Fire Came Down

Darkness for Light

Those Who Perish

Yulia Yakovleva

Punishment of a Hunter